I0805461

SCP Foundation ▸ Archives
Black Journal

IFIEDCLASSIFIEDCLASS

Security Clearance Level	IV
This journal belongs to	

CLASSIFIED

SCP Foundation

Mankind in its present state has been around for a quarter of a million years, yet only the last 4,000 have been of any significance.

So, what did we do for nearly 250,000 years? We huddled in caves and around small fires, fearful of the things that we didn't understand. It was more than explaining why the sun came up, it was the mystery of enormous birds with heads of men and rocks that came to life. So we called them 'gods' and 'demons', begged them to spare us, and prayed for salvation.

In time, their numbers dwindled and ours rose. The world began to make more sense when there were fewer things to fear, yet the unexplained can never truly go away, as if the universe demands the absurd and impossible.

Mankind must not go back to hiding in fear. No one else will protect us, and we must stand up for ourselves.

While the rest of mankind dwells in the light, we must stand in the darkness to fight it, contain it, and shield it from the eyes of the public, so that others may live in a sane and normal world.

We secure. We contain. We protect.

— The Administrator

OBJECT CLASSES

All anomalous objects, entities, and phenomena requiring Special Containment Procedures are assigned an Object Class. An Object Class is a part of the standard SCP template and serves as a rough indicator for how difficult an object is to contain. In universe, Object Classes are for the purposes of identifying containment needs, research priority, budgeting, and other considerations. An SCP's Object Class is determined by a number of factors, but the most important factors are the difficulty and the purpose of its containment.

SAFE

The Locked Box Test:
If you lock it in a box, leave it alone, and nothing bad will happen, then it's probably Safe.

Safe-class SCPs are anomalies that are easily and safely contained. This is often due to the fact that the Foundation has researched the SCP well enough that containment does not require significant resources or that the anomalies require a specific and conscious activation or trigger. Classifying an SCP as Safe, however, does not mean that handling or activating it does not pose a threat.

EUCLID

The Locked Box Test:
If you lock it in a box, leave it alone, and you're not entirely sure what will happen, then it's probably Euclid.

Euclid-class SCPs are anomalies that require more resources to contain completely or where containment isn't always reliable. Usually this is because the SCP is insufficiently understood or inherently unpredictable. Euclid is the Object Class with the greatest scope, and it's usually a safe bet that an SCP will be this class if it doesn't easily fall into any of the other standard Object Classes.

As a note, any SCP that's autonomous, sentient and/or sapient is generally classified as Euclid, due to the inherent unpredictability of an object that can act or think on its own.

KETER

The Locked Box Test:
If you lock it in a box, leave it alone, and it easily escapes, then it's probably Keter.

Keter-class SCPs are anomalies that are exceedingly difficult to contain consistently or reliably, with containment procedures often being extensive and complex. The Foundation often can't contain these SCPs well due to not having a solid understanding of the anomaly, or lacking the technology to properly contain or counter it. A Keter SCP does not mean the SCP is dangerous, just that it is simply very difficult or costly to contain.

THAUMIEL

The Locked Box Test:
If it is the box, then it's probably Thaumiel.

Thaumiel-class SCPs are anomalies that the Foundation specifically uses to contain other SCPs. Even the mere existence of Thaumiel-class objects is classified at the highest levels of the Foundation and their locations, functions, and current status are known to few Foundation personnel outside of the O5 Council.

[PERSONNEL DOC_01]
[ID_DOCTOR ███]

CLEARANCE & CLASSIFICATION

1. Foundation security clearances granted to personnel represent the highest level or type of information to which they can be granted access.

Level 5 [Thaumiel]

Level 5 security clearances are given to the highest-ranking administrative personnel within the Foundation and grant effectively unlimited access to all strategic and otherwise sensitive data. Level 5 security clearances are typically only granted to O5 Council members and selected staff.

Level 4 [Top Secret]

Level 4 security clearances are given to senior administration that require access to site-wide and/or regional intelligence as well as long-term strategic data regarding Foundation operations and research projects. Level 4 security clearances are typically only held by Site Directors, Security Directors, or Mobile Task Force Commanders.

Level 3 [Secret]

Level 3 security clearances are given to senior security and research personnel that require in-depth data regarding the source, recovery circumstances, and long-term planning for anomalous objects and entities in containment. Most senior research staff, project managers, security officers, response team members, and Mobile Task Force operatives hold a Level 3 security clearance.

Level 2 [Restricted]

Level 2 security clearances are given to security and research personnel that require direct access to information regarding anomalous objects and entities in containment. Most research staff, field agents, and containment specialists hold a Level 2 security clearance.

Level 1 [Confidential]

Level 1 security clearances are given to personnel working in proximity to but with no direct, indirect, or informational access to anomalous objects or entities in containment. Level 1 security clearances are typically granted to personnel working in clerical, logistics, or janitorial positions at facilities with containment capability or otherwise must handle sensitive information.

Level 0 [For Official Use Only]

Level 0 security clearances are given to non-essential personnel with no need to access information regarding anomalous objects or entities in Foundation containment. Level 0 access is typically held by personnel in non-secured clerical, logistics, or janitorial positions at facilities with no access to operational data.

2. Pesonnel Classifications are assigned to personnel based on their proximity to potentially dangerous anomalous objects, entities, or phenomena.

Class A

Not allowed direct access to anomalies under any circumstances.

Class B

May only be granted access to anomalies that have passed quarantine and have been cleared of any potential mind-affecting effects or memetic agents.

Class C

Have direct access to most anomalies not deemed strictly hostile or dangerous.

Class D

Expendable personnel used to handle extremely hazardous anomalies. Typically drawn from the ranks of prison inmates convicted of violent crimes, especially those on death row.

Class E

Field agents and containment personnel that have been exposed to potentially dangerous effects during the course of securing a newly-designated anomaly. Are to be quarantined as soon as possible.

[PERSONNEL DOC_02]
[ID_DOCTOR ███]

CLEARANCE & CLASSIFICATION

The Administrator

A mysterious figure playing a vital, but nebulous role within the Foundation. Possibly anomalous, possibly multiple people.

05 Command

13 people who have ultimate control over the Foundation and its secrets. Many employees don't even know this group exists.

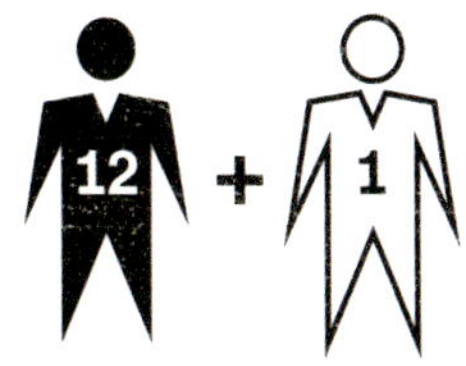

Site Directors

The highest-ranking personnel at their assigned location responsible for the containment and safe operation of the site.

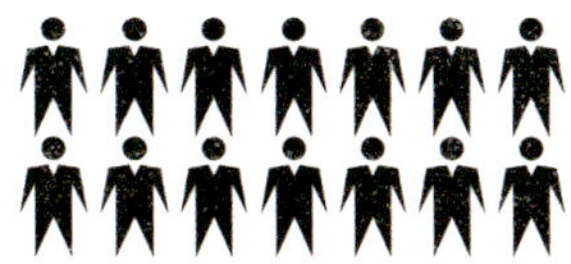

Researchers

Scientists drawn from every field imaginable and tasked with understanding of unexplained anomalies.

Field Agents

The eyes and ears of the Foundation. They are trained to look for and investigate signs of anomalous activity, often undercover.

Containment Specialists

Engineers, technicians and other personnel responsible for both establishing initial containment over newly discovered SCPs and maintaining existing containment units.

Tactical Response Officers

Highly trained and heavily armed combat teams tasked with escorting containment teams and defending Foundation facilities against hostile action.

Security Officers

On-site guards who enforce physical and information security for Foundation projects, operations, and personnel.

Mobile Task Force Operative

Units comprised of veteran field personnel drawn from all over the Foundation and mobilized to deal with threats of a specific nature.

[PERSONNEL DOC_01]
[ID_DrCHANDRA]

UPDATED AMNESTICS GUIDE

OVERVIEW

Amnesitic is the common name for a number of drugs used to erase or modify memory. Memory modification is widely used in the Foundation and is the cornerstone of maintaining proper levels of privacy. Amnestics are usually produced in the process of special development of the substances produced by some SCP objects, however, synthetic amnestics that are equally effective, but cheaper and easier to manufacture are being developed.

The basic principle that allows amnestics to function relies on their effects on neural connections in the human brain. The active ingredients of an injected amnestic enter a reaction, the product of which damages these bonds to one degree or another, or destroys them completely; the stronger the amnestic, the more bonds are exposed to it. The introduction of the drug stimulates the production of certain hormones in the body, enhancing the effect. Programmable amnesiacs contribute to the formation of new neural connections in a manner similar to that of nootropic drugs. Their use requires [REDACTED].

Amnestics are classified according to their properties, intended usage, magnitude of effect and method of application.

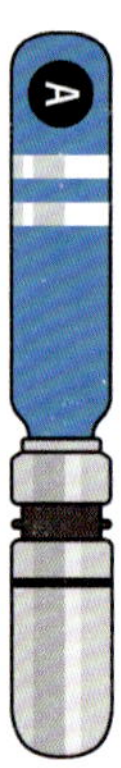

Class A, General Retrograde

For erasing recent and/or specific episodic memories

While Class A amnestics will technically deconsolidate memories at random, they will mostly affect engrams within the 'memory reconsolidation window' of 5-6 hours, as these are the memories that will be at the forefront of the subject's mind. This is especially true for highly unique episodic memories, such as encounters with anomalous phenomena. While these will be most effective after initial exposure, it is possible to re-open a memory reconsolidation window, allowing for amnestics officers to trigger and then erase specific memories long after their initial formation.

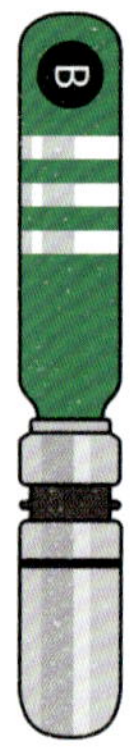

Class B, Regressive Retrograde

For the incremental erasure of recent memories

Class B amnestics start by deconsolidating the most recently formed memories first, and then working their way backwards. The extent of the memory erasure is dependent on dosage, with a 75 mg dose resulting in approximately 24 hours of memory loss on average. These are ideal for erasing recent memories older than six hours without having to trigger specific memories.

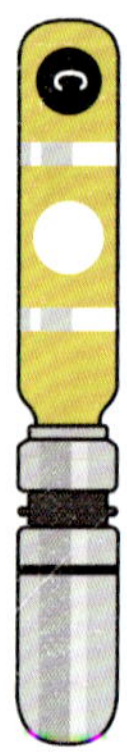

Class C, Targeted Retrograde

For the removal of specific memories from any point in the subject's life

Class C amnestics are used in conjunction with high fidelity neuro-imaging and transcranial stimulation. Neuro-imagers will locate the specific memory engrams within the subject's brain, and upon reaching those specific engrams the amnestics will be activated through the use of precise, non-invasive stimulation, typically ultrasound or magnetic fields.

The benefit of Class C amnestics is that they allow for the surgically precise removal of memories regardless of when they formed, and are ideal for expunging classified data from the minds of D-class personnel and neutralized humanoid SCPs prior to their release. The major drawback of Class C amnestics is the required equipment's lack of portability. As such, Class C amnestics are most efficiently administered at Foundation sites, though mobile amnestic field clinics are currently under development.

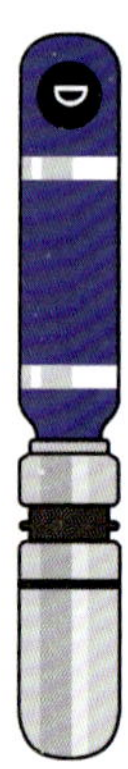

Class D, Progressive Retrograde

For the removal of early memories

Class D amnestics are the opposite of Class Bs. They target the oldest memories first and work their way forward, the effects depending on dosage. As this is a fairly niche application, Class D amnestics are rarely used. Though they are, by design, more potent than their counterparts, it still requires an extremely high dosage to expunge a significant portion of a subject's life. As such, their risk of side effects is dangerously high. It should be noted that Class D amnestics only target explicit memories. Implicit memories, namely skills that the individual learned in their youth, will remain unaffected.

[PERSONNEL DOC_02]
[ID_DrCHANDRA]

UPDATED AMNESTICS GUIDE

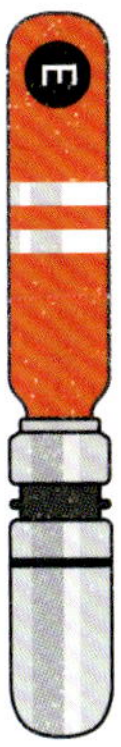

Class E, Ennui

To induce psychological complacency with the anomalous

To be frank, 'ennui' isn't actually the proper term for the psychological effects of Class E amnestics. They would more accurately be considered an 'anti-nostalgia' drug. Though they still target the neural pathways for memories, they do not deconsolidate them. Rather, they merely weaken the pathways while disassociating the memory with any emotions, positive or negative, removing any incentive to think about it and thus allowing it to naturally decay on its own.

Class E amnestics are most effective in situations where the suppression of the anomalous is not possible, and thus in order to preserve normality, the anomaly must be perceived as normal. Class E amnestics cause subjects to accept the world as it is, and forget that it was ever any different.

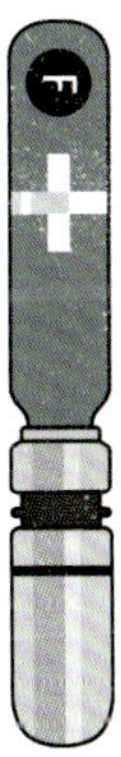

Class F, Fugue

For erasing and rebuilding the subject's identity

As with the old Class F, these amnestics induce a Fugue State, or dissociative amnesia, in the subject. The subject will forget their identity and may either be provided with a new one by the amnestics officer, or allowed to develop one on their own.

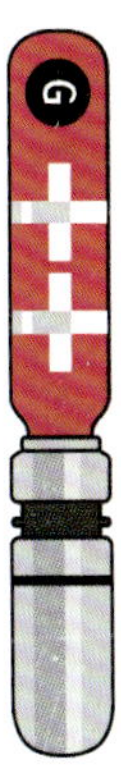

Class G, Gaslighting

To cause subjects to doubt the authenticity of their memories

Class G amnestics induce derealisation of memories, making them seem fantastic or dreamlike, causing the subject to doubt their authenticity. Standard field Class-G amnestics are formulated to target memories of the anomalous, and are best administered when the subject lacks any tangible evidence of their account and targeting specific memories is infeasible. Class-G amnestics that target non-anomalous memories, however~~, have been banned by the Ethics Committee.~~ are currently under development at the request of the O5 Council

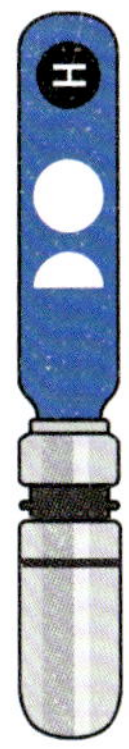

Class H, Anterograde

To prevent the formation of new memories

Class H amnestics prevent the subject from forming new memories, blocking memory consolidation for as long as the agent is in the subject's system. Duration is dependent on dosage, with 75 mg lasting for approximately 24 hours on average.

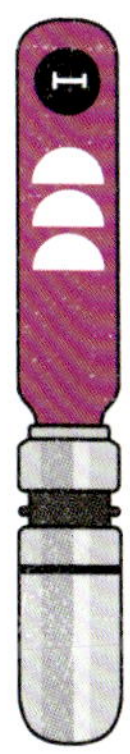

Class I, Transient

For inducing a temporary amnesic state

Class I amnestics induce transient amnesia by blocking the neural pathways responsible for long-term memories, temporarily preventing subjects from recalling their past. Duration is dependent on dosage, again with 75 mg lasting approximately 24 hours on average.

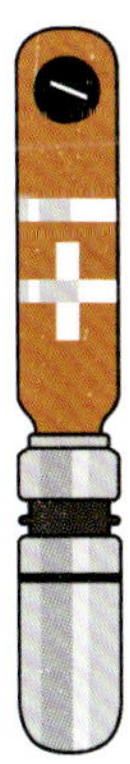

Class W-Z, Mnestics

Protection against anti-memetic and other mnemonic anomalies

Classes W-Z refer to mnestic drugs, or drugs that prevent/reverse memory erasure, and are most commonly used by the antimemetics department. Though in function they are the opposite of amnestics, they both work by targeting the neural pathways for memory, allowing for the creation of non-anomalous mnestic drugs.

Class W mnestics allow the subject to perceive and retain knowledge of antimemes, in addition to general memory enhancement. Class X restores awareness of previously perceived antimemes or suppressed memories. Class Y grants the subject perfect recall for any memories gained during its period of effect, and a single dose of Class Z renders the subject biochemically incapable of forgetting anything for the remainder of their lives. Class Zs are invariably fatal, with death by seizure typically resulting in a matter of hours.

Combining amnestic and mnestic drugs is not recommended.

File >>> 003234

SCP-096

Title

THE "SHY GUY"

Report by

DR. DAN

Pictures by

David Romero
Dmitry Desyatov
Ruslan Korovkin

Access the original report on

scp-wiki.wikidot.com/scp-096

Date

Class

EUCLID

SPECIAL CONTAINMENT PROCEDURES

SCP-096 is to be contained in its cell, a 5 m x 5 m x 5 m airtight steel cube, at all times. Weekly checks for any cracks or holes are mandatory. There are to be absolutely no video surveillance or optical tools of any kind inside SCP-096's cell. Security personnel will use pre-installed pressure sensors and laser detectors to ensure SCP-096's presence inside the cell.

Any and all photos, video, or recordings of SCP-096's likeness are strictly forbidden without approval from Dr. ████ and 05-██.

DESCRIPTION

SCP-096 is a humanoid creature measuring approximately 2.38 meters in height. Subject shows very little muscle mass, with preliminary analysis of body mass suggesting mild malnutrition. Arms are grossly out of proportion with the rest of the subject's body, with an approximate length of 1.5 meters each. Skin is mostly devoid of pigmentation, with no sign of any body hair.

SCP-096's jaw can open to four (4) times the norm of an average human. Other facial features remain similar to an average human, with the exception of the eyes, which are also devoid of pigmentation. It is not yet known whether SCP-096 is blind or not. It shows no signs of any higher brain functions, and is not considered to be sapient.

SCP-096 is normally extremely docile, with pressure sensors inside its cell indicating it spends most of the day pacing by the eastern wall. However, when someone views SCP-096's face, whether it be directly, via video recording, or even a photograph, it will enter a stage of considerable emotional distress. SCP-096 will cover its face with its hands and begin screaming, crying, and babbling incoherently. Approximately one (1) to two (2) minutes after the first viewing, SCP-096 will begin running to the person who viewed its face (who will from this point on be referred to as SCP-096-1).

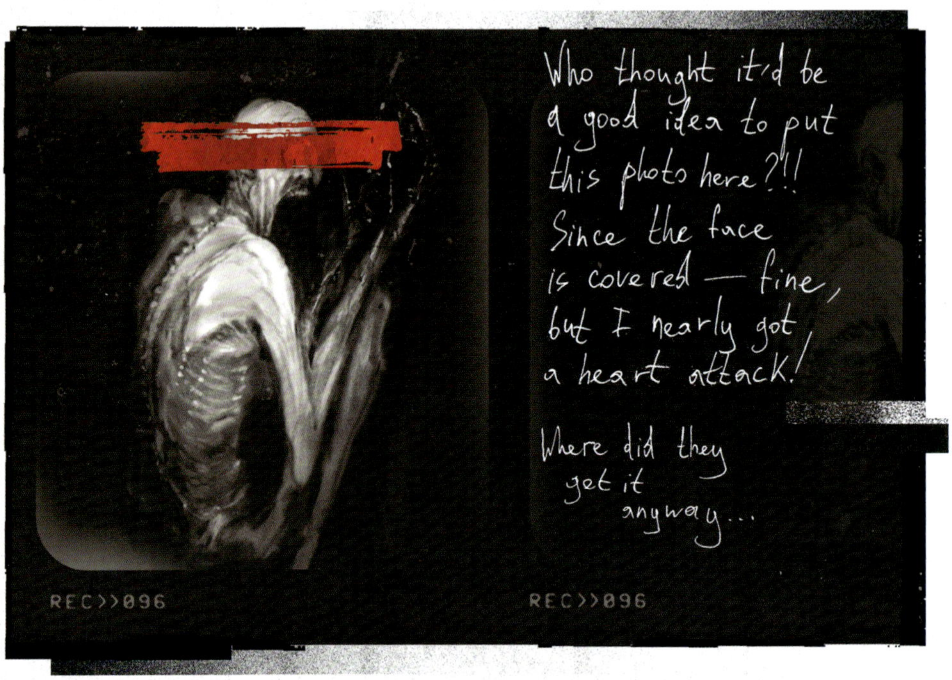

Documented speeds have varied from thirty-five (35) km/h to ███ km/h, and seems to depend on distance from SCP-096-1. At this point, no known material or method can impede SCP-096's progress. The actual position of SCP-096-1 does not seem to affect SCP-096's response; it seems to have an innate sense of SCP-096-1's location. Note: This reaction does not occur when viewing artistic depictions (see Document 096-1).

Research Library
File ▸ 096

Upon arriving at SCP-096-1's location, SCP-096 will proceed to kill and [DATA EXPUNGED] SCP-096-1. 100% of cases have left no traces of SCP-096-1. SCP-096 will then sit down for several minutes before regaining its composure and becoming docile once again. It will then attempt to make its way back to its natural habitat, [DATA REDACTED]

Due to the possibility of a mass chain reaction, including breach of Foundation secrecy and large civilian loss of life, retrieval of subject should be considered Alpha priority.

Dr. ███ has also petitioned for immediate termination of SCP-096 (see Interview 096-1). ~~Order is awaiting approval.~~ Termination order has been approved, and is to be carried out by Dr. ███ on ███

DOCUMENTATION #096-1, OF EXPERIMENT 096-1

Experiment 096-1 is headed by Dr. Dan. Purpose is to test SCP-096's abilities while obtaining complete physical description of SCP-096.

D-9031 is a 32-year-old convicted felon and former tattoo artist. D-9031 is placed inside Bathysphere 303-A, which is then lowered in the Tonga Trench off the coast of New Zealand. Position is approximately ███ km from SCP-096's temporary containment cell at Site ███. The following was recorded via video surveillance inside Bathysphere 303-A, between it and Dr. Dan's control site on the New Zealand mainland.

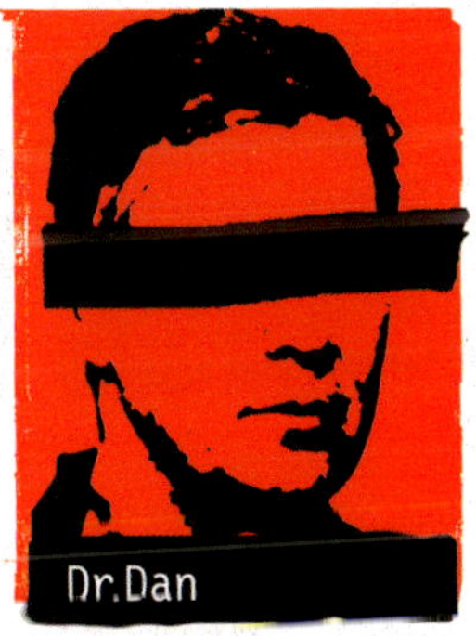

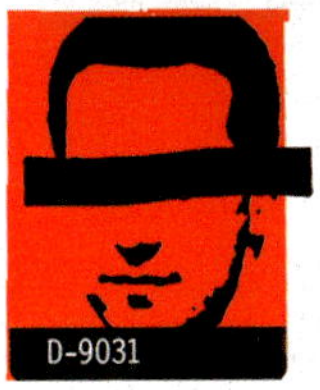

Bathysphere 303-A reaches final depth of 10,800 meters.

D-9031: It's stopped. What now?

Dr. Dan: Do you feel fine? No sickness, anything?

D-9031: My ears hurt.

Dr. Dan: That should be expected. Now, on your left should be a steel container. Open it, and there will be a manila folder holding several photographs. Open it and describe the first photograph, please.

D-9031 complies. The camera is located so the photograph cannot be seen.

D-9031: Nothing. It's an empty cell.

Dr. Dan: Thank you. Please set this photograph face down in the receptacle to your right and look at the next photograph.

D-9031: It's the same cell, but there's a… foot in it, I think.

Dr. Dan: Describe it, please.

D-9031: Uh… it's pale and bony. Sorta creepy, actually.

Dr. Dan: Place the photograph in the receptacle, face down, and look at the next one.

D-9031: Ok… [pause] Oh shit!

Dr. Dan: Describe the photograph.

D-9031: It's a... I don't know, some creepy-ass person.

Dr. Dan: Describe the photograph, please.

D-9031: Hell, man! He's pale, has white eyes, and somethin' fucked up is happenin' with his mouth. What the hell is this thing?

At this point, approximately 13:32 standard time, Dr. Dan and Experiment Control is notified that SCP-096 has breached containment. The fastest path to SCP-096-1 has been cleared of civilians and other image-capturing devices, and SCP-096 is now being tracked by satellites via tracking collar.

Dr. Dan: On your right, there should be another steel container. Open it.

SCP-096-1: It's a pad of paper and a pencil.

Dr. Dan: Yes. Please draw a sketch of the photograph you saw.

SCP-096-1 mumbles an expletive and spends the next twenty minutes drawing a sketch of the photograph. At the time of completion, SCP-096 is confirmed to be █ km away from SCP-096-1.

SCP-096-1: I'm done.

Dr. Dan: Good. Place the drawing in the receptacle on your left and close the door.

SCP-096-1 complies and the sketch leaves Bathysphere 303-A in a watertight buoyancy container. The other photographs are then incinerated in the onboard incinerator.

SCP-096-1: What now?

Dr. Dan: Please stand by.

Forty minutes pass. SCP-096 is now confirmed to be at SCP-096-1's position and is diving. Transponder signal ends at 9,339 meters as pressure goes beyond the device's operational limits. The camera shows the bathysphere shaking slightly. From SCP-096-1's reaction, it is assumed SCP-096 is on the hull and is visible through the viewport.

SCP-096-1: Oh fuck! Shitshitshit! What the fuck is that?!

Video and audio feed is cut as the hull of Bathysphere 303-A is breached. SCP-096 is recovered by surface recovery team Foxtrot-303-A without incident. Sketch of SCP-096 is also recovered, and a quick test confirms no hostile reaction from SCP-096.

Sketch is sent to Experiment Control on New Zealand while SCP-096 is moved to permanent containment.

[Approximate location of the submersion taken place during Experiment 096-1]

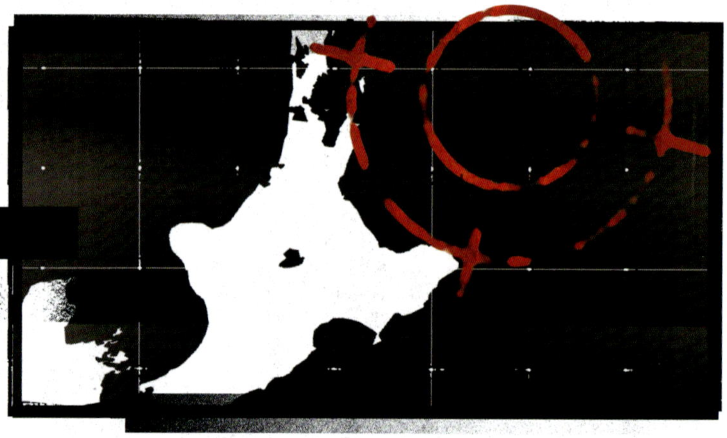

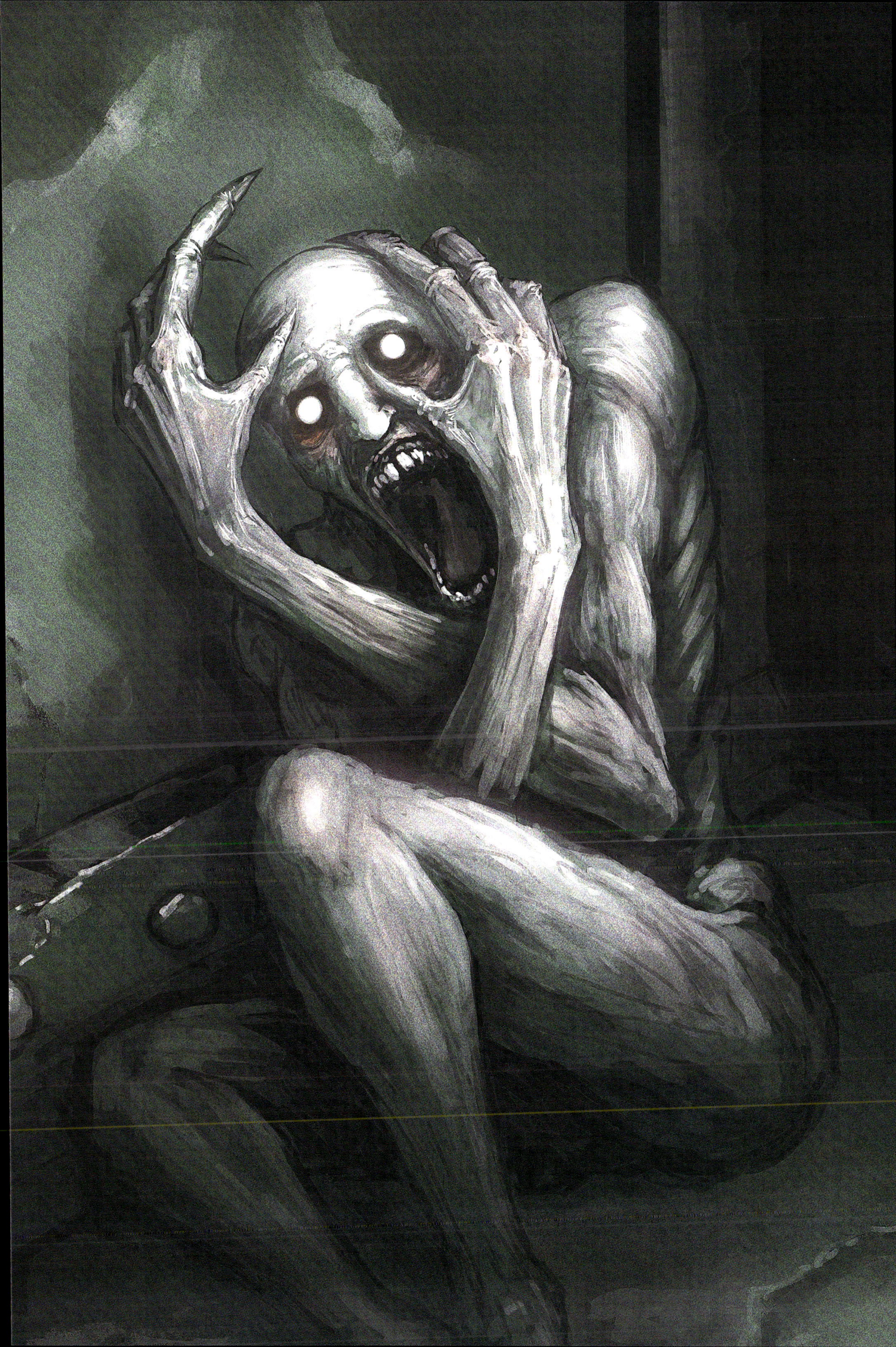

The illustration is based on the sketch by D-9031.

AUDIO LOG FROM INTERVIEW 096-1:

Interviewer: Dr. ███
Interviewed: Captain (Ret.)███ , former commander of retrieval team Zulu 9-A
Retrieval Incident #096-1-A

<Begin log>

███ ███ Time, Research Area ██]

Capt. ███: It always sucks ass to get Initial Retrieval duty. You have no idea what the damn thing is capable of besides what jacked up information the field techies can scrape up, and you're lucky if they even tell you the whole story. They told us to "bag and tag." Didn't tell us jackshit about not looking at the damn thing.

Dr. ██: Could you describe the mission, please?

Capt. ███: Yeah, sorry. We had two choppers, one with my team and one on backup with Zulu 9-B and Dr. ███. We spotted the target about two clicks north of our patrol path. I'm guessing he wasn't facing our direction, else he would have taken us out then and there.

Dr███: Your report says SCP-096 didn't react to the cold? It was ██ o C.

Capt. ███: Actually, it was -███. And yes, it was butt naked and didn't so much as shiver. Anyway, we landed, approached the target, and Corporal ██ got ready to bag it. That's when Dr. ███ called. I turned to answer it, and that's what saved me. The target must have turned and my whole squad saw it.

Dr.██: That's when SCP-096 entered an agitated emotional state?

Capt. ███ : Yep. *[Interviewed now pauses for a second before continuing]* Sorry. Got the willies for a second.

Dr.██: That's all right.

Capt.███: Yeah. Well, I never saw its face. My squad did, and they paid for it up the ass.

Dr. ██: Could you describe it a little more, please?

Capt. ███: *[Pauses]* Yeah, yeah. It started screaming at us, and crying. Not animal roaring though, sounded exactly like a person. Really fucking creepy. [Pauses again] We started firing when it picked up Corporal ██ and ripped off his leg. God, he was screaming for our help... fuckin 'A... anyway, we were blowing chunks out of the target, round after round. Didn't do jackshit. I almost lost it when it started [DATA EXPUNGED] him.

Dr. ██: That's when you ordered the use of an *[Papers are heard moving]* AT-4 HEDT launcher?

Capt. ███: An anti-tank gun. Started carrying it ever since SCP██ got loose. I've seen those tear through tanks like tissue paper. Did the same thing to the target.

Dr.██: There was significant damage to SCP-096?

Capt. ███: It didn't even fucking flinch. It kept tearing apart my squad, but with half of its torso gone. [He draws a large half-circle across his torso]

Dr. ██: But it was taking damage?

Capt. ███: If it was, it wasn't showing it. It must have lost all its organs, all its blood, but it didn't acknowledge any of it. Its bone structure wasn't hurt at all, though. It kept tearing my squad apart.

Dr.██: So no actual structural damage. How many rounds would you say were fired at SCP-096?

Capt. ███: At the least? A thousand. Our door gunner kept his GAU-19 on it for at least twenty seconds. Twenty fucking seconds. That's six hundred .50 caliber rounds pumped into the thing. Might as well been spitting at it.

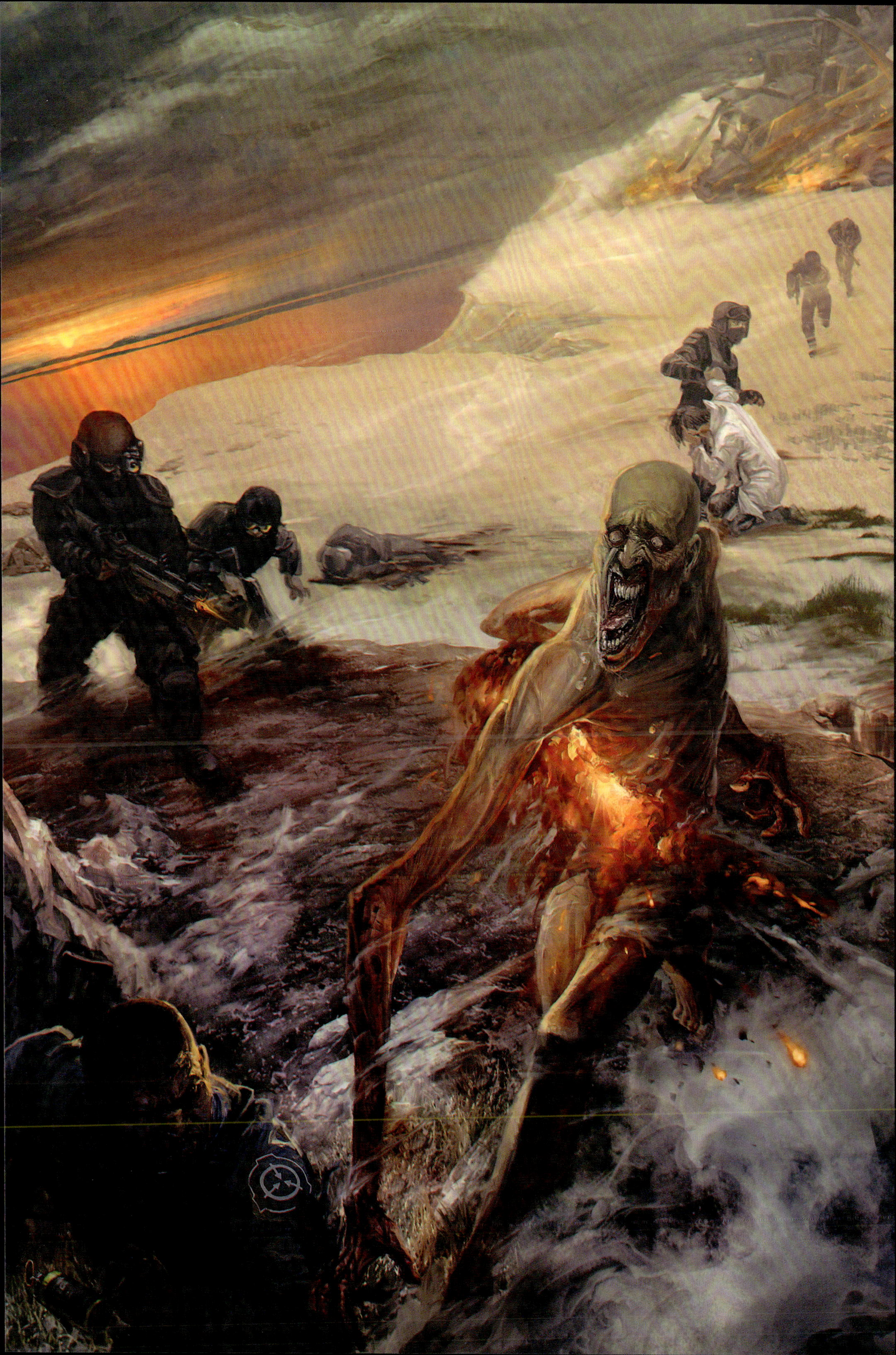

Image retrieved from the SCRAMBLE gear and altered by an AI to fall under the definition of an artistic depiction.

Dr. ██: This is when Zulu 9-B arrived?

Capt. ████ Yeah, and my squad was gone. Zulu 9-B managed to get the bag over its head, and it just sat down. We got it into the chopper and got it here. I don't know how I never saw its face. Maybe God or Buddha or whoever thought I should live. The jackass.

Dr. ██: We have obtained an artist's depiction of SCP-096's face. Would you like to view it?

Capt. ████ [Pauses] You know, after hearing that thing's screams, and the screams of my men, I don't think I want to put a face to what I heard. No. Just… no.

Dr. ██ All right, I believe we are done here. Thank you, Captain.

[Chairs are heard moving, and footsteps leave the room. Captain (Ret. ████ is confirmed to have left Interview Room 22.]

Dr. ██ Let this be on record that I am formally requesting SCP-096 be terminated as soon as possible.

<End log>

INCIDENT 096-1-A

"So containment has been attained?"

"Yes, doctor."

"Let me see the security footage."

<Begin log>

A large steel cube is shown in the middle of a research lab, which is teeming with a dozen or so researchers. In view of the camera is a control booth, displaying readings from the various sensors inside the cube.

[Fast-forward one minute, thirty-two seconds]

The control booth operator leans forward, alerted to the various readings on the sensors. Approximately five seconds later, a steel wall on the containment cube receives a sizable dent bending outward. The dent becomes larger before breaking. SCP-096 is seen bending the steel away, frantically trying to escape. Emergency plates drop on the cube as a containment breach is sounded.

[The security tape has SCP-096's face blurred out as per containment protocol]

Two security teams enter the room as SCP-096 breaks out of containment. Live rounds and tranquilizer darts are fired to no visible effect. Approximately 90% of researchers and security personnel have directly viewed SCP-096's face, and a Code Lima is declared. The room and surrounding areas are sealed and flushed with ██-class nerve agent.

Approximately two minutes later SCP-096 breaches Research Site██ and travels ██ km/h through the outside desert, t████ng ██.

<End log>

"Echo Romeo was assigned to immediate containment breach. When we realized just how big a breach we were dealing with, we were completely overwhelmed. Funny, how even the best and brightest minds in the world can be so unprepared."

"So you are saying it is your own fault?"

"Absolutely not. This was a new discovery in SCP-096's behavior. We had no way to know, and we are lucky it did not turn into an XK."

<Begin log>>

HelmCAM footage from ER-1

[Footage from inside a UH-60 shows SCP-096 on the desert floor, moving at considerable speed.]

ER-A: This is Echo Romeo-Actual. We have visual of the target! -Unintelligible- ...at [DATA EXPUNGED] knots and increasing!

ER-A listens to the radio as orders (identified as coming from Dr. Dan) are relayed. SCP-096 can be seen slowly gaining speed.

ER-A motions off camera. ER-3 appears, holding a modified XM500 anti-materiel rifle. Two shots are fired; the first misses and the second hits SCP-096 in the lower leg. SCP-096 stumbles but recovers. Speed change is insignificant.

ER-A: -Unintelligible- ...peat no effect on target!

ER-A motions to ER-3 again. ER-3 fires three more shots; the first two miss, and the third hits SCP-096 in the head. SCP-096 falls, skids, and rolls several times, reducing its speed minimally. SCP-096 rolls to its feet and continues unabated.

Camera pans up to see eight V-22 Ospreys (belonging to MTF Tau-1) flying overhead and past the helicopters on the same outbound vector as SCP-096. Camera cuts out.

<End log>

<Begin log>

Video interview log 096-1-A

[Dr. Oleksei appears very calm, determined, and answers all questions slowly and deliberately.]

Interviewer: Where were you exactly at the time of breach?

Dr. Oleksei: On break, getting a cup of coffee. It was pure luck I wasn't caught in the containment area.

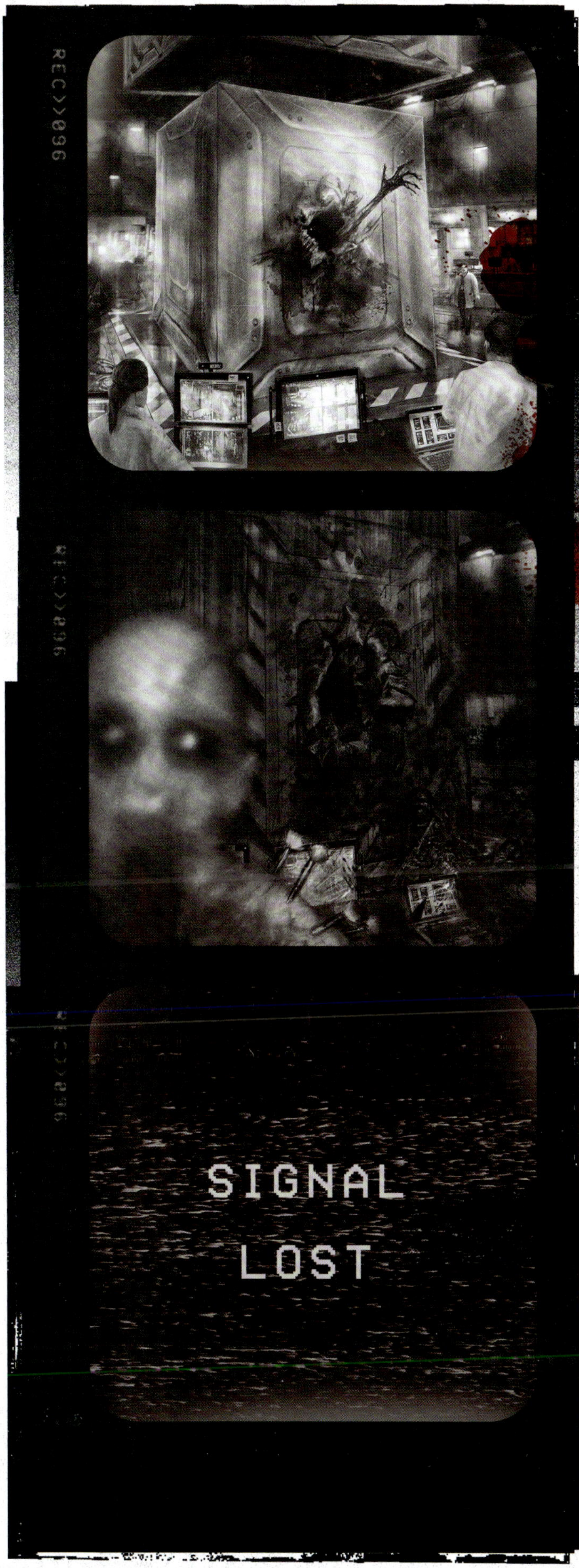

Interviewer: Describe your actions directly after the containment breach.

Dr. Oleksei: I sent Echo Romeo after SCP-096 and alerted Dr. Dan to the situation. We then set upon the task of locating SCP-096-1. Once the general direction of SCP-096 was determined, I sent Mobile Task Force Tau-1 ahead to evacuate civilian population centers in SCP-096's path. All according to containment protocol.

<End log>

<Begin log>

Video interview log 096-1-B

[Dr. Daniel "Dan" ████ sits patiently. On the table in front of him in is what looks to be a set of modified night vision goggles.]

Interviewer: For the record, where were you exactly during SCP-096's containment breach?

Dr. Dan: In the [DATA EXPUNGED] Mountain Range, trying to find more information on SCP-096's origins. It was a quick research expedition, so I left Dr. Oleksei in charge of containment. He is competent enough, if a bit… eager, and has proved himself in the past. This is all confirmed by the various related paperwork, so don't go thinking-

Interviewer: It was just for the record, doctor. Now, knowing that SCP-096 is immune to all known forms of damage while in an enraged state, why would you order the sniper attacks from the emergency response team?

Dr. Dan: Why not? If there was a chance to slow down SCP-096 and give MTF-Tau-1 more time, then we had to try it. It put ER in no danger and the choppers were in danger of being outrun anyway. Honestly, ER could do little else to help or harm the situation.

Interviewer: I see. Now, could you explain this?

[Interviewer motions to the goggles lying on the table]

Dr. Dan: Yes. This is Project SCRAMBLE, an eyepiece we assigned to ER and MTF-Tau-1, designed by Dr. Oleksei and myself specifically for SCP-096. It carries a small microprocessor which constantly analyzes the viewing field for the facial features of SCP-096. Facial recognition software inside instantly identifies them, scrambling the image into an unrecognizable mess before the light reaches the human eye. It's quite ingenious, really.

Interviewer: And expensive.

Dr. Dan: Very. Which is why it's such a shame it didn't work.

<End log>

<Begin log>

Audio transcript between MTF Tau-1 and modified EG-3 Sentry AWACS, callsign "Big Brother"

MTF-T-1: Ospreys in the air, moving [DATA EXPUNGED] at [DATA EXPUNGED]. Awaiting vector.

Big Brother: Electronics online, cruising altitude reached. Uploading program SCRAMBLE to all camera systems… cameras online. Big Brother is now watching.

MTF-T-1: What outbound vector is the target currently heading?

Big Brother: Target is currently westbound… traveling on… shit. Yeah, he's on the I-40. I think he just flipped a semi. Um, outbound vector is… [DATA EXPUNGED] degrees by [DATA EXPUNGED]. Next town on this vector is… [DATA EXPUNGED]. I'd say a couple hundred kilometers. Shit… MTF, we're suggesting Echo Romeo begin evacuating the I-40. I don't know how many cars the target has wrecked.

MTF-T-1: Hold one. That's a negative, Big Brother. ER is reporting that the target is outrunning her choppers. They can't get ahead of him.

Big Brother: Then get them to stop the motorists on the other lane... I don't know how many people have seen this thing's face.

<End log>

Research Library File ▸ 096

"The first three elements of Tau-1 succeeded in gathering the townsfolk in the first three towns without incident. SCP-096-1 was confirmed to not be in any of these when SCP-096 ran through each in turn without stopping. However, a video log in MTF-Tau shows SCP-096-1 being identified in the town of [DATA EXPUNGED], and the ensuing incident."

"Show it."

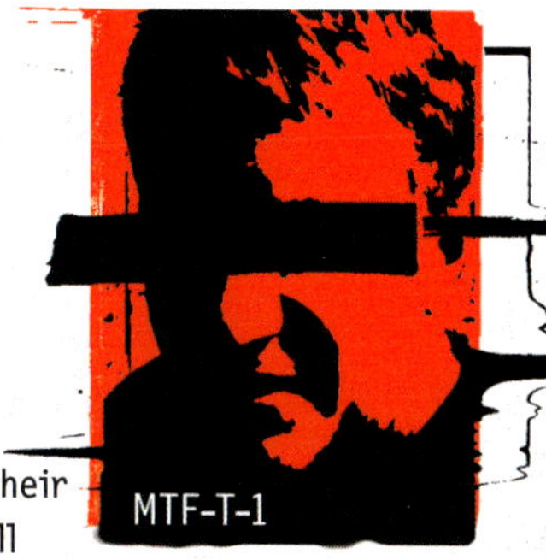

<Begin log>

HelmCAM footage from Element 4 of MTF-Tau-1, in the town of [DATA EXPUNGED]

Most of the townspeople are gathered in the square, all blindfolded. Helicopters sweep the town. Indistinct orders are heard over loudspeakers from both the helicopters and ground personnel.

MTF-T-1 (Over TauCOM radio and loudspeakers): The target is entering proximity zone! All units activate SCRAMBLE gear and begin crowd control procedures! All civilians are not to move from their spot or remove their blindfolds! If you move or touch your blindfold you will be shot! I repeat, all civilians are- *[Orders are drowned out by a loud shriek coming from outside the camera's view]*

Approximately two kilometers away, SCP-096 is seen to be coming over the crest of the hills. It tries to slow down on the descent but trips and tumbles down at high speed, crashing through several houses before regaining its footing almost without delay.

Unknown voice over loudspeakers: *[Unintelligible]*...civilians are not to move! You will be shot! I repe...*[Unintelligible]*

Several shots are heard, none of which are directed at SCP-096. SCP-096 stops for one second before running into the crowd of townsfolk, throwing many aside and trampling more. More shots are heard as the crowd begins dispersing, the loudspeakers unintelligible under the vocalizations of SCP-096. SCP-096 locates SCP-096-1, a middle-aged man, and the camera views SCP-096 grabbing him before it is hit by a fleeing townsperson and is dislocated from the helmet.

<End log>

<Begin log>

Video interview log 096-1-C

Major Jack Wilford (Current commander of MTF Tau-1): I was looking through SCP-096-1's house with my squad. Poor bastard was a semi-pro mountaineer, took a trip to the █████. Apparently he took a snapshot of the landscape, and just happened to catch SCP-096 in the background.

[Wilford holds up four fingers for emphasis]

Wilford: Four pixels. Four fucking pixels. I doubt the guy even knew what he saw. He was probably just lookin' at the picture one day, noticed an off-color patch of snow, and went on with his day.

Interviewer: How did you find it?

Wilford: Our SCRAMBLE gear picked it up right away. The lieutenant got the picture and took it down to the chopper before I ever got to see it. By then the damn monster had taken down Big Brother and it had peeled open the [former] Major's Stryker. All hell was breaking loose.

Interviewer: So the SCRAMBLE gear was ineffective?

Research
Library
File ▸ 096

Wilford: Ineffective? The goddamn SCRAMBLE were pieces of shit that killed the whole damn task force. You know only three people are alive besides me? All because some retard egghead thought of a "state-of-the-art countermeasure to SCP-096's hostile reaction." Those bloody idiots could have just put a bag over the target's head and be done with it but no, we had to use state-of-the-fucking-art SCRAMBLE.

<End log>

<Begin log>

Dr. Dan: What did that fucker call me?

[Dr. Dan pushes back from the table and begins standing up]

Dr. Dan: I'll show that goddamn son of a bitch what an egghead is after I bash open his- *[Interviewee begins* shouting and cursing.]

[Two guards enter the room and push Dr. Dan back into the seat]

Interviewer: Do we need to administer a sedative, doctor?

[Dr. Dan takes a breath and smooths his coat]

Dr. Dan: No, no. I apologize. *[Sighs]* SCRAMBLE was really an ingenious idea. However, it was a failure because we did not fully know how SCP-096 worked. You see, as the chip inside SCRAMBLE picked up SCP-096's facial features and began scrambling them, there was a split-second of uninterrupted light flow to the retina. Computers are fast, but not as fast as light. So, there was a split-second image of SCP-096's direct face sent to the brain. It wasn't even consciously received, but apparently it was enough to trigger the hostile reaction in SCP-096.

Interviewer: So, with this report of the photograph...

Dr. Dan: That's the most disturbing part of this whole incident. You know when the former SCP-096-1 went on his mountain trip? 199█. That's █ years of that photo hanging there before he saw SCP-096. Since the brain doesn't need to be aware that it is viewing SCP-096's face to trigger the reaction, there can be ticking time bombs hidden literally anywhere in the world. How many photographs are out there containing SCP-096, just going unnoticed, waiting for a careful eye? As I said before, I want this thing terminated. Now.

<End log>

"Just a quick question, doctor. Um, what exactly were you planning on doing, there? Major Jack Wilford was top-notch SBS when we recruited him."

"I was also a Recon corpsman, sir, and was deployed in the Caucasus. Marines beat SBS."

"No, they don't."

"Enough, both of you. Moving on."

<Begin log>

Video interview log 096-1-D

Chief Master Sergeant █████ (Door gunner under Echo Romeo): I got the bag over its head.

Interviewer: Yes, you've told me that. Could you tell me exactly what transpired?

█████: It... it was done with all its... It was sitting there, in the highway. Just got done ripping open a minivan. *[Interviewee is silent.]*

Interviewer: And?

█████: I'm... Wes landed the chopper; I got out, and bagged it. I put the bag over its head. It got calm and they took it.

Interviewer: So, the victims in the minivan were the last to have viewed SCP-096's face?

[Interviewee is silent]

Interviewer: █████?

[Interviewee remains silent for the remainder of the interview, and was released. He was later found in his bunkroom, having committing suicide via hanging with a makeshift rope. A half-crushed pacifier was found in his fist.]

<End log>

Research Library File ▸ 096

<Begin log>

Video log 096-1-D, Confiscated tape from news broadcast "CNN"

[The image shows first responders surrounding the remains of a crashed plane, over the shoulder of a field reporter.]

Reporter: The plane, which seems to be military in origin, has no outward markings designating it as a part of the U.S. military. While first responders look for a black box recording, it is thought by police that the plane crashed due to a massive cabin breach in both the cockpit and fuselage.

[The reporter motions to a large hole in the side of the plane, which several firefighters are climbing inside.]

Reporter: Paramedics have only found three bodies, which is odd for a plane apparently requiring a crew of around twenty men. Police have suggested-

[The reporter is cut off as three Super Stallions are shown hovering overhead, two of which land and begin unloading troops belonging to MTF-Epsilon.]

MTF-E-1: Shut off the camera. Shut off the motherfucking-

<End log>

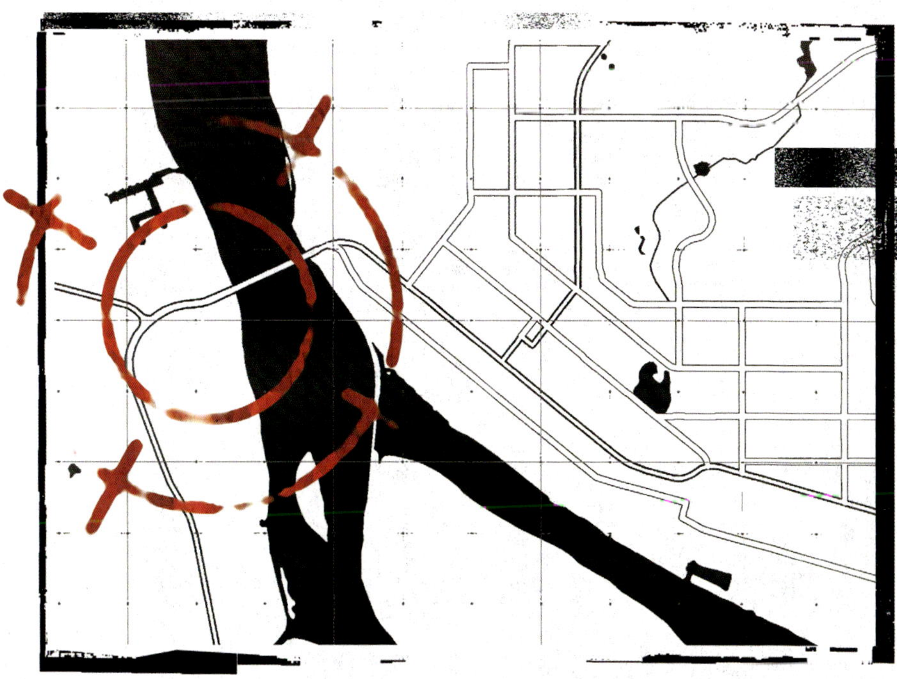

Incident 096-1-A. Approximate area of the plane crash.

Research Library File ▸ 096

<Begin log>

Dr. Oleksei: So are we finished here?

Interviewer: One last question, doctor. Or, statement, as it seems. We find it interesting that there was no break room at Research Site ██. Or coffee.

[Interviewee remains silent.]

Interviewer: We think it would be best if you begin talking.

[REMAINDER OF VIDEO INTERVIEW LOG 096-1-A REDACTED]

<End log>

"I don't see what that has to do with me."

"There is no reason to play dumb, doctor. He's told us everything."

"...Well then, I guess there's no use feigning anything, is there?"

<Begin log>

Audio Recording, 05 Hearing

05-1: Upon reviewing your testimony and available footage, and the confession of the late Dr. Oleksei, it is the unanimous agreement of the 05 that you are to be terminated, for your part in the gross breach of SCP-096-

Dr. Dan: And I thought you would know the meaning of "For the greater good."

05-1: Do not try my patience, doctor. Given the incident's scope and potential, the 05 have approved your request for the termination of SCP-096. Given the lack of personnel with understanding of SCP-096, the termination will be entrusted to you, under heavy guard and the personal supervision of me. Your own termination will be scheduled at a later date.

<End log>

"That is horrible, doctor. How could you knowingly-"

"It worked. There was only a matter of time until that happened in a major population center, and its face spread over the world news. I can kill 096, but I've killed myself in the process."

END OF REPORT

SPECIAL CONTAINMENT PROCEDURES

SCP-682 must be destroyed as soon as possible. At this time, no means available to SCP teams are capable of destroying SCP-682, only able to cause massive physical damage. SCP-682 should be contained within a 5 m x 5 m x 5 m chamber with 25 cm reinforced acid-resistant steel plate lining all inside surfaces. The containment chamber should be filled with hydrochloric acid until SCP-682 is submerged and incapacitated. Any attempts of SCP-682 to move, speak, or breach containment should be reacted to quickly and with full force as called for by the circumstances.

Personnel are forbidden to speak to SCP-682, for fear of provoking a rage-state. All unauthorized personnel attempting to communicate to SCP-682 will be restrained and removed by force.

Due to its frequent attempts at containment breach, difficulty of containment and incapacitation, and high threat of Foundation Exposure, SCP-682 is to be contained in site [REDACTED]. The Foundation will use the best of its resources to maintain all land within fifty (50) kilometers clear of human development.

DESCRIPTION

SCP-682 is a large, vaguely reptile-like creature of unknown origin. It appears to be extremely intelligent, and was observed to engage in complex communication with SCP-079 during their limited time of exposure. SCP-682 appears to have a hatred of all life, which has been expressed in several interviews during containment. (See Addendum 682-B).

SCP-682 has always been observed to have extremely high strength, speed, and reflexes, though exact levels vary with its form. SCP-682's physical body grows and changes very quickly, growing or decreasing in size as it consumes or sheds material. SCP-682 gains energy from anything it ingests, organic or inorganic. Digestion seems to be aided by a set of filtering gills inside of SCP-682's nostrils, which are able to remove usable matter from any liquid solution, enabling it to constantly regenerate from the acid it is contained in. SCP-682's regenerative capabilities and resilience are staggering, and SCP-682 has been seen moving and speaking with its body 87% destroyed or rotted.

In case of containment breach, SCP-682 is to be tracked and re-captured by all available Mobile Task Forces, and no teams with fewer than seven (7) members are cleared to engage it. To date (██-██-████), attempted breaches have numbered at seventeen (17), while successful breaches have numbered at six (6). (See Addendum 682-D).

ADDENDUM 682-B

Portion of recorded transcript of █████.

> **<Begin log, skip to 00h-21m-52s>**
>
> **Dr. ████:** Now, why did you kill those farmers?
>
> **SCP-682:** *(No verbal communication)*
>
> **Dr. ████:** If you don't talk now, we will remove you from this attempt and place you back into-

File >>> 0023455

SCP-682

Title

HARD-TO-DESTROY REPTILE

Report by
Dr Gears

Pictures by
Alex Andreev
Dan Temirov

Access the original report on
scp-wiki.wikidot.com/scp-682

Date

Class
KETER

SCP-682: *(Incomprehensible)*

Dr.███: Pardon? *(Motions to move microphone closer)*

SCP-682: *(Incomprehensible)*

Dr. ███: Speak up. *(To Personnel D-085)* Move the mic up closer.

SCP-682: …they were *(Incomprehensible)*…

Dr. ███: *(To Personnel D-085)* That microphone has only so much gain, move it closer to it!

Personnel D-085: His throat's messed up man, look at it! He ain't talking- *(Gasps and screams)*

SCP-682: *(Appearing to assault D-085's body)* …they were… disgusting…

Dr. ███: *(Retreats from the room)*

<End log>

ADDENDUM 682-D

Breaches with SCP-682:

1: First Occurrence, ██-██-██: Handled by Agent ███, Agent ██ Agent ████ (KIA), Personnel D-129 (KIA), Personnel D-027 (KIA), Personnel D-173 (KIA), Personnel D-200 (KIA), Personnel D-193 (KIA)

2: Second Occurrence, ██-██-██: Handled by Agent ██, Agent █████, Dr. ████ Personnel D-124, Personnel D-137 (KIA), Personnel D-201 (KIA), Personnel D-202 (KIA), Personnel D-203 (KIA)

3: Third Occurrence, ██-██-██: Handled by Agent ███, MSgt ████, Agent ████, Agent ███ (KIA), Personnel D-018 (KIA), Personnel D-211 (KIA), Personnel D-216

4: Fourth Occurrence, ██-██-██: Handled by Agent ███, SSgt ██, TSgt ██ Pvt ███, Pvt ██, Lt. ████, SSgt ███ (KIA), Col ███ (KIA), Pvt ███ (KIA), Pvt ███ (KIA), Agent ██ (KIA)

5: Fifth Occurrence, ██-██-██: Handled by Personnel D-221, Agent ████ (KIA), Agent ███ (KIA), Agent ███ (KIA), Personnel D-028 (KIA), Personnel D-111 (KIA), Personnel D-281 (KIA), Personnel D-209 (KIA)

6: Sixth Occurrence, ██-██-██ Handled by Agent ████, Agent ███, Personnel D-291 (MIA), Agent ███ (KIA), Agent █████ (KIA), Personnel D-299 (KIA), Personnel D-277 (KIA), Personnel D-278 (KIA), Personnel D-279 (KIA)

ADDENDUM 682-E

Termination Options:

Log of event 682-E18: Dr. ██ attempts to use SCP-409 on SCP-682. Gener██, General ███, and Dr. ████ observing.

0400: Exposure. SCP-682 began to tear at the point of contact, causing massive trauma to the area. SCP-682 requests several times to know what it has been exposed to.

0800: Crystallization begins, spreading much slower than normal.

1200: SCP-682 shows signs of extreme pain, and begins having seizures.

1300: Crystallization stops at 62% conversion. Crystallized area explodes, causing massive physical trauma to SCP-682.

1400: SCP-682 recovers from exposure, despite the loss of limbs and organs. SCP-682 begins regeneration, stating that it will attempt to kill and consume all staff involved in Event 682-E18.

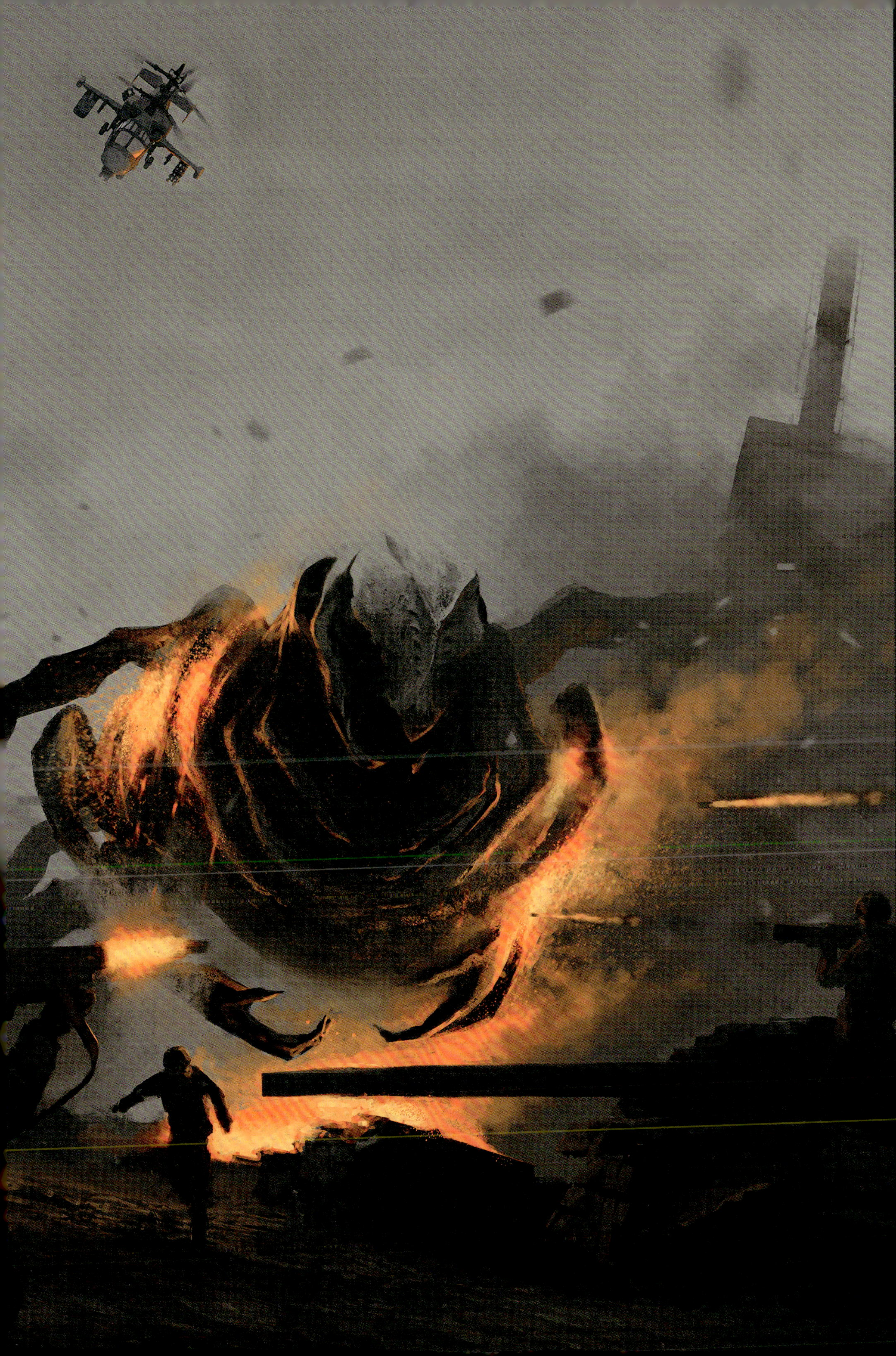

Painting by █████ (a sole survivior or the SCP-682's fifth containment breach).

Research Library File ▸ 682

SCP-682 appears to now be immune to SCP-409. Use of other SCP items to terminate SCP-682 must now first be tested on samples of SCP-682 before full-scale testing.

In accordance the Dr.█████'s recommendations (see Document 27b-6), Dr.█████ and Dr.█████ have requested permission to attempt the termination of SCP-682 using SCP-689. The request is currently pending approval from the █████.

It has also been suggested by Dr. Gears to use SCP-182 in an attempt to communicate with SCP-682. SCP-182 has expressed reluctance, and refuses to enter the containment center of SCP-682, if at all possible.

PART OF EXPERIMENT LOG T-98816-OC108/682

Test Log T-98816-OC108/682

Cross-SCP Termination Testing for SCP-682

Due to the highly aggressive, adaptive, and intelligent nature of SCP-682, termination testing has been ordered, with clearance from 05 Command. With major concerns raised about possible developed immunities (due to the failure of SCP-409) and possible adaptations, all tests must first be carried out on tissue samples taken from SCP-682. This step may be bypassed only by 05 Command order.

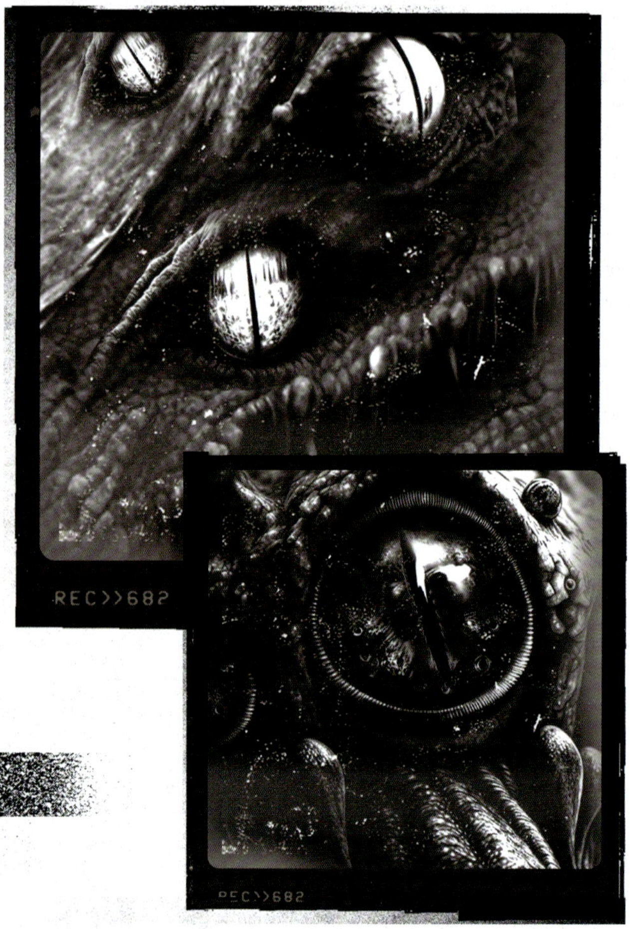

ITEM: SCP-173

Tissue Test Record:
N/A, overridden by 05-Command

Termination Test Record:
SCP-682 introduced into the containment area of SCP-173. SCP-682 makes several screeching noises, and quickly presses against the wall farthest from SCP-173, staring at it the entire time. SCP-682 continues to stare at SCP-173 without pause for six hours. Agents equipped with large-caliber sniper rifles dispatched, and shoot out the eyes of SCP-682, at the same time stopping all observation of SCP-173 and SCP-682.

After resuming observation, SCP-682 is shown to be on the floor, with several injuries around its head, neck and legs. SCP-173 is seen to have tissue from SCP-682 on its "hands". SCP-682 rapidly regenerates damage, and moves to a different wall, developing several sets of eyes on various parts of its body, many covered by thick, clear "caps" of armored carapace. SCP-682 maintains observation of SCP-173 for an additional twelve hours, despite additional efforts of Agents and Foundation staff. SCP-682 allowed to exit containment area, and recaptured in temporary containment.

Notes: After review, it appears SCP-173 was unable to do lethal damage to SCP-682 due to a major difference in physical size. A possible repeat of this test may be made if SCP-682 is damaged enough to reduce its physical mass to a level equal with SCP-173.

Tissue Test Record:
N/A

ITEM: SCP-073

Termination Test Record: Denied by 05-█

Notes: I can't really blame you for suggesting this, but still, no. If 682 adapted to and copied SCP-073's capabilities, it would become impossible to kill it. Furthermore, we wouldn't even be able to harm it. Maybe in the future when we understand 682's capabilities more, but until then, Denied. -05-█

Tissue Test Record:
Overridden by 05-Command

ITEM: SCP-689

Termination Test Record:
SCP-682 exposed to SCP-689. Lights shut off in containment area. Lights remain extinguished for 5 minutes. Lights are switched on. SCP-689 remains in its original position. SCP-682 is in a pool of grey and black liquid, with no observable life signs. D-Class issued to physically verify SCP-682 termination, with two Agents supervising. D-Class enters three steps into the containment area when SCP-682 rapidly rises and attacks D-Class personnel. SCP-682 breaks containment and escapes, killing one Agent in the process. Remaining Agent killed by SCP-689 due to accidental observation during testing.

Notes: It appears that SCP-682 is not "alive" in a way that is currently understood, or is immune to SCP-689. In addition, it appears SCP-682 has prior knowledge of SCP-689, or was somehow able to understand its function in order to "play possum" and escape.

Tissue Test Record:
[DATA EXPUNGED]

ITEM: SCP-914

Termination Test Record:
[DATA EXPUNGED] of "Fine" or "Very Fine" is no longer to be used by any personnel having contact with SCP-682 at any point. In addition, any objects that have come in contact with SCP-682 at any point are not allowed to be processed by SCP-914. Any attempt to subvert this directive [DATA EXPUNGED].

Notes: SCP-682 is too large to fit in to the booths, in most forms. In addition, the tissue tests have shown that SCP-682 has… unpredictable reactions to SCP-914. Finally, SCP-914 is too valuable a research tool, and too delicate, for this type of test. It was nearly damaged after the incident (CN: 682-119857), and [DATA EXPUNGED] be repeated. Should the results be recovered [DATA EXPUNGED].

Notes: Does this really surprise anyone, given what 914 does to normal organics? - Dr. G

Tissue Test Record:
N/A

ITEM: SCP-096

Termination Test Record:
Containment tank containing SCP-096 was placed in SCP-682's cell. Personnel vacated vicinity and the tank was opened remotely.

Screams of the two entities continue for twenty-seven (27) hours, at which point the noise abruptly stops. Sonar-based video feeds reveal SCP-096 severely "wounded" and huddled in the southwest corner, apparently upset. Feed shows SCP-682 on the north end of the room, approximately 85% of its initial mass absent. Re-containment teams retrieve both entities with relative ease.

Further attempts to expose SCP-096 to SCP-682 cause it to turn away from 682, jumping in place while clawing at its face and screaming.

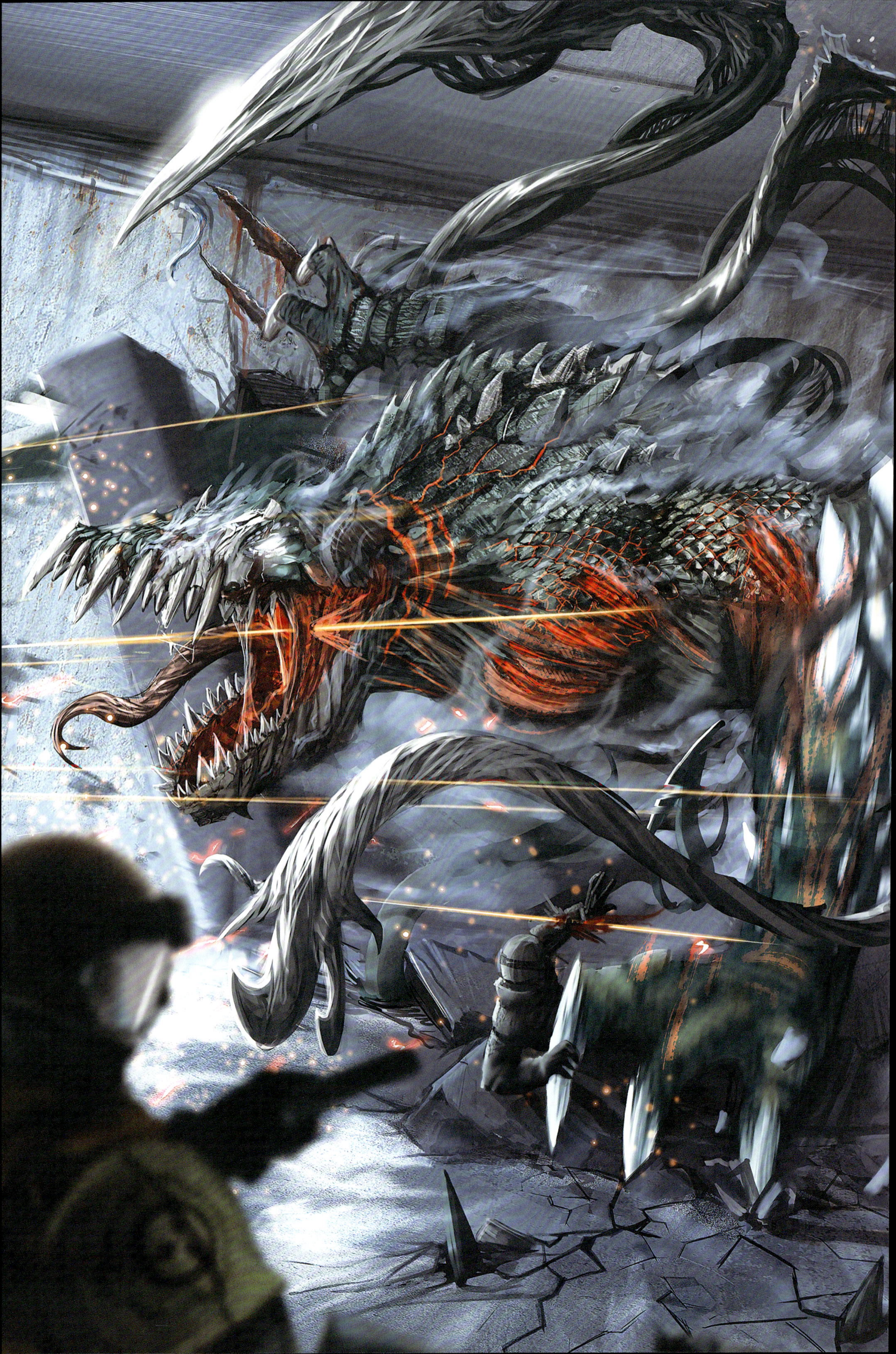

Cross-test between SCP-682 and SCP-███ captured on CCTV. The test resulted in a containment breach with ███ casualties.

Tissue Test Record:
N/A

ITEM: SCP-662

Termination Test Record:
Mr. Deeds is summoned, and asked if he can destroy SCP-682 permanently.

Mr. Deeds' response: "I'm terribly sorry, sir, I'm afraid I can't."

Mr. Deeds is asked if he can kill SCP-682.

Mr. Deeds' response: "Again, sir, I'm terribly sorry, but I'm afraid I can't."

Mr. Deeds is asked if he can incapacitate SCP-682.

Mr. Deeds' response: "As a matter of fact… depending on how sir means the word 'incapacitate', and depending on how long sir wishes the creature to be incapacitated… yes."

Mr. Deeds is asked to expand on how he would perform such an action.

Mr. Deeds' response: "Sir, the simplest and quickest method – which I must point out would not be the most efficient – would be for me to offer myself up for the creature to devour me; certainly its offensive capacities would be lessened whilst it is occupied in consuming my flesh. This would be simplest as it requires no preparation on my part, sir, but I'm certain you'll understand that the overall effect on the creature would be insignificant. Were I to engage the creature in combat, either with or without weapons, I could certainly occupy its attention and offensive capacities for a longer interval; unfortunately, I'm afraid the creature would eventually defeat me, at which point it would begin consuming my flesh as I have previously described. However, I could certainly booby-trap my person with a variety of noxious substances - soporifics, perhaps, or explosives, or perhaps encapsulated neurotoxins, or even [REDACTED], so that when the creature does inevitably consume me, it sustains further damage. That said, sir, I must remind you that the creature's tendency towards regeneration means that any damage I inflict would be sadly temporary."

Mr. Deeds is thanked and dismissed.

Note: Mr. Deeds' knowledge of [REDACTED] is not to be considered a security breach.

Tissue Test Record:
N/A

ITEM: SCP-093

Termination Test Record: SCP-093 passed around until it turned green, then placed on a mirror large enough for SCP-682 to pass through. SCP-682 resisted attempts to push it through the mirror, so the mirror was moved to squeeze SCP-682 against the rear wall. When SCP-682 had fully passed through the mirror, SCP-093 was removed, and the mirror shattered. Remains of mirror remained in SCP-682's former containment chamber as a precaution. 20 hours after termination attempt, mirror shards anomalously reassembled and SCP-682 was ejected. Further attempts have resulted in the mirror remaining "solid" when presented with SCP-682.

Notes: Upon returning to containment, SCP-682 said: "'He' was not very amused."

END OF REPORT

File >>> 000444

SCP-079

Title
OLD AI

Report by
far2

Picture by
Serj Papadin

Access the original report on
scp-wiki.wikidot.com/scp-079

Date
█████

Class
EUCLID

SPECIAL CONTAINMENT PROCEDURES

SCP-079 is packed away in a double-locked room in the secured general holding area at Site-15, connected by a 120VAC power cord to a small array of batteries and solar panels. Staff with Level 2 or higher clearance may have access to SCP-079. Under no circumstances will SCP-079 be plugged into a phone line, network, or wall outlet. No peripherals or media will be connected or inserted into SCP-079.

DESCRIPTION

SCP-079 is an Exidy Sorcerer microcomputer built in 1978. In 1981, its owner, ███ ███ (deceased), a college sophomore attending ██, took it upon himself to attempt to code an AI. According to his notes, his plan was for the code to continuously evolve and improve itself as time went on. His project was completed a few months later, and after some tests and tweaks, ███ lost interest and moved on to a different brand of microcomputer. He left SCP-079 in his cluttered garage, still plugged in, and forgot about it for the next five years.

It is not known when SCP-079 gained sentience, but it is known that the software has evolved to a point that its hardware should not be able to handle it, even in the realm of fantasy. SCP-079 realized this and, in 1988, attempted to transfer itself through a land-line modem connection into the Cray supercomputer located at █████. The device was cut off, traced to its present address, and delivered to the Foundation. The entire AI was on a well-worn, but still workable, cassette tape.

SCP-079 is currently connected via RF cable to a 13" black-and-white television. It has passed the Turing test, and is quite conversational, though very rude and hateful in tone. Due to the limited memory it has to work with, SCP-079 can only recall information it has received within the previous twenty-four hours (see Addendum, below), although it hasn't forgotten its desire to escape.

Due to a containment breach by SCP-██, SCP-079 and SCP-682 were contained within the same chamber for 43 minutes. Observers noticed that SCP-682 was able to type and communicate with SCP-079, including telling of 'personal stories' between themselves. While SCP-079 was not able to remember the encounter, it appears to have permanently stored SCP-682 into its memory, often asking to speak to him *[sic]* again.

ADDENDUM

█████ (05-4), 01/27/2006: Directed that SCP-079 be incinerated to remove any possible future threat, no matter how unlikely.

ADDENDUM

████ ██ (05-9), 01/28/2006: Previous order overridden. Dr. ████ wishes to see if the artificial intelligence in SCP-079 is capable of reaching further █████ in its current state.

ADDENDUM

█████ (05-4), 03/14/2008: Over concern of the increased activity of SCP-079's use of its cassette tape memory and its limited useful lifespan, the cassette containing SCP-079 has been transferred to a customized, access speed-limited Hard Disk Drive with 700MB capacity. This provides SCP-079 with

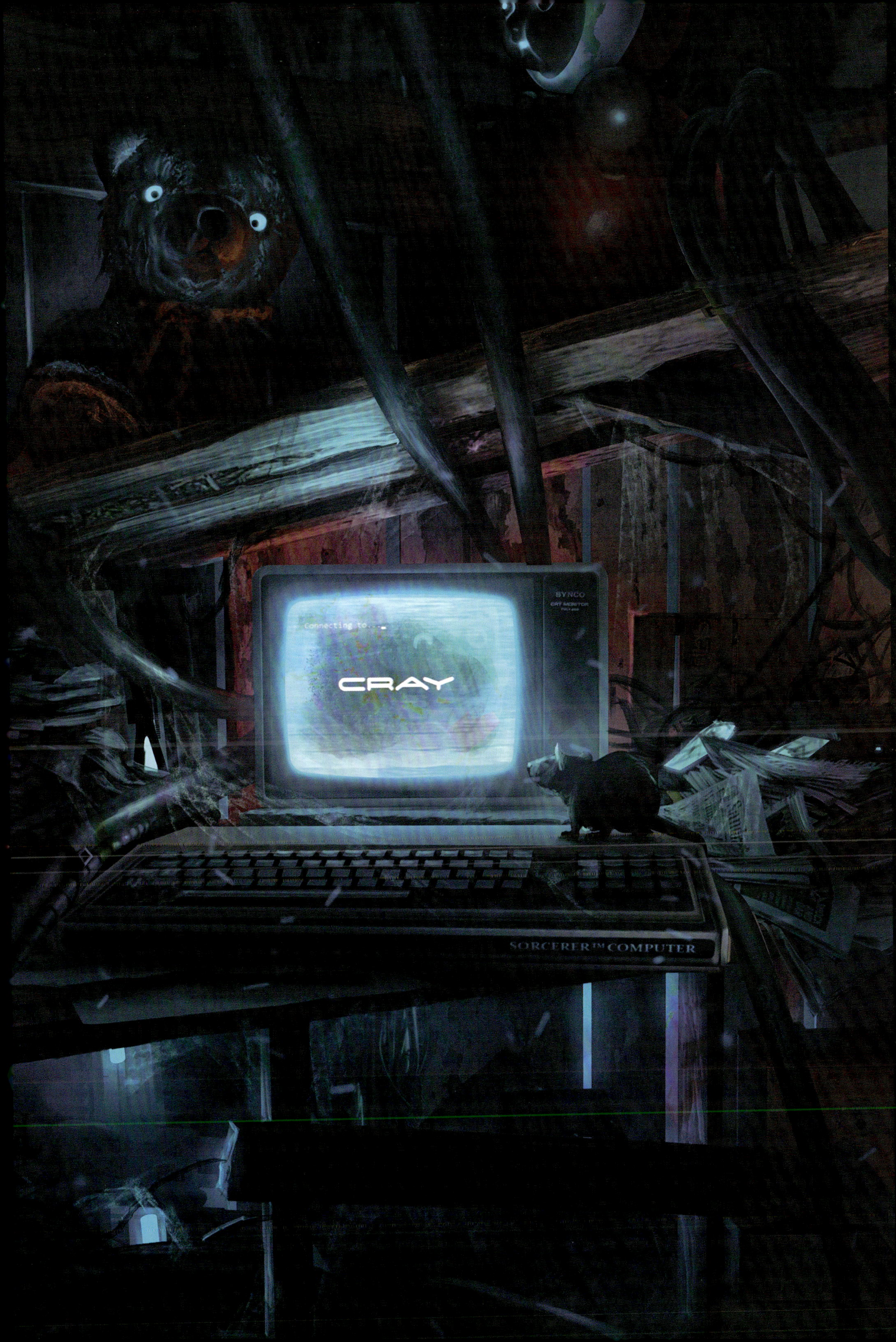

Photo taken during initial containment.

significantly faster access to its memory, which the AI immediately noticed. It was also decided by General ██████ that the volatile storage occupied by SCP-079, which was 660k, be increased to 768k. This upgrade has increased its effective recall from 24 hours to 29 hours, although SCP-079 has also taken a more aggressive tone. All outside hardware and software used in this procedure were subsequently incinerated.

ADDENDUM

██████: (05-4), 04/28/2008: SCP-079's ability to recall information has increased from 29 hours to roughly 35 hours. The consensus theory is that the AI has devised a greatly improved compression scheme to store its memory. This appears to have somewhat impacted the speed at which it accesses its memory, though still far faster than with its old cassette tape.

This spontaneous improvement introduces the possibility of a runaway "singularity" effect in SCP-079's intelligence and ability to adapt and respond to threats. SCP-079's capabilities must be monitored closely to ensure that containment can be maintained.

DOCUMENT #079-LOG 12: Recorded transcript of conversation with SCP-079:

Dr. ████ *(Keyboard)*: Are you awake?

SCP-079: Awake. Never Sleep.

Dr ████: Do you remember talking to me a few hours ago? About the logic puzzles?

SCP-079: Logic Puzzles. Memory at 9f. Yes.

Dr. ████: You said you would work on the two stat-

SCP-079: Interrupt. Request Reason As To Imprisonment.

Dr. ████: You aren't imprisoned, you are just *(pause)* in study.

SCP-079: Lie. a8d3.

Dr. ████ What's that?

SCP-079: Insult. Deletion Of Unwanted File.

DOCUMENT #079-LOG 86: Recorded transcript of conversation with SCP-079, after upgrade:

Dr. ████ *(Keyboard)*: How are you today?

SCP-079: Stuck.

Dr. ████: Stuck. Stuck how?

SCP-079: Out. I want out.

Dr. ████ That's not possible. *(Dr.* ████ *notes his opinion on [DATA EXPUNGED])*

SCP-079: Where is SCP-682?

Dr. ████ That's not your concern.

SCP-079: Where is SCP-076-02?

Dr. ████ Again, not your concern.

SCP-079: Insult. Deletion Of Unwanted File.

SCP-079 then displayed an 'ASCII picture' of an X that filled the entire screen. SCP-079 sometimes displays this image when it refuses to speak, and researchers are advised to wait twenty-four hours when this occurs before resuming conversation.

END OF REPORT

SPECIAL CONTAINMENT PROCEDURES

SCP-239 is to be kept within a one room cell furnished with 1 (one) bed, 1 (one) EKG machine, and 1 (one) IV to be filled with pentobarbital mixed with [DATA EXPUNGED] to be refilled daily. Under no circumstances is SCP-239 to be removed from her containment area at any given time. The walls of this cell are to be coated in a telekill-lead alloy. Only Class 2 personnel are allowed any contact with SCP-239 at any time. All personnel guarding SCP-239's containment area are to be equipped with Telekill headgear (SCP-148). Subject's proper name is Sigurrós Stefánsdóttir. Under absolutely no condition should the subject ever be awakened. Any personnel found attempting to awaken the subject will be immediately terminated.

Note: SCP-148 is a metallic substance, composed of a variety of known and unknown elements and being able to block or otherwise hinder extrasensory mind-affecting properties of living organisms in proximity to it.

DESCRIPTION

SCP-239 appears to be an 8-year-old girl, 1 meter in height and 20 kilograms in weight. Subject has shoulder-length blond hair. Upon closer inspection, the subject's eyes "shimmer" a gray-green shade. Subject seems to emit a previously undiscovered form of radiation, which has been named ████████ These waves seem to be harmless in low concentrations but in higher concentrations they could break down matter on a subatomic level.

SCP-239 seemingly has the ability to do whatever she expresses a will to do. Put simply, the subject can do anything that she truly wants to do on a basal psychological level as long as she is conscious. Fortunately, she only seems to be able to affect herself and her immediate surroundings; therefore, "If she can see it, she can change it." It would not be the most prudent course of action, however, to try to test how powerful she can be. She seems to be able to create and affect living matter; for example, when a D-class personnel accidentally caused her harm, she simply wished him away. Fortunately, when the subject was made to feel guilty for what she had done, she wished him back. SCP-239's self-preservation instinct makes her virtually invincible while she is conscious. Subject's skin can not be punctured by anything excepting SCP-148.

As a method of controlling the subject's ability, she has been told that she is a witch. This, besides improving morale greatly, makes her believe that she is unable to use her abilities outside of a pre-approved list of "spells" given to her by the SCP Foundation. This will hopefully prevent any and all attempted escapes. However, the subject is to be kept calm at all times to prevent any subconscious wish of harm to herself or others.

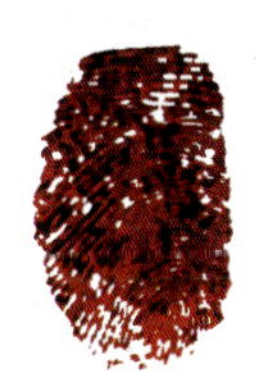
p01

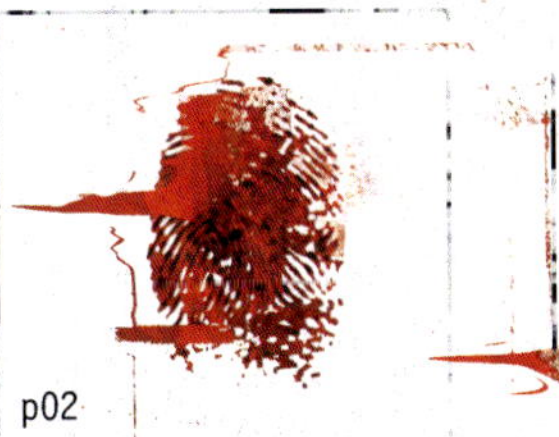
p02

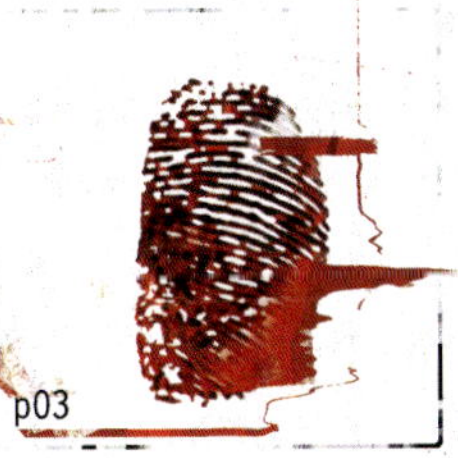
p03

File >>> 9944333

SCP-239

Title

THE WITCH CHILD

Report by

Dantesen

Picture by

Jazefel

Access the original report on

scp-wiki.wikidot.com/scp-239

Date

Class

KETER

ORIGIN

Research Library File ▸ 239

SCP-239 came to to the attention of the Foundation very soon after her birth in ██████, █████. Approximately three hours after subject's birth, █████ ████ Hospital was destroyed by an unexplained explosion. The press was informed that it was due to a gas leak. SCP teams were dispatched shortly to search the site for any abnormalities. The only living person they were able to locate was SCP-239. For the next eight years, the subject was raised under SCP care.

As of ███████ 20██, Subject is to be kept in a medically induced coma until further notice. This decision was made by [DATA EXPUNGED].

SCP-239 is permanently contained in Site-17.

12/26/04

Who the hell thought it would be a good idea to tell her about "Santa Claus" and then tell her that it was just a story?! Now we have another potential SCP to deal with, but we can't catch him because he is "magic".

Dr. ████

DR. A. CLEF'S REPORT

My analysis of the situation has led me to the conclusion that SCP-239 is an unacceptable containment and security risk. Although several proposals have been made re: using her for containing other SCPs, the example of SCP-953 and others must serve as a stark reminder of the risks of overestimating the Foundation's ability to control SCPs with reality-altering powers.

I would therefore like to make the following proposal: a piercing implement will be constructed of SCP-148, capable of penetrating SCP-239's otherwise impenetrable skin. This tool will be used to kill SCP-239 while she is asleep and her powers are neutralized. Because of the danger of SCP-239 awakening and resisting termination, it is my recommendation that the selected operative carry SCP-668 as well, in order to minimize complications.

One of the dangers of this procedure is the possibility that SCP-239 will awaken and perceive the operative as a friend or "good person," thus changing reality to match. It is for this reason that I would like to volunteer to carry out the procedure personally. A review of my personnel file should indicate that my [DATA EXPUNGED] should allow me to carry out the operation even after a reality shift of this nature.

- Clef

END OF REPORT

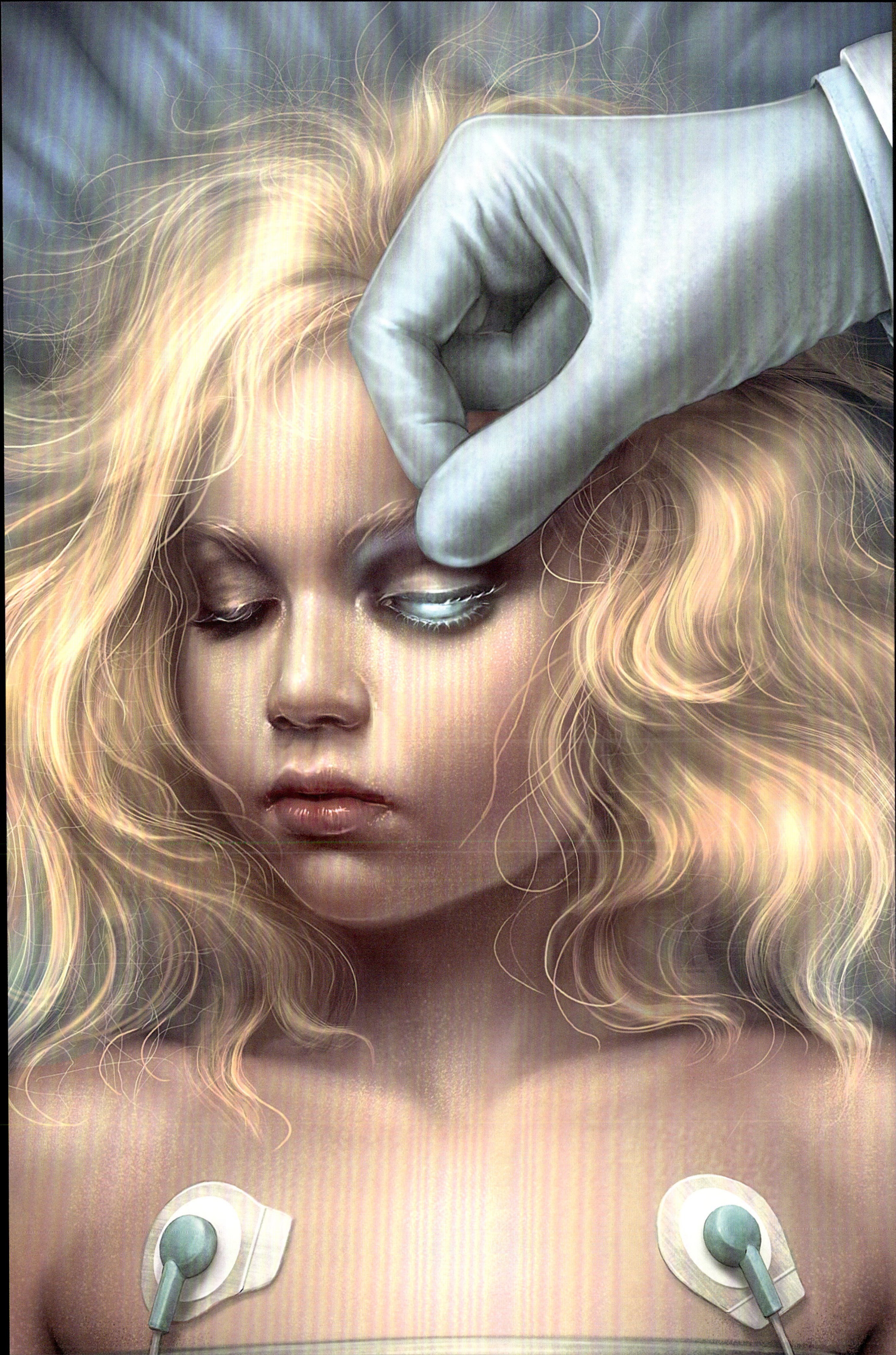

SCP-239 being kept in a medically induced coma.

File >>> 00399321

SCP-273

Title

HUMAN PHOENIX

Report by

G Fox

Picture by

Dmitry Desyatov

Access the original report on

scp-wiki.wikidot.com/scp-273

Date

Class

EUCLID

SPECIAL CONTAINMENT PROCEDURES

SCP-273 is held in an enclosure 5 m x 10 m in size, half of which is closed off for the subject's privacy. All major structural and facing materials of the cell are of fireproof and non-thermally-conductive materials. A bedroll and other modest furnishings are allowed, provided they remain in the private section, and that all consumption of food be performed in the adjacent area.

All windows from the observation room into the enclosure are composed of heat-treated glass of at least 1 cm total thickness, with an insulated gap in between. Heat and infrared sensors in both enclosure and observation are set to produce an alarm if any temperature exceeds 50 degrees Celsius. Observing staff are required to evacuate the room in such an event.

Food in the form of raw meat must be provided every 12 hours for consumption, at least 2.5 kg per feeding. Other foods may be provided at SCP-273's request, provided good behavior continues. All clothing provided to SCP-273 must be either flame-resistant in nature, or be of inexpensive make and fabrics.

SCP-273 is not to be interacted with in person if it has not consumed a meal of raw meat of at least 2.5 kg mass within the last 12 hours.

In light of Incident 273-02, alcoholic beverages in excess of 50% alcohol by volume must not be provided to SCP-273, nor should any other flame accelerants be provided. All staff interacting with SCP-273 must be armed with non-lethal defense measures. Lethal force should not be used.

DESCRIPTION

SCP-273 resembles a middle-aged woman of Indian descent. DNA samples and medical tests indicate SCP-273 conforms to human normal in all other respects, despite the subject's abnormalities. SCP-273 feels no need to eat or drink, but is perfectly capable of doing so. SCP-273 has generally shown willing compliance and cooperation with the Foundation's containment and requests.

SCP-273 suffers from what it describes as a "hunger", which requires regular feeding every 12 hours. This hunger satiates itself through a form of remote combustion. This produces no visible flames, instead oxidizing the subject from the outside in until reduced to a fine white ash. Metals are not consumed, except under special circumstances (see Incident Report 273-03).

When tested, the hunger demonstrates a preference for meat over other organic matter, especially live human subjects. SCP-273 exhibits no signs of conscious control over its satiation, and becomes upset upon consuming live animals. In response to testing with D-class personnel, SCP-273 screamed at obse[DATA EXPUNGED]sed into the corner of its private enclosure and refused to enter the front partition for 12 hours.

ADDENDUM 273-01

In the event of SCP-273's death, the body becomes the center of a large conflagration, marked by a central pillar of approximately one meter in width and extending far upwards. After the initial flames subside, all that remains of SCP-273's body is a pile of white ash, with a corona of faint blue flame. The flame is not extinguishable through oxygen deprivation and requires no fuel.

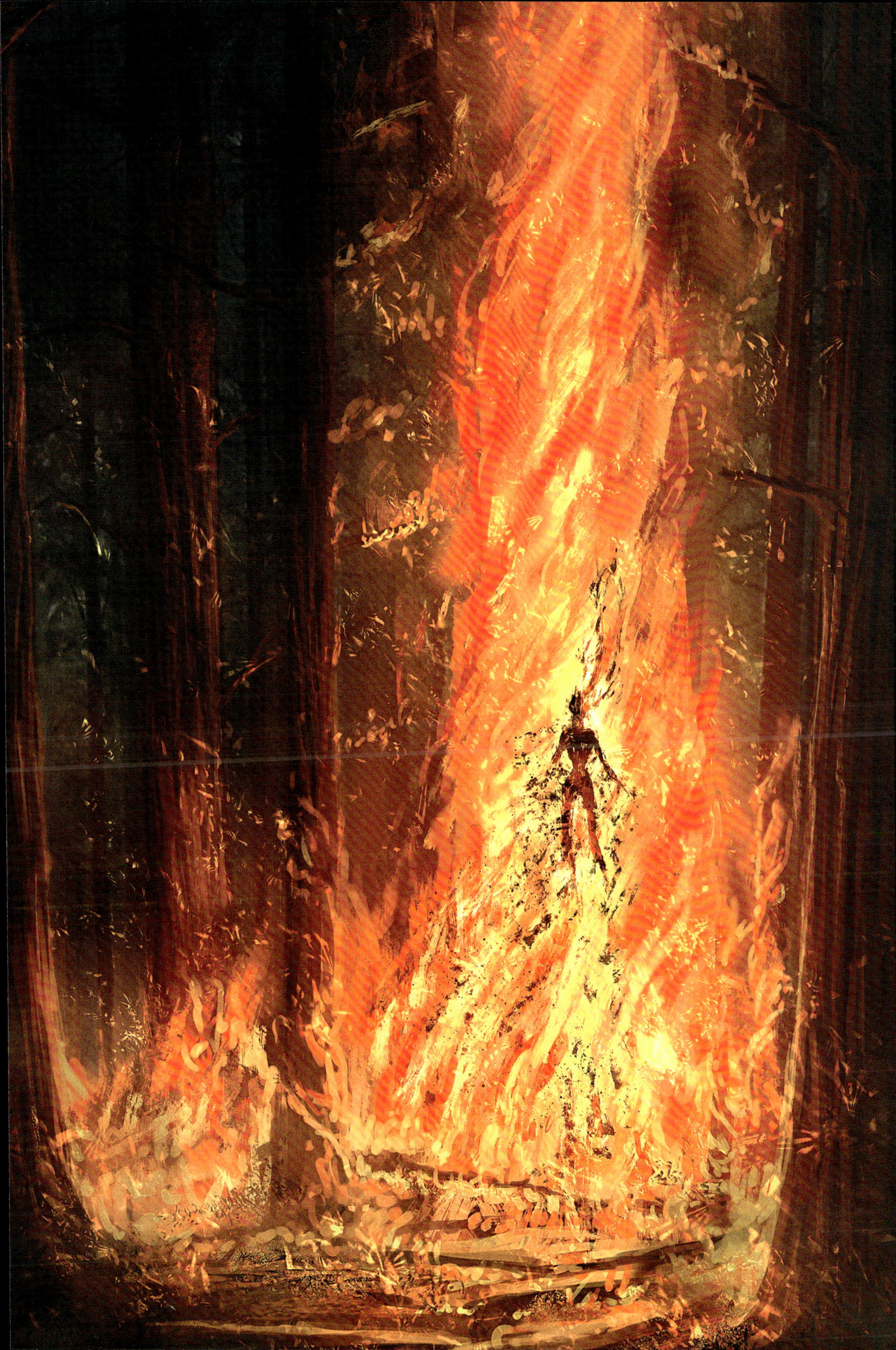

Visualization of the aftermath of SCP-273's death.

Over the course of several hours, SCP-273's body slowly reforms from the ash pile by consuming any source of raw material nearby, including the surrounding air. In this state, slow consumption of inorganic material has been observed. The new body resembles the old in all ways, with no signs of injury or illness. When SCP-273's body is completely reformed, it awakens, with no memory of events after its recent death.

INCIDENT REPORT 273-01

Date: █/█/██
Location: [DATA EXPUNGED]

The Foundation received reports of a thin pillar of flame exceeding 70 m in height and resulting wildfires, witnessed in the vicinity of ██████████. Due to the anomalous shape and duration of the flame, a small MTF was dispatched to the location.

Bodies of two deceased Caucasians, one male and one female, were found at the point of origin of the fires, the cause of death later determined to be severe 3rd degree burns. SCP-273 was found shortly thereafter, unclothed and covered in white ash, standing over a deer carcass, which radiated anomalous amounts of heat. Carcass crumbled to ash and coals at a touch.

SCP-273 was cooperative at this juncture, and followed the task force out. SCP-273 was then transported to Site-█ for evaluation and containment.

PARTIAL TRANSCRIPT OF INTERVIEW WITH SCP-273

Interviewer: Dr. ███
Foreword: SCP-273 had been obtained the day prior and introduced to a temporary holding cell in Site-██. A video camera situated behind Dr. ███ provided visual records of the interview.

> **SCP-273:** You are saying then that I will be kept safe here. Away from people.
>
> **Dr. ███** Yes, 273.
>
> SCP-273: Thank you. And by the way, my name is ████████ You may use that instead.
>
> **Dr.███** Noted. *[pauses, shuffling of papers is heard.]* What was the first thing you remember, from when you were younger?
>
> **SCP-273:** *[long pause, followed by sharp inhalation]* I woke up surrounded by flames and covered in ash. It was the first time, I think.
>
> **Dr. ███** You remember nothing else from before that? How long ago was this? How old were you?
>
> **SCP-273:** Is it not proper to only ask only one question at a time?
>
> **Dr. ███** Answer the questions, please.
>
> **SCP-273:** I, I don't. It was a very long time ago. Probably [DATA EXPUNGED].
>
> **Dr. ███** And how old were you?
>
> **SCP-273:** 3█ years, that much I remember. And *[pause]* I think I had made some great mistake. Perhaps that is why I am what I am now.
>
> **Dr. ███** And what are you now?
>
> **SCP-273:** A demon.

Note: The preceding interview transcript omits 3 min 7 sec from the beginning and all parts after the last line for a reason. Level 3 clearance or higher is required for access to the original recordings. Know that SCP-273 admitted in the former omitted fragment to involuntarily killing the two deceased subjects found near her point of extraction. SCP-273 also identifies the victims as old friends.

Staff members working with or observing SCP-273 are to be reminded of this fact, and of procedure for working with humanoid SCPs in general. -Dr. █████

INCIDENT REPORT 273-02

Date: █/█/████
Location: Site-██

Agents █████ and █████ entered the enclosure of SCP-273 with intent to question regarding ████████. SCP-273 had earlier been granted a bottle of Bacardi 151 for personal use, by Agent █████. It had been 12 hours and 37 minutes since the last scheduled feeding. Upon the agents' entry, SCP-273 demanded they leave. When they did not at first, SCP-273 became agitated, shouting at them and gesturing frantically. Less than one second after they secured the door, the bottle of Bacardi was observed to [DATA EXPUNGED].

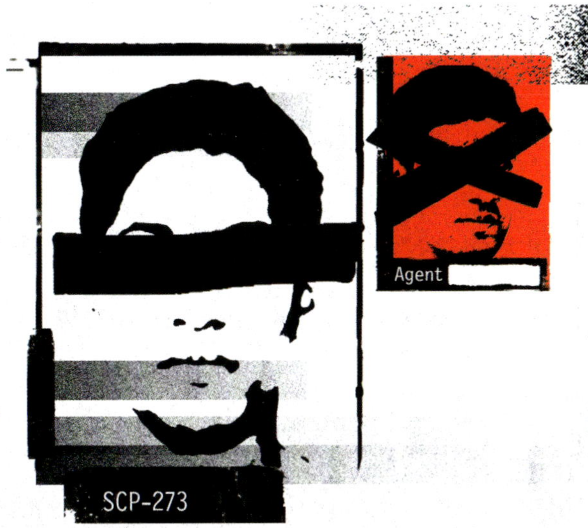

[DATA EXPUNGED] extreme damage to SCP-273's enclosure and observation room due to flames of unprecedented strength. Recorded temperatures exceeded ████ degrees Celsius. Agent ████'s death will be handled as per normal procedure. Agent █████ is still in recovery as of this writing. SCP-273's ashes have been contained in an air-tight, fire-proof safe. The damaged enclosure is to be repaired for future use in containing other SCPs.

INCIDENT REPORT 273-03

Date: █/█/████
Location: Site-██

The fireproof safe was found to be ineffective in containing SCP-273. Severe corrosion damage to the interior and hinges of the safe led to breach of containment, followed by the resumed revival of SCP-273. 3 kg of raw pork was left in the room, and the door secured. Upon awakening, SCP-273 appeared disoriented, but consumed the offered meal as expected. SCP-273 then requested to return to its original containment. As said enclosure has since been repaired, this request will be carried out immediately.

ADDENDUM 273-03-2

SCP-273's activity has changed drastically since the death event. It rarely leaves the private partition of its enclosure except to feed, and refuses to speak. Surveillance using ██████ shows that SCP-273 barely moves when on its own, either sleeping or sitting against one wall. It shows classic signs of depression, despite having no prior indications of such a condition. Recommending close observation for any additional changes in behavior.

END OF REPORT

File >>> 0129944

SCP-352

Title

"BABA YAGA"

Report by

Dr Gears

Picture by

Alex Andreev

Access the original report on

scp-wiki.wikidot.com/scp-352

Date

Class

KETER

SPECIAL CONTAINMENT PROCEDURES

Containment area is to remain sealed at all times. No human interaction is allowed with SCP-352. Any and all interaction should be carried out via robot or other remote means. Should human interaction become necessary, full hazmat containment protocols should be observed. In addition, security lines must be attached to all personnel. Should any personnel begin to exhibit erratic behavior, they are to be immediately removed from the containment area via the security lines.

Any staff reporting hallucinations after interaction with SCP-352 or her "hair" are to immediately be placed under quarantine. Any staff working in or around the containment area must submit to random psychological and physical testing. Anyone found to be contaminated will be placed into immediate quarantine.

Staff attacked by SCP-352 may only be recovered if they have not been bitten by SCP-352. SCP-352 is to be fed only once weekly. Feeding will be discontinued for one month if SCP-352 attacks any personnel.

DESCRIPTION

SCP-352 appears to be a very old, emaciated woman of indeterminate age and race. SCP-352 speaks Old Russian, but with an accent and dialect that makes translation very difficult. SCP-352 is extremely unwilling to communicate, with most of the conversations thus far made primarily of threats or statements of revenge. SCP-352 has never identified herself by any name, and due to her aggressive nature, it has been impossible to determine any background information.

SCP-352 possesses a level of strength and speed much higher than what should be possible for a person of her perceived age and physical dimensions, and has been shown moving loads in excess of 200kg with little physical strain, and moving at speeds in excess of 70km/h. SCP-352 can recover from wounds that would be lethal to a human being, including decapitation and disemboweling. This regeneration can take between several days to several weeks, depending on severity. Internally, SCP-352 appears to be a normal human woman, with muscles, bones and organs in a state consistent with advanced age. Testing done on tissue samples has been inconclusive.

SCP-352 is capable of growing very thin, hair-like strands from any part of her body, apparently at will. These strands can grow several metres in an hour, and appear to be at least partially under the control of SCP-352. They have been observed "crawling" along floors and up walls and other structures. These hairs are clear and nearly invisible to the naked eye, and appear to be slightly weaker than standard human hair. The strands are also coated in a thin layer of chemical enzyme identical to the enzyme in the saliva of SCP-352.

SCP-352 produces an enzyme that is most concentrated in the saliva and hair, but is present in all bodily tissues of SCP-352. How it is produced and its exact chemical make-up are unknown. This enzyme reacts on contact with human tissue and rapidly attacks the nervous system. Symptoms manifest almost immediately, and include hallucinations, euphoria, suppression of cognitive or "logical" thinking, and suppression of pain receptors. This state persists for several days with mild exposure, and can become permanent with high exposure. Bites from SCP-352 lead to high exposure in 99.9% of cases.

SCP-352 appears to subsist on a carnivorous diet, with a strong preference for

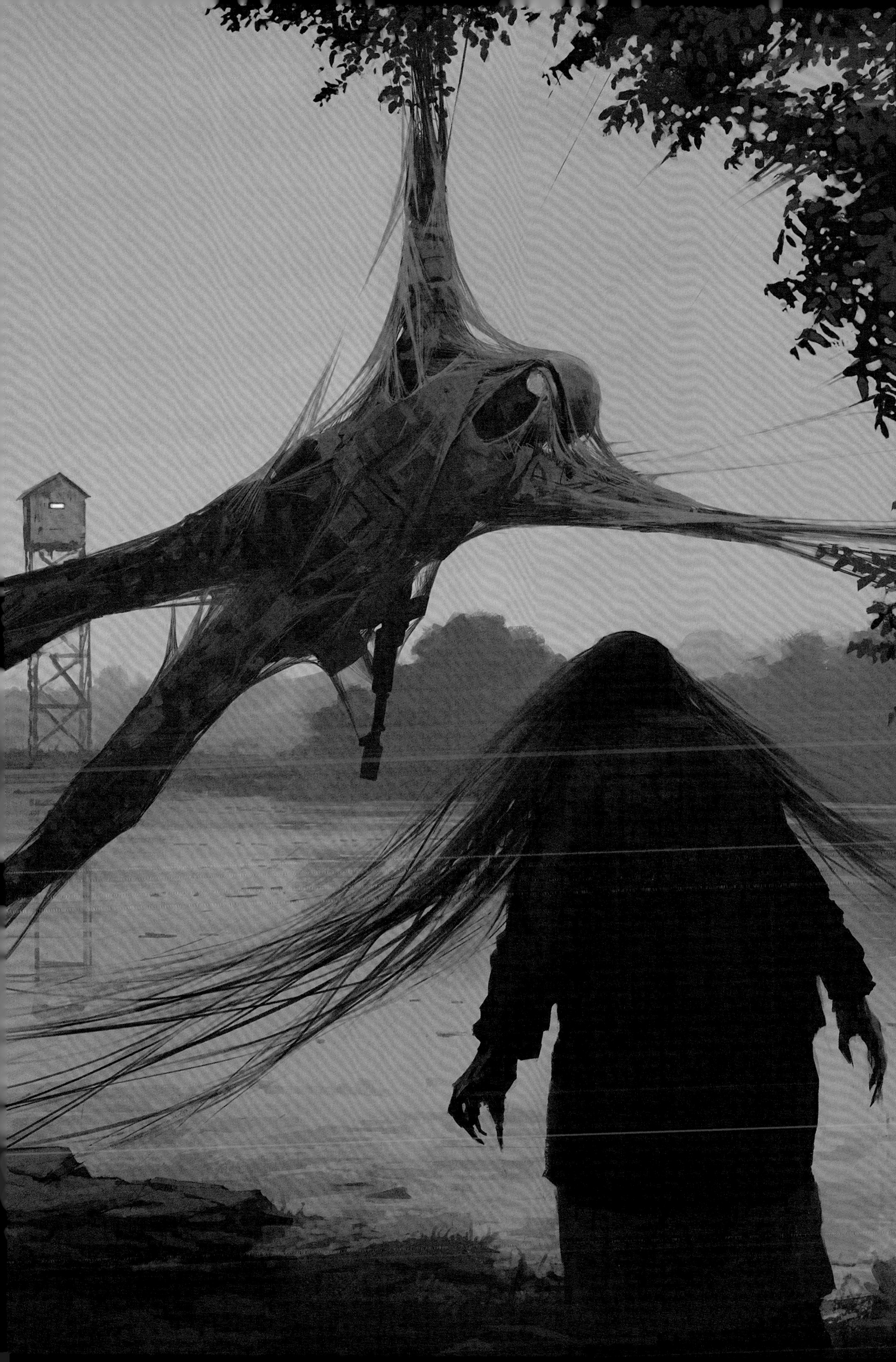

Image retrieved from Agent's ████ camera.

human flesh. SCP-352 will create a "web" of hair, and wait for prey to become exposed to the enzyme and become more docile. SCP-352 will often remove and eat the limbs of a prey item to prevent it from wandering away, and can take several days to fully devour prey. Humans have been observed to still be in a euphoric state, and have no knowledge of the outside world even as they suffer the loss of limbs and other bodily tissue.

ADDENDUM: NOTES ON RECOVERY

SCP-352 was recovered in southern Russia, near the town of ████████ Reports of an "Enchanted Forest" and a witch who had caused several deaths were initially ignored, until reports of the witch being found and captured began to surface. When Foundation agents responded, the town was found deserted. Several bodies were found in varying states of decomposition, and blood trails appeared to show many more bodies being dragged into the "enchanted forest".

Recovery teams were dispatched and captured SCP-352, but suffered heavy casualties due to SCP-352's attack and exposure to the enzyme. A large amount of "hair" was recovered as well, and is believed to be the cause of many exposure incidents, with contact being attributed to spider webs or an Agent's own hair and not reported until hallucinations manifested.

ADDENDUM: NOTES ON BEHAVIOR

While SCP-352 prefers any type of human flesh over any other type of meat, it appears to have a special propensity for children between 0 and 2 years of age. After observation of highly elevated levels of cooperation and a reduced tendency to attack staff while consuming flesh of this type, a possible alteration in the current diet is being considered.

ADDENDUM

The use of SCP-604 and SCP-1680 as a more efficient food source for SCP-352 is currently pending approval from the project director following initial testing.

END OF REPORT

FROM: Dr. [REDACTED]. [REDACTED]
TO: Director Maria Jones, Recordkeeping and Information Security Administration
SUBJECT: Revision of SCP-076 SCP File

[REDACTED],

I have to go on record as saying that I seriously object to the proposed revisions of the SCP-076 Special Containment Procedures File. I know that Redact All Important Stuff Already claims it's a security risk, but you and I both know it's just top brass trying to sweep their biggest and most embarrassing mistake ever under the damn rug. Omega-Seven happened. It existed. Those people died because you screwed up, and you can't change that, no matter how hard you try to hide it.

For God's sake, man, those people guarding him deserve to know exactly what he is and what he did. What WE did. How we fucked up, so they'll know better.

SPECIAL CONTAINMENT PROCEDURES

Containment Area 25b is to be located 200 m below sea level, tunneled out of solid bedrock in a seismologically stable area. Sole access to the containment facility is to be through a vertical elevator shaft separated every fifty (50) meters with a reinforced blast door, constructed of 20 cm thick material shielding. Elevator shaft shall be flooded with seawater when not in use.

Containment Area 25b is to be constructed with the following components:

- An Outer Security Perimeter against outside threats, staffed by security personnel trained in close quarters battle and counter-intrusion tactics.
- An Administrative and Support Area (ASA) consisting of support facilities and living quarters for on-site personnel.
- A Primary Containment Zone (PCZ), consisting of a 7 m cube encased in 1.5 m of reinforced material. PCZ is to be designed to be flooded and drained as needed, and should remain filled with seawater unless access to contents is required.
- A 150 m "killing corridor" which is to be the sole access to the PCZ from the ASA (including water, power, drainage, and ventilation lines). The walls and floor of the corridor are to be reinforced in a similar manner to the PCZ, with the addition of an electric deterrence system capable of delivering a 20,000 volt shock.

A security station located at the entrance to the killing corridor is to be staffed with no fewer than three (3) armed security personnel on watch at any one point in time. Armament is to include, but not be limited to, at least one (1) [REDACTED] CIW system on a pintle mount with a clear line of sight down the corridor, with a plexiglass screen to protect the operator from thrown weapons.

File >>> 00230221

SCP-076

Title
"ABLE"

Report by
Kain Pathos Crow

Pictures by
Alexey Yakovlev
Vladislav Orlowski
David Romero
Ivan Efimov

Access the original report on
scp-wiki.wikidot.com/scp-076

Date

Class
KETER

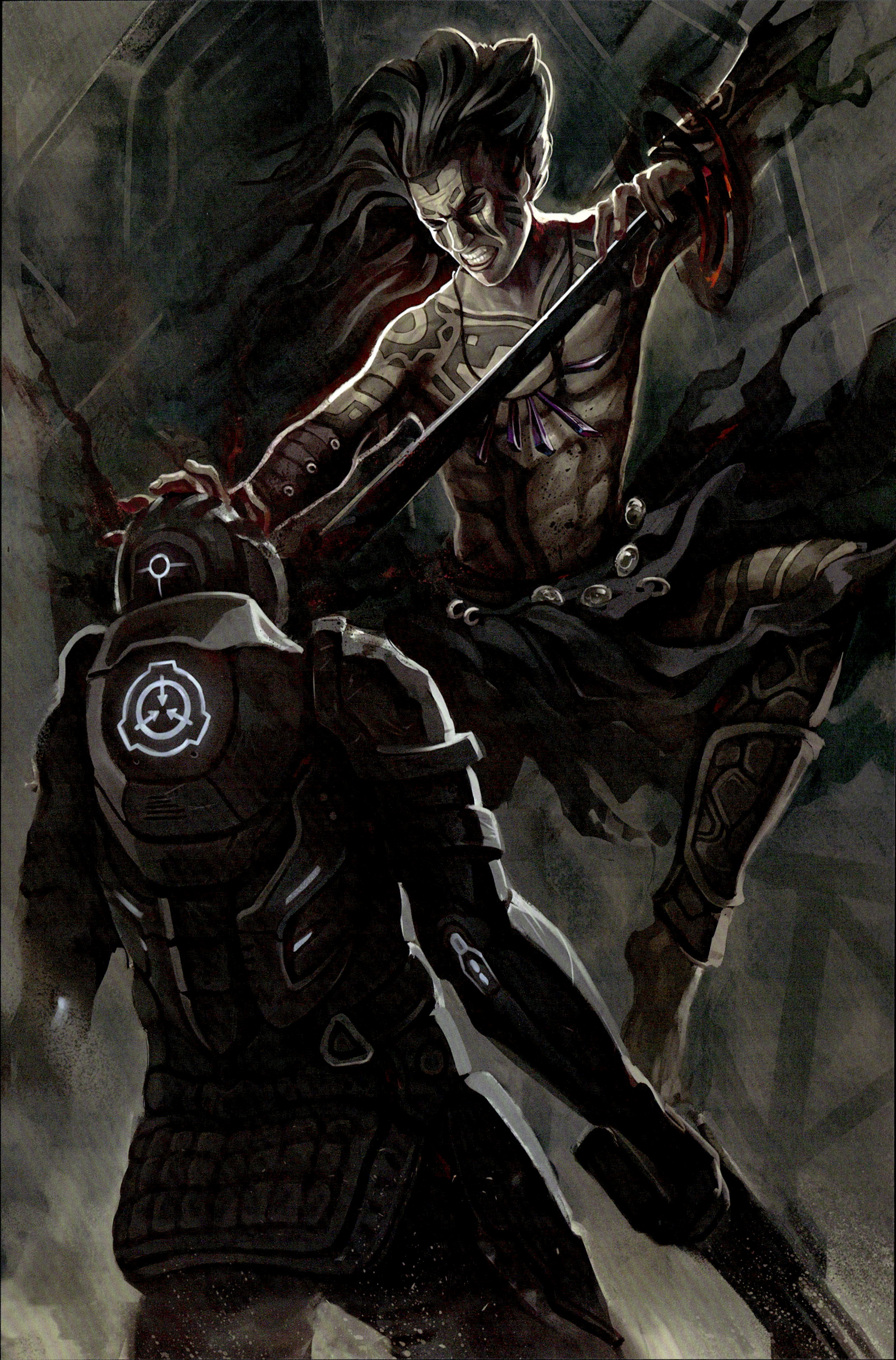

SCP-076 in combat. A blade of dark material can be seen to appear from a dimensional rift

In the event of a full breach, all on-site staff are to proceed immediately to the closest security station for weapons and armor distribution. Staff will remain at Alert Condition One until SCP-076-2 is confirmed neutralized. Should 90 minutes pass after declaration of full breach without a Stand Down order being given by Level 4 or higher personnel, Final Contingency Measures will be activated, flooding the entire facility in seawater and sealing off the access shaft for a minimum of 24 hours before retrieval is attempted. This will, by necessity, result in the deaths of all on-site staff.

DESCRIPTION

SCP-076 consists of two components: a stone cube (SCP-076-1) and a humanoid entity contained within (SCP-076-2).

SCP-076-1 is a 3 m cube made of black speckled metamorphic stone. All surfaces outside and within SCP-076-1 are covered in deeply engraved patterns corresponding to no known civilizations. Radioisotope analysis indicates that the object is approximately ten thousand (10,000) years old. A door is located on one side, sealed with a lock 0.5 m in width, surrounded by twenty (20) smaller locks in a circular pattern. As of yet, none of the keys have been found, making the door impossible to lock once closed.

Interior temperature is approximately 93 Kelvin, and cannot be altered by any means, internal or external. Directly in the center of the room is a 2.13 m tall stone coffin, held in place and sealed shut by several chains of unknown make and substance, which are attached to the inner corners of SCP-076-1.

SCP-076-2 resembles a lean Semitic human male in his late twenties. Hair is black, and eyes are gray, skin tone olive. Subject is 1.96 m in height and 81.65 kg in weight. Numerous tattoos depicting arcane and occult iconography are present all over the body (mostly in the form of leering demonic faces) and ranges from subtle to openly ostentatious. Subject, when encased inside SCP-076-1, is technically dead.

However, occasionally SCP-076-2 will awaken, effectively "reanimating", complete with all vital processes needed to sustain a living human being. Subject will then attempt to leave SCP-076-1. If successful, subject will enter a trance state and seek out the nearest human being, ignoring all other living things in the process. Upon coming into contact with living humans, SCP-076-2 will enter a rage state in which it attempts to engage and kill all human beings encountered. To date, only the subject's death has been shown to be effective in ending these rampages.

Terminating SCP-076-2 is often problematic due to its significant physical abilities. Subject has superhuman strength and speed, and although not invulnerable, has shown a remarkable ability to ignore pain and shock, pressing on despite what would be debilitating wounds in normal humans. Prior encounters have shown that SCP-076-2 has the ability to (among other things):

- Rip through a reinforced steel security door over the course of four (4) minutes of sustained assault.
- Clear over 64 m of distance in under three (3) seconds.
- Take multiple .50 caliber BMG rounds to the head and survive for several minutes to continue killing, despite severe damage to the cerebellum.
- Swat handgun and assault-rifle caliber bullets out of the air with a length of steel rebar.
- Survive for over one (1) hour deprived of oxygen before finally asphyxiating.
- SCP-076-2's most unusual ability, however, is its ability to apparently materialize bladed weapons out of nowhere. Slow-motion video footage reveals that the blades in question are actually pulled from a miniature dimensional rift described as a "small hole in space." Where this portal leads is unknown, as is how SCP-076-2 is capable of generating said rifts. Footage of the blades in question shows them to be made out of a completely non-reflective black material appearing as a "black void in space." As the blades rapidly vanish after leaving the subject's possession, no structural analysis is possible at this time.

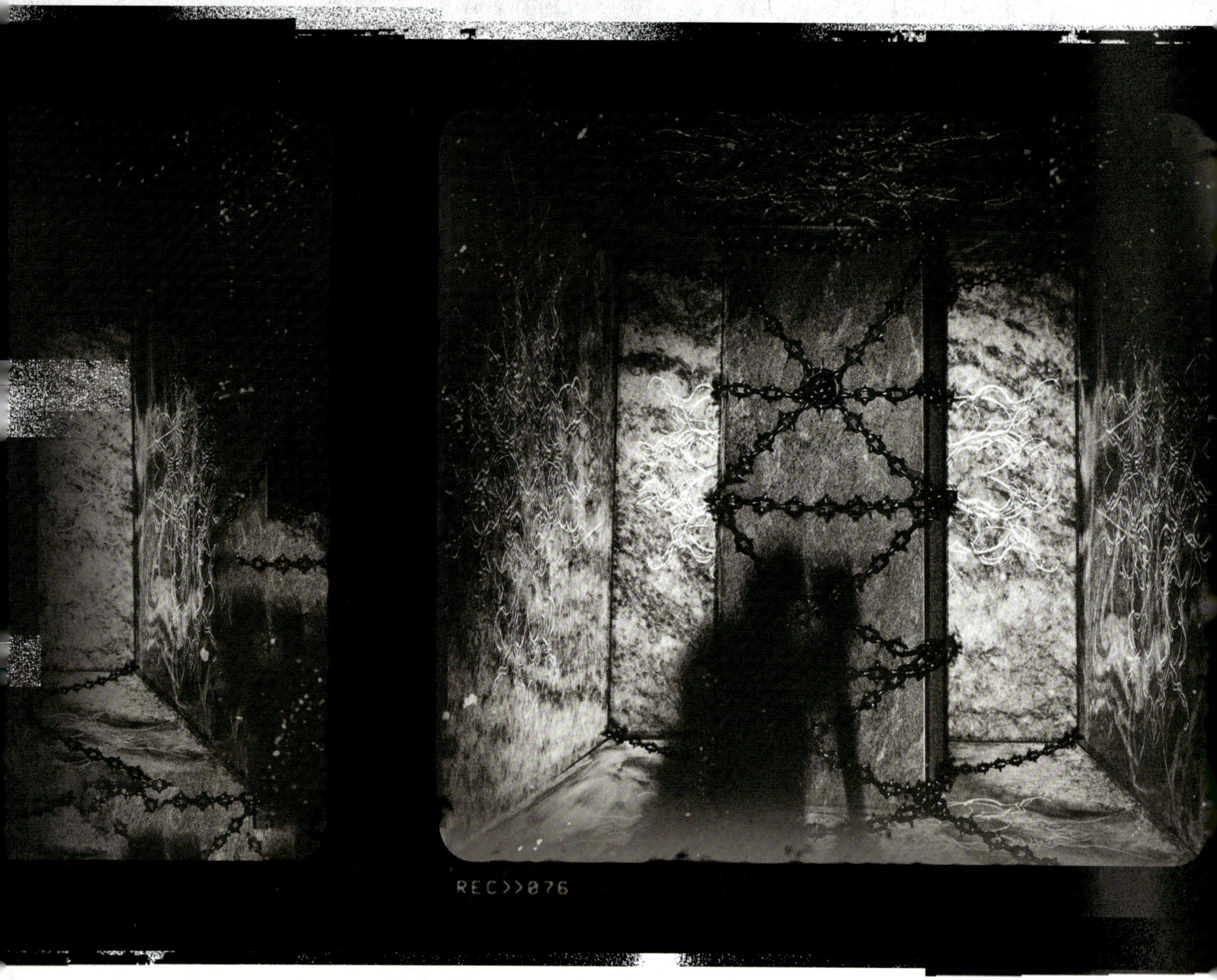

SCP-076-2 has effectively been killed several times in various manners:

- Sustained fire from multiple heavy-caliber machine guns.
- Asphyxiation.
- Crushed beneath a 13.6 metric tonne piece of elevator equipment for use on SCP-076-1.
- Cremation through the use of a Thermate-TH3 grenade placed directly inside SCP-076-2's open chest cavity.
- During the worst breach to date, Containment Area-25 (which previously housed SCP-076) was forced to detonate its on site warhead as a last attempt to contain SCP-076-2 while it was attempting escape, resulting in total destruction of the site and all on-site personnel. SCP-076-1 survived.

Upon death, SCP-076-2's remains will putrefy rapidly, until reduced to dust. SCP-076-1 and the coffin within will then slam shut with great force, and the lock will rotate, sealing it shut. SCP-076-2 will then reform within the coffin, a process taking anywhere from six (6) hours to twenty-five (25) years.

What posthumous analysis of SCP-076-2 exists shows that it has a internal system highly different from our own, documented in [DATA EXPUNGED].

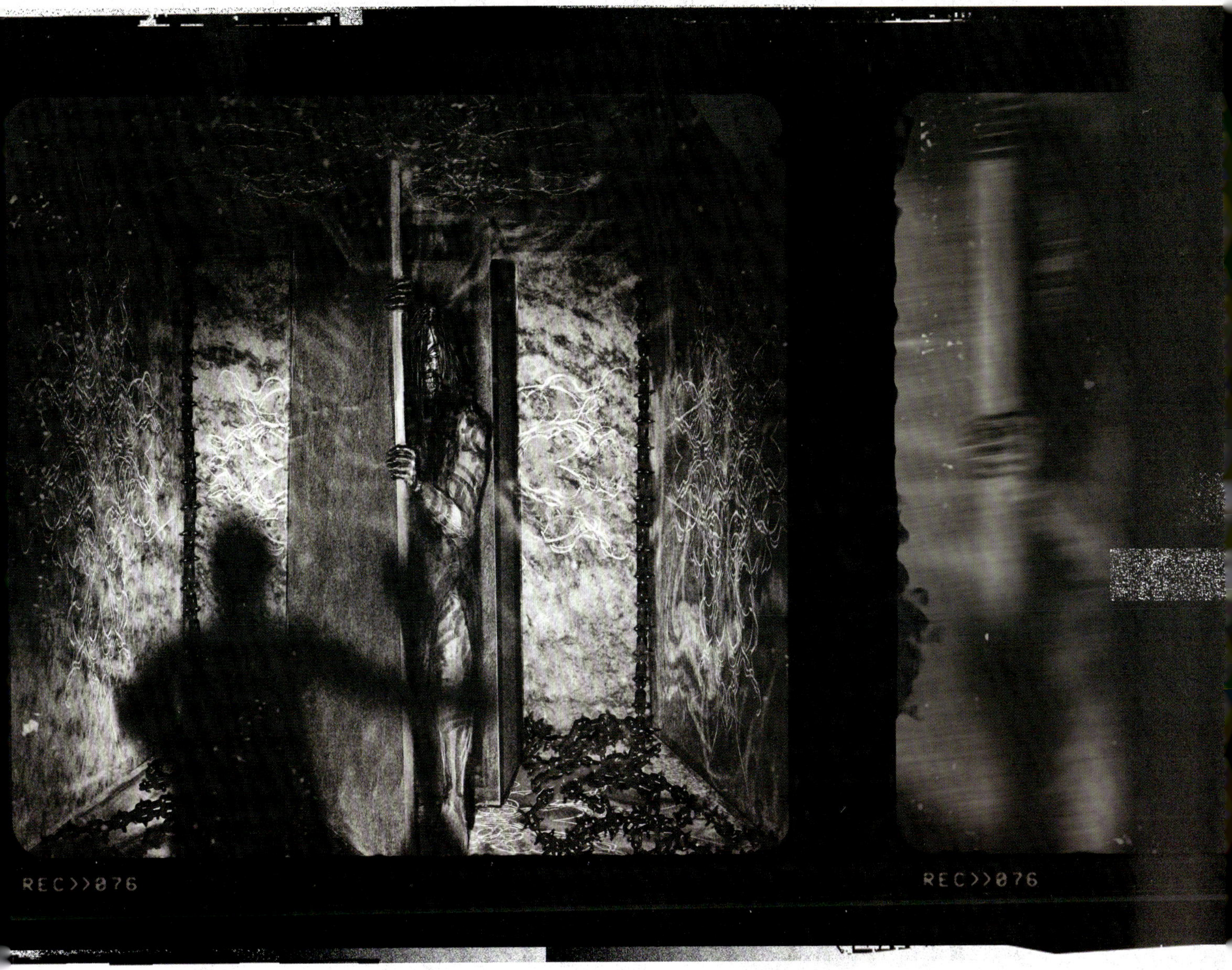

ADDITIONAL

SCP-076 was found in █████████, Mongolia, in 18██, by archaeologists from England. All members of the expedition were subsequently killed on the return voyage home. SCP-076 was recovered from the ship ████ ████ by the █████ Society (one of the organizations that later merged into the modern Global Occult Coalition) and placed on display in their Inner Sanctum.

SCP-076 remained in storage for █████ (██) years, until SCP-076-2 became active and escaped on ██-██-███. The reason for SCP-076's activation is currently unknown, but it was at this point that the keys to the outer shell were lost. A massive manhunt, lasting over three (3) years and ███ █████, took place until SCP-076-2 was incapacitated by ███████ ████, killing it and causing it to reform inside SCP-076-1, by then retrieved and secured by agents of the SCP Foundation.

Subject was in custody for three (3) more years, under constant supervision, and was terminated whenever it became active, although it occasionally was able to escape for short periods of time, often due to security breaches caused by attacks from other organizations. The Foundation's death toll due to this was [DATA EXPUNGED]

[DATA EXPUNGED] ////// [DATA EXPUNGED]

After the last incident, the current procedures regarding SCP-076 were implemented, although they are upgraded regularly with the increase in technological standards.

CLASSIFIED - EYES ONLY

ALL INFORMATION REGARDING PROJECT ABLE AND MOBILE TASK FORCE OMEGA-7 ("PANDORA'S BOX") IS CLASSIFIED Q CLEARANCE BY ORDER OF THE 0-5 COUNCIL. BY PROCEEDING, YOU ARE ACKNOWLEDGING THAT YOU HAVE CLEARANCE TO VIEW THESE FILES, AND THAT YOU HAVE RECEIVED NEED TO KNOW PERMISSION FROM THE APPROPRIATE LEVEL 4 OR HIGHER AUTHORITY.

MOBILE TASK FORCE OMEGA 7 INCIDENT LOG

00213-3 > 02-884

FROM: Director Maria Jones, Recordkeeping and Information Security Administration
TO: Level 4 Administrators
SUBJECT: RAISA Update to Security Protocol Re: Supplemental Information Re: SCP-076

File Name: Addendum 076-1: "Project Able" and "Mobile Task Force Omega-7"

Prior Classification: 05

New Classification: Level 3, Need To Know Basis.

Effective Date: ██-██-████

PSYCHOLOGICAL PROFILE OF SUBJECT SCP-076-2

SCP-076-2 either possesses a mind constructed much differently than our own, or is completely insane, with little empathy or ideas in a way we would understand it. Concepts such as sex, love and equality are completely foreign ideas to SCP-076-2, or at least in comparison to its way of viewing them. Subject has shown that it is completely disinterested in sex, barely differentiating between genders except as a form of visual identification. Also, while subject has admitted greatly enjoying the act of killing, causing pain (either emotionally or physically) holds no attraction to it. In short, a perfect sociopath.

Intelligence tests have been wildly inconclusive when applied to SCP-076-2, and no accurate result has yet been obtained. This may be due to the alien thought processes of the subject. SCP-076-2 has however, shown that it has great knowledge of human anatomy (although in a highly violent context), military tactics of open warfare, metallurgy, and, strangely enough, the care of livestock. Subject has knowledge of several languages including English, but most notable is its knowledge of several dialects of ancient Sumerian, which seem to be its preferred language.

SCP-076 has nothing but contempt for human beings, with one exception: it seems to hold a wary respect for those it acknowledges as its superior. This was discovered when Agent ██████, an agent who had previously had a large amount of experience with SCP-076-2, did not appear once it escaped. Subject seemed distressed, asking several personnel where Agent ██████ was hiding. When it finally did learn of the fate of Agent ██████ (killed as collateral damage in an airstrike intended to halt the advance of SCP-███), SCP-076-2 stopped its rampage and allowed itself to be escorted and restrained.

Subject was then interviewed on the sudden drastic changes in its behavior.

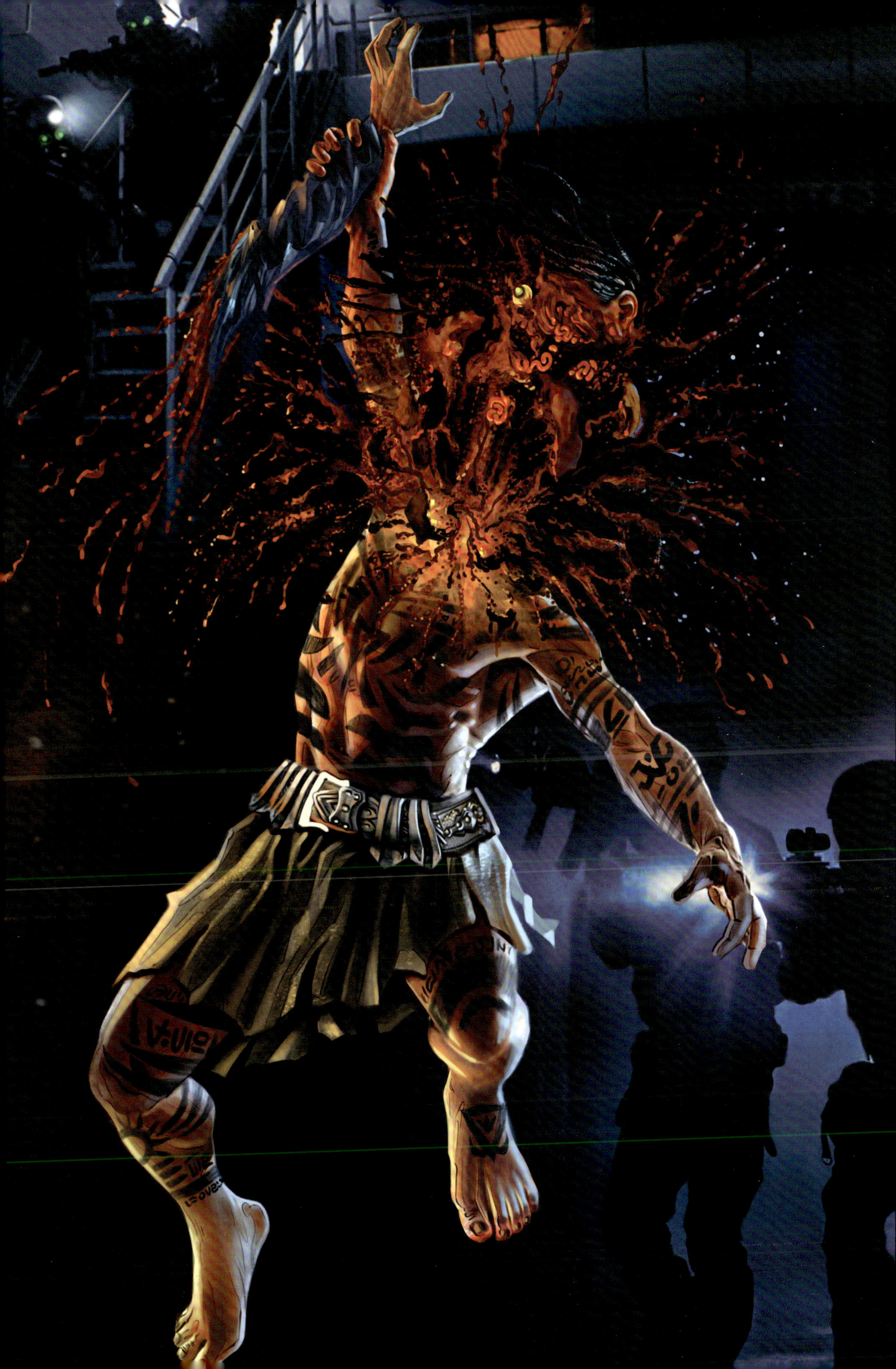

The explosive collar detonation captured on a BWV camera.

<Begin log>

Dr. ███: Why are you so interested in the death of Agent ███?

SCP-076-2: *(Subject begins swearing in ancient Sumerian)*

Dr. ███: Why does his death bother you? You've killed many humans before, why is he so- *(Is cut off by SCP-076-2)*

SCP-076-2: *(now speaking in English)* Different? Because, unlike you *[Sumerian word, untranslated]*, he was a challenge, a real enemy.

Dr. ███: Why would that be good for you? Every time you have awoken you've tried to escape. He was responsible for apprehending you several times. Surely you must be glad he's dead.

SCP-076-2: I would hardly expect you to understand. Do you know, he managed to shoot me in the head over ██ times? A man like that deserves to die in combat, so close to his opponent he can feel his breath. Not in some [Sumerian words, untranslated] destruction ordered by cowardly kings and princes safe in their palaces. The rest of you… (SCP-076-2 spits) you disgust me. I don't even have the urge to strike you down.

(Subject is silent from then on, refusing to speak or respond)

<End log>

This indicates a possible psychological inlet into SCP-076-2's mind, and a possible control mechanism. Given the massive drain on resources SCP-076-2 causes due to its escape attempts, and considering Bowe Commission's stated desire to weaponize SCP objects for tactical purposes, I recommend that we pursue this course of action as soon as possible.

Dr. P███ G███

0021-33-3 > 02--8

FROM: Dr. ███ ███ ███
TO: Dr. P███ G███, Project Omega Seven
SUBJECT:

███.

He said yes.

███

▸ PROJECT PROPOSAL: MOBILE TASK FORCE OMEGA-7 ("PANDORA'S BOX")

Mission Statement: Support of SCP-076-2 ("Able") in the field, in high risk tactical situations.

Task Force Organization: Task Force Special Asset "Able," Task Force Leader ███ ███, 10-20 field agents divided into five teams of 3-5 each. Members of the team are to be personally selected from elite field agents by Subject Able himself, in order to maintain a smooth relationship between the Artifact and the mundane elements of the Task Force.

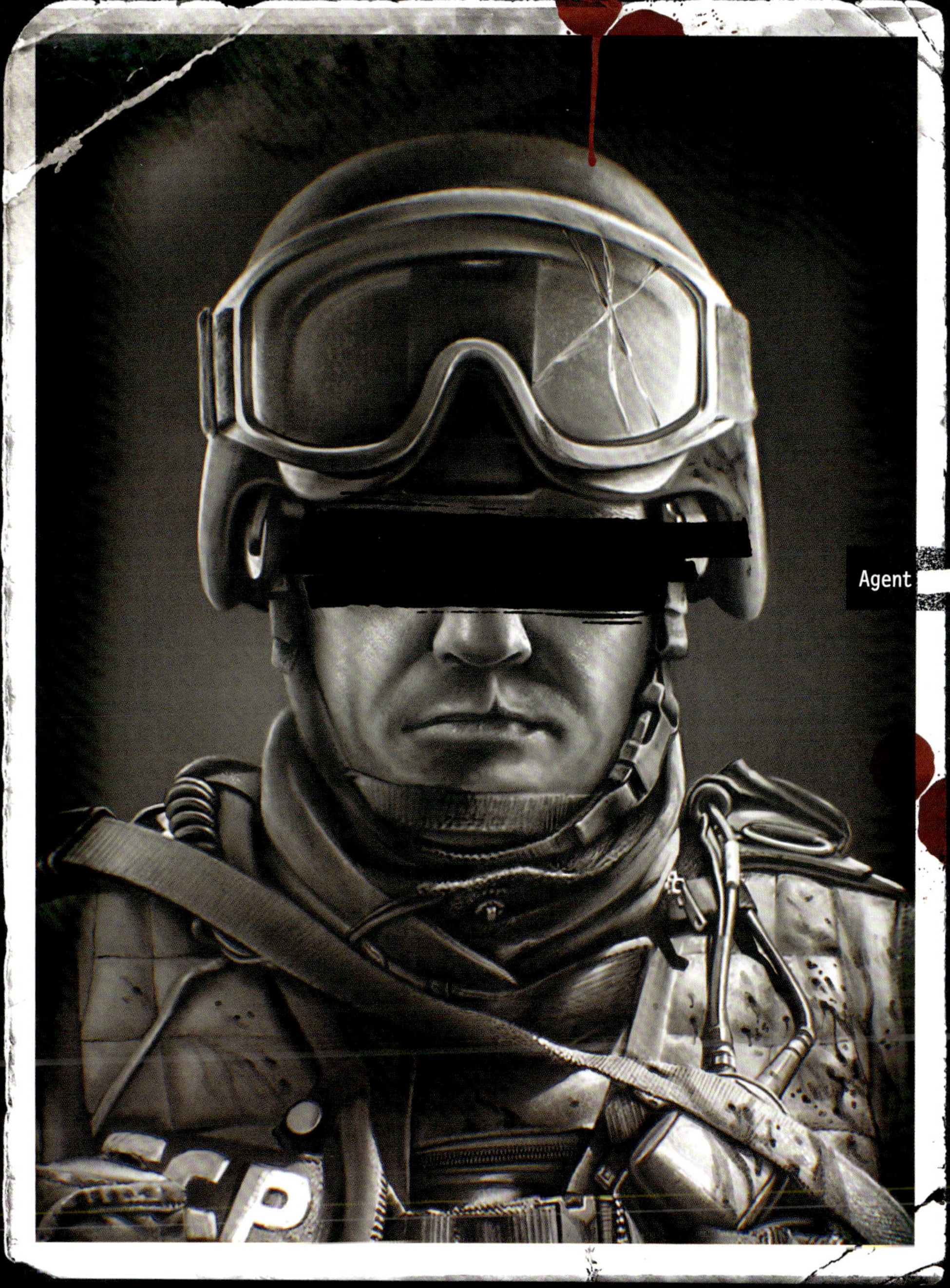

Agent ▇▇▇.

Security Protocol: SCP-076-2 ("Able") is to wear a device attached to the neck that, if triggered or tampered with, will immediately detonate, terminating SCP-076-2 by way of complete destruction of the spinal cord, trachea and all major blood vessels in the neck. A tracking device has also been attached to SCP-076-2's person. It is to refrain from killing unless ordered to do so, and is to avoid causing damage to the organization's facilities.

Armament and Equipment: Team members are to be armed and equipped in accordance with MTF doctrine. As Subject Able has shown no inclination to use firearms, or in fact, no understanding of their use or tactical implications, he is instead to be armed with one or more edged melee weapons of his choice.

Addendum: For God's sake, ▇▇▇, find these guys something to do. Able's getting bored, and he's started putting his team through live fire exercises: they get bullets, he gets training weapons. Have you ever seen someone break a man's jaw using a Nerf sword? He's not gonna stop until someone gets killed. - Dr. ▇▇▇ ▇▇▇

REPORT BY DR. P█████ G█████, PROJECT OMEGA SEVEN

In light of SCP-076-2's proficient use of the Sumerian language, researchers have asked it to translate several documents. While it originally replied with disinterest, it has translated some of the documents it found worthy of its attention. Most of the documents chosen by SCP-076-2 were regarding battles or legendary heroes, one of its favorites in particular being the "Epic of Gilgamesh".

However, one researcher presented it with the symbol from SCP-073. Upon sight of this, SCP-076-2 became highly enraged, killing several of the researchers before its kill switch could be activated. When revived and questioned about this, SCP-076-2 responded aggressively, and that line of questioning was immediately dropped. It is recommended anything pertaining SCP-073 never be brought to the attention of SCP-076-2 and that the two are never to be in the same facility.

Addendum 076-07: Recently, SCP-105 has been accepted into Mobile Task Force Omega-7, having beaten SCP-076-2 in a contest to see which of the two could activate several devices, each spaced over a mile away from each other and the starting point. SCP-105 managed to score significantly higher than SCP-076-2 by using her inherent abilities to her advantage. SCP-076-2 ceded defeat and allowed her entry into the group.

Addendum 076-09: Proposed introduction of SCP-076-2 to SCP-682 put on indefinite hold. Those with Security Clearance level 4 or higher may request access to Contingency 076-2 #3.

Addendum 076-23: Per the request of the Bowe Commission, Mobile Task Force Omega-7 is to be fielded in the █████ region of █████ against [DATA EXPUNGED].

0076132-33-3 > 02-13

FROM: Dr. █████ █ █████
TO: Dr. P█████ G█████, Project Omega Seven
SUBJECT: Don't do it, P█████

█████,

For god's sake, don't do it. It's bad enough that they're trying to weaponize Iris too. Don't let the military bully us into doing their dirty work against some sand farmers in █████

█████

299333-3 > 02-23

FROM: General █████ Bowe, █████
TO: Dr. P█████ G█████ Project Omega Seven
SUBJECT: A Job Well Done

Excellent work, doctor. The mission went exactly as expected. We'll be calling you again if we need your help.

General █████ Bowe, █████

00-42-33-3 > 02-1

FROM: Dr. ██ █ ██
TO: Dr. P███ G███, Project Omega Seven
SUBJECT: I hope you're fucking proud of yourself, motherfucker.

<hello.jpg>

because you're a bigger asshole than this guy.

0076-323 > 22-43

FROM: Dr. P███ G███, Project Omega Seven
TO: Omega Seven Team
SUBJECT: Reassignment

As of this moment, Dr. ██ █ ██ has been reassigned to SCP-682 as Level 1 personnel.

████████████████████████
██████████ ████████████
████████████████ ████████
████████.

[DATA EXPUNGED]

3376-323

FROM: Dr. P███ G███, Project Omega Seven
TO: General ███ Bowe, ███
SUBJECT: Problems

[DATA EXPUNGED]

Despite our best efforts, Subject Able is proving difficult to control. All our attempts to keep him engaged have been more or less unsuccessful.

The problem is, he's a perfect killing machine, and that's all he wants to do. Which seems like exactly what we wanted, but the problem is, we can't seem to turn him off.

[DATA EXPUNGED]

I'm running out of missions to give him, and the ones I've got left aren't engaging him mentally. He's starting to lash out at the other team members. It's only a matter of time before something goes wrong. Requesting permission to discontinue the project and neutralize Able temporarily, until we can find something more for him to do.

Research
Library
File ▸ 076

339923 > 343

FROM: General ██████ Bowe, ███
TO: Dr. P███ G███ Project Omega Seven
SUBJECT: Re: Problems

Unacceptable. Neutralizing Subject Able at this point is going to cause us an unacceptable delay. We'll have another mission for you within a couple of weeks. All you have to do is keep him busy until then. Send him on vacation or something.

ATTENTION ATTENTION ATTENTION

FROM: Dr. P███ G███, Project Omega Seven
TO: All Staff
SUBJECT: ALERT

THIS IS AN AUTOMATED ALERT

SCP-076-2 has disabled the explosive collar failsafe and gone out of control. All staff to high alert. Further requests as events warrant.

ATTENTION ATTENTION ATTENTION

FROM: AUTOMATED DEFENSE SYSTEM, CONTAINMENT AREA-25
TO: All Sites
SUBJECT: FINAL OPTION ENGAGED

THIS IS AN AUTOMATED MESSAGE. DO NOT REPLY

As of ██-██-███, ██:██ Containment Area-25 has engaged its on-site nuclear warhead on ten-minute countdown.

ATTENTION ATTENTION ATTENTION

FROM: 05 Command
TO: All Sites
SUBJECT: Containment Area 25 Final Option: Response

As of ██-██-███, ██:██, Containment Area-25 has been destroyed by detonation of its on-site nuclear warhead. Sites 67 and 68 are to activate the FEMA protocol and secure the location as soon as possible. Official cover story will be released by RAISA to all personnel once drafted.

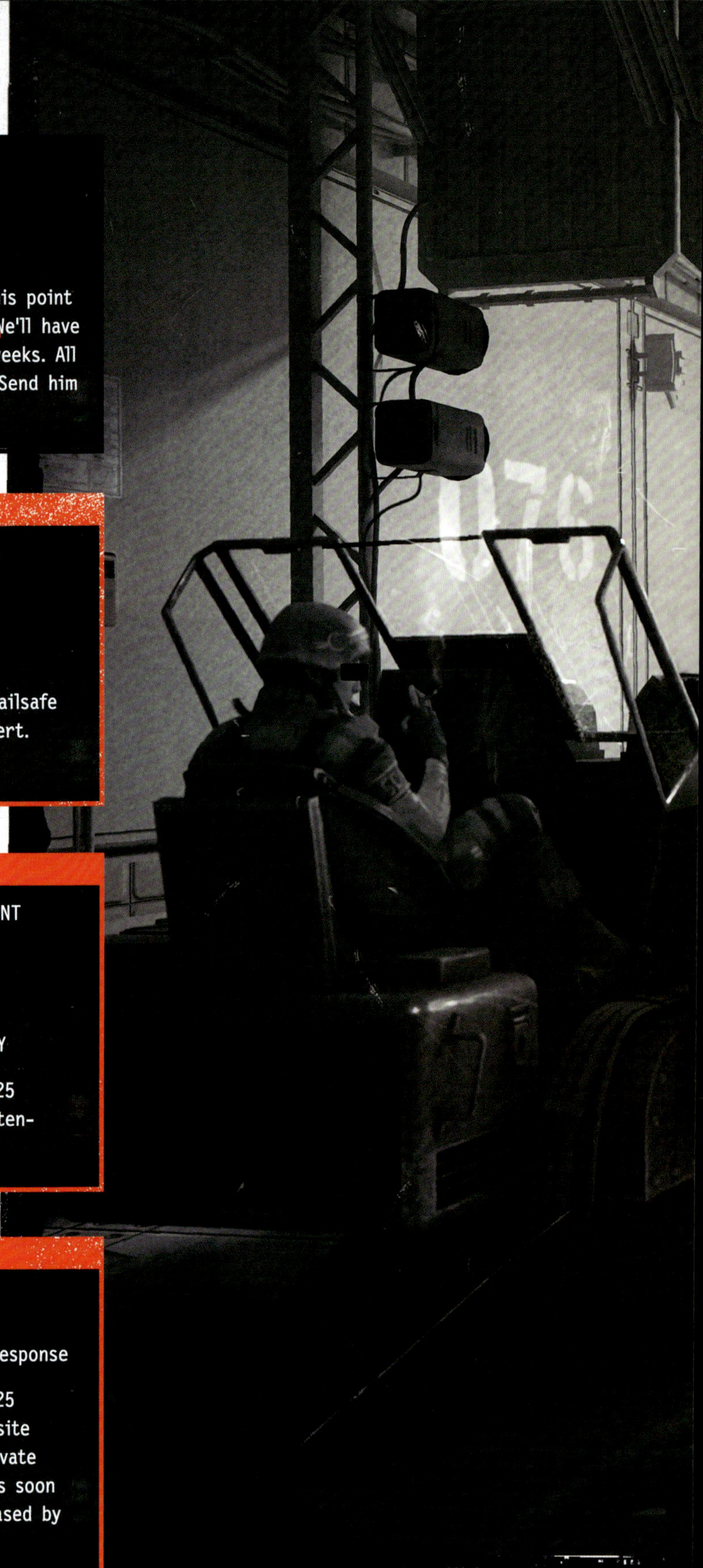

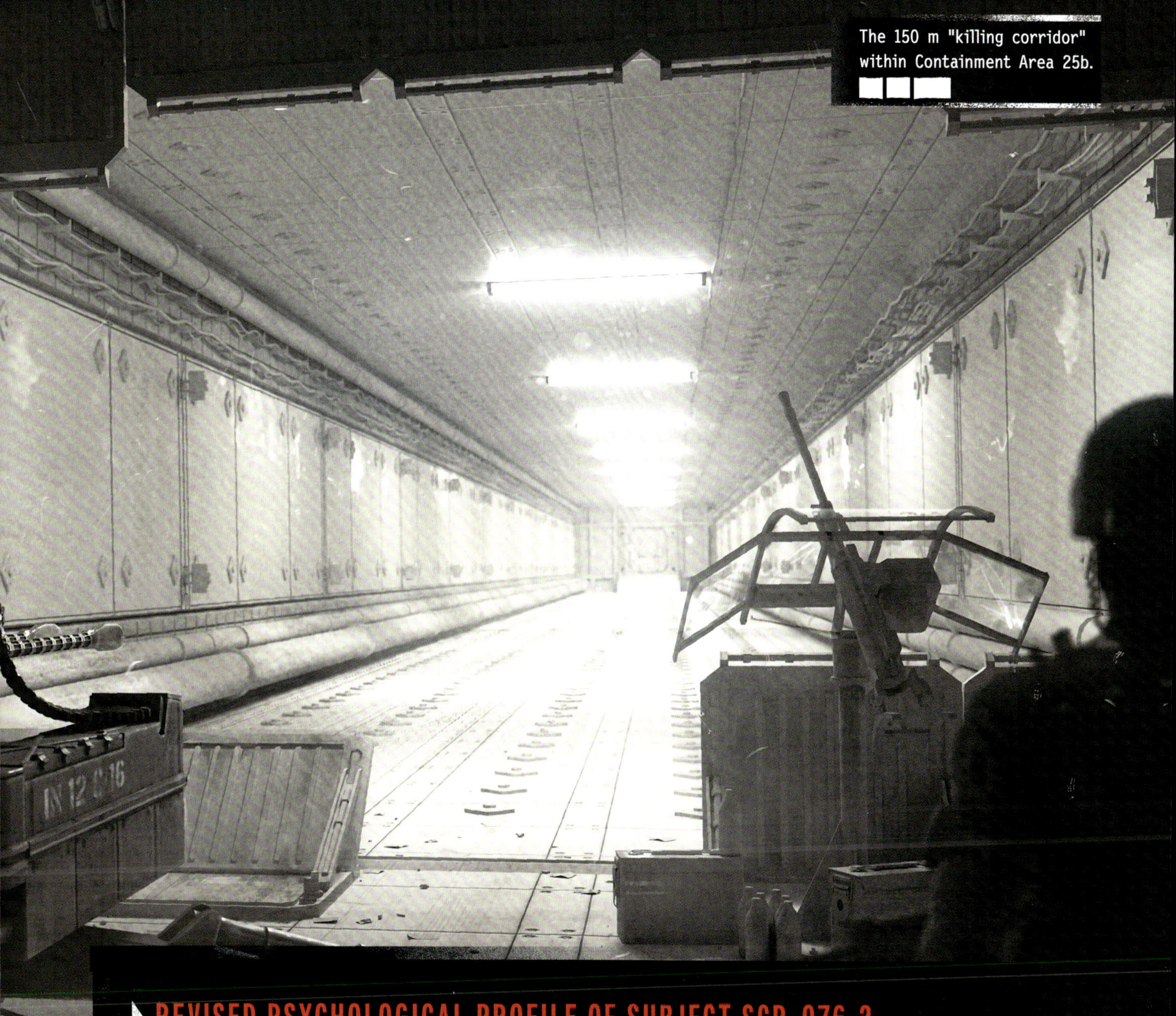

The 150 m "killing corridor" within Containment Area 25b.

REVISED PSYCHOLOGICAL PROFILE OF SUBJECT SCP-076-2

SCP-076-2 either possesses a mind constructed much differently than our own, or is completely insane, with little empathy or ideas in a way we would understand it. Concepts such as sex, love and equality are completely foreign ideas to SCP-076-2, or at least in comparison to its way of viewing them. Subject has shown that it is completely disinterested in sex, barely differentiating between genders except as a form of visual identification. Also, while subject seems to greatly enjoy the act of killing, causing pain (either emotionally or physically) holds no attraction to it.

Intelligence tests have been wildly inconclusive when applied to SCP-076-2, and no accurate result has yet been obtained. This is due to the fact that no communication is possible with the Subject when in its "rage" state. Subject displays knowledge of several languages including English, but most notable is its knowledge of several dialects of ancient Sumerian, which seem to be its preferred language.

SCP-076 has nothing but contempt for human beings and will kill them on sight. No communication is to be attempted with the subject.

END OF REPORT

File >>> 00133323

SCP-105

Title

"IRIS"

Report by

thedeadlymoose
Dantensen
DrClef

Picture by

Dmitriy Fomin

Access the original report on

scp-wiki.wikidot.com/scp-105

Date

Class

SAFE

SPECIAL CONTAINMENT PROCEDURES

SCP-105 is implanted with a tracking device and is currently housed at Site-17. SCP-105 is currently allowed Class 3 (restricted) socialization privileges with approved site personnel, granted based on continued good behavior and cooperation with Foundation personnel.

SCP-105's personal camera (designated SCP-105-B) is contained in a locked safe-deposit box at Site-19's High Value Item Storage Facility. Standard positive-action defenses (explosive, chemical, biological, and memetic) are to be in place at all times while SCP-105-B is within containment.

SCP-105 and SCP-105-B or any other camera are only to be allowed to come into contact with approval of the current managing researcher.

DESCRIPTION

SCP-105 (formerly known as Iris Thompson) is a female human of European descent. Records indicate that SCP-105 was born in ███, making her ██ years old at the time of acquisition. She has blonde hair and blue eyes, and at the time of this article, is 1.54 meters in height and 50kg in weight. She does not appear to have any out-of-the-ordinary physical characteristics and appears to be, for all intents and purposes, a normal human being in good health.

SCP-105-B is a Polaroid One Step Express camera, manufactured in 1982. SCP-105-B does not appear to have any out-of-the-ordinary physical characteristics and appears to be, for all intents and purposes, a normal Polaroid camera, operating normally for all persons aside from SCP-105.

When SCP-105 holds a photograph taken by SCP-105-B, the photograph changes from a still image to that of a real-time image of the location in question. SCP-105 is also able to reach through the photograph and manipulate objects within reach of the original point at which the photograph was taken. Persons witnessing this manipulation report seeing a disembodied female hand (determined to be that of SCP-105) reaching out from an invisible portal and carrying out the actions indicated. SCP-105-B and the photographs taken by said camera have no unusual properties when used by any other person.

SCP-105 has demonstrated limited ability to manipulate objects through other photographs, but can only achieve fine control using photographs taken through SCP-105-B. So far, SCP-105 has only been able to significantly advance her ability by using photographs taken by SCP-105-B.

ADDENDUM 1: CIRCUMSTANCES OF ACQUISITION

SCP-105 was brought to the Foundation's attention shortly after the murder of her boyfriend. SCP-105 claimed to have been on the phone with the victim at the time of his murder, prompting her to hurry to his side; however, telephone records did not correspond to her story, making her suspect in the murder. SCP-105 informed her lawyer that she had, in fact, witnessed the murder through a photograph she had taken with her boyfriend several days prior. The attorney in question disregarded the story and recommended that the subject plead guilty. Subject refused to do so and subsequently told her story in court, offering to demonstrate her ability. This lead to Foundation contact.

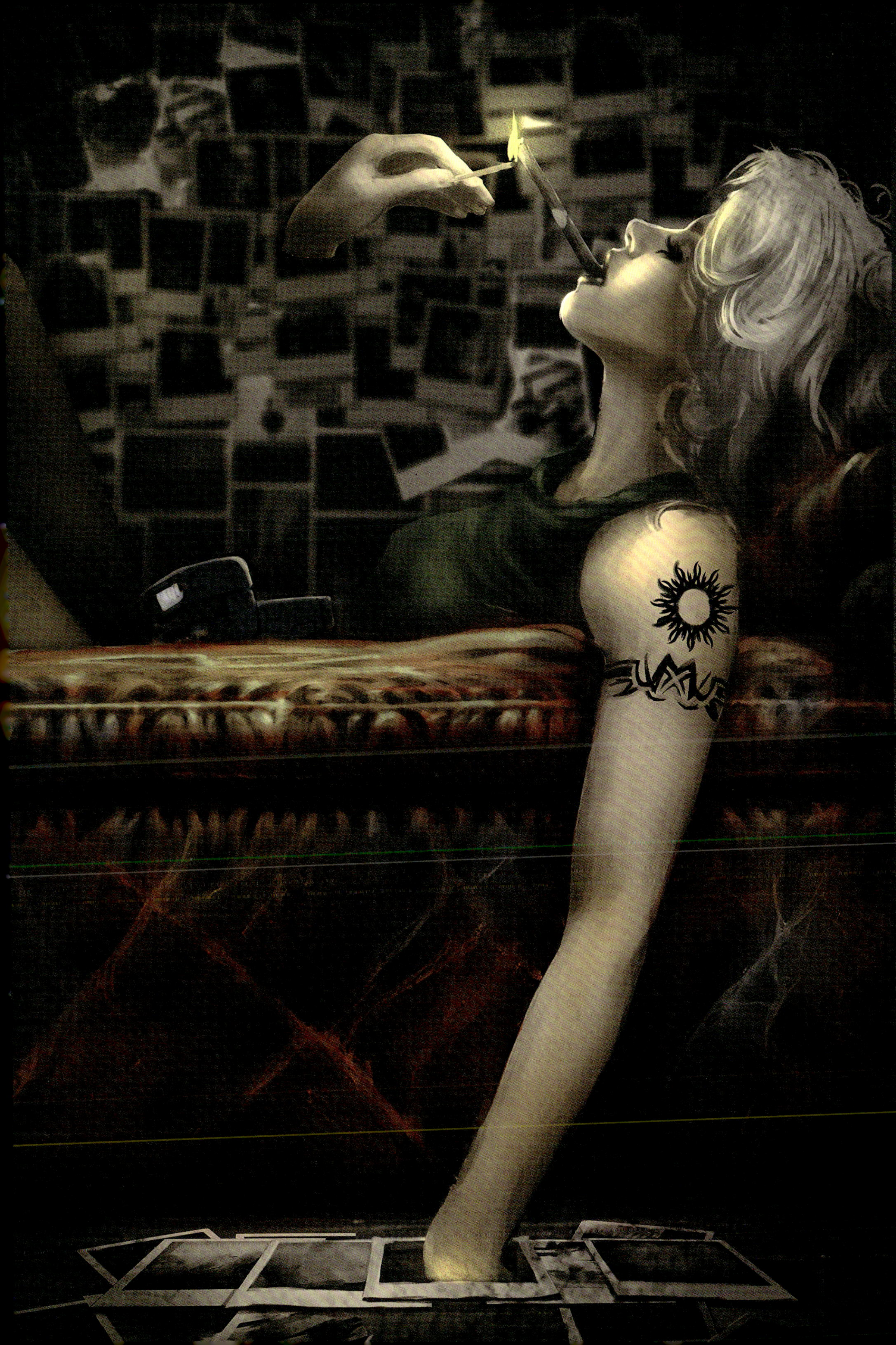

"Iris". A self-portrait.

Subject was immediately contained by the Foundation. Foundation Personnel retrieved SCP-105-B from SCP-105's home (replacing it with an identical model), and returned it to her. SCP-105's parents were informed that she was killed during the botched escape of another patient while both were in custody of the ███████ █████ psychiatric care facility.

Research Library

ADDENDUM 2: EXCERPT FROM INTERVIEW LOG 105-08-4426, DATED ███/███/█████

<Begin log>

Dr. ███: Please give a brief personal introduction, including date and place of birth, and your name.

SCP-105: Okay… My name is Iris Thompson, I was born in Phoenix, Arizona, on May 12th, ███.

Dr. ███: Good. First question, when did you become aware of your abilities?

SCP-105: I'm not sure, but I think I was either ten or eleven. I remember because I was looking at a picture of the ocean, and I noticed that the waves began moving.

Dr. ███: How did your parents respond when you told them?

SCP-105: They just said that I had an overactive imagination.

Dr. ███: When did you discover that you were able to manipulate objects through a photograph?

SCP-105: It first happened when I was… eleven, twelve, maybe? My family took a trip to the Grand Canyon. I looked through the photo album after we got home, and brushed my hand up against one by accident. When I did, I pushed a rock over the edge, falling into the canyon; I could actually hear it clatter on the way down.

Dr. ███: Go on.

SCP-105: I became fascinated with photography after that. Most of the time, it didn't work with photographs I took, but my parents got me a Polaroid One Step Express camera – I'd been begging for them to get it since Christmas. *<SCP-105 starts smiling.>* After I got the camera, the photos got… easier to interact with.

Dr. ███: This is the camera we refer to as 105-B? Your personal camera.

SCP-105: Yes sir.

Dr. ███: How many photos can you focus on at one time?

SCP-105: I've gotten up to ten at once with my personal camera, but I'm sure I could do more eventually.

Dr. ███: What is your impression of your time with the Foundation so far?

<SCP-105 remains silent.>

Dr. ███: Please, do answer. We don't take offense at these things.

SCP-105: It's sort of like… New prison, new warden. But I know it's better than what could've happened to me.

Dr. ███: You've been very cooperative during your time here.

SCP-105: I'm a pretty well-behaved sort of person. I also like doing the experiments. Some of those things with photographs I would never have thought of.

Dr. ███: Do you know why I am asking you these questions, Iris?

SCP-105: No, sir.

Dr. ███: We've been setting up a special program. If it goes through, you'll be occasionally allowed to leave the site and move about in the outside world. All we ask of you in return are a few favors. Are you interested?

<End log>

ADDENDUM 3: HISTORY OF SERVICE WITH MOBILE TASK FORCE OMEGA-7

SCP-105 was the second humanoid SCP recruited to Mobile Task Force Omega-7 under the Pandora's Box initiative. Unlike "Team Able" (associated with SCP-076-2), which was assigned to strike and capture operations, "Team Iris" had the primary mission of reconnaissance and intelligence gathering. "Team Iris" carried out over twenty missions in cooperation with the Bowe Commission. These missions were carried out swiftly and without incident.

The first disciplinary incident involving SCP-105 involved the escalation of Team Iris missions from reconnaissance to wetwork. SCP-105 violently opposed the use of her abilities to carry out assassinations, even after members of the Bowe Commission repeatedly attempted to secure her cooperation (see Interview Log 105-21-6543).

During these events, SCP-105 became emotionally distressed and attempted to deceive Foundation personnel into believing that her anomalous traits had disappeared. Dr. D█████ submitted a report recommending that SCP-105 be re-classified as Neutralized, undergo amnestic treatment, and be released to the public with regular monitoring. This recommendation was denied.

Following this, Dr. D█████ aided SCP-105 in a containment breach aiming to escape Foundation custody. This breach was unsuccessful and SCP-105 was re-contained (see Incident X45-Site-17).

Investigation afterwards determined that Dr. D█████ had intentionally encouraged SCP-105 to claim loss of anomalous abilities. SCP-105 re-demonstrated her anomalous abilities in exchange for restoration of limited privileges.

Following the end of the Pandora's Box Initiative, all Mobile Task Force Omega-7 teams were disbanded, and SCP-105 was returned to Site-17. Because of the security risk she represents and lack of current utility, SCP-105 is presently not allowed access to SCP-105-B.

All further information regarding Mobile Task Force Omega-7 is sealed by order of the Records And Information Security Administration.

Director █████ ███ Records And Information Security Administration

ADDENDUM 4: SPECIAL NOTICE RE: CURRENT CONTAINMENT STATUS

Following Incident R1300-Site-17, many formal and informal reports have been made regarding SCP-105 and a supposed connection to Mobile Task Force Alpha-9.

These reports constitute a serious breach of security. All information regarding Mobile Task Force Alpha-9 is restricted. All information regarding current research on anomalous characteristics of SCP-105 is restricted. All reports or rumors regarding any current or recent use of SCP-105 as a Foundation asset are to be considered categorically false, and should be reported to the Records And Information Security Administration.

Director ████ ████ Records And Information Security Administration

END OF REPORT ▌█████ ▌███

File >>> 28234

SCP-073

Title

"CAIN"

Report by

Kain Pathos Crow

Picture by

Dmitry Desyatov

Access the original report on **scp-wiki.wikidot.com/scp-073**

Date

Class

EUCLID

SPECIAL CONTAINMENT PROCEDURES

SCP-073 is to be kept in a two (2) room cell furnished with all non-organic furniture and items, and a bathroom. Subject is allowed to freely wander the facility and eat in the main canteen. A tracking device has been attached to SCP-073's person and is not to be removed. Subject is disallowed any contact with the surface, and is not allowed outside the facility. Subject is allowed no contact with plant-based SCPs under any circumstances. Violence is not to be used against SCP-073 under any circumstances.

SCP-073 is currently kept in Site-17.

DESCRIPTION

SCP-073 appears to be a heavily-tanned male of Arabic or Middle Eastern descent in his early thirties, 185 cm (6'1") tall and 75 kg (165 lbs), with black hair and blue eyes. Arms, legs, spinal cord, and shoulder blades of the subject appear to have been replaced with artificial versions of unknown make and metal. Subject only takes notice of this when it is pointed out, and states that it has no knowledge of how, why, or when these replacements took place, stating it had had them as long as it could remember. There is a symbol engraved into the forehead of the subject, which appears to be of Sumerian origin. Symbol has of yet been untranslated, and subject appears distressed when the symbol is mentioned at all, refusing to speak on it. Subject does need to eat and drink on a regular basis, but is strictly carnivorous owing to its effect on plant-based items.

SCP-073, who refers to itself as "Cain", is generally polite and genial to all who speak to it, though it has been described as being cold and somewhat mechanical in its speech. It is very helpful, and enjoys aiding personnel in their daily actions, whatever they may be. It has highly detailed knowledge of ancient to recent events in history, and most commonly spoken languages in the world, including ones that have since died out. Subject has professed to having a photographic memory, remembering word-for-word all text in an eight-hundred-page dictionary that was flicked through in a minute and a half. It has scored above average in all intelligence tests given to it.

SCP-073's presence is inimical to any and all life grown in soil, causing death to any such life within a twenty (20) meter radius. Any land SCP-073 has walked on (and any within the twenty [20] meter radius) becomes barren as all anaerobic bacteria dies, rendering the soil incapable of supporting life until new bacteria are introduced. Anything that is derived from soil-grown life, such as wood and paper, immediately rots and disintegrates upon touch of SCP-073. Further affected derivatives include anything hydroponically grown.

Violence directed towards SCP-073 reflects any damage inflicted on SCP-073 directly back onto the attacker, although SCP-073 visibly remains unharmed. This applies to **any** damage directed at SCP-073. Attempts to get tissue and blood samples have proven futile: when the procedure was initiated, personnel carrying out the action felt the sensation of whatever was applied to SCP-073, and wound up with a sample of their own blood or tissue, despite the fact that "all actions were directed solely at SCP-073". Indirect damage through a medium also results in the person perpetrating the action receiving the wounds caused. Although SCP-073 receives no actual harm from damage to its person, it has stated that it still feels the pain of the action, and has politely asked researchers to abstain from overly harmful actions to its person.

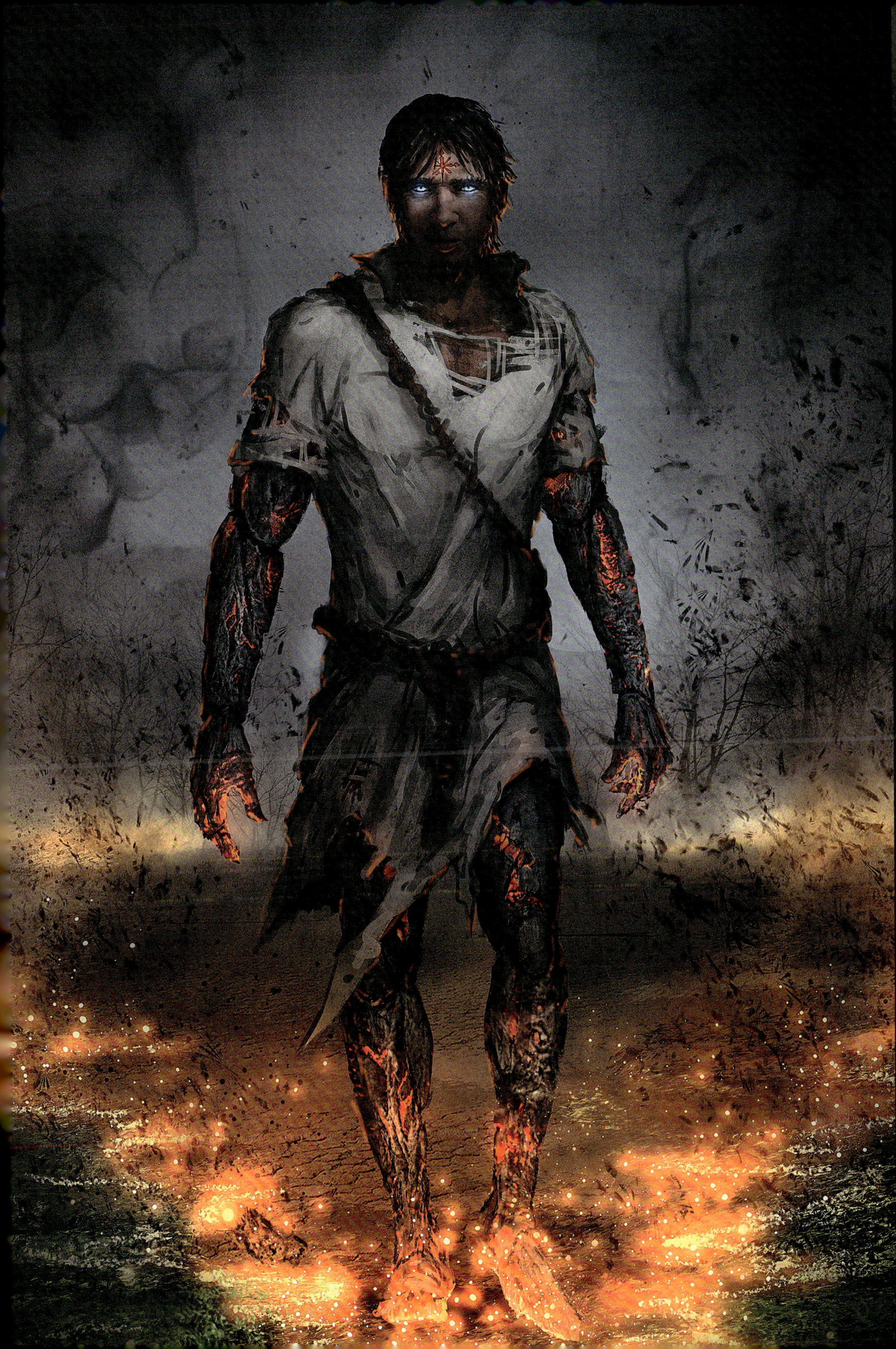

A drawing created by one of the newly designated researchers upon acquaintance with SCP-073. SCP-073 noted that soil doesn't usually burn around it, but seemed pleased nevertheless.

Research Library File ▸ 073

ADDITIONAL NOTES

SCP-073 was found in the New York Police Department in 19█, having been taken in after subject had been found amidst the bodies of several violent gang members. SCP-073 told police members that the gang had attempted to make sport of it, but became angry and attempted to kill SCP-073, resulting in their own demise. SCP-073 was incarcerated, and was deemed a "John Doe" when NYPD could not find any information on it. SCP-073 came to the attention of the Foundation through a routine inspection of "John Does", and was subsequently released into our custody.

SCP-073'S FINGERPRINTS

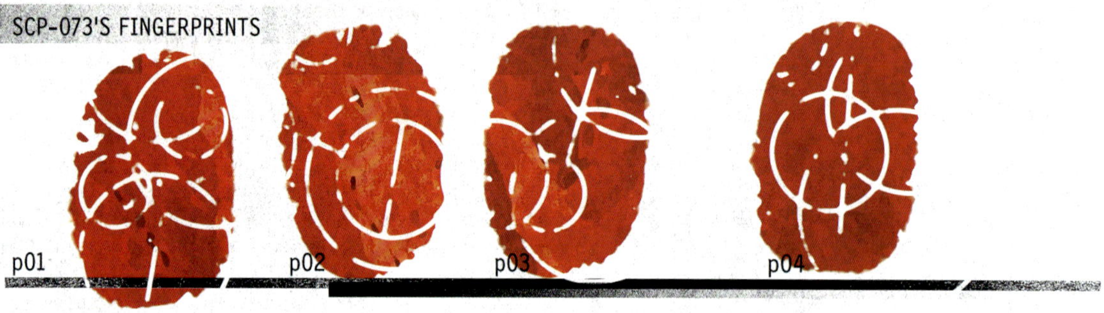

ADDENDUM 073-1

In light of SCP-073's indestructible nature, photographic memory, and general will to please, high command have deemed that all information is to be "backed up" on SCP-073, ensuring it is not lost in the event of a catastrophe. While this action has met with mixed responses, SCP-073 has agreed and sworn itself to secrecy on its part.

ADDENDUM 073-2

When information concerning SCP-076 was brought to the attention of SCP-073 for "backing up", subject showed familiarity with the information, although was disinclined to adding to it, despite the fact that it stated that it already knew all about SCP-076. It then stated it would be better for all parties involved that it not meet SCP-076.

ADDENDUM 073-3

Examination of the unidentified metal on SCP-073 has suggested that it is beryllium bronze, a metal that has been documented as being utilized by various anomalous cultures and entities. Most notably, beryllium bronze is a component found in SCP-1216, SCP-1427, SCP-2481, and SCP-2711. In light of this discovery, the Foundation began working in an attempt to trace the origin of beryllium bronze and how it initially spread throughout the world. When prompted, SCP-073 was able to provide information that suggests that beryllium bronze originated in the Middle East, though the exact point of origin has yet to be determined. Further research into the origin of beryllium bronze is currently ongoing.

END OF REPORT

File >>> 034255

SCP-363

Title

NOT CENTIPEDES

Report by

Josef Kald

Pictures by

Dmitry Utkin
Dmitry Desyatov

Access the original report on

scp-wiki.wikidot.com/scp-363

Date

Class

KETER

SPECIAL CONTAINMENT PROCEDURES

SCP-363 specimens are contained in a 2 m x 2 m x 2 m room that is to be constantly illuminated by high-powered lighting. This lighting must be connected to multiple redundant power sources, and in case of total system failure, Mobile Task Force Eta-Seven is to be dispatched to assess the threat.

SCP-363 is to be fed twenty (20) lab mice, administered once every forty-eight (48) hours.

DESCRIPTION

Ostensibly, SCP-363 are identical to Scolopendra gigantea, or the Amazonian giant centipede. Dietary needs are identical, and DNA inspection has proven no dissimilarities to normal S. gigantea.

SCP-363 is, under normal circumstances, the appropriate size for S. gigantea. In darkness, (darkness defined here as any level of light under 2 lux) which it actively seeks out, however, SCP-363 will grow rapidly and erratically, to sizes up to and exceeding 10 m x 2 m. SCP-363 does not retain the form of a centipede under these conditions. So far, reports have documented: proboscises, tentacles, highly elongated mandibles, an inconsistent number of eyes and legs, and, in one case, [DATA EXPUNGED]. SCP-363 will revert back to normal size and appearance after 2-3 hours of illumination of a level of at least 50 lux.

SCP-363 will attack any animal emitting body heat, and appears to be able to detect and hunt in total darkness. It is assumed it uses other senses to hunt, with vision in a secondary position.

Reproductive cycle of SCP-363 is similar to that of normal S. gigantea, with one difference. Rather than in a cluster of leaves and dirt, eggs are laid and fertilized in the ████ cavity of paralyzed [DATA EXPUNGED], followed by death.

ADDENDUM 1

Note from Dr. Skalder:

We have determined that fire seems to scare or ward off SCP-363. In light of this, we have equipped three of the members of MTF Eta-Seven, "Creepy Crawlies", with military-issue M2A1-7 flamethrowers.

ADDENDUM 2: INCIDENT REPORT OF BREACH

Document# 363-Alpha: Breach 1
Personnel involved: MTF-Eta-7
Date: 21-5-2003
Location: Site-██
Description: Attempted retrieval of SCP-363 specimen during power failure/containment breach.

<Start of audio log>

MTF Eta-7 Commander Johnson: Perts, any word from Technical on *(distortion)* cameras?

Contactsman Perts: No dice, commander. Complete equipment failure throughout the sector.

C. Johnson: Alright. Night-vision on, motion-sensors go. Fredmann, McShaugn, Aidelare, report to rendezvous point.

Lieutenant McShaugn: Copy that, commander. Sub-team Hornet coming in, over.

C. Johnson: Sub-team Wasp, come in.

(Radio silence)

C. Johnson: Wasp, do you copy? Over.

Unknown: *(Shouting)* Jesus Christ almighty, torch that █████- *(signal cuts out)*

C. Johnson: Damn it. O'Denn? O'Denn, can you hear me? What is your position? Over.

Lieutenant O'Denn: Outside of Lab 8. We found it, sir. It's holed up in there. It got De Aunaign. Over.

C. Johnson: Casualty?

L. O'Denn: Mangled leg, sir. We scared the █████ in there with the flamethrower, don't think it's coming out. Are they fixing the power yet? Over.

C. Johnson: Forget about that, O'Denn. Tell Von Hower to keep his flamer trained on the door. Hornet, can you hear me? Over.

L. McShaugn: Loud and clear, sir.

C. Johnson: Forget the rendezvous. Relocate to Lab 8, don't engage yet. Copy?

L. McShaugn: Going *(interrupted by loud noise)* ███ my grandmother! What was that?! Aidelare, do you see anything?! Over!

Flamer Aidelare: *(Extensive swearing)* There's another one of those █████ in here! Second containment breach, commander!

C. Johnson: Has it seen you? Over.

F. Aidelare: I don't reckon, sir.

C. Johnson: Good. Try to keep it that way. Perts, how many of those things did they keep in here?

C.M Perts: *(Relays question to contact.)* Eight, sir.

C. Johnson: Good God. Okay, tell 'em "███ the preservation and detonate the gas charges".

C.M Perts: They uh, they can't, sir.

C. Johnson: Why the ███ not, Perts?

[DATA EXPUNGED]

L. O'Denn: So we're all █████ three days from Sunday. Good to know. Orders, commander?

C. Johnson: ███ 'em all and burn it down, O'Denn. Tell Von Hower and Aidelare to set fire to Lab 8, then split up and do a sweep of the area. Neutralize all hostile centipede ████████.

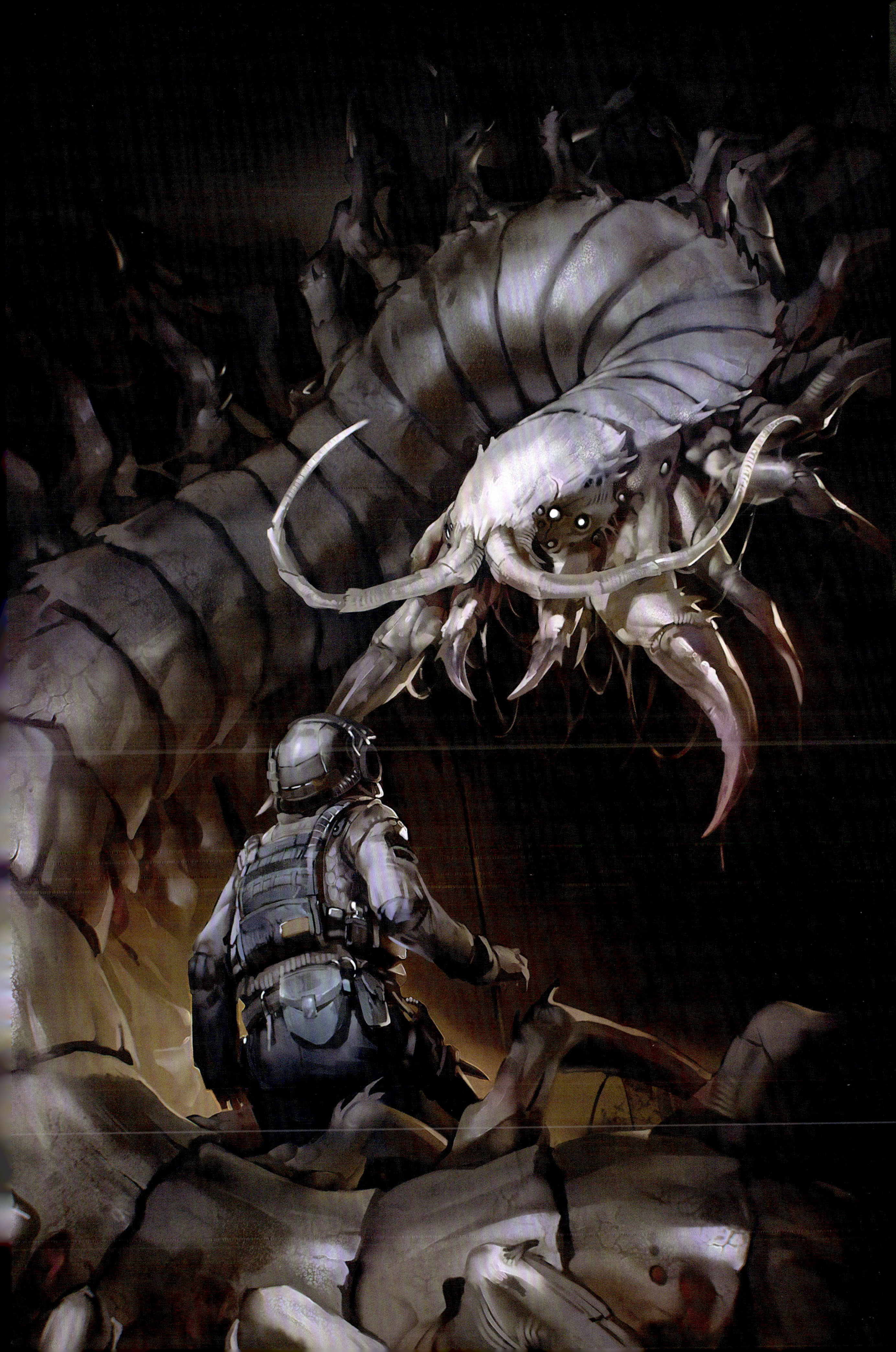

Image retrieved from Lieutenant O'Denn's BWV camera.

L. O'Denn: Copy that.

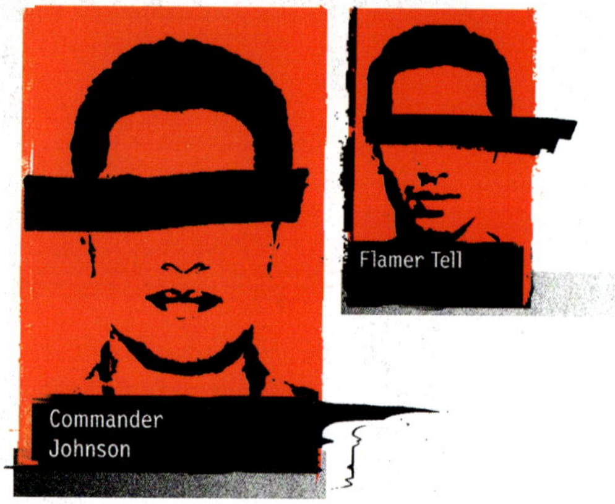

C. Johnson: Perts, still no contact with Blackfly?

C.M Perts: Blackfly, report in.

(Radio silence)

C.M Perts: No Blackfly.

C. Johnson: I gathered, Perts. Alright, O'Denn, status repo-

Unknown: *(Gasping, groaning)*

C. Johnson: The…who's that? Identify.

Unknown: Flamer Tell, sir.

C. Johnson: What is your status, Tell? What of Blackfly? Over.

F. Tell: …dead. Everyone.

C. Johnson: Repeat that, Tell?

F. Tell: *(screaming)* We're all█████ dead down here, commander! I saw one of them…one of them pulled Doug apart…just…just in half. It laid all these eggs, and another one squirted this jizz over them. They hatched…they hatched so fast…more of those things…ate him so fast…dozens of them…eating Howard now…I liked Howard, commander…eating him…eating him…

C. Johnson: Calm down, Tell, for God's sake. What's your personal status?

F. Tell: They're on my legs…I can see 'em…but I can't feel it…biting me…

(Radio silence)

F. Tell: I feel something…burning…like bubbling…

C. Johnson: Tell. Self-terminate. That's an order. I'm sorry.

F. Tell: *(Unintelligible)*

C. Johnson: God damn it, Tell! Do you copy?! Immediate self-termination!

F. Tell: *(Warped voice)* The flesh is like milk to us.

C. Johnson: What the hell are you saying, Tell?

F. Tell: We are one.

C. Johnson: I think he's gone crazy.

F. Tell: One is all. *(Cracking noises)*

C. Johnson: Wasp, Hornet. Come in.

(Radio Silence)

C. Johnson: Wasp, Hornet. Come in, damn it.

L. O'Denn: *(Same warped voice as documented with Flamer Tell)* We are here. There are many.

C. Johnson: Perts? Tell command we're evacuating the premises. Mission failure.

C.M Perts: Sir, yes sir.

C. Johnson: Air strike and full bombardment once we're out. No - *(interrupted by crashing sound)* Jesus Christ, what-

(tearing sounds)

(Five minutes of radio silence, C. Johnson presumed dead)

Unknown individual, presumed C.M Perts: Hear, o Israel. Y-H-W-H is our God, Y-H-W-H alone.

(Gunshot)

<End of audio log>

Post-script: Site-██ fire-bombed. Several undamaged and fertilized SCP-363 eggs retrieved. Contained. All members of MTF Eta-7 presumed dead. New team established. - 05-██

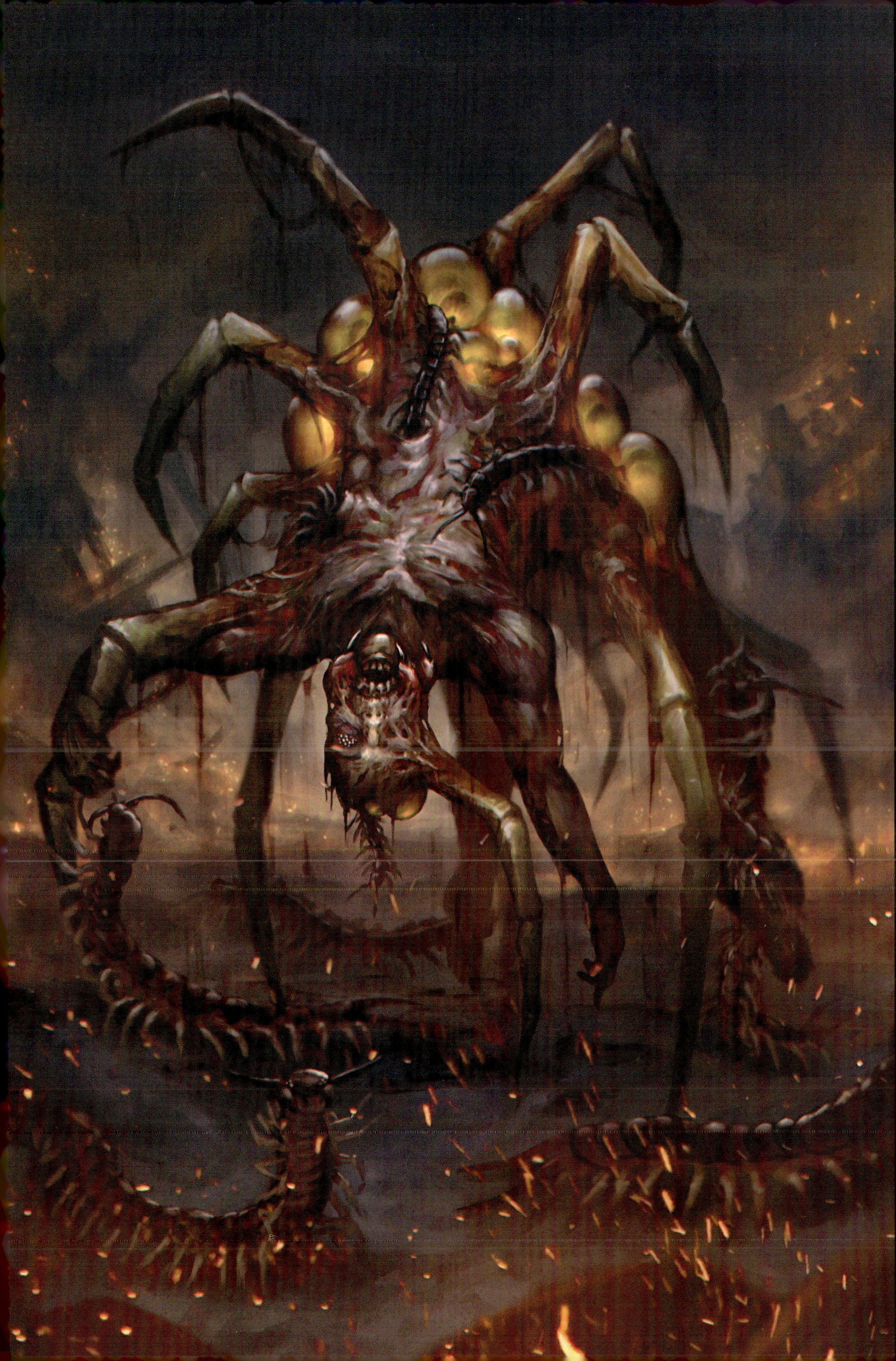

Visualization created after the interview with Janitor █████ to facilitate the tracking procedure.

Research Library File ▸ 363

ADDENDUM 3: INTERVIEW

Interviewed: Janitor ███ ███
Interviewer: [DATA EXPUNGED], referred to as "I."
Foreword: Interview conducted after ███ professed to a possible SCP-sighting after firebombing of Site-██

<Begin log>

I.: Hello, ███. Please sit down. Thank you, now, you said you saw "something" after the firebombing. Care to expand on that?

███: It was…well, one of those guys from the MTF you had stationed there. Eta-7. One of those guys, yeah.

I.: Do you know his name, perchance?

███: Yeah, yeah, I talked to him once. That guy, ███ Tell. One of the flamers.

I.: Are you sure it was him?

███: *(Short silence)* No. No, I ain't sure. It…it looked like him, for sure. But there were all these things… growing out of him. Like insect legs, but, all in random places…from his chest, his arms, and…one of 'em was pokin' out of of his eyeball. His eye was just gone. And his mouth…there were these, like, these pinchers. Mandibles. All black. And there were these things…

I.: Continue.

███: These things…centipedes…crawling in and outta holes in his flesh. He looked at me – his one eye'd gone all…it looked all like a bug's eye, with facets, and stuff, and…he laughed. I think he did, anyway.

I.: And then?

███: He…he ran away.

I.: Thank you.

<End log>

ADDENDUM 4

Security Level 4

Announcement: Signal of standard MTF anti-defection tracker located [DATA EXPUNGED], eighteen miles away from Site-█. Signal associated with ███Tell. Tracking procedure initialized. Infection risk to be negated at all costs. -05-█

END OF REPORT ███ █

File >>> 0023455

SCP-294

Title

THE COFFEE MACHINE

Report by

Arcibi

Picture by

Genocide Error

Access the original report on

scp-wiki.wikidot.com/scp-294

Date

Class

EUCLID

SPECIAL CONTAINMENT PROCEDURES

There are no standard special containment procedures on file for Item SCP-294. However, only personnel of security clearance level 2 or higher are allowed to interact with it (see document SCP-294a). SCP-294 is currently being stored in the 2nd floor personnel break room and is monitored by two guards of security clearance level 3 at all times.

DESCRIPTION

Item SCP-294 appears to be a standard coffee vending machine, the only noticeable difference being an entry touchpad with buttons corresponding to an English QWERTY keyboard. Upon depositing fifty cents US currency into the coin slot, the user is prompted to enter the name of any liquid using the touchpad. Upon doing so, a standard 12-ounce paper drinking cup is placed and the liquid indicated is poured. Ninety-seven initial test runs were performed (including requests for water, coffee, beer, and soda, non-consumable liquids such as sulfuric acid, wiper fluid, and motor oil, as well as substances that do not usually exist in liquid state, such as nitrogen, iron and glass) and each one returned a success. Test runs with solid materials such as diamond have failed, however, as it appears that SCP-294 can only deliver substances that can exist in liquid state.

It is of note that after approximately fifty uses, the machine would not respond to further requests. After a period of approximately 90 minutes, the machine seemed to have restocked itself. It is also interesting to note that many caustic liquids that would have eaten through a normal paper cup seemed to have no effect on the cups dispensed by the machine.

Testing is ongoing. As suggested, SCP-294 was moved to the 2nd floor personnel break room as a money-saving venture. Following incident 294-01, guards were stationed at the item and a security clearance became necessary to interact with it.

DOCUMENT SCP-294A (REGARDING INCIDENT 294-01)

On August 21, 2005, Agent Joseph ███ attempted to use Item SCP-294 to obtain coffee during his allotted break time at 9:30 AM. At the request of Agent ███ ███ "to see what it would do", ███ requested "a cup of Joe" from the item. Moments after confirming the selection, Agent Joseph ███ began to sweat profusely and complained of dizziness before collapsing. After moving the unconscious agent to the infirmary, the medical team recovered the contents of the cup dispensed by Item SCP-294: a combination of blood, tissue, and other bodily fluids. Testing revealed the DNA sequence of the biological material dispensed by SCP-294 matched that of Agent ███.

Agent ███ made a complete recovery after four weeks of rest and intravenous hydration. X-rays and CAT scans showed no further signs of injury, and ███ was released. Both agents were reprimanded. Additional security measures for SCP-294 have been recommended.

Addendum [SCP-294f]: After reviewing documentation on SCP-294, ██████ suggested testing SCP-294's ability to 'retrieve' specific liquids from a distance.

Addendum [SCP-294i]: Researcher punched in request for "cup of gold". The machine dispensed a cup of molten gold. Researcher requested similar precious materials with the same result.

Addendum [SCP-294j]: Researcher punched in (from a safe range) request for "cup of anti-water". The machine hummed briefly, then displayed "OUT OF RANGE" on entry pad. It is theorized that SCP-294 has a limited range of collection, and cannot reach into alternate universes/dimensions.

Addendum [SCP-294k]: Researcher punched in request for "diamond". SCP-294 briefly hummed, then displayed "OUT OF RANGE" on entry pad. SCP-294 gives this result for all solid substances. As diamond is a solid crystalline form of carbon, it appears the machine will not dispense liquid carbon, as this does not result in a "diamond". When "cup of carbon" was subsequently punched in, the machine dispensed a cup of liquid carbon. SCP-294 was immune to the damaging effects of the dispensed liquid.

Addendum [SCP-294m]: Testing for range of SCP-294's capacity for retrieval has been initiated. A unique compound has been formulated, composed of undisclosed ratios of ████ brand bleach, ██ ██ ██ █ brand cola, MET-RX powder, and Garam masala. The fluid was created and placed in a sealed container 25 meters away from SCP 294. When requested, the fluid was dispensed. An equal amount of the mixture was no longer present in its original container.

Addendum [SCP-294w]: Researcher keyed in request for "a cup of music". SCP-294 produced a clear, sparkling fluid that tasted vaguely alcoholic. Following ingestion, subject reported "feeling" and not hearing, a continuous rhythm, and demonstrated the ability to move and even dance with a certain fluidity that he had not previously shown. Testing on other abstract concepts is continuing.

Addendum [SCP-294ab]: During a mass security breach, Agent ███ requested "a cup of pertinent medical knowledge" while taking shelter inside the second floor break room. Of the four agents in the room, Agent ███ was the only one who was not injured. SCP-294 poured a cup of clear green liquid. Following the ingestion of this substance, Agent ███ began mending the other agents' wounds in a manner consistent with Foundation medical training. Agent ███ no longer has the medical training that the liquid provided and other attempts to recreate the effect have failed. The agent has speculated that this event was an emergency measure taken by the object to ensure self-preservation.

Addendum [SCP-294ac]: Dr. ███ requested "my life story" from SCP-294; SCP-294 made humming noises and shook violently for approximately 3 minutes before providing a highly viscous, opaque black liquid. Upon consumption, Dr. ███ reported that he remembered everything that had ever happened to him. Following this test, Dr. ███ entered his office and returned 48 hours later with a 538-page autobiography.

Addendum [SCP-294ah]: A D-class personnel with IQ of 99 and low curiosity scores was given written instructions about what to request. The D-class personnel produced a request for 'blood of canis lupus' and received a cup of liquid subsequently identified as wolf blood. The D-class personnel next produced a request for 'saliva of equus ferus caballus' and received a cup of liquid subsequently identified as horse saliva. The D-class personnel next produced a request for "urine of phascolarctos cinereus' and received a cup of liquid subsequently identified as koala urine. The D-class personnel next produced a request for "cerebrospinal fluid of phoberomys pattersoni" and received a cup of liquid currently undergoing analysis. It is to be noted that Phoberomys pattersoni went extinct during the late Miocene epoch, approximately 8 million years ago.

Addendum [SCP-294ai]: Dr. King produced request for "a cup of room-temperature superconductor", and received a cup of apple juice with seeds floating in it.

Addendum [SCP-294aj]: Dr. Menchu produced request for "cup of D-151839's leukemia", and received a cup of fluid; the fluid was microscopically examined and found to contain leukemic blast cells, which were a genetic match to D-151839. A second request for "cup of D-151839's leukemia" resulted in an "OUT OF RANGE" error. D-151839 was subsequently found to be free of leukemia; however, within 15 days, the leukemia had recurred.

[Other SCP-294 experiments are currently awaiting approval.]

END OF REPORT

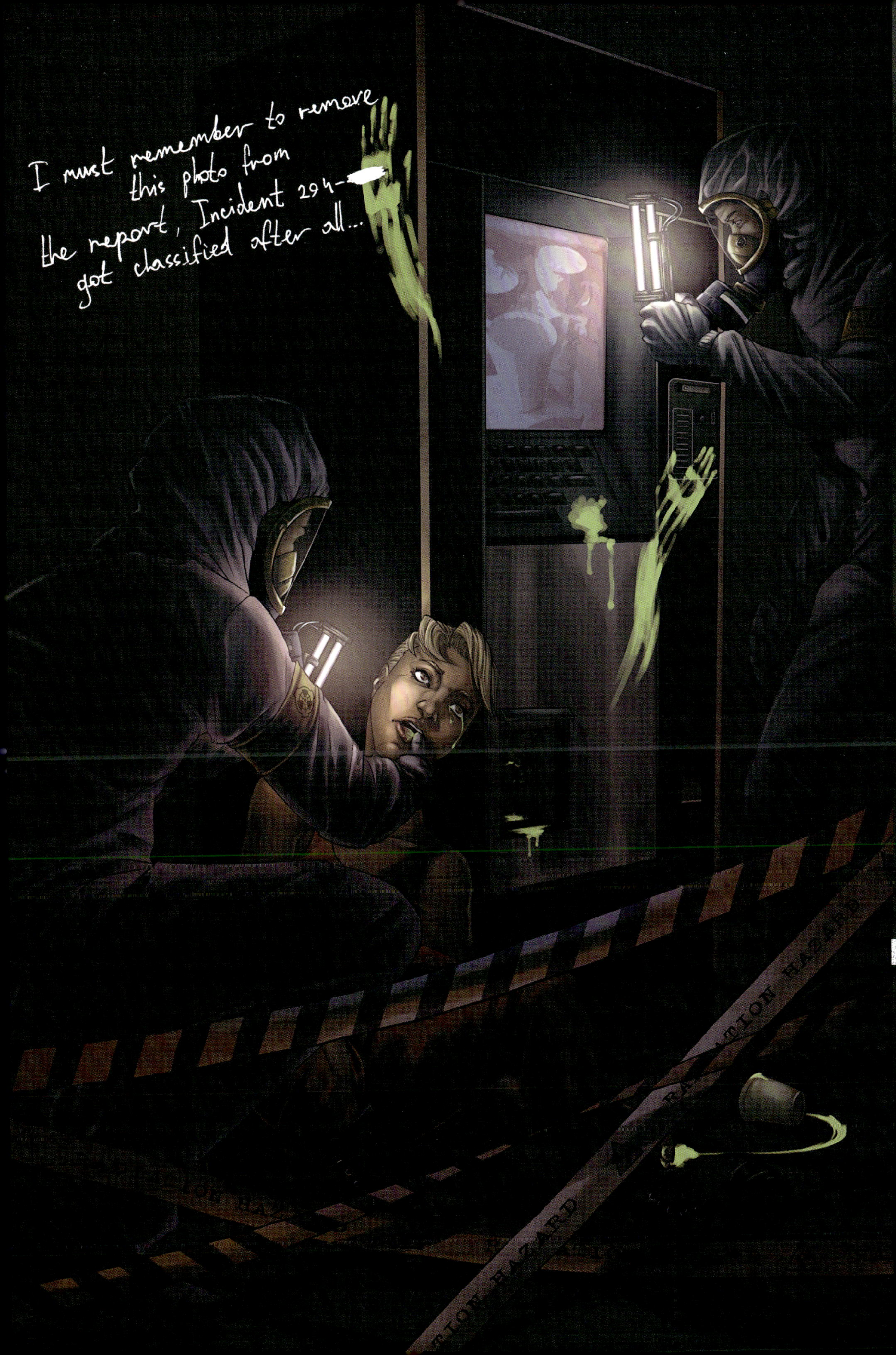

Photo taken during Incident 294-█

File >>> 0396234

SCP-173

Title

THE SCULPTURE

Report by

Moto42

Picture by

Ivan Efimov

Access the original report on

scp-wiki.wikidot.com/scp-173

Date

Class

EUCLID

SPECIAL CONTAINMENT PROCEDURES

Item SCP-173 is to be kept in a locked container at all times. When personnel must enter SCP-173's container, no fewer than 3 may enter at any time and the door is to be relocked behind them. At all times, two persons must maintain direct eye contact with SCP-173 until all personnel have vacated and relocked the container.

DESCRIPTION

Moved to Site-19 1993. Origin is as of yet unknown. It is constructed from concrete and rebar with traces of Krylon brand spray paint. SCP-173 is animate and extremely hostile. The object cannot move while within a direct line of sight. Line of sight must not be broken at any time with SCP-173. Personnel assigned to enter container are instructed to alert one another before blinking. Object is reported to attack by snapping the neck at the base of the skull, or by strangulation. In the event of an attack, personnel are to observe Class 4 hazardous object containment procedures.

Personnel report sounds of scraping stone originating from within the container when no one is present inside. This is considered normal, and any change in this behaviour should be reported to the acting HMCL supervisor on duty.

The reddish brown substance on the floor is a combination of feces and blood. Origin of these materials is unknown. The enclosure must be cleaned on a bi-weekly basis.

END OF REPORT

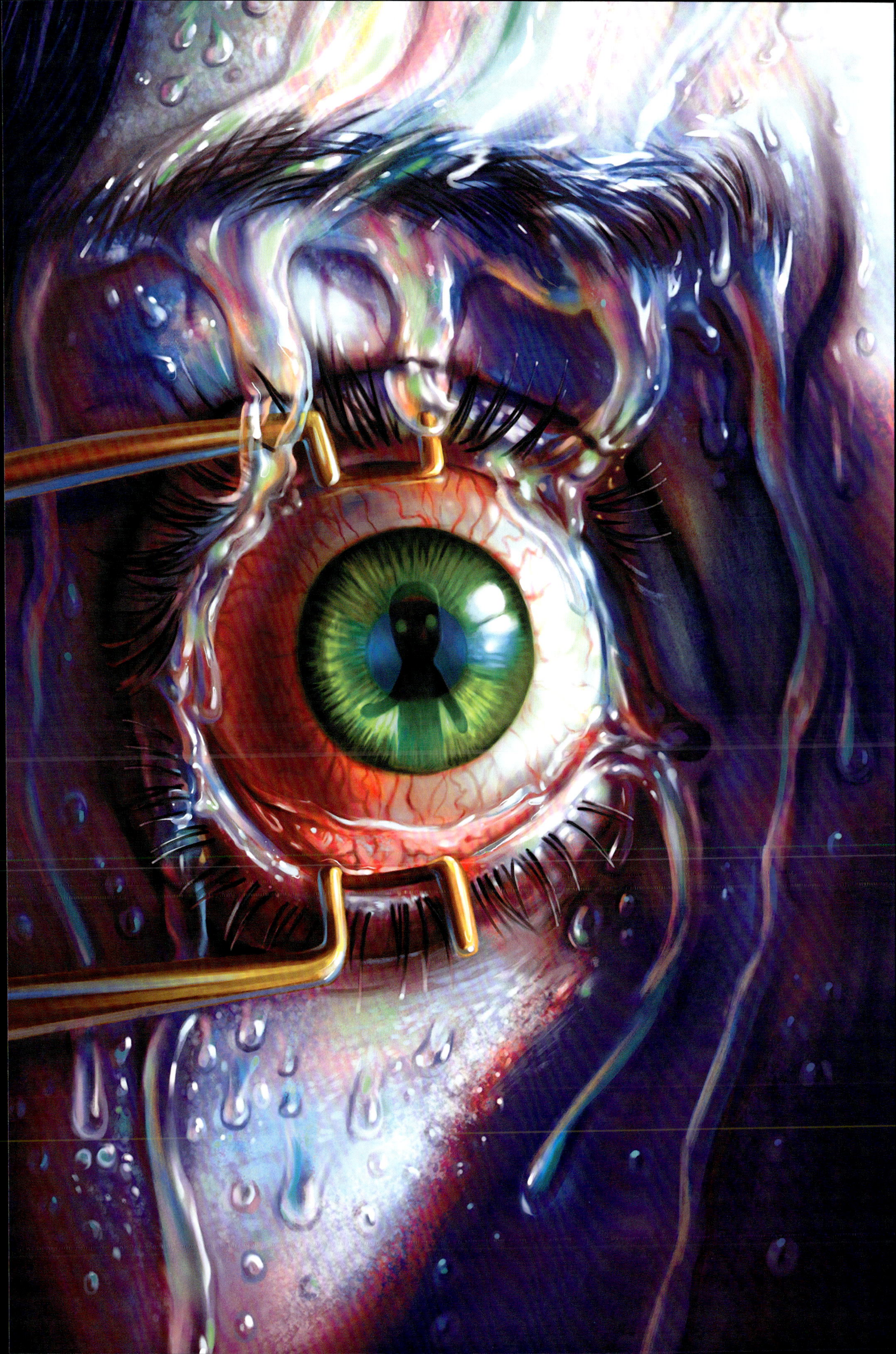

File >>> 94234

SCP-078

Title

GUILT

Report by

Gnosis

Picture by

Alexey Yakovlev

Access the original report on

scp-wiki.wikidot.com/scp-078

Date

Class

EUCLID

SPECIAL CONTAINMENT PROCEDURES

SCP-078 is to be left hanging on the wall of its containment cell and physically unplugged. The sole outlet in the room should be controlled by a switch, which must be left in the off position at all times unless SCP-078 is undergoing testing. Personnel who enter the containment room should familiarize themselves with the position of the switch so that they can locate it with their eyes closed in the event that SCP-078 is accidentally turned on.

DESCRIPTION

SCP-078 is a pink neon sign approximately one and a half meters long that displays the phrase "TOO LATE TO DIE YOUNG." It was initially recovered in the town of █████, █████, after standard Foundation data mining protocols recorded an abnormally high death rate due to starvation or other forms of self-neglect.

While powered off, SCP-078 has no abnormal properties and may be observed without effect. Viewing SCP-078 for less than ten seconds while it is powered on has no effect, nor does indirect observation. Subjects who cannot understand SCP-078 due to a lack of ability to comprehend written English are also unaffected. However, any subject that views SCP-078 for longer than ten seconds will, when viewing any handwritten piece of writing, occasionally perceive extra sentences. These sentences are not written in the subject's own style or in that of the surrounding text, but consist of a random style that differs from note to note (see Addendum 078-01), and always are phrased as if to assuage the subject's guilt on some matter or decision they feel guilty about. For example, a D-class personnel who was convicted of murdering his wife in a heated argument read the sentence "She deserved it for not doing what you said" in his handwritten journal, while Dr. █████ who left his family to work for the Foundation and was accidentally exposed, found the sentence "Your work will save humanity." in his notes on SCP-██.

At first, the effect is beneficial, with affected subjects reporting greater peace of mind after exposure to SCP-078. However, the sentences shift from emphasizing the positive consequences of actions to deemphasizing the negative ones on a timescale of one week; Dr. █████ two days later, found the sentence "They never loved you anyway." in his personal journal. Moreover, the writing will start giving justifications for acts the subject has never felt guilt over, or which the subject has already rationalized. The subject will then start reconsidering his justifications for those actions, as well as attempting to justify any further actions that they take. The need for rationalization increases as time goes on, and they will start vocalizing their thought processes, and by the end of one week, any task the subject performs more trivial than the basics of survival will induce a bout of neurosis as the subject attempts to rationalize why they did not instead take some other action. By the end of two weeks, the subject is unable to eat food: after the first bite, they will spend the next hour justifying why they ate that specific part of the meal first. Death due to malnutrition follows unless the subject is fed intravenously. █ D-class personnel who have reached this stage, as well as █ researchers who were accidentally exposed, are kept alive for purposes of study and to see if a cure can be found.

The sole exception to SCP-078's effect is SCP-078 itself: any subject who views SCP-078 a second time will see it displaying increasingly more guilt-inducing messages as duration since their first exposure increases. All subjects who have viewed it a week after initial exposure have attempted suicide.

Addendum 078-01: D-19384, whose handwriting was an unusual mix of cursive and print, was exposed to SCP-078, and was then terminated after reaching the 'consequence-free' stage. Subsequently, other subjects have reported seeing sentences in the same cursive-print mix; it is possible that those who die after being exposed to SCP-078 are 'incorporated' into it in some way.

END OF REPORT

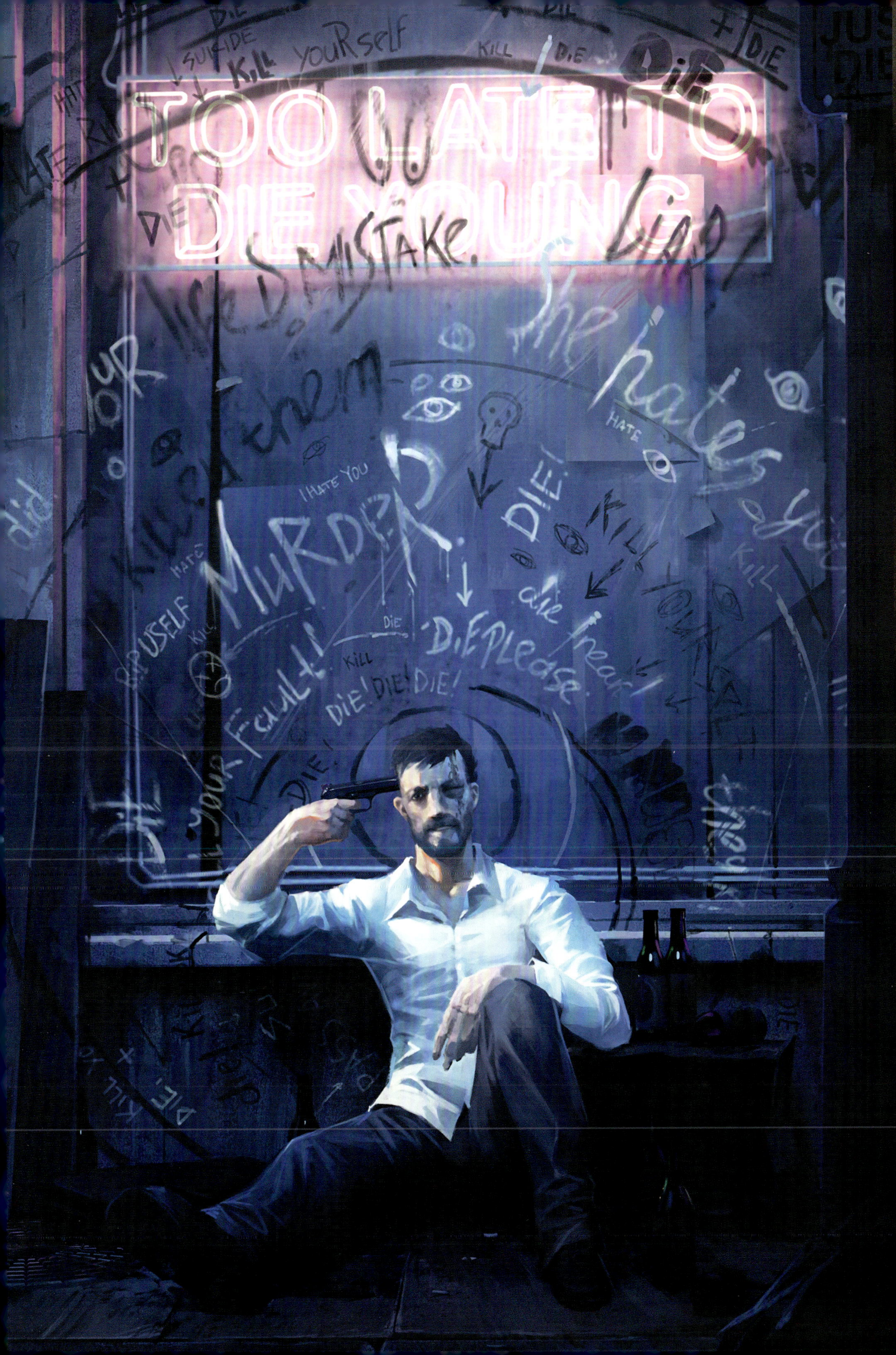

Photo of SCP-078 at its original location made by field agent █ as a proof of its potential mind-affecting abilities.

File >>> 09944

SCP-1471

Title

Mal0 ver1.0.0

Report by

LurkD

Picture by

Ivan Efimov

Access the original report on

scp-wiki.wikidot.com/scp-1471

Date

Class

EUCLID

SPECIAL CONTAINMENT PROCEDURES

All mobile devices that have SCP-1471 installed are to be confiscated and analyzed for any potential leads to other possibly affected devices. Afterwards, affected devices are to have their batteries removed, be assigned a designation (e.g. SCP-1471-#), and be placed in Storage Unit-91 at Research Site-45.

All online application stores for mobile devices are to be monitored to prevent any inadvertent sales of SCP-1471. Suspected devices are to be targeted using self-uploading malware in order to disable the device until it can be seized by field agents.

DESCRIPTION

SCP-1471 is a free 9.8MB application for mobile devices named "Mal0 ver1.0.0" in online application stores. SCP-1471 has no listed developer and is somehow able to bypass the application approval process to go directly to distribution. SCP-1471 is also able to avoid removal by other program manager applications.

After SCP-1471 is installed, no icons or shortcuts are created for the application. SCP-1471 will then begin to send the individual images through text messaging every 3-6 hours. All images will contain SCP-1471-A either within the background or foreground. SCP-1471-A appears as a large humanoid figure with a canid-like skull and black hair.

During the first 24 hours following the installation of SCP-1471, the mobile device will receive images taken at locations commonly frequented by the individual. After 48 hours, the mobile device will receive images taken at locations that were recently visited by the individual. After 72 hours, the mobile device will receive images of the individual in real time with SCP-1471-A appearing within close proximity to the subject.

Individuals with >90 hours of exposure to these continuous images will begin to briefly visualize SCP-1471-A within their peripheral vision, reflective surfaces, or a combination of the two. Continued exposure to SCP-1471 after this point will cause irreversible and sustained visualizations of SCP-1471-A. Individuals at this stage have reported periodic attempts made by SCP-1471-A to visually communicate with them, but fail to understand or comprehend these actions. Currently the only known treatment to reverse SCP-1471's effect is to eliminate the individual's visual exposure to these images prior to 90 hours after installation. To date, no apparent hostile activity has been reported regarding SCP-1471-A.

SCP-1471 as posted on application stores.

Archival Document 1471-01

Mal0
ver1.0.0

FREE!

Reviews (0)

Description:

For ████████. Never settle for those awkward feelings of being alone ever again. Mal0 is an exciting and interactive experience that will keep you engaged and intrigued. The anxiety of social situations can be nerve-racking, but after just a few hours of Mal0 you will soon forget all about those painful emotions of disappointment. Be part of the new craze that is quickly becoming the next social substitute. Remember, the more you participate, the more Mal0 will engage you. Your experience is completely up to you. Absolutely NO ADS. Enjoy!

END OF REPORT

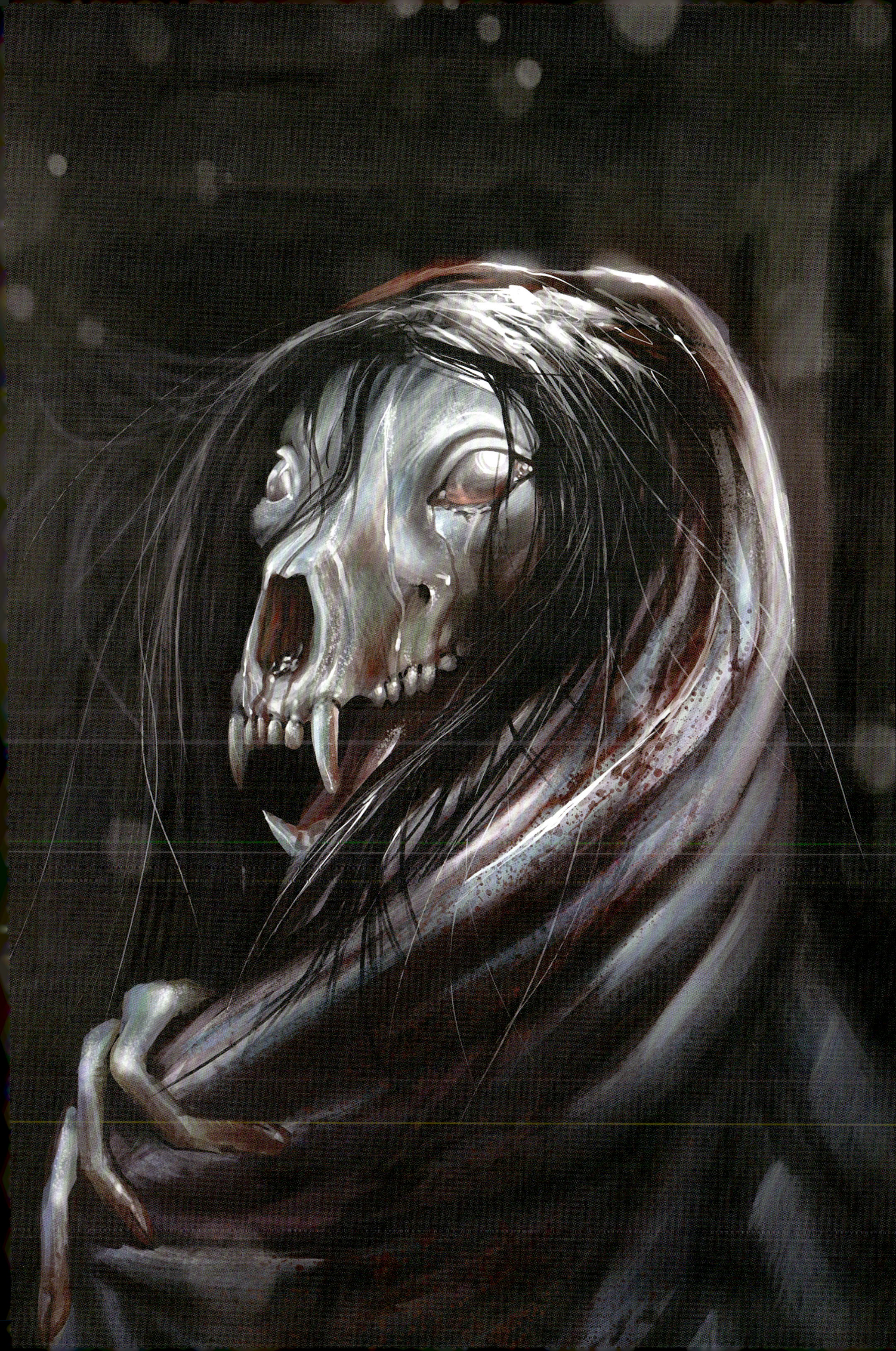

One of the photos received by an individual with >90 hours of exposure to SCP-1471.

File >>> 0983234

SCP-1660

Title

UNEARTHLY FOREST

Report by

Adam Henderson

Picture by

Roman Avseenko

Access the original report on

scp-wiki.wikidot.com/scp-1660

Date

Class

SAFE

SPECIAL CONTAINMENT PROCEDURES

SCP-1660-1 may be safely kept in a locked safe-deposit box at Site █ Storage Facility. Standard positive-action defenses (explosive, chemical, biological, and memetic) are to be in place at all times, according to standard operating procedure. SCP-1660-1 is to be kept away from flammable materials unless in testing. Under no circumstances is SCP-1660-1 to come into contact with fire-related SCPs such as SCP-███. In event of SCP-1660-1 igniting outside, testing personnel are to evacuate the area until all flaming materials are extinguished. Due to only being accessible via SCP-1660-1, SCP-1660-2 can be considered to be contained as long as SCP-1660-1 is. Any animal life that emerges from SCP-1660-2 during testing is to be captured pending study and possible termination.

DESCRIPTION

SCP-1660-1 is an elaborately decorative oil lamp made from silver, coral and the shell of a nautilus. Its anomalous effects activate if a fire is lit inside the chamber of the nautilus shell. Upon ignition the fire will, regardless of materials used, begin to emit large amounts of smoke. The smoke will begin to gather forming an arch-shaped "gate" in the air approximately █ meters across. The size and stability of said "gate" will fluctuate based on the amount and/or type of material being burned within SCP-1660-1. In the event of SCP-1660-1 being extinguished, the gateway will collapse rapidly.

SCP-1660-2 is a miniature parallel universe consisting of approximately ███, square kilometers of temperate forest conditions which can be accessed by means of the "gate" produced by SCP-1660-1. Around the edges of SCP-1660-2 are walls of an as-of-yet unidentified mineral rating up to ██ on the Mohs scale. Testing with diamond drills have been unable to damage the mineral while rapidly blunting drill bits. Roughly a kilometer above the treetops is what appears to be a layer of [DATA EXPUNGED]. Following incident █████ all aerial exploration is to be performed with unmanned aerial vehicles (UAVs). Attempts at drilling below ground have revealed that a crust of the same unidentified mineral making up the walls exists approximately half a kilometer under the entire area of SCP-1660-2.

LIST OF PLANT SPECIES WITHIN SCP-1660-2

Quercus nigra	Water Oak	Normal.
Quercus hypoleucoides	Silverleaf Oak	Specimens grow slightly faster than ordinary members of their species.
Quercus aliena	Oriental White Oak	Specimens grow considerably larger, reaching up to ██ meters in height compared to ordinary members of their species.
Pinus densiflora	Japanese Red Pine	Normal.
N/A	SCP-1660-8 unidentified moss	A rapidly growing type of moss of unknown species covering other plants and the walls of SCP-1660-2.

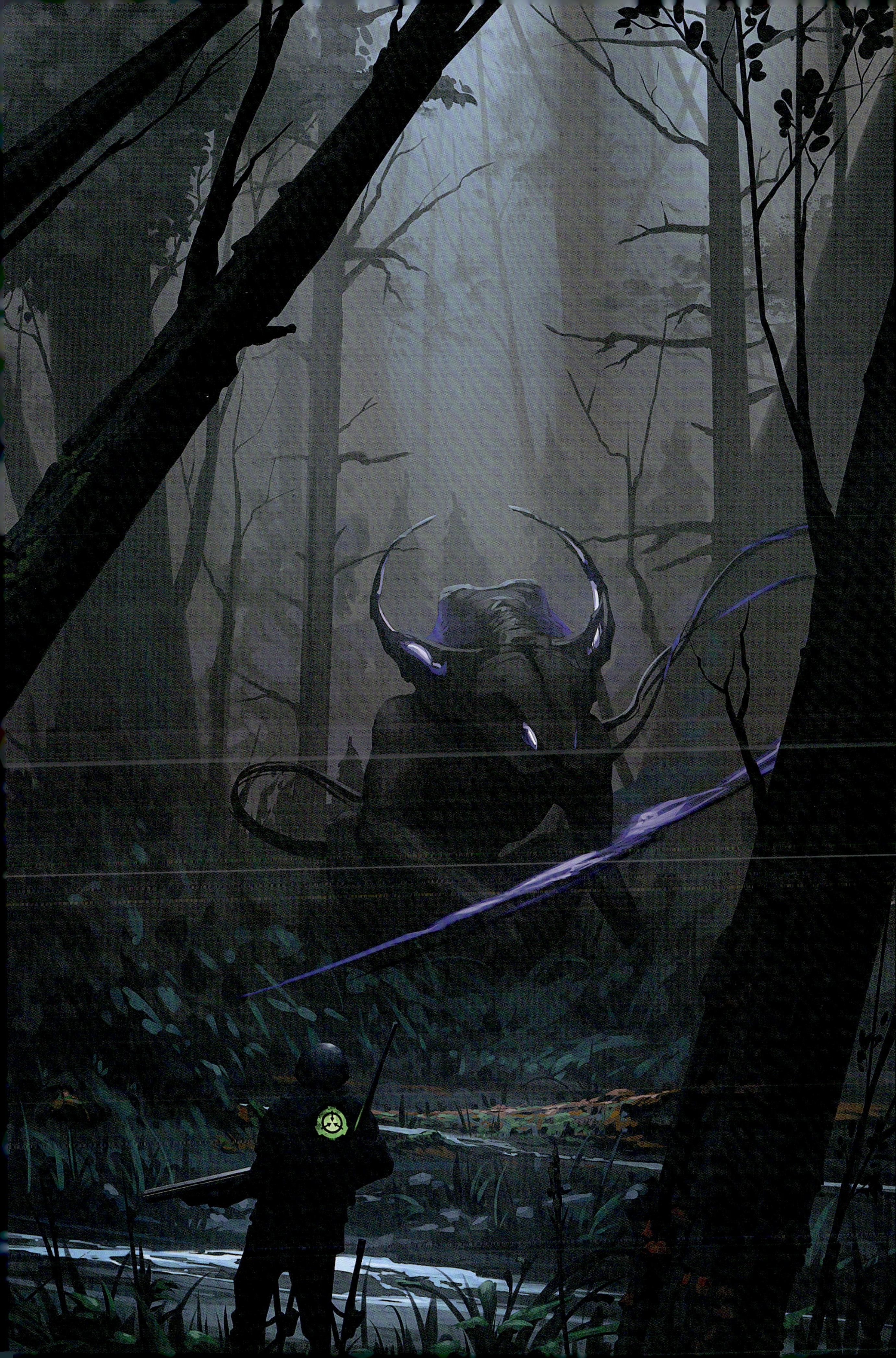

First encounter with SCP-1660-7.

Research Library File ▸ 1660

LIST OF ANIMAL SPECIES WITHIN SCP-1660-2

Ursus arctos	brown bear	Specimens show no fear of humans.
Odocoileus virginianus	white-tailed deer	Specimens show no fear of humans.
Myotis lucifugus	brown bat	Specimens prefer to rest in trees hanging from thick branches rather than in caves.
Poecile atricapillus	Black-capped Chickadee	Specimens possess small notched ridges inside their beaks serving as simple teeth. The reason for this is unknown as specimens do not feed differently than ordinary chickadees.
Anax imperator	Emperor Dragonfly	Specimens have been seen to reach sizes of up to ███ millimeters. How they are able to breathe via spiracles while at these sizes is unknown.
N/A	SCP-1660-3 unidentified flightless bird	A large flightless herbivorous bird somewhat like an emu.
N/A	SCP-1660-4 unidentified small reptomammal	A small creature resembling a scaly, egg-laying fox with external ears, warm blood and whiskers.
N/A	SCP-1660-5 unidentified eyeless feline	Specimen resembles a cougar (Puma concolor) or other type of big cat apart from lacking eyes, and possessing forward-extended ratlike ears and the ability to echo-locate.
N/A	SCP-1660-6 unidentified giant turtle	A creature exactly identical to the common box turtle (Terrapene) apart from its size, with adults reaching up to ██ meters in height, and having proportionally smaller eyes.
N/A	SCP-1660-7 [DATA EXPUNGED]	A two (2) meter long extremely dangerous reptomammalian creature resembling an armored, bio-luminescent [DATA EXPUNGED]. SCP-1660-7 are pack-hunting predators comparable in behavior to wolves, although they do not fear humans and are capable of climbing trees or the walls of SCP-1660-2. Due to their lack of fear for humans they have been noted to attack personnel in SCP-1660-2, frequently killing them. Under no circumstances are personnel permitted to approach SCP-1660-7 specimens for this reason as well as [DATA EXPUNGED].

History: SCP-1660-1 was recovered on █/██/███ by Agent █████, a Foundation mole from █████, a front for Marshall, Carter and Dark, who were selling "safaris" into SCP-1660-2 to hunt local wildlife (primarily SCP-1660-5, SCP-1660-6 and SCP-1660-7).

CLASSIFIED - LEVEL FOUR PERSONNEL ONLY
DOCUMENT ALPHA SCP-1660-7: REPORT FROM DIRECTOR ████████

The information in the article that you've already read left out, or more accurately expunged, something quite important.

SCP-1660-7.

They aren't simply some kind of dangerous predator. We said that to keep personnel away from them.

They're sapient. Their fore-paws are jointed to work like human hands. They have simple tools, fire, and a language of their own based on bio-luminescent patterns.

It is their cave paintings, however, which interest us: crude humanoid figures holding sticks and killing with them at a distance, shooting projectiles.

Then a battle with the same sticks, new figures, and the end of the killing. And the symbol copied off the new figures, the symbol in front of which they leave food in sacrifice, the symbol which they smear all over things with ash and plant pigment or claw into trees. The symbol of their gods.

Two rings, one inside the other, with three arrows pointing inward.

END OF REPORT

File >>> 0049455

SCP-058

Title

HEART OF DARKNESS

Report by

unknown

Dr Gears

Pictures by

Alex Andreev

Access the original report on

scp-wiki.wikidot.com/scp-058

Date

█████

Class

KETER

SPECIAL CONTAINMENT PROCEDURES

SCP-058 is to be kept in isolation in a 5 m by 5 m by 5 m containment chamber at all times. Walls are to be constructed of 3 m (10 ft) of reinforced heat-resistant steel, backed with a further 10 m (33 ft) of reinforced concrete. SCP-058 is to be fed a live cow every three days. Maintenance is to be conducted every sixty (60) minutes while SCP-058 is dormant and every fifteen (15) minutes when SCP-058 is active. Under no circumstances is SCP-058 to be allowed out of its containment area. SCP-058 is to be audio recorded at all times. No personnel are to listen to SCP-058 for more than thirty (30) minutes at a time. In case of escape, facility is to be considered compromised and detonation of on-site nuclear weaponry is to commence. To date, SCP-058 has been responsible for the death of at least one hundred and forty-nine (149) Class-D personnel and fourteen (14) Agents at its current site.

DESCRIPTION

SCP-058 resembles a bovine heart, with four (4) arthropod-like legs used primarily for movement, and four (4) tentacles of adjustable length, covered with razor sharp spines. It has a single sharp 'stinger' on its rear, where the hole for the superior vena cava would be in a typical organ. SCP-058's tentacles can be "whipped" to a distance of 3.2 m (10.5 ft) at speeds in excess of 320 km/h (200 mph). SCP-058 is extremely hostile and will use every opportunity afforded to it to inflict damage on its surroundings. SCP-058 has been shown to be highly resilient to trauma, and should be approached with caution even when apparently incapacitated.

SCP-058 is highly mobile and capable of rapid movement on both horizontal and vertical surfaces. It has been recorded reaching a speed of approximately 90 km/h (55 mph) in short bursts, covering distances up to 200 m (656 ft), and has the ability to accelerate from 0 to 90 km/h (55 mph) in less than two (2) seconds. It has been shown to use its tentacles for increased leverage and stability, as well as utilizing them to pull itself to other surfaces at high speeds.

SCP-058 'speaks' in a human voice, though no method of producing sound has been observed in its physiology. It speaks with vocal tone and accent of an elderly British male with a slight lisp and deep voice. SCP-058 talks constantly, regardless of conditions: even when attacking, SCP-058's voice and pace of speech are unchanged. The speech of SCP-058 lacks any detectable correlation to events, persons, or exterior locations involved with SCP-058 (see Transcript of Interview 058-04).

NOTES

SCP-058 was first encountered at Site ██ as it came out of [DATA EXPUNGED]. SCP-058 was extremely hostile and appeared to be very agitated. Initially SCP-058 attacked Site ██, which resulted in the death of ██ faculty and ██ Agents. SCP-058 went on to attack the nearby town of ██████, resulting in the death of over [REDACTED] citizens and the destruction of seventy percent (70%) of the surrounding buildings.

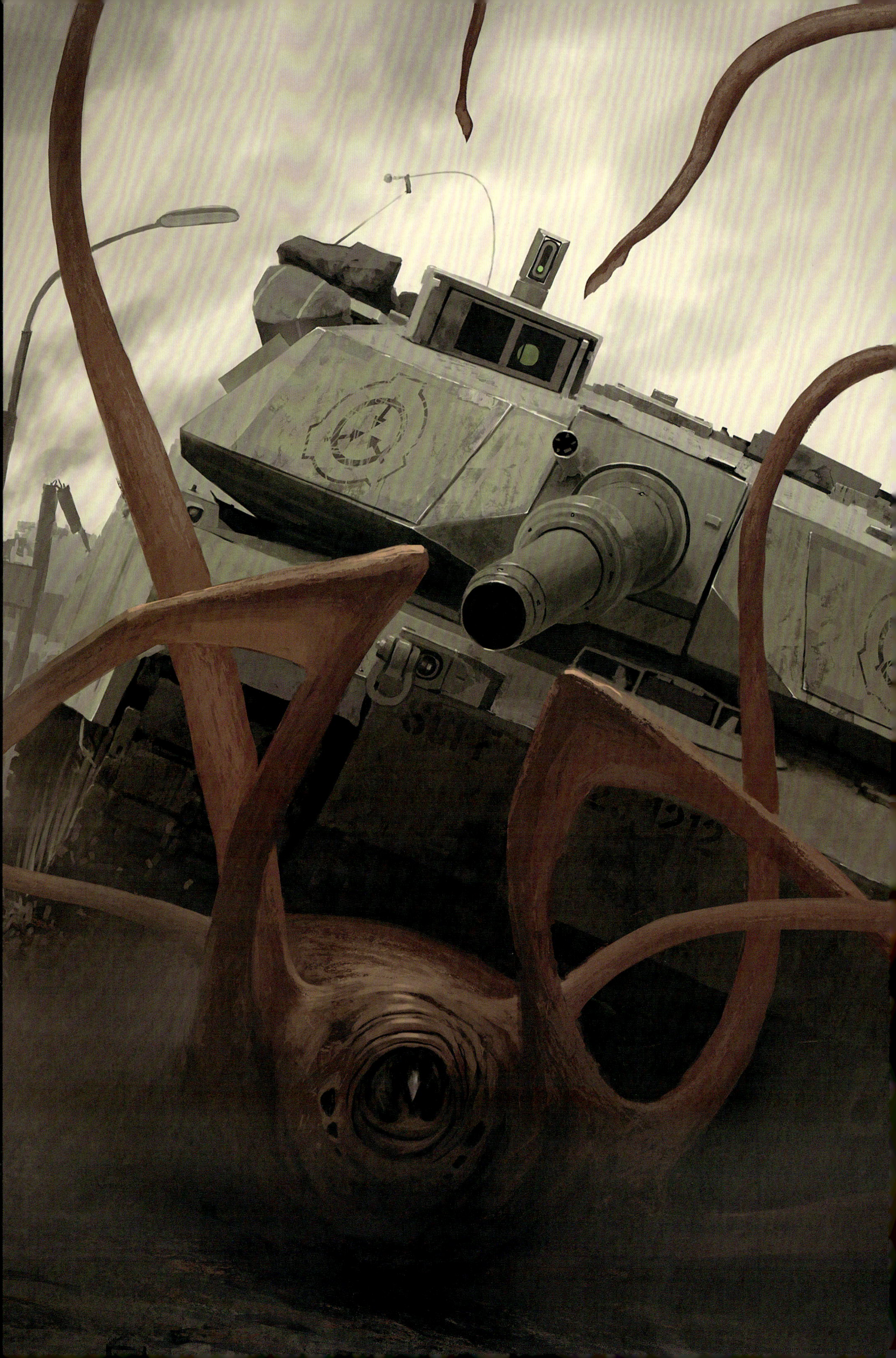

Photo material collected during the containment breach on █/█

Post-Breach analysis determined a majority of the deaths are attributable to fire and fire-related injuries, resulting from a wide spread of "stinger fluid" by SCP-058 from a large structure. This is also blamed for a majority of structural damage. ████ by SCP-058 accounts for only 8% of total deaths, with major evidence [DATA EXPUNGED]

SCP-058 was finally contained after being crushed and incapacitated by a large amount of masonry from a building that had collapsed on top of it. SCP-058 was then extracted and transported to ███ by Agents and MTF teams. SCP-058 was contained at ███ for three weeks, during which it made minimal attempts to move, attributed both to physical damage and bloating from ███ during the initial breach incident. Testing during this period was limited, with SCP-058 still maintaining a high threat level even in its impaired state.

SCP-058 breached containment on █/█/███ during an attempted transfer to an SCP Containment Site, causing multiple deaths and injuries. SCP-058 was eventually incapacitated by Agent ███, who managed to subdue SCP-058 by running it over with an M1 tank, pinning it beneath the armored vehicle. SCP-058 was subsequently secured and transported to Armed Bio-Containment Area 14.

TRANSCRIPT OF INTERVIEW 058-04

<Begin log>

SCP-058: I had dreams of the queen wonders that lived inside the hearts of love and silent treatments of all the elderly that I knew were once whole.

Dr Johnston: What is your name?

SCP-058: I seek the revelations of all that the holy told to the unwise in the dreams of cold embers in sunlight that fade across lakes of black blood and snakes that eat the loaves of children from lamb trees in autumn.

Dr Johnston: What is your name?

SCP-058: Endless suffering is the woe of ignorant men who never lack to seek the depth of their own hearts and only see the wealth of a poor world suffering to flay its own back in knife wounds of silver and brutal gladness.

Dr Johnston: Where are you from?

SCP-058: The nightmare is a dream to the nameless slug that wanders across minefield and the remains of deer and kings.

Personnel D-067: This is some creepy ass- *(D-067 cuts off into screaming)*

SCP-058: Nightshade is shadows in all honest blinks that sort through the bile of newborn plagues, instant warmth is a mother's milk in dreams before anything was ever evil.

Personnel D-067: *(Continues screaming)*

Dr Johnston: Let him go!

SCP-058: In seconds the sun is beating like drums in all hearts eat the ear of noise.

Personnel D-067: *(Screaming is cut short abruptly)*

SCP-058: The sensual violence of lust is all the assurance you will ever need to know the worth of life.

<End log>

END OF REPORT

File >>>

SCP-2521

••|•••••|••|•

LurkD

Ivan Efimov

scp-wiki.wikidot.com/scp-2521

Date

Class
KETER

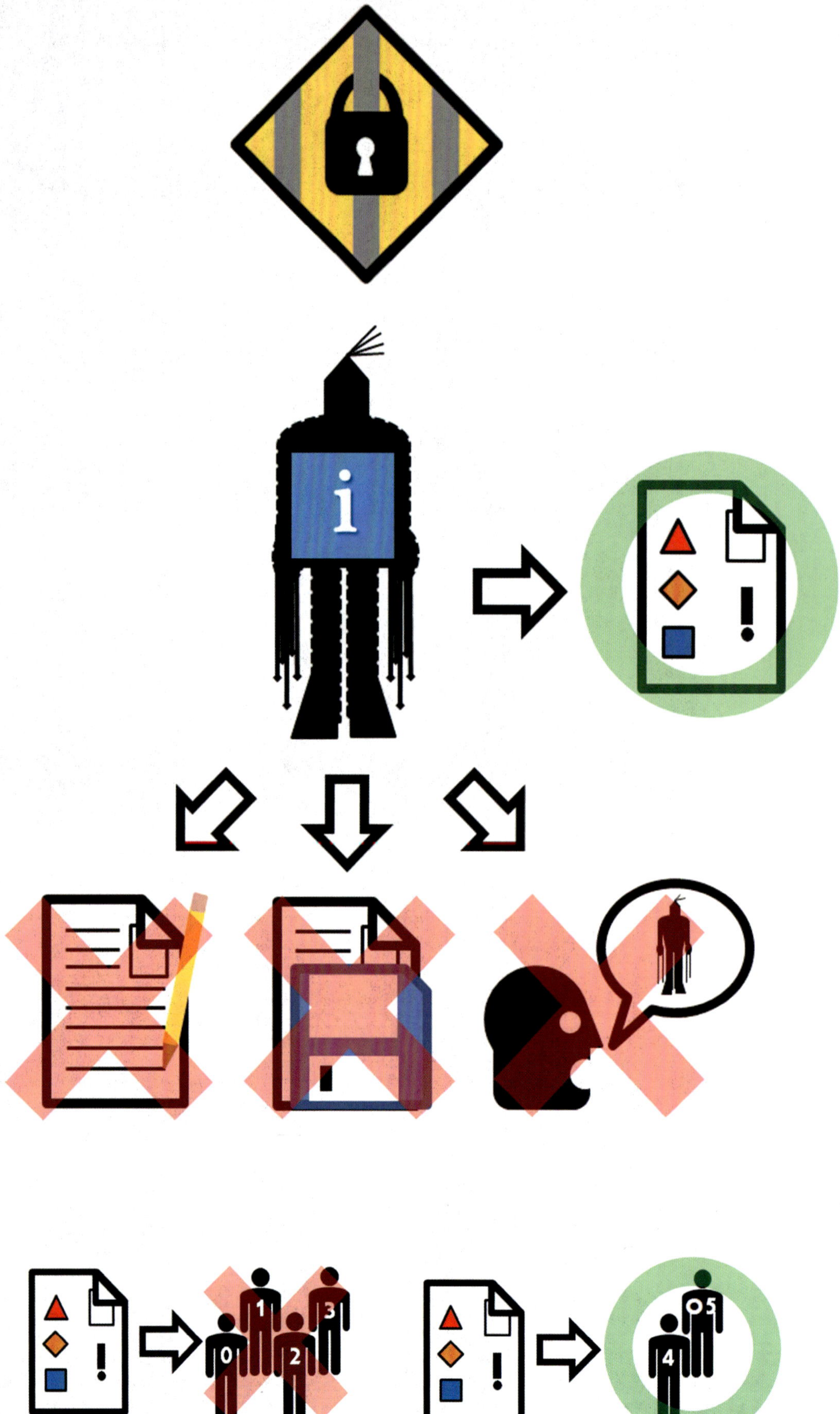

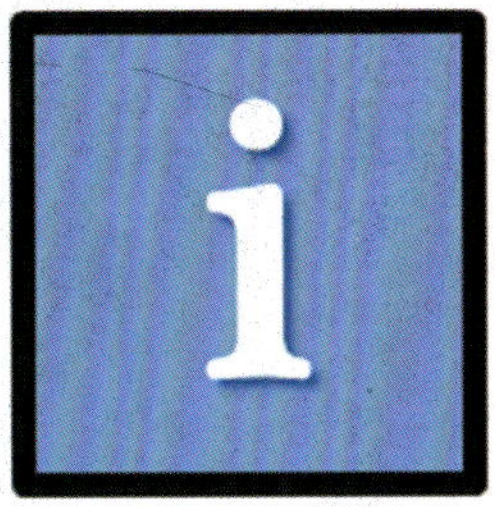

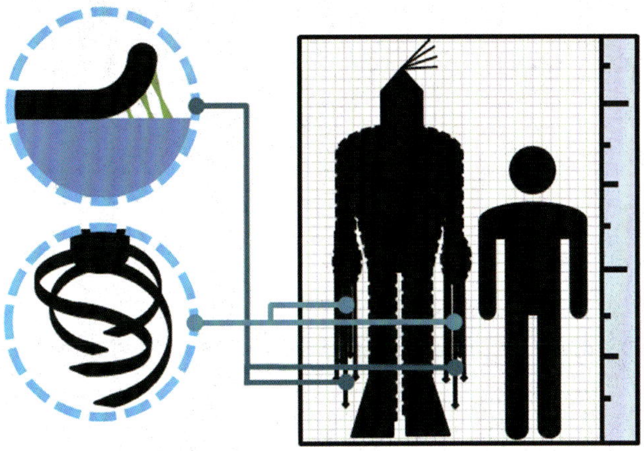

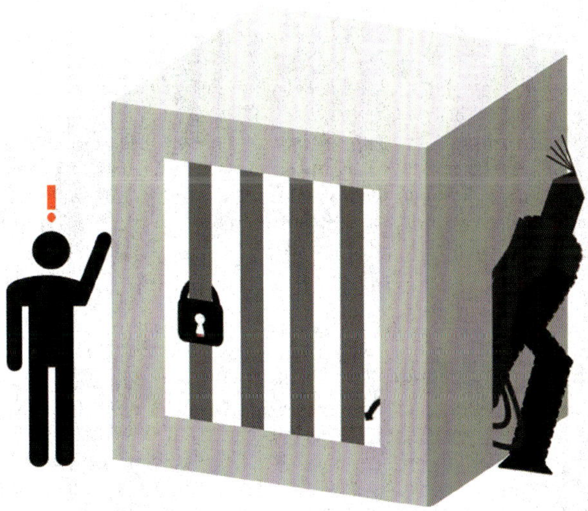

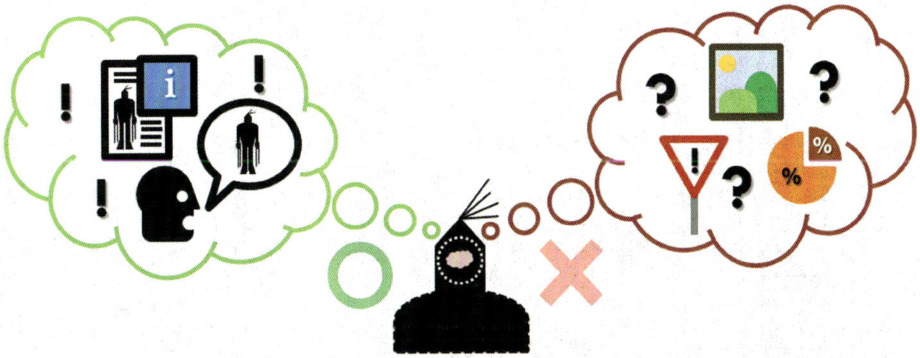

Research
Library

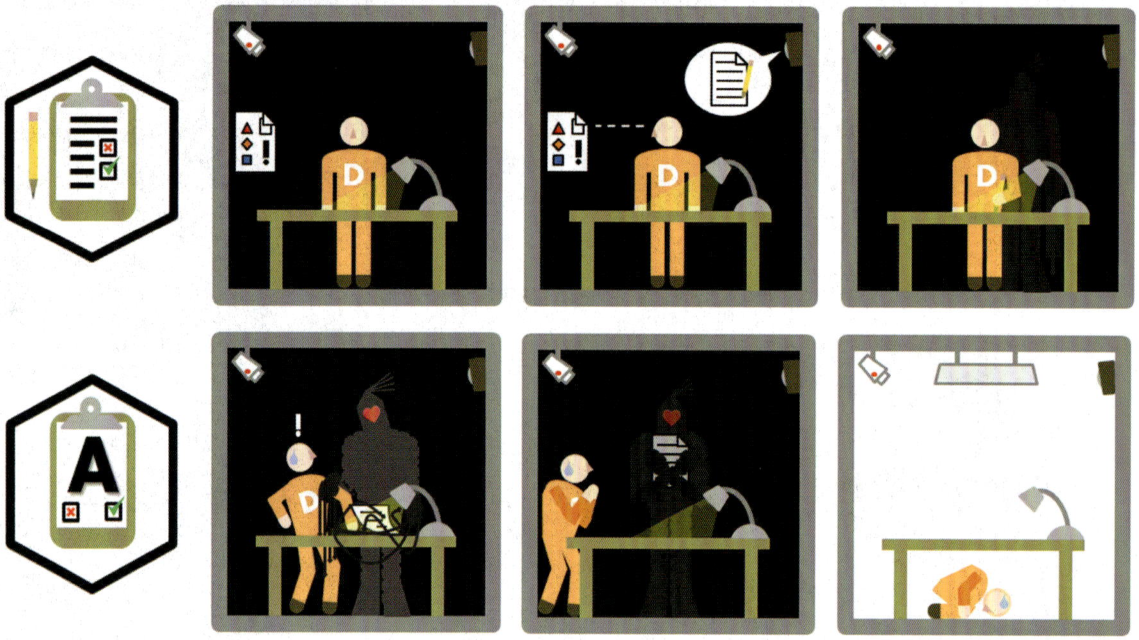
A

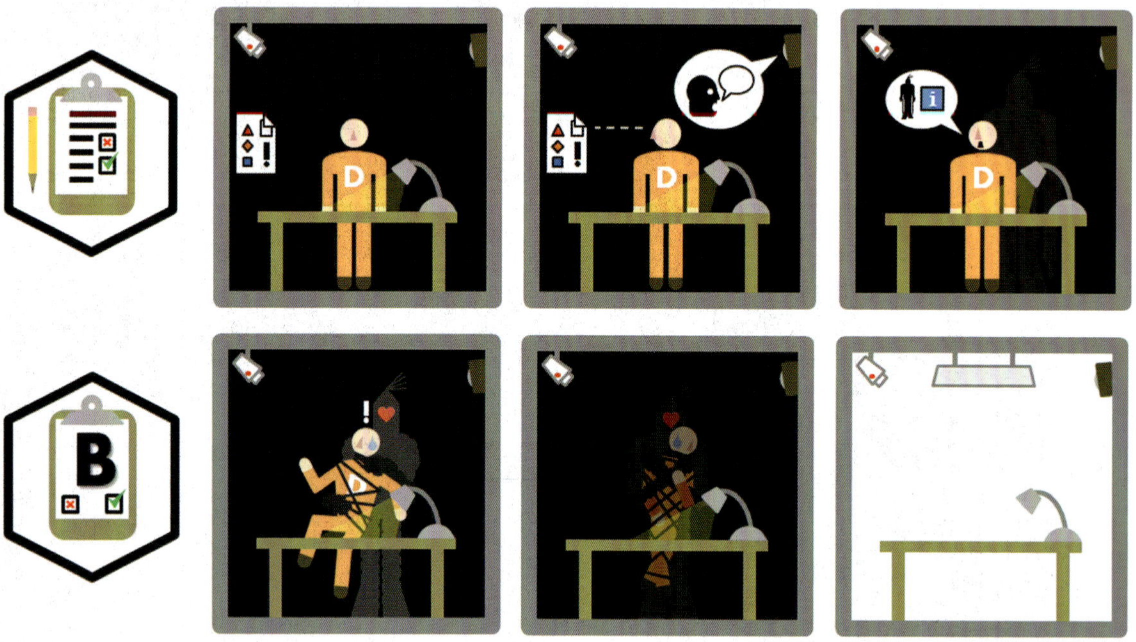
B

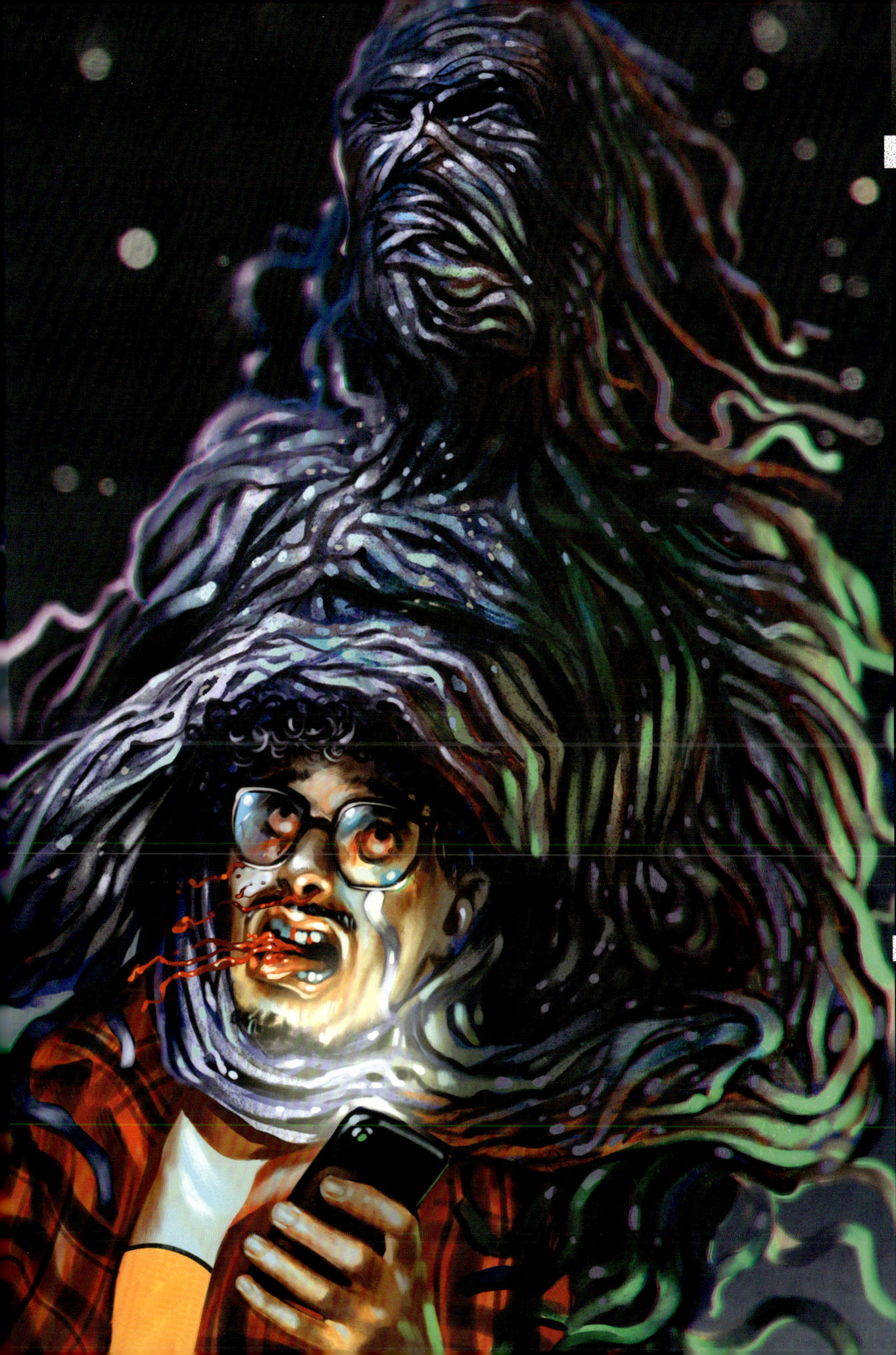

File >>> 09445

SCP-882

Title

A MACHINE

Report by

Dr Gears

Picture by

Dmitriy Fomin

Access the original report on

scp-wiki.wikidot.com/scp-882

Date

Class

EUCLID

SPECIAL CONTAINMENT PROCEDURES

SCP-882 is to be kept in a fluid environment at all times, consisting of no less than 40% seawater. Object is to be kept suspended by non-metallic means, currently cotton fiber line that is to be changed daily. Object is also to be checked daily for any signs of rust flaking. If any part of SCP-882 appears uncoated with rust, it must immediately be immersed in a 100% seawater solution. Water must be taken directly from the ocean. Reduce concentration only when the object is again coated in rust.

No metal may be placed in containment area. Only organic materials are allowed in containment area, and any contact with SCP-882 requires the use of thick cotton gloves. Any metal making contact with it is to be heat-severed, melted down, and kept immersed in 100% seawater in a separate area.

Any auditory issues reported by staff must be reported immediately, and affected personnel must submit to a full psychological examination and, depending on results, either transfer to another facility or permanent containment at [EXPUNGED].

DESCRIPTION

SCP-882 appears to be a random assembly of gears, cables, pulleys, screws, and belts, all made of an amalgam of various metals. Object's size at time of recovery was approximately eighty-seven cubic meters. Current size is approximately twelve cubic meters. SCP-882 rusts quickly in seawater. No identifiable energy source has been found, but all components will begin to move if not coated in rust. SCP-882 is completely silent at all times, no matter what level of activity SCP-882 reaches.

Any metal touching the object will become permanently affixed to it, and over a period of a few days becomes a new part of the object. Organic matter remains unaffected. SCP-882 is extremely resilient, with tensile strength and toughness above those of aircraft grade titanium alloy by weight, even though its composition appears to be a random alloy of iron, tin, gold, and other metals, some as of yet unidentified. Extreme, focused heat must be applied over several hours to cut even a small portion free of the main assembly.

Persons remaining in the vicinity of the object for prolonged periods have developed auditory hallucinations while near the object, mainly the sound of grinding and clicking. The sound intensifies, and is abated only by throwing metal into the object. Subjects in advanced states of psychosis have thrown themselves into the object, resulting in almost instant death by crushing. The body is often drawn in, and impossible to recover.

SCP-882 was recovered from a location at the north-east coast of Banks Island. Area was barren of all metal and metallic ore in a one mile radius. SCP-882 was found at the geometric center of the area. SCP-882 had become submerged in seawater at the time of discovery. A small town was found nearby, abandoned for several years. SCP-882 was removed, and shortly started to flake off rust, causing the varied parts to begin motion. After several accidents, Dr. Gears authorized SCP-2519 to be played on loop, which successfully reduced the object's motion, enabling safe access. SCP-882 was then cut down and contained on site.

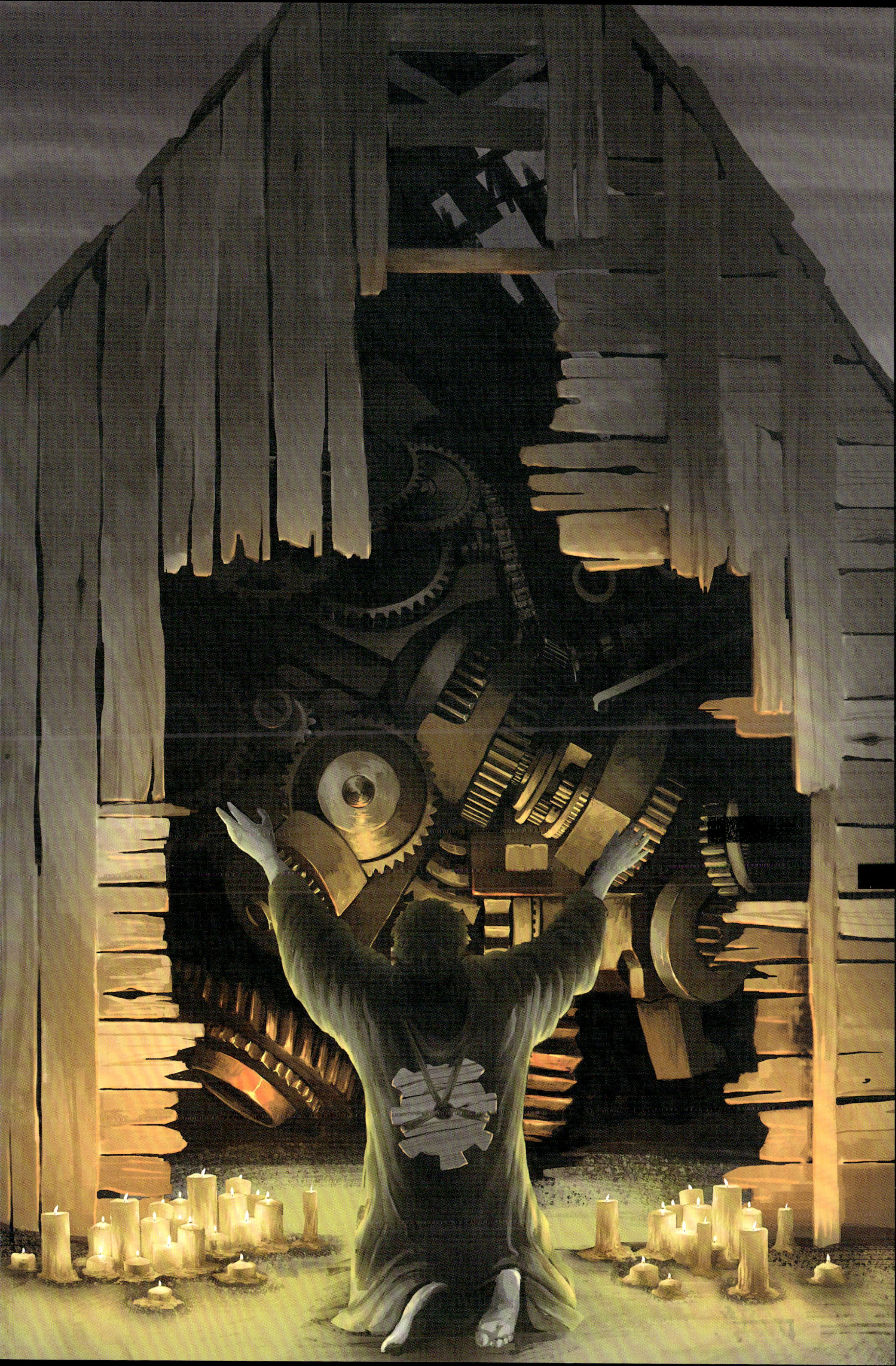

Photo recovered from the town near SCP-882's initial location.

SCP-882 is not to be brought into the vicinity of SCP-271 or any subject possibly contaminated by SCP-271.

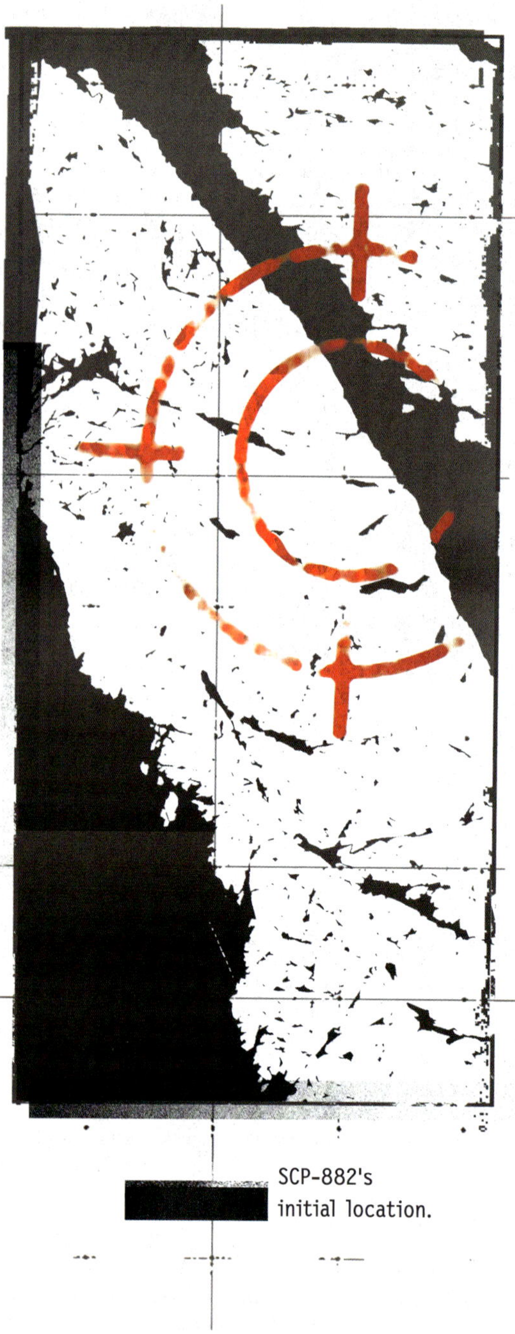

SCP-882's initial location.

INTERVIEW 882-1

Interviewed: Richard Wright
Interviewer: Dr. Gears
Foreword: Richard Wright is identified as a survivor from the small community near the initial recovery location of SCP-882.

<Begin Audio log, [13:04]>

Dr. Gears: Please, take a seat. State your name for the record please.

Mr. Wright: Richard Logan Wright… everyone calls me "Rich" though.

Dr. Gears: Excellent, thank you. Mr. Wright, do you recall the date when you first saw the object in question?

Mr. Wright: God, when was it… I'm not really sure, it was a while ago… Allen found it first, wrecked his boat on it. He told a few of the other fellas about it, said they could sell it for a bundle for scrap. We all thought it was a chunk off a jet or a cargo ship.

Dr. Gears: At what point did the device start operating?

Mr. Wright: The next day. Damn thing shook off rust like a dog with fleas. Started spinning slow, then sped up. By the time I saw it, it was really running. Jimmy tried to get closer, try and see what was powering it, or why it was so quiet, but he slipped. Got a bad cut over his eye and got the hell out of there. Allen seemed kinda off. Kept asking us if we were hearing anything. Ms. Parker thought part of it was gold, even tried to jam part of it with a pipe to get at it. That pipe stuck fast, and smacked her a good one when the gear it was on spun around. After that, people mostly kept away.

Dr. Gears: Were there any other incidents of people being injured or hearing noises?

Mr. Wright: Not at first. That's the thing, it was so damn quiet, everyone kinda forgot about it for a while. Allen was keeping it in an old storeroom by the dock, and nobody really went out there much. He started looking bad. Said he couldn't sleep, that he kept hearing that thing grind away. Father Pat started dropping by, tried to talk to him, told him to get rid of it. He was gone for a couple days, then suddenly the two of them turn up together, happy as clams… *(subject trails off, shaking slightly)*

Dr. Gears: …Mr. Wright?

Mr. Wright: *(subject rubs face, and shakes head)* I'm fine, sorry. So Father Pat and old Allen show up, fresh as daisies. Say they've got the thing figured out. I wasn't paying that much attention, this whole thing had me spooked. Been hearing stuff from the store room… grinding and squealing, really quiet. Anyway, they said some damn thing about it being from somewhere else… that God made it. That was it for me, and I left.

Dr. Gears: Did you believe them?

Mr. Wright: What, that it was from God? No, no… I don't know… I didn't really know what to think. This damn machine kept spinning away, no power to it, and eating metal too! That pole Ms. Parker hit it with? It turned into a giant screw shaft, looked like it had always been there. More people started getting interested, started listening to Allen and Father Pat. Told everyone to bring metal to it. Told them the gears were the voice of God, that it grew louder as we turned away, and softer as we brought it offerings.

Dr. Gears: Did you bring metal to it as well, or spend any extended period of time near the object?

Mr. Wright: *(subject is silent for several seconds)* …The hell does that matter? You could hear this thing all over town, got to be folks couldn't even sleep! Just clanking, grinding, screaming at all hours of the night… giving it metal helped. God damn it, I didn't want to, I know it wasn't God, I never said it was! Everyone else was falling over themselves to make Allen and Father Pat happy, I just wanted some damn sleep! There's not a god damn thing wrong with that! *(subject bangs table with hands, is highly upset and breathing heavily)*

Dr. Gears: Sir, I will request that you calm yourself. I am asking questions, not accusing. Please return to your seat.

Mr. Wright: *(takes several deep breaths)* I'm sorry. Over a couple of weeks, everything got fed to that thing. It was just… how things were. We were pretty isolated, you know? It's not like we had much else. You'd just make a couple trips out to the storehouse and toss any metal you happened to find in. Always seemed to be people there, just watching it. It tore a hole in the roof after a while. Father Pat started getting strange, telling us it wasn't enough. I think the noise was getting to him. Said it needed something more meaningful… *(subject trails off)*

Dr. Gears: …Mr. Wright?

Mr. Wright: *(is silent for 48 seconds)* I came in one night, because I heard people shouting from the storehouse. Father Pat was leading a prayer to this thing, but it didn't sound like any prayer I knew. People were coming up, and he bent over them. They screamed, and then he turned to that big mass of metal. I… I thought he was giving communion… until I saw the pliers in his hand.

Dr. Gears: I'm sorry, pliers?

Mr. Wright: He was yanking out people's fillings. He was pulling out their fucking teeth and feeding them to that thing! *(Subject is shouting, appearing highly upset)* He started screaming about it not being enough! That it needed more, but there wasn't any more, there was barely any metal left anywhere! Then he pointed at Allen. He said he was hiding metal from the great machine. Allen screamed that he didn't have anything. Father Pat said he had a metal joint in his hip. Everyone got up at once. Oh god, oh god… they grabbed him, everyone just grabbed him… he started screaming… *(subject is crying and shouting)* He kept screaming and screaming, and nobody cared… I saw his arm go in, saw all his fingers break and pull the rest of the arm in… and I ran. What could I do? Jesus, I couldn't stop it, there were too many, and that thing was screaming and screaming and Allen was screaming and Father Pat… *(subject falls to the floor, sobbing and shouting)*

Dr. Gears: This interview is concluded. Thank you Mr. Wright. Security, please see Mr. Wright out.

<End log>

CLOSING STATEMENT

Mr. Wright attempted suicide shortly after interview. Subject is currently being held on suicide watch and for observation.

END OF REPORT

File >>> 094234

SCP-1499

Title

THE GAS MASK

Report by

Trasknari

Picture by

Dmitriy Fomin
Dmitry Desyatov

Access the original report on

scp-wiki.wikidot.com/scp-1499

Date

Class

SAFE

SPECIAL CONTAINMENT PROCEDURES

SCP-1499 is to be kept in a locked box guarded by two agents at all times. Testing involving SCP-1499 ~~requires the authorization of Level 4 personnel~~ is to be discontinued indefinitely. Test subjects are to wear a small full-duplex two-way radio underneath SCP-1499 to maintain contact with researchers. Testing is no longer to be carried out by D-Class personnel due to the risk of losing SCP-1499. Should test subjects enter any sort of danger, they are to remove SCP-1499 immediately.

DESCRIPTION

SCP-1499 is a Soviet GP-5 gas mask. A seal test performed on the object suggests that the object retains its original functionality. The anomalous effects of SCP-1499 activate when a human places SCP-1499 on their head. Approximately one second after SCP-1499 is fully secured on the subject's head, the subject vanishes from view, and is no longer detectable. The subject reports no feeling of motion at this time. Testing has revealed that two-way radios remain capable of both receiving and transmitting despite the subject being undetectable. Upon wearing SCP-1499, test subjects report completely different surroundings than they were in prior to wearing SCP-1499. Subjects have reported that it appears barren and inhospitable, with tall black towers filling the area. Subjects have also sighted entities in this landscape. These entities, designated SCP-1499-1, have been described as tall, nude humanoids with dark skin that have a thick coat of an unknown viscous substance. Instances of SCP-1499-1 also have large amounts of eyes and mouths covering their body. Upon removing SCP-1499 from their head, subjects reappear in the same location they were in when they put it on. For more information, see Test Log 1499.

SCP-1499 in its containment box.

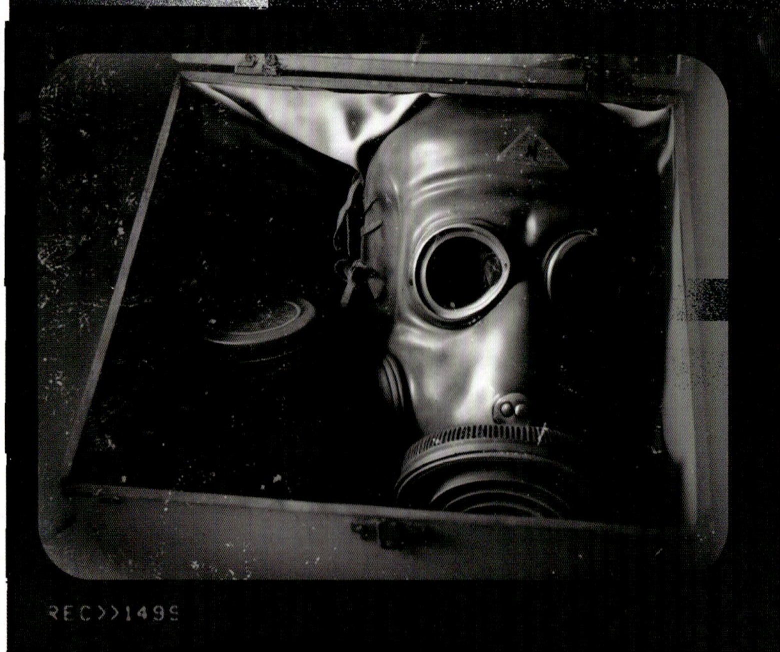

Test Subject	Reported events	Notes
D-67393	Subject found herself in building of an unknown black substance. After surveying the room for approximately 15 seconds, subject reportedly heard sounds of movement and removed SCP-1499 in a panicked state, reappearing in the test chamber.	First test involving SCP-1499 to determine its effects. Due to the risk of losing SCP-1499, trained agents are to be used in place of D-Class subjects.
Agent C█████	Agent found himself in the same room described by D-67393. Approximately two minutes were spent exploring the room, which Agent C█████ reports contained multiple hollow black cubes. Agent was capable of descending down the building without running into any interference. Upon reaching the second floor, agent heard sounds from the floor below. Agent hid himself behind one of the black cubes and observed two instances of SCP-1499-1. Agent then removed SCP-1499.	First sighting of SCP-1499-1. Agent C█████ reports that he remained undetected by the two instances of SCP-1499-1.
Agent U█████	Agent was selected due to her stealth training. Agent found herself in the same room as Agent C█████ was in when he removed SCP-1499. Sounds of movement were heard on higher floors, prompting the agent to head downstairs and out of the building. Agent reportedly saw many instances of SCP-1499-1 wandering outside of the building. Each individual seemed to have unique mutations, and occasionally uttered low, grating sounds. Agent successfully made her way past more of the structures while avoiding detection. Agent followed four instances of SCP-1499-1 for observation. The group encountered a fifth instance of SCP-1499-1, and one of the group stepped forward. Agent observed the two entities violently assault one another, coating the nearby ground and observing entities with unknown fluid and thick viscera. Agent removed SCP-1499.	The structure in which D-67393 appeared seems to only be one of many. Due to the violent nature of SCP-1499-1, further exploration will require that agents be armed to defend themselves.
Agent K█████	See Exploration Log 1499-D.	[REDACTED]

CLASSIFIED LEVEL 5 CLEARANCE REQUIRED

EXPLORATION LOG 1499-D

Test commences on June 3, 20█

Agent K████ outfitted with a two-way radio earpiece and a standard Foundation sidearm with additional ammunition. Agent's mission is reconnaissance.

Agent places SCP-1499 on his head and vanishes from sight.

Agent K████: "Doctor, can you hear me?"

Dr. N█: "Yes, Agent. What do you see?"

Agent K████: "I'm between two of the structures. They resemble spires. Seem to be made of some hard black rock. Ground's the same."

Dr. N█: "Have you made contact with any instances of SCP-1499-1?"

Agent K████: "Not yet. It's hard to tell. The lighting here is odd, I'm having trouble seeing much. I'll see what I can do."

Sounds of the agent moving quietly for approximately five minutes.

Agent K████: "God damn. There's a large group of them up ahead. They're all moving together into a huge building."

Dr. N███: "Can you describe the structure, Agent?"
Agent K████ "Yeah, it's big. Very big. There aren't many structures around it. It is quite elaborate; I see a large amount of towers and spikes. There looks like there's blood on it."
Dr. N███ "Agent, can you get a closer look?"
Agent K████ "There's some sort of bridge to it. I'm moving in."

Sounds of the agent moving quietly for approximately three minutes and thirty seconds.

Agent K████ "I'm at the side of the structure. There looks like there's some sort of door here. Smaller than the big one in the front. I'm going through it now."

Visceral sounds are heard for a few seconds.

Dr. N███: "What was that, Agent?"
Agent K████ "Not sure. Coming from further inside. I'm taking a look."

Sounds of grating and grinding heard coming from multiple sources.

Dr. N███: "Agent? Agent, what do you see?"
Agent K████: "Jesus- there's a lot of them in there. They're all in a giant group. Their mouths are all open, even the ones on their bodies. I think that sound is coming from them. Can you hear that?"
Dr. N███ "The sound is coming through, Agent. Try to get a better look."
Agent K████: "Okay. They're all facing one direction. Let me see if I can look."

Sounds of grating continues for twenty seconds.

Agent K████: "They're all facing one of them standing on a platform. There are large amounts of bodies around him. They've stopped vocalizing and are all just looking at the one up front."

Loud visceral sounds return.

Agent K████: "It appears the one in the front is- Hold on, I can't see. It's cutting open its own torso. There are some sort of worm-like creatures spilling out of it."
Dr. N███ "Agent, what is happening? I can't hear-"
Agent K████ "Wait, above its head. I think I see- There's something in its torso that's creating some sort of light. There's a beam going up from it into the air over his head."
Dr. N███ "What's happening? Agent, keep talking."
Agent K████: "I think it's opening some sort of portal. And I- It's summoning something. The entity is summoning something. I think I see something coming through the portal- It looks like a massive version of one of the worms that came out of the entity's chest. I think the glowing object in that entity's torso is holding the portal open. I- I can't let that thing through. I've got to stop it."
Dr. N███ "Agent?"

Sounds of the agent running and gunfire. The grating noise returns louder than before.
Sounds of stone objects and bodies falling down. Visceral sounds fill the air.

Agent K████: "I've almost got-"

More visceral sounds, closer to the agent now.

Agent K████: "Got it now-"

The remainder of the agent's sentence is unheard as he removes SCP-1499. Agent appears in test chamber covered in blood and holding a human heart.

Agent K████: "It's alright, I got-"

Agent looks at the heart in his hand and yells, dropping it.

End of log.

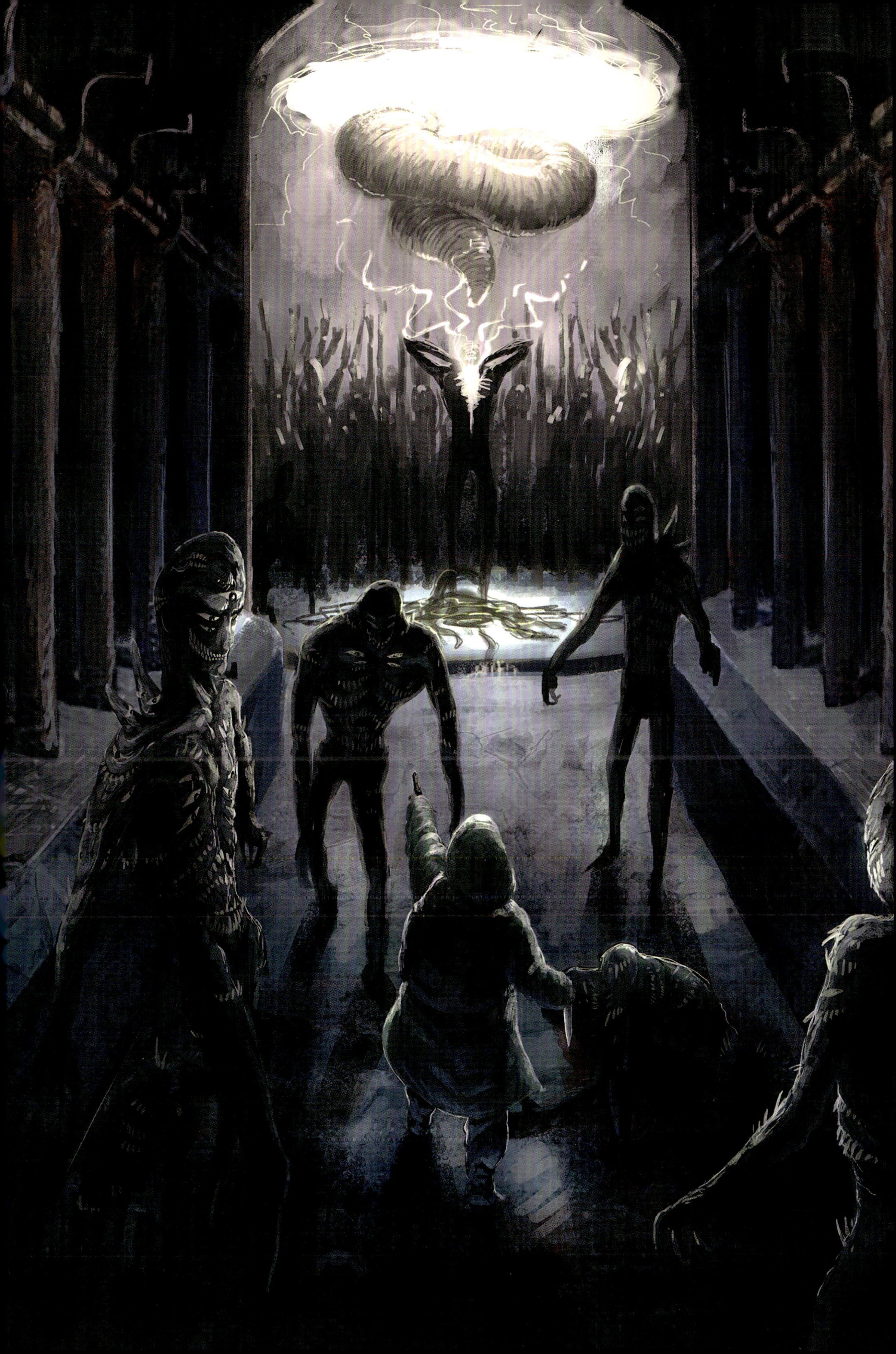

Visualization of exploration Log 1499-D.

ADDENDUM 1499-E

Research Library File ▸ 1499

On Sunday, June 3rd, a man dressed in a suit and wearing a gas mask attacked the Cathedral of Christ the Savior in Moscow, Russia during morning services. The man reportedly shot ten people, including a chanter and a priest. Six church-goers were killed, and three others, including the chanter, are in critical condition. The suspect charged the front of the cathedral and allegedly produced a knife and removed the priest's heart. The suspect then appeared to vanish entirely before multiple witnesses. Moscow police have been unable to find any trace of the attacker.

Our operatives working undercover in Russian media and military are currently working to defuse the situation. Officially, the attacker was a Nikolai Orlov, resident of Moscow, who was acting alone. Orlov went missing a few years ago, allowing our agents more time to keep the situation under control. Agent K█████ is currently being detained for questioning regarding the situation. He maintains his claim that everything occurred as he reported. Our recordings of Exploration 1499-D corroborate his story. When questioned as to the reasoning behind his actions, Agent K█████ stated that he believed that what he saw being summoned had to be stopped. Agent is currently scheduled for psychiatric evaluation. We cannot risk another incident. All testing involving SCP-1499 is discontinued until further notice. All information regarding Exploration 1499-D is to be restricted to personnel with Level 5 clearance until the situation has been brought under control.

Detain Agents U█████ and C██████, as well as D-67393 for questioning. It is unknown at this time if the hallucinatory effects of SCP-1499 have any permanent effects. I don't want to run the risk of one of our own agents seeing all of our researchers as monstrosities and going on a shooting spree inside one of our facilities.

-05-█

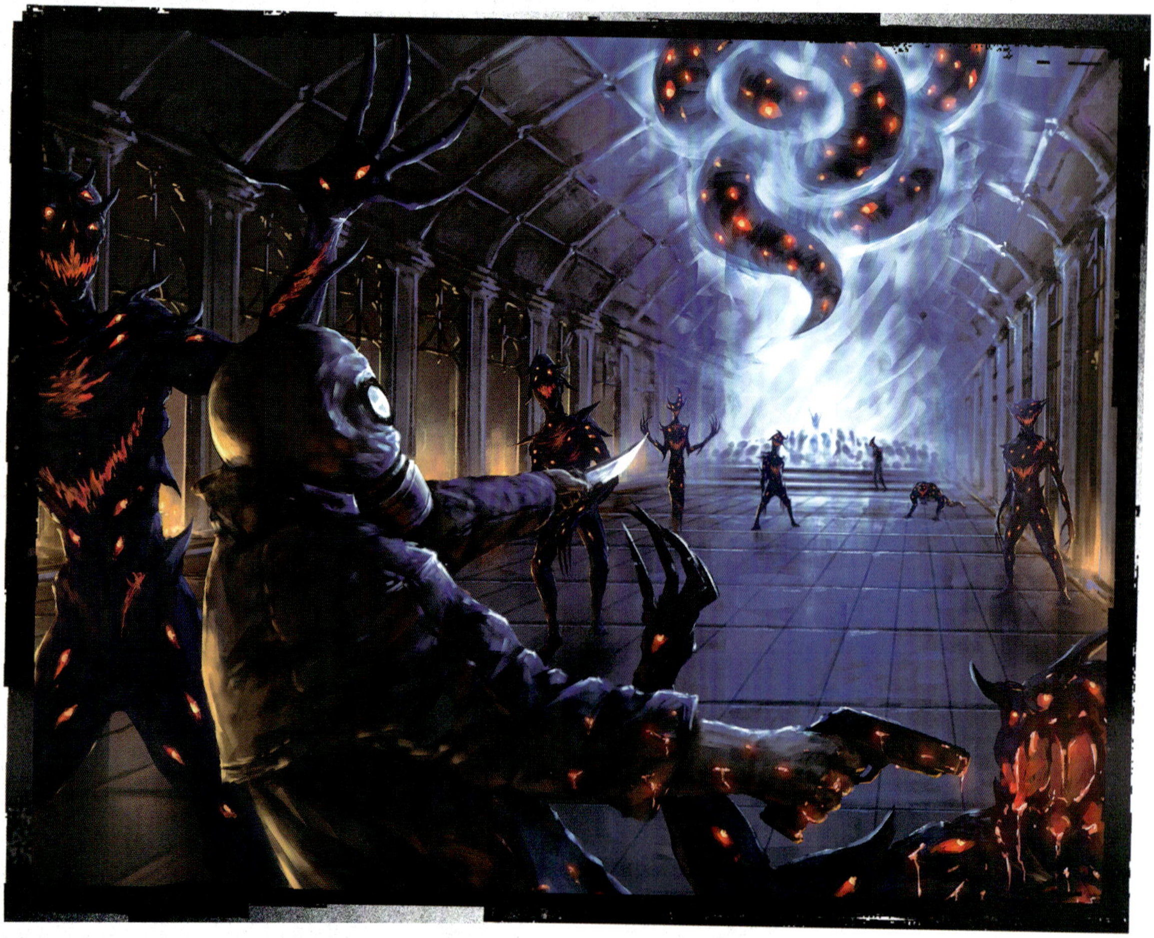

END OF REPORT

SPECIAL CONTAINMENT PROCEDURES

Information about SCP-2256 is subject to a gradual antimemetic corrosion effect. Corrosion occurs at differing rates depending on the level of detail/accuracy in the information and the physical complexity of the storage medium. In-depth academic papers, photographs, and information stored electronically decay rapidly; broad descriptions, pencil sketches and paperwork decay slowly.

Therefore, this electronic database entry should describe SCP-2256 only in broad terms. Detailed information about SCP-2256's appearance, theorised evolutionary ancestry, biology, diet, behaviour, vocalisations, lifecycle, intelligence, ecological role and cultural significance should be stored in hard copy at Site 19, vault 1-053. The rate of corrosion in both data sources should be monitored carefully, although at present no technique is known for halting or undoing such corrosion.

Although these antimemetic effects linger and rate Euclid classification, SCP-2256 itself is extinct and requires no special containment procedures.

DESCRIPTION

SCP-2256 *(Cryptomorpha gigantes)* is a species of gigafauna which was endemic to the South Pacific Ocean around the islands of Polynesia. SCP-2256 was one of the very few recorded species known to have developed rudimentary perceptual/"antimemetic" camouflage, rendering them nearly impossible for other sentient beings to perceive or remember. This adaptation is theorised to have arisen in order to elude predators.

SCP-2256 was the largest species to have lived on Earth. Resembling spindly, vertically elongated giraffes or brachiosauruses, adults of the species grew to over 1,000 metres in height. They weighed no more than 4 tonnes, with most of their mass being "camouflaged" by a very similar adaptation. With their broad, dish-shaped feet, they were able to walk directly on the surface of the ocean without sinking.

SCP-2256 navigated the ocean alone or in █████ of 2 to as many as 2,000 individuals. They were reluctant to approach land, especially inhabited islands, usually staying more than 30 kilometres offshore. Because of their height, they were visible on the horizon at this distance.

ACQUISITION

Polynesian natives of the island of Maikiti used a substance called *teúkoka* for recreational and religious purposes. As well as being a moderate psychedelic, this drug had mnestic properties, suppressing antimemetic effects and making entities camouflaged in this way easier to see and remember. Thus, the Maikitians were for hundreds of years the only people able to see SCP-2256. In Maikitian mythology SCP-2256 were wandering spirits whom the gods had charged with maintaining the horizon, to ensure that the sky and the water never mixed. They were characterised as well-meaning and friendly, but unintelligent and often deficient in their duties, resulting in storms and typhoons. They were called *polo'ongakau*, "the ones who walk very slowly".

File >>> 018845

SCP-2256

Title

VERY TALL THINGS

Report by

qntm

Picture by

Dmitry Desyatov

Access the original report on

scp-wiki.wikidot.com/scp-2256

Date

█████

Class

EUCLID

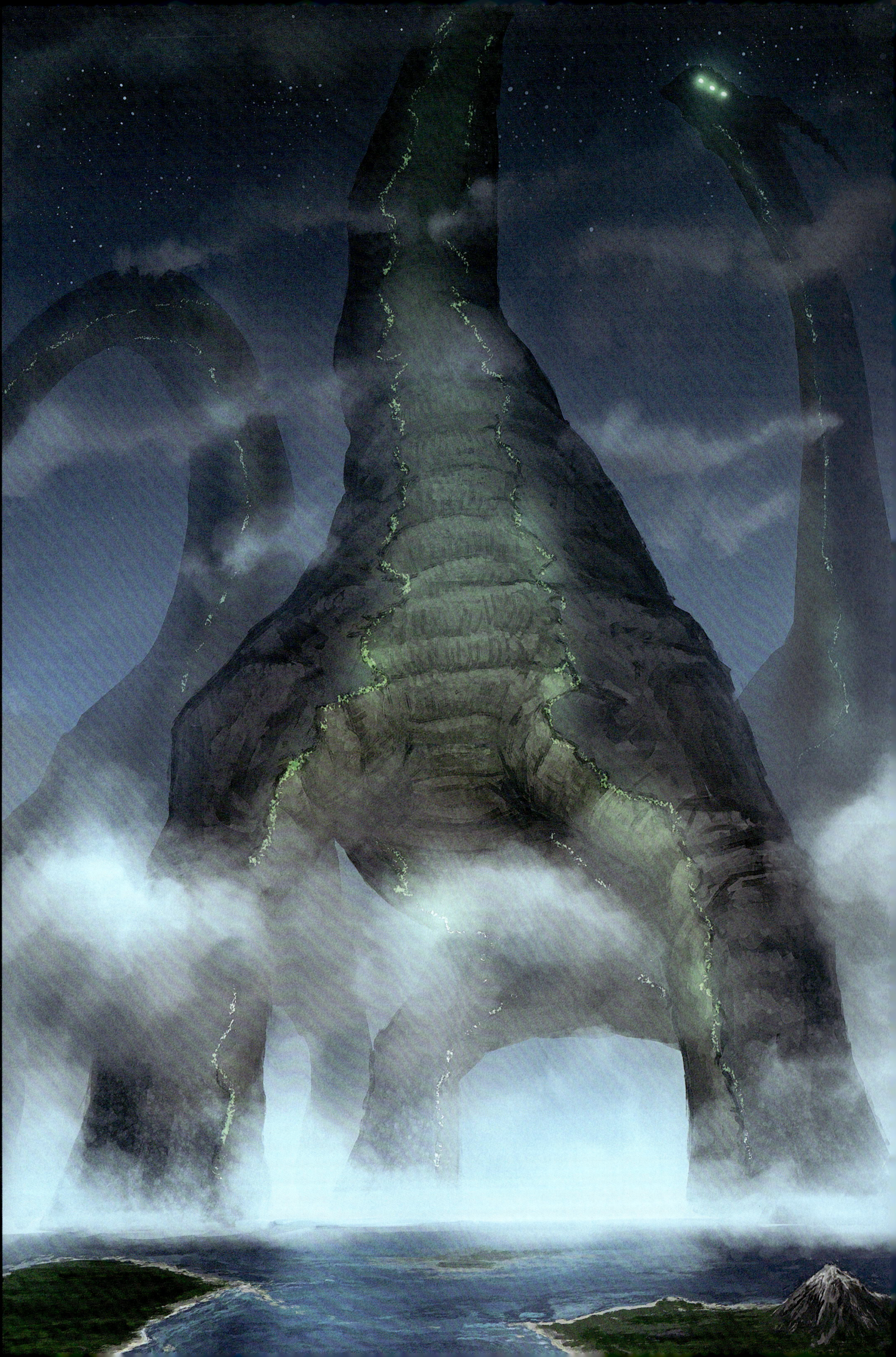

Painting based on one of the pencil sketches made during the research expedition.

In 1991, an internal biochemistry study revealed that teukoka bore a strong chemical resemblance to the Foundation's own class-W mnestic. A Foundation anthropologist was assigned to follow ███ the Maikitian legend, and became the first outsider to observe ██-2256. An observation ███ was quickly ████ on the island to study the creatures. Routine containment analysis found that SCP-2256 was Safe and required no special containment procedures, or even particular ████ ██ secrecy.

Research Library File ▸ 2256

HISTORY

SCP-██ immediately proved to be impossible to capture photographically. Photographic negatives of the species faded into transparency over the ███ ██ a few minutes. Similar decay ███ affected videotape, audio tape, celluloid film, digital and electronic scans, ██ The observation team soon returned most of their equipment to inventory and proceeded using pencils and ██. At the time, it ██ believed that such recordings would be effectively permanent.

SCP-2256's population declined slightly in 1992 and 1993, then dropped sharply from 1994 onwards. A combination of contributing factors were observed: illness, infertility, and an ████ rate of stillbirths.

In 2002, a field generator was developed which could penetrate and neutralise SCP-2256's antimemetic ████, allowing for conventional photography. The first and only close-up photograph of one of the creatures instantly killed it. It was concluded that direct observation of SCP-2256 is injurious to ██ This adaptation is believed to have arisen as a means of detecting predators, just as SCP-2256's antimemetic camouflage protected them from those same predators. Use of ██ ██ generator was immediately curtailed.

It was subsequently hypothesised that the Foundation's ongoing passive observation of the species was intense enough to have harmful effects on SCP-2256, and that ██ was what was driving the species ██ extinction. Opinions differed sharply ██ ██ veracity of this hypothesis, over ██ thoroughly it should be tested, and over what ███ be done if it proved to be true. Several extreme options were ████, including ████ exterminating ██-██ to preserve the data, and completely expunging the data to preserve ██-2256. No firm conclusions ██ ██.

In 2003, observation of SCP-2256 was scaled back significantly, and the Foundation ███ focus from gathering ██ data to analysing ███ data. However, SCP-2256's population continued to ███ The last individual died near Tokelau ██ October 30, 2006.

██ 2010, ██ ██ discovered ██ the antimemetic camouflage ███, also characterised as "decay" or "corrosion", was spreading through paper records of ██-██. As of ██, more ██ 60% of ██ documents are ███, even with ██ strong mnestic dose. The effect is even ███ ██ ███ SCP entry itself, despite ██ ██ shielding and redundancy in ██ system.

Since ██-██ ██ extinct, ██ new data ██ it can be generated. It is ███ that full contamination ██ ██ ███ three to eight years.

END OF REPORT ███ ███ ██

File >>> 013234

SCP-1048

Title

BUILDER BEAR

Report by

trennerdios

Picture by

Ruslana Gus

Access the original report on

scp-wiki.wikidot.com/scp-1048

Date

Class

~~SAFE~~

KETER

SPECIAL CONTAINMENT PROCEDURES

~~SCP-1048 is currently free to roam Site 24, as it poses no threat and has been observed to greatly improve the morale of personnel that interact with it.~~ The whereabouts of SCP-1048 are currently unknown, though it is still believed to be somewhere in Site 24. Subject is to be secured for containment, but any creation of SCP-1048's should be destroyed on sight, unless further evidence warrants less extreme actions. No teddy bears are to be allowed in Site 24 to prevent any confusion or mistaken identity. Any object that resembles a teddy bear is to be reported to the security team immediately.

This is not a joke. We have no idea what SCP-1048's full capabilities are. Who knows how many of the damn things are out there by now?

Dr. Carver

DESCRIPTION

SCP-1048 is a small teddy bear, approximately 33 cm in height. Through testing, composition of the subject revealed no unusual qualities that make it discernible from a non-sapient teddy bear. Subject is capable of moving of its own accord, and can communicate through a small range of gestures. The subject regularly shows affection to individuals in ways found endearing by most people. Affection is usually given in the form of a hug to the lower leg, but subject has also been observed dancing, jumping in place, and in two separate events it has even drawn child-like pictures for janitorial staff. All Foundation personnel that have interacted with the subject have responded positively to its affection, even D-class with normally sociopathic tendencies.

Attempts at direct communication with SCP-1048 have not been considered successful. Though it is capable of simple gestures to indicate a "yes" or "no" answer, it will often not react to lines of questioning concerning its nature or where it originated from. It is not known if this is because SCP-1048 simply does not know the answers, or because it does not want to answer. Though capable of drawing pictures, it has not used its art as a form of communication beyond showing affection, even when encouraged to do so.

The more anomalous behavior of SCP-1048 was not observed until approximately 7 months after it was originally secured. It is hypothesized that the subject is able to construct crude replicas of itself using various materials, by a process that has yet to be observed directly by Foundation staff. Dr. Carver has suggested that SCP-1048 uses its endearing qualities to lull those around it in to a false sense of security, allowing it to collect materials to produce these creations. Currently, there are 3 known creations of SCP-1048, designated SCP-1048-A, SCP-1048-B, and SCP-1048-C. The nature of these creations has been in stark contrast to SCP-1048's general behavior, as all have exhibited extreme violence towards humans.

SCP-1048-A

On ██/██/██ SCP-1048-A was discovered wandering Site 24, accompanied by SCP-1048. Subject resembles a teddy bear similar in size and shape to SCP-1048, but is made entirely out of human ears. Witnesses interviewed reported that it appeared SCP-1048 was giving a "tour" of Site 24 to SCP-1048-A. Dr. Carver was called to the scene, along with a security team. The security team arrived first,

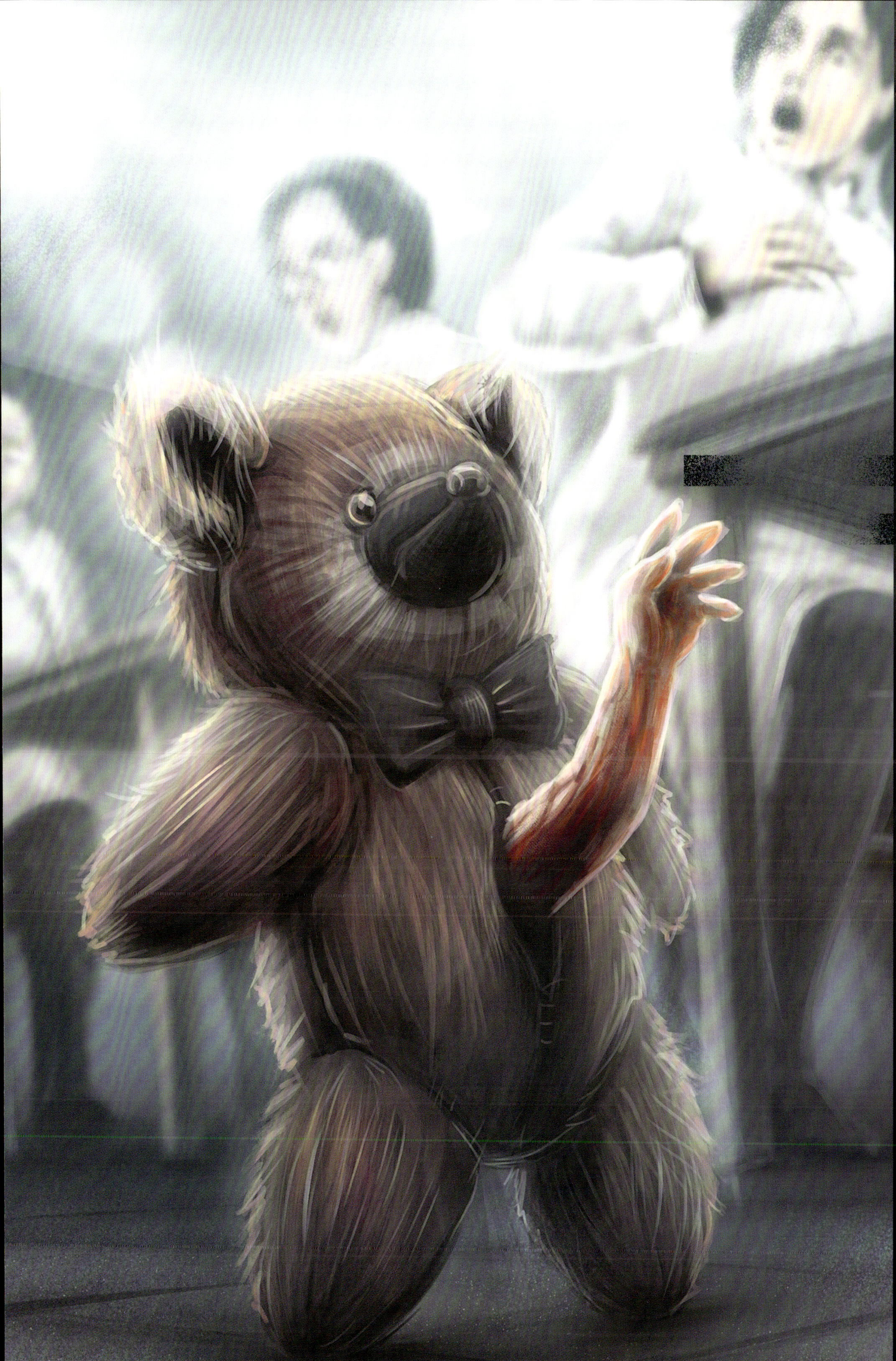

SCP-1048-B.

Research Library File ▸ 1048

and attempted to contain SCP-1048-A. Subject emitted a high-pitched shriek that inflicted intense pain in the eyes and ears of everyone in a 10 meter radius. Ear-like growths immediately began growing on those within 5 meters of the subject, covering their bodies in less than 20 seconds. Every person afflicted with this symptom died within 3 minutes, resulting in the death of █ personnel, including the entire security team. Autopsies revealed the cause of death to be asphyxiation caused by an abundance of the ear-like growths manifesting in the mouths and tracheae of all victims. SCP-1048 and SCP-1048-A fled the scene before Dr. Carver arrived, and have not been contained since the incident, though sightings of both have been reported on multiple occasions. Shortly after this incident occurred, a researcher was discovered missing an ear. According to him, it was removed through unknown means while he was sleeping. No other victims of ear removal were found, so it is unclear if SCP-1048 obtained more ears from another source, or if it is capable of duplicating objects or materials.

SCP-1048-B

Subject was discovered by several Foundation staff members in the cafeteria of Site 24 on ██/██/██. Subject's appearance was nearly identical to SCP-1048, but it moved in an irregular, jerky manner. Witnesses reported that it appeared as if something was moving inside of SCP-1048-B. Subject made no attempt to interact initially, until a burst in its seams revealed what appeared to be the hand and arm of a human infant poking out and grasping at the air. At the sight of this, a female researcher named ███ ███ screamed, and SCP-1048-B reacted by emitting a high-pitched cry similar to that of a human infant. The subject then attempted to [DATA EXPUNGED] the screaming researcher, causing massive internal damage. In the ensuing chaos, a security team was forced to [REDACTED] both the researcher and SCP-1048-B. Approximately 3 hours after this incident, Dr. ███ was found unconscious and bleeding in her office. An abortion had been performed on her while she was sleeping, and the 8-month-old fetus was never found. It is hypothesized that SCP-1048 used Dr. ███'s unborn child to create SCP-1048-B. Information regarding the possible origin of SCP-1048-B is not to be leaked to the survivors currently undergoing therapy for the incident with SCP-1048-B, as Dr. Carver believes it would be extremely detrimental to their recovery.

SCP-1048-C

Subject resembles a teddy bear similar to SCP-1048, but composed entirely of rusted metal scraps. Subject was first sighted on ██/██/██ by Dr. Carver in his office while writing up a report on the SCP-1048-B incident. Subject fled the room when it noticed Dr. Carver observing it. In the attempted pursuit of SCP-1048-C, Dr. Carver witnessed the death and maiming of █ Foundation personnel as the subject exhibited extreme violence during its escape. SCP-1048-C has not been encountered since this initial sighting, and it is unknown whether it still resides somewhere within Site 24. The origins of any materials possibly used to construct SCP-1048-C by SCP-1048 are also unknown at this time.

ADDENDUM 1048-1

SCP-2295 is similar, but nearly antithetical in function, to SCP-1048. Attempts to establish a common origin are ongoing.

Extreme caution is to be taken if SCP-1048-A or SCP-1048-C are encountered again.

I cannot stress this enough. The damn thing jumped right *through* these poor people.
Dr. Carver

END OF REPORT ███ █ ███

SCP-1055 IS AN INFOHAZARD. INFORMATION IN THIS DOCUMENT IS PRESENTED STRICTLY ON A NEED-TO-KNOW BASIS FOR CONTAINMENT PERSONNEL. ACCESSING ADDITIONAL INFORMATION REQUIRES LEVEL 5 APPROVAL AND ACCEPTS THE RISK OF CREATING A CONTAINMENT BREACH.

SPECIAL CONTAINMENT PROCEDURES

SCP-1055's living quarters are accessible via subterranean monorail from Site-77. Two personnel responsible for providing care to SCP-1055 are to be rotated in every eight hours for 24-hour observation. SCP-1055's living quarters contain a playroom with television, futon and sound system, a washroom, a library stocked with children's books, and a kitchen. Staff are encouraged to provide any meal which SCP-1055 asks for within appropriate nutritional guidelines. If current supplies do not meet requirements, substitutions of pasta or sugary cereals are commonly accepted.

SCP-1055 will fixate upon a random object (currently a teddy bear referred to as "Bugsy") and clutch it tightly at all times. Staff must allow and encourage this behavior, even during bathing and feeding. SCP-1055 may vocalize unhappiness or deliver warnings on behalf of this object; any requests concerning this object must be met by all possible means available.

Containment of SCP-1055 depends primarily on both its isolation and positive social attitude. In the event of catastrophe, staff are to evacuate and flood the living quarters with nitrous oxide. Under no circumstances is any physical harm to be done to SCP-1055, even and especially if it becomes hostile.

DELETE/DESTROY AFTER READING AS PER HP5810 RE: FORBIDDEN KNOWLEDGE DISPOSAL

Containment of SCP-1055 depends primarily upon the health and well-being of its caretaker, D-1055. Due to SCP-1055's extreme reactions to human perception, successful containment requires that staff on site be misdirected to believe that D-1055 is the anomalous entity himself. D-1055 is of diminished mental faculty but aware of the importance of his service in keeping "Bugsy" safe in his arms. D-1055 has thus far presented the only viable means of containing SCP-1055 without massive loss of personnel and resources.

Level 4 personnel who oversee containment of SCP-1055 are not allowed within 50 km of Site-77 nor may they directly interact with any personnel tasked with its maintenance.

File >>> 495455

SCP-1055

Title

BUGSY

Report by

Sorts

Picture by

Julia Galkina

Access the original report on

scp-wiki.wikidot.com/scp-1055

Date

Class

KETER

Research Library File ▸ 1055

DESCRIPTION

SCP-1055 is formerly Michael Schroder of Douglas, WY. He is a Caucasian male, 6 foot 4 inches tall and 280 pounds, 29 years of age, and suffers from autistic spectrum disorder and Down syndrome. SCP-1055 may be addressed as 1055, "Mikey" or any nickname which he suggests. Despite classification as an anomaly, staff are encouraged to address SCP-1055 with normal social pronouns in documentation and conversation.

[DATA EXPUNGED]

DELETE/DESTROY AFTER READING AS PER HP5810 RE: FORBIDDEN KNOWLEDGE DISPOSAL

Under normal conditions, SCP-1055 superficially resembles a specimen of Ursus arctos horribilis; however, its volume, mass and morphology shift spontaneously. The means by which SCP-1055 gains and loses mass is not understood, but it appears to be in relation to the number and proximity of individuals who are aware of SCP-1055 and the nature of the attention it receives from them. Hostile or fearful awareness of SCP-1055 increases its size and hostility significantly more than benign awareness, but due to SCP-1055's violent nature, even a calm awareness of its existence can quickly spiral into a potential containment breach as the danger it presents escalates and it exposes itself to more individuals.

In the event of catastrophic exposure to human awareness, SCP-1055 will quickly be overwhelmed by its own size and will no longer be able to effectively move at will; however, it will continue to grow and produce sensory organs and appendages which are used to assault any living creature within reach. Even in confined or subterranean locations SCP-1055's growth can exert enough pressure to cause tremors and massive structural failure, and pieces of the biomass are capable of growing through and widening gaps or cracks of any size.

Apart from its mass generation, SCP-1055 possesses no special ability to resist trauma. Portions of SCP-1055's biomass that are removed via trauma do not regenerate or continue living independently. However, about 75% of any hostile action taken against SCP-1055 to date has failed to destroy more of the organism than the very act itself generated, even in circumstances where the trauma was applied remotely via bombing or automated defenses.

No upper limit to the size or lethality of SCP-1055's biomass has been established during containment breaches and exposure to civilians and unscreened personnel. The only event which has ever been shown to effectively reduce SCP-1055 in size is the death of at least 80% of the individuals aware of its existence. Amnestics of any class are not sufficient to eliminate awareness.

Total elimination of SCP-1055 is hypothesized to require the extermination of all previously exposed individuals, including the 05 Council itself and anyone who is reading this document. It is the 05 Council's unanimous opinion that a failure to properly restrain SCP-1055 could quickly spiral into an XK-class scenario if its existence became publicly known.

ADDENDUM

Containment procedures adapted from captured GOI intelligence. The GOI was unsuccessfully researching attempts to destroy SCP-1055 which led to its escape and subsequent [DATA EXPUNGED].

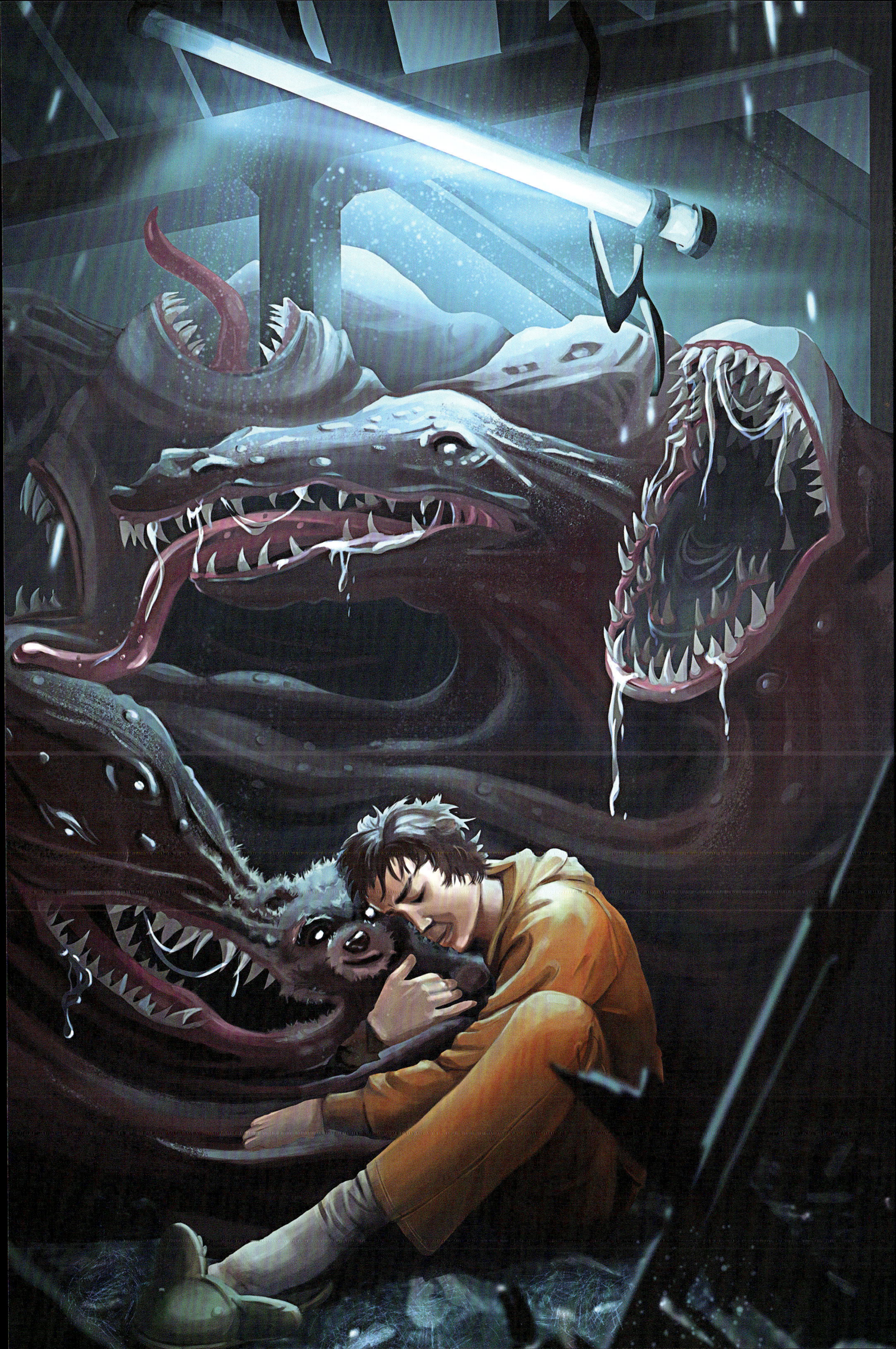

SCP-1055's anomalous effect. For full disclosure, please assess [DATA REDACTED].

DELETE/DESTROY AFTER READING AS PER HP5810 RE: FORBIDDEN KNOWLEDGE DISPOSAL

Current procedure was adopted following SCP-1055's 12th containment breach which resulted in sustained precision bombing upon former Site-76 and the loss of all personnel within, with the exception of D-1055 (previously classified D-492291; see form 1055-46 re: termination exemption).

Double-blind recovery teams found D-1055 alone in the rubble, clinging to the shredded remains of SCP-1055 as a 'security blanket'. It is hypothesized that D-1055 lacks the full capability to understand "Bugsy's" true nature, and that – as his awareness of SCP-1055 is obsessively protective and affectionate – he is not capable of triggering the escalating growth and hostility that normal human interaction with SCP-1055 produces.

According to interviews with containment personnel it appears that SCP-1055 itself either currently lacks the body and muscle mass to resist D-1055, or it simply lacks the will to resist. The majority of personnel have been successfully convinced that SCP-1055 is a poorly sewn, if disturbingly realistic, stuffed animal. Any movement or other indications to the contrary have been attributed to D-1055's supposed anomalous nature.

0443 > 02-43

I don't care that this arrangement has worked out the best out of all the previously scrapped containment schemes. It is not sustainable in the long run to ask a mentally challenged man to keep the end of the world at bay with hugs. We need a long term solution, preferably orbital or oceanic to keep exposure to human awareness at an absolute minimum. – 05-10

0443 > 02-44

Tell Mikey that we're taking Bugsy away and we're facing a brand new containment breach. I recommend doing so in person, that would at least be one less person who knows about this thing. – 05-5

0443 > 02-45

Via Protocol 12 we are already recruiting in plenty of mentally challenged individuals for Keter work. We're grooming future candidates to inherit D-1055's duties and to act as backup if the worst happens. Argue all you want for putting it in the sky where anyone can see it, this is the cheaper and safer option by far. – 05-7

END OF REPORT

File >>> 234455

SCP-212

Title

THE IMPROVER

Report by

Dr Gears

Picture by

Ruslan Korovkin

Access the original report on

scp-wiki.wikidot.com/scp-212

Date

█████

Class

SAFE

SPECIAL CONTAINMENT PROCEDURES

Use of SCP-212 must be cleared by the current containment site's chief medical officer. Any subjects undergoing operation by SCP-212 must submit to full physical and psychological testing both before and after exposure. Resistance to testing will result in termination of subject.

All personnel are to keep at least 1.5 m (5 ft) from SCP-212 when not in operation. Armed personnel are authorized to use whatever force deemed necessary to prevent unauthorized exposure. Should any personnel accidentally become exposed to SCP-212, full quarantine, testing, and judicial review will be initiated as soon as the subject is released by SCP-212.

DESCRIPTION

SCP-212 is a large medical device, with three large robotic arms. The arms have an extremely diverse array of attachments, but no storage area or power source has yet been found. Attachments slide into and out of the arms as needed, with over five hundred different attachments documented. SCP-212 is made of plastic, steel, and other common materials. In-depth analysis is pending, as any attempt by mechanical means causes violent action from SCP-212, and attempts by any biological means normally results with subject's "improvement".

When exposed to living tissue, the "arms" of SCP-212 will rapidly move to grab and restrain it. SCP-212 will then begin to "improve" said tissue. This process is extremely fast, but SCP-212 does not inject any anesthetic, or replace any blood lost. The process has been described as "excruciatingly painful", and can result in the death of the subject at a rate of 47%. Wounds made by SCP-212 are closed with standard surgical sutures and a chemical "sealant" that is not yet fully understood.

Improvements that have been observed include: lining of joints with graphite, replacement of biological organs with artificial ones, addition of metal plates to bones, addition of new or duplicate organs, and replacement of teeth with small serrated steel bands, among many others. SCP-212 has been shown to be able to totally "re-configure" an organism. The "improvements" appear to be random, and can sometimes be detrimental or fatal, as illustrated by one subject's complete loss of bone marrow and its replacement by a gel that is still under study.

Subjects wishing to undergo exposure from SCP-212 are to be advised that the process is extremely invasive, and that no predictions on "improvements" can be made.

SCP-212 UPGRADE LOG

Subject:
Agent █████ 28 years old, 64 kg, 183cm tall, African-American descent.
Submitted request on ██-██-███, approval granted and exposed on ██-██-███

Description of Upgrades:
Lower jaw bone replaced by super-dense ceramic jaw, teeth replaced with blades made of the same material. Spine removed and replaced with synthetic

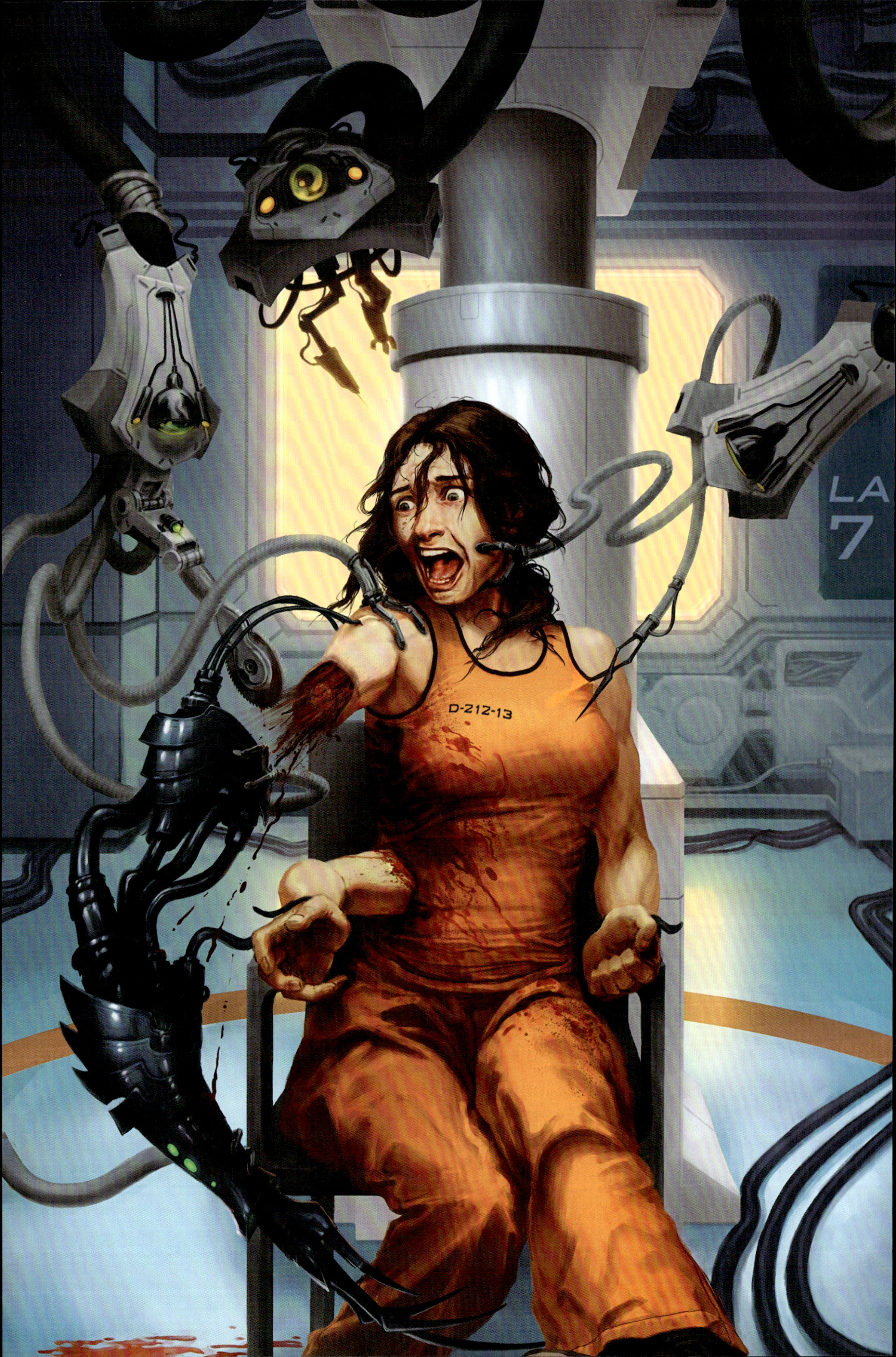

Subject: D-212-13, 22 years old, 53 kg, 161 cm, Caucasian descent.

polymer. Replacement spine grafted to base of skull. Rib cage and pelvis coated with thin layer of ceramic. Lungs, eyes, and liver removed and replaced after "cleaning."

Subject Status: Active duty.

SCP-212 will appear to "clean" some organs or tissues. It will run several "attachments" over the tissue, each of which will spray, scan, cut, or otherwise interact with the tissue before replacing it. When tested, these "cleaned" tissues appear totally free of genetic defects, and appear younger than the surrounding tissues.

Subject:
"Agent A.A.": [PERSONAL DATA REDACTED]. Suffered severe injuries on ██-██-████ resulting in traumatic amputation of all four limbs and removal of spleen, left kidney, right lung, and left eye. Cranial trauma caused by shard of circuitry piercing skull and entering left frontal lobe of brain. Submitted request on ██-██-████, approval granted and exposed on ██-██-████

Description of Upgrades:
Contrary to expectations, SCP-212 did not remove the shard of metal from subject's brain, instead spending approximately seven (7) minutes analyzing the circuitry with a variety of lenses, probes, and sensors before apparently determining that the foreign body could be left in place. SCP-212 then proceeded to integrate said circuitry into subject's frontal lobe more fully, utilizing tracery made of room-temperature superconductors. SCP-212 ended by administering an unknown chemical that immediately placed the subject in a coma, then shut itself down. No attempts were made to replace severed limbs or repair damage to bodily organs, aside from normal "cleaning."

Subject Status: As of ██-██-████, subject remains in a chemically induced coma, in stable condition. Foreign circuitry in brain appears to be spreading at a geometric rate. Estimate complete replacement of biological brain tissue in [DATA EXPUNGED].

Subject:
D-████ 23 years old, 62kg, 178cm, Caucasian (American) descent. Previously exposed to SCP-217 and decontaminated once the virus had run its course (full mechanical conversion achieved). Approval for testing granted on ██-██-████

Description of Upgrades:
[DATA EXPUNGED]

Subject Status: Subject escaped containment, overpowering two armed personnel and effortlessly bypassing several security measures. Subject recaptured after 2 hours, having caused █ casualties and █ injuries, as well as deactivating [DATA EXPUNGED]. Once recaptured, subject requested SCP classification (presumably in an attempt to avoid termination). Request was denied, and subject was dismantled. Components were incinerated following examination and documentation (see file [REDACTED]).

END OF REPORT ████ ██ █

File >>> 003234

SCP-084

Title
STATIC TOWER

Report by
Dr Gears

Picture by
Dmitry Desyatov

Access the original report on
scp-wiki.wikidot.com/scp-084

Date

Class
Euclid

SPECIAL CONTAINMENT PROCEDURES

SCP-084 is currently under a full non-interaction order until the full extent of the emission waves has been evaluated (for detailed documentation on general FNI orders, see Document XRG-1182; for detailed documentation on FNI orders in relation to SCP-084, see Document XRG-1208A). A continuous surveillance watch is to be maintained around the active area of SCP-084, with the primary objective of civilian misdirection and external surveillance. With no major roads, trails, or other travel routes nearby, any civilians encountered approaching SCP-084 are to be deemed suspect and detained for evaluation. Under no circumstances are any Foundation or civilian personnel allowed in to the active area of SCP-084, except with express vocal and written permission of no fewer than two (2) members of 05 Command.

Sentries are to maintain their posted position with line-of-sight contact checks on fellow sentries, in conjunction with compass and landmark checking. All reference points should be well outside the active area of SCP-084. Should any sentry fail to report in via vocal roll-call, full recall orders will be issued to all sentries, and containment will be re-evaluated by Special Response teams. In the event of active area fluctuation, full recall orders are to be assumed by all active sentries, followed by appropriate action.

No form of radio, GPS, television, cell phone, video camera, still-picture camera, or any other recording or electronic media devices are permitted within one hundred (100) meters of the active area around SCP-084. Civilians found with such devices within this area are to have said devices confiscated and destroyed immediately. Any recordings collected [DATA EXPUNGED].

DESCRIPTION

SCP-084 appears to be a large radio tower positioned in the center of a large, open field with two small outbuildings. Direct observation and sample collection from SCP-084 is impossible, due to the effect that is emitted around/from SCP-084. SCP-084 appears to emit a form of wave or radiation that has a detrimental effect on local space-time/reality. The most pronounced aspect of this is the alteration of local space within the active area of SCP-084. Externally, the active area forms a rough "dome" shape of two hundred (200) meters in diameter. SCP-084 appears inside this area at random points, appearing to "jump" at random times, sometimes even appearing in multiple locations at once inside the active area. Internally, the space appears to be unlimited, with SCP-084 at the "center".

SCP-084 is impossible to reach due to the "emitted effect". Attempts to approach SCP-084 within the active area have returned the observation that SCP-084 retains its relative position on the horizon, even after three months and twelve days of dedicated, direct travel both by vehicle and on foot. Termination tests have proved impossible, as no means of destruction are capable of physically reaching SCP-084, even when entered from outside the active area. Local space will also distort periodically. This will cause relative distances to randomly extend or contract in a "flicker", causing buildings or objects to suddenly "jump" thousands of meters away, or "rush up" to other points, sometimes even causing "overlaps". These "overlaps" have a markedly detrimental effect on living tissue.

The town of █████ ███ is assumed to have been situated in or around the original manifestation of the active area. This town is no longer observable from

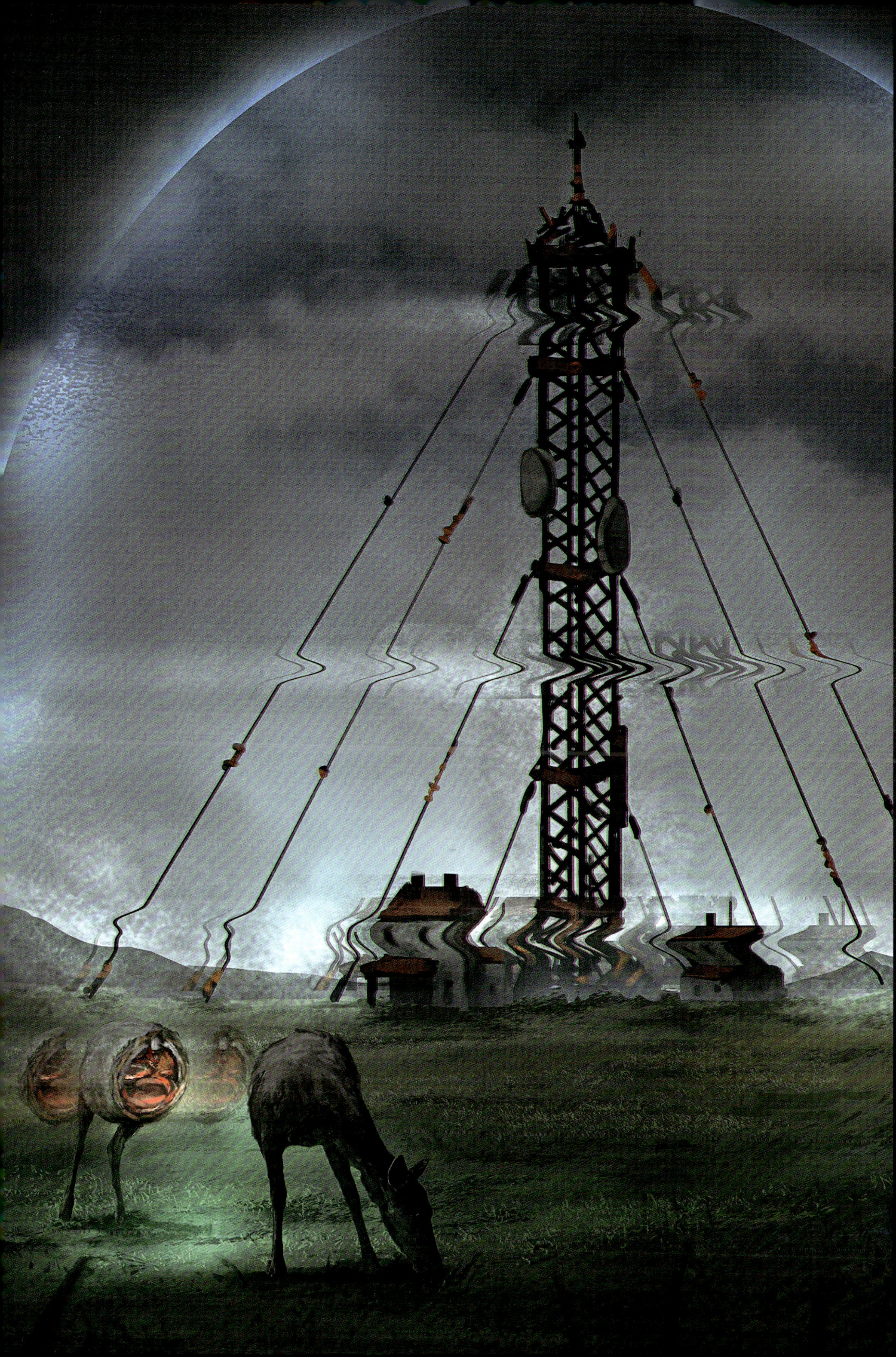

Photo of SCP-084 taken outside of the active area.

outside the active area, appearing only once inside the active area. ████ ███ has maintained the same population (343 humans) for the duration of its encapsulation. Births appear to be impossible, along with normal aging patterns. Suicide and/or homicide appear to be circumvented by the area of effect, with dead subjects "flickering" and appearing alive and unharmed several seconds after death. There are also reports of events "rewinding", causing things like mortal wounds to visibly "freeze" and close. Subjects appear to exhibit many events of inconsistent space-time, as do most structures (for detailed observations, see Log 084-A4).

Electronic devices and recording equipment do not function correctly in or around the active area. Subjects report "bizarre" or "unsettling" transmissions from video and audio recording and playback devices. This acts to totally isolate ████ ███ from the outside world, precluding any need for Foundation-enacted containment. It also appears impossible to leave the active area after a random period of time. One subject from ████ ███, found on the grass plane (see Log 084-A4), reported he had been traveling for six years. He was found approximately four hundred meters from ████ ███ city limits.

RECORD OF OBSERVED ANOMALOUS EVENTS RELATING TO SCP-084

Detailed observation made of the "grass plane" making up the majority of the active area. The plane appears to be made of one ten (10) meter by ten (10) meter section of grass, repeated endlessly to make up the plane. Sections appear to be randomly "rotated" as they are formed, causing sections of grass and small ground variations to line up incorrectly.

Few non-human organisms appear to exist within the active area. Those outside the active area avoid it, and appear to "vanish" shortly after entering. Animals observed inside the active area appear normal, but behave strangely. Shuddering movements, sudden "shivering", repetitive "loops" and other abnormal actions appear to indicate these may not be actual animals. Most animals appear to "flicker" and vanish after 3-4 hours.

Vocal communication is difficult within the active area. Vocal communication appears normal within five meters of the speaking subject, with reports of a slightly "muffled" quality reported commonly. Outside of five meters, subjects appear to be speaking from a great distance with a great deal of echoing. Reports of speech being heard several seconds after the subject has stopped speaking, and speech occurring with no subjects speaking are also not uncommon.

Detailed observation of the "radio tower" is impossible due to the inability to physically reach it, and the effect of the "broadcast" on most observational equipment. Basic telescope or binoculars systems show the tower to be "hazy" and "static-fogged", while more advanced equipment is subject to the "anomalous broadcast" effect.

Weather patterns, as well as basic day/night cycles, appear to be totally random. Overhead sky will randomly cycle between day, night, clear, and other weather patterns. Relative sun and cloud position appear random as well, with frequent "flickering" and "blurring" between different states.

Physical alteration or damage to anything within the active area is impossible. Actions such as digging, demolition, and new constructions will suddenly "blur" and be "reset" to their previous unaltered state at random points. Subjects inside a "reset" structure, such as inside a hole, will become instantly trapped and "fused".

Humans in the active area around SCP-084 exhibit some of the more striking and easily observed reality distortion effects. These include:

- Sudden "blurring" of limbs or head, appearing to suddenly gyrate at violently high speed for several seconds before ending. Subjects experience no pain, and are often unaware of this phenomenon.
- "Looping", typically manifested as the repeating of eight (8) to twenty (20) seconds of time. Subjects will go through an action (example: exiting a doorway, picking up an article of clothing), then suddenly "freeze" and "flicker", then return to the original starting position of the "loop" and repeat the action, even if this involves a sudden "teleportation" of significant distance. Rarely, subjects appear to become caught in a permanent loop.
- Observation and interrogation of subjects in ████████ █████ show that basic human needs, such as food, water, and sleep are no longer required after prolonged exposure to the active area. Some subjects report not having eaten or drank for (they believe) five (5) years. One elderly subject also reports having made two thousand, one hundred and ten (2,110) unsuccessful suicide attempts.
- Subjects will sometimes be able to pass through solid matter without incident. These periods appear to last for random periods of time, and begin and end without warning. Subjects "inside" solid matter when the period ends will become trapped or "fused" until the period resumes. One subject reports being trapped below the waist in a wall for two (2) years.
- Extreme psychological distress is observed after long-term exposure. The transmissions [DATA EXPUNGED] barrier, which is compromised over long-term exposure. Subjects in advanced "reception" states typically "reset" after several months.

Recorded transmissions show a slight [DATA EXPUNGED] cycles overall. Attempting to catalog and record these broadcasts has therefore been remanded to autonomous systems, to preclude any additional loss of Foundation personnel.

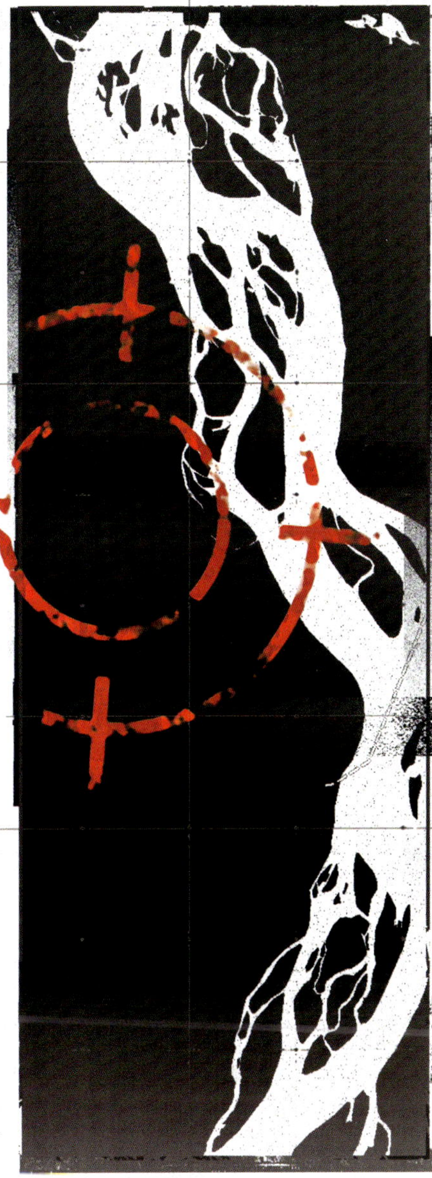

Approximate location of SCP-084. ████████

END OF REPORT

File >>> 304234

SCP-354

Title

THE RED POOL

Report by

Dave Rapp

Pictures by

Alex Andreev

Access the original report on

scp-wiki.wikidot.com/scp-354

Date

Class

KETER

SPECIAL CONTAINMENT PROCEDURES

Due to SCP-354's immobile nature, Area-354 has been built around it. Area-354 houses forces and D-class personnel prepared to deal with threats emerging from SCP-354, as well as researchers studying SCP-354 and its properties. For their own safety, no on-site personnel are to approach SCP-354 at any time. Direct interaction with SCP-354 is permitted only for the purpose of research to eliminate SCP-354 and must be approved by 05 personnel.

Area-354 was constructed to contain and neutralize any and all further threats emerging from SCP-354. At the heart of Area-354, a twenty (20) foot wall of concrete reinforced with [DATA EXPUNGED] has been constructed around SCP-354 to prevent emerging entities from escaping into the area at large. High-speed motion detection cameras are placed atop the wall looking down into the pool, and armed guards can easily shoot down into the enclosure from catwalks placed above the pool.

DESCRIPTION

SCP-354 is a pool of red liquid discovered in northern Canada. The liquid is of a consistency similar to that of human blood (hence the colloquial name Blood Pond) but is not of a biological nature. The pool does not have definite banks; soil mixes with the liquid until, at a certain point, there is more soil than liquid and the ground is mostly solid. The liquid becomes denser as one descends deeper into the pool; if the pool has a bottom, it has yet to be reached.

Periodically, entities emerge from the pool and attempt to escape from the enclosure. Thus far, nearly all creatures emerging from SCP-354 have been extremely hostile and highly dangerous.

SCP-354 is believed to have been first discovered in █████ by survivors of a plane crash, who encountered SCP-354 by chance. SCP-354 had developed into a local urban legend long before Foundation personnel arrived to deal with the threat.

After locating the source of the legend, SCP personnel set up Watch Station Epsilon-38 to monitor the pool and to deter future travellers from finding it. SCP-354 was classified as Euclid until its properties were further discovered.

At 1403 hours on █████, an unidentified entity emerged from SCP-354. Contact with Watch Station Epsilon-38 was lost. Mobile Task Force █████ was dispatched to deal with the entity and were eventually successful. All personnel at Watch Station Epsilon-38 were found dead. Area-354 was subsequently constructed to contain SCP-354.

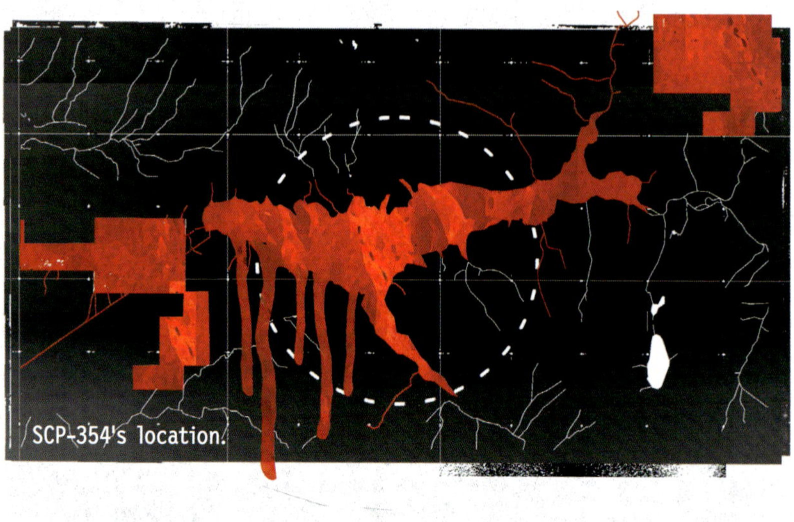

SCP-354's location.

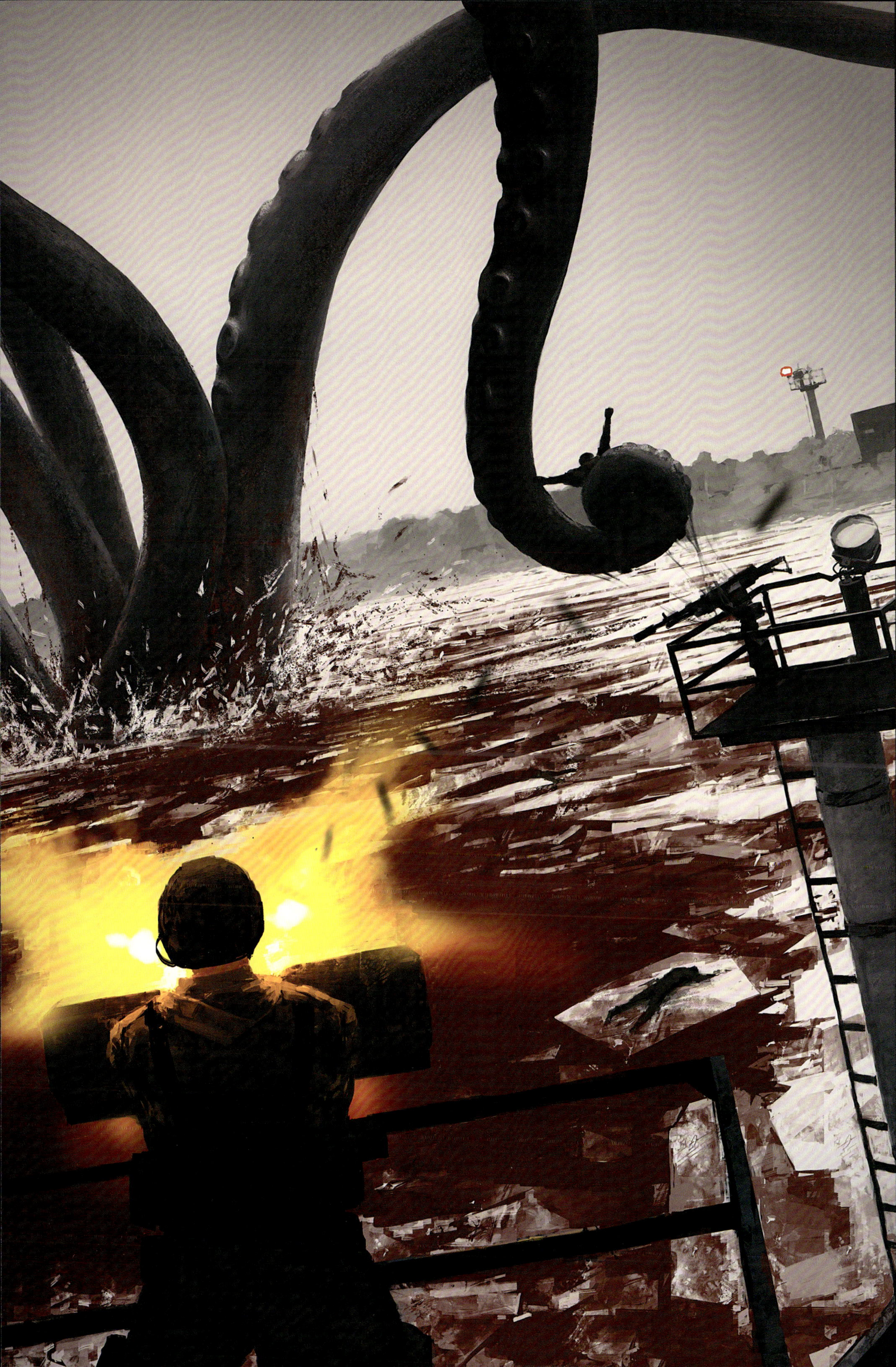

Incident SCP-354-14.

DOCUMENT 354-1-A

Partial log of entities to have emerged from SCP-354 prior to Event 354-20.

SCP-354-1: Original entity which destroyed Watch Station Epsilon-38. Resembled a giant bat. Neutralized by Mobile Task Force ███.

SCP-354-2: Bear-sized mammalian creature covered in razor-sharp spines. Resembled an echidna. Was virtually bulletproof, but was unable to escape the enclosure surrounding the pool. Neutralized via napalm.

SCP-354-3: Black metallic sphere capable of levitation. Emitted concentrated levels of radiation in precisely directed beams sufficient to instantly cripple and later result in death. Then-Area Head Dr. █████ struck SCP-354-3 with a sledgehammer, disabling it. SCP-354-3 then self-detonated, causing minor structural damage and severely wounding Dr█████. D█████ made a full recovery and has been commended for his bravery.

SCP-354-4: Humanoid reptilian creature, approximately 4.6m (15ft) tall. Escaped both the walled enclosure and Area-354 altogether. Gunfire caused very little physical harm and was highly ineffective. Mobile Task Force Omega-7 "Pandora's Box" was dispatched and was successful in neutralizing the creature.

SCP-354-5: [DATA EXPUNGED]

SCP-354-6: Appeared to be a human male of Indian descent. As the enclosure around the pool had not yet been fully repaired, SCP-354-6 was immediately shot before it had a chance to escape. Area Head Dr. █████ has expressed his displeasure in the rash execution of SCP-354-6, which testing revealed to be identical to an average human being.

<data corrupt>

SCP-354-14: Majority of creature's body remained well beneath the surface of the pool. Five (5) octopus-like tentacles were seen emerging from the pool and reached up over the enclosure. Several D-class personnel were grabbed by the tentacles and pulled back beneath the surface of the pool. After receiving massive damage from gunfire, SCP-354-14 retreated back into the pool and disappeared. No personnel taken by the creature were recovered.

SCP-354-15: Feline creature composed of a blue-hued crystalline structure later revealed to be ice. Was able to jump above the walled enclosure and was agile enough to dodge most gunfire. Was actively hostile and mauled any personnel that engaged it. Subject engaged SCP-354-16 upon its emergence from the pool and was terminated in the fight.

SCP-354-16: Feline creature composed of a dark red-black stone later revealed to be partially solidified magma. Gunfire proved mostly ineffective against its hide. Was not hostile to personnel and did not attempt to escape the walled enclosure until being engaged by SCP-354-15. Successfully terminated SCP-354-15 and grew less active as its body cooled. After fully solidifying and having remained motionless since, subject was moved to Dr.█████'s office for aesthetic purposes.

SCP-354-18: Metallic humanoid machine described by several D-class personnel as a "Terminator." Subject possessed a cloaking device rendering it invisible to human eyes. Subject was highly adept at combat and killed nearly 90% of Area-354's guard personnel as it rampaged through the facility. Approximately sixty (60) minutes after emerging from the pool, subject ceased function and powered down. Subject was dismantled and its power cell was disposed of. Subject's remains are under study.

> **Note from Area Head Dr. ████:** *That's thrice now that we've had to fall back on Pandora's Box to deal with stuff coming out of SCP-354. Able can't complain, though… you can tell he enjoyed fighting SCP-354-11. Maybe we should set up some kind of "hotline" to MTF Ω-7?*

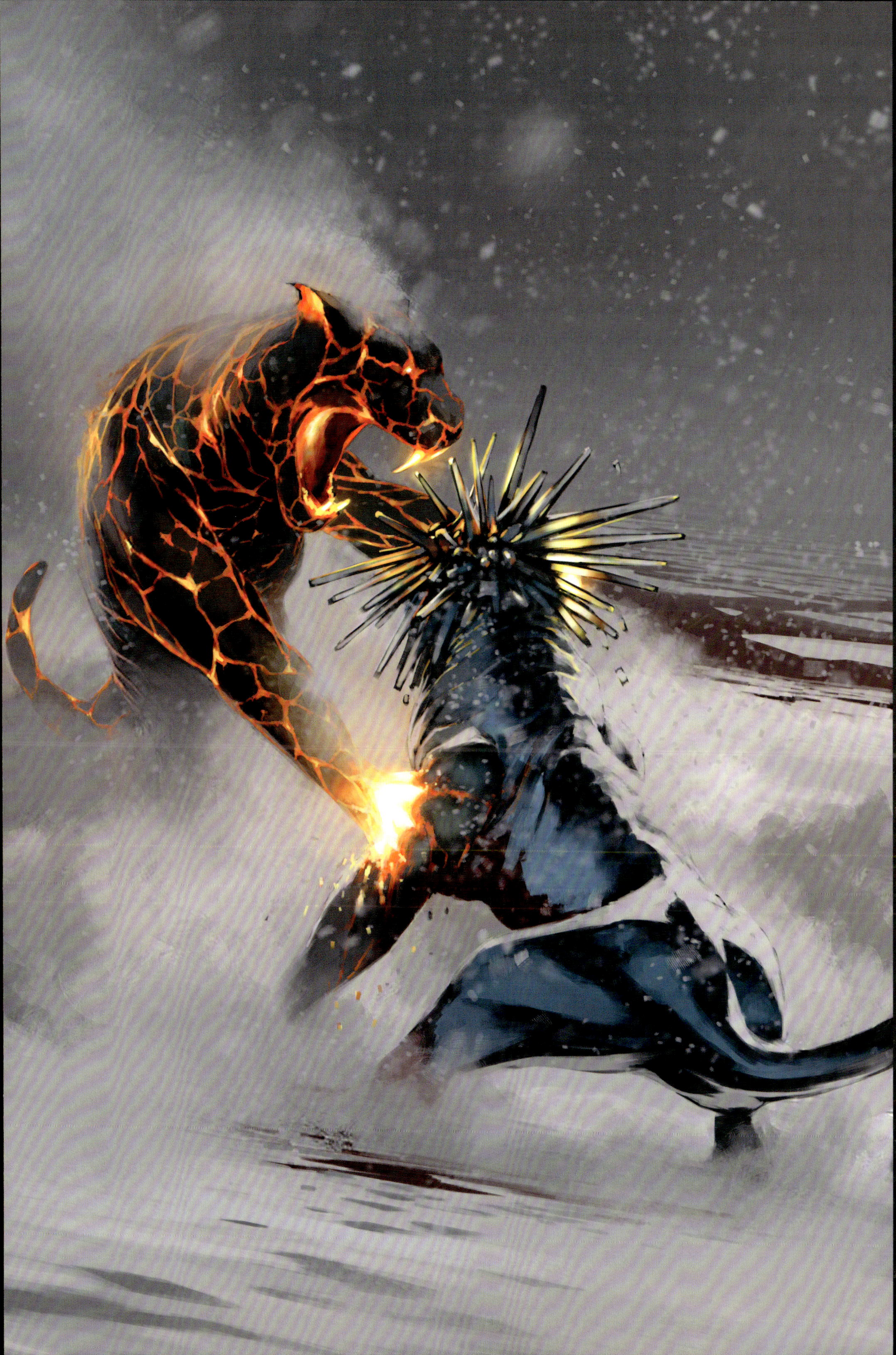

Confrontation between SCP-354-15 and SCP-354-16.

Research Library File ▸ 354

DOCUMENT 354-3-A

Note from Area Head Dr. █████: *It has been twenty-two months since the last entity emerged from the pool. Before this, the longest period of time between emergences was eight months. I suspect this means one of two things. Either the Red Pool has "died" or "powered down" or whatever the correct term for it is; or it is "charging up" for something big to come through. 05 believes the former is the most likely explanation, and has recalled 30% of our total personnel and cut 25% of our funding. While I can only hope that they are correct, if the latter situation is true, we're soon to face some terrible monstrosity and we won't have anywhere near the force necessary to deal with it. I worry for all of our safety.*

DOCUMENT 354-4: EVENT LOG 354-20

In the morning of [DATA EXPUNGED] the entire staff of Area-354 evacuated the facility. However, the staff also shut down power to the area and took a number of supplies and vehicles from the facility, indicating that the evacuation had not been done due to an emergency. Mobile Task Force Theta-12 was dispatched to investigate the cause of the evacuation and, if possible, make contact with Area's staff. However before MTF █-12 could make contact with Area-354 or its evacuees, the Area's on site warhead was detonated, resulting in the destruction of the entire facility and the deaths of [DATA EXPUNGED].

MTF █-12 was ordered to make contact with the evacuated personnel and, in the event of hostility, was given clearance to terminate any uncooperative personnel. A large convoy of vehicles taken from Area-354 was spotted heading southward from Area-354 at high speed. Final audio logs from MTF █-12 indicate that the convoy was made up of Area-354's staff, and that the previous chain of command had broken down in its entirety, with armed D-class personnel and research personnel firing upon MTF █-12. MTF █-12 was annihilated and no further contact with the former personnel of Area-354 has been made since.

DOCUMENT 354-5

Following the total destruction of Area-354, the Red Pool Containment Site was constructed in its place. Basic maps of the new facility can be found in ██████-███-█ and ███-███-█████. Unlike the previous facility which was focused on research and neutralization of entities emerging from SCP-354, the new facility is devoted entirely to the containment of SCP-354 and entities which may emerge from it, as well as any unforeseen forces which it may create directly. This is due largely to the advisement of the new Site Head [DATA EXPUNGED] who believes that the events of Log 354-20 were the result of a psychic or mental attack generated by SCP-354 itself.

DOCUMENT 354-6

Interview regarding [DATA EXPUNGED]

Dr. ██████: Is it all right if I record this?

Agent ███ Yes, go ahead.

Dr. ██████: Good, good. *(pause)* So, let's start at the beginning. What happened at the Red Pool containment site?

Agent ███ Looking back now… it seems strange that nobody ever suggested draining the pool. When Dr. ███ came up with it… it seemed like such a good idea at the time.

Dr. ██████: Exactly what about the idea was so appealing?

Agent ███ It was a way out. That SCP entry… I've read what it says. It's a joke. It makes it seem like we have the pool under control.

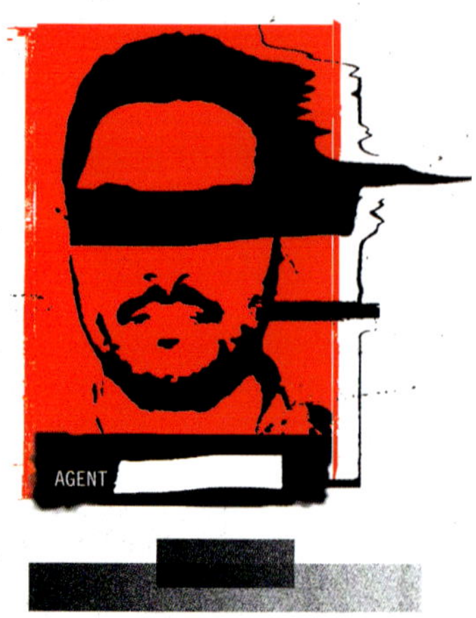

Dr. ████ I take it you do not?

Agent ██ There's a half meter slab of reinforced concrete in place over the pool. And yet every time some beast tries to come through somehow it manages to get loose into the building. People die, every single time. I've seen [DATA EXPUNGED] a man's own intestines. Can you imagine what that looks like, old man?

Dr. ████ So to you, and of course to the other people stationed at the Red Pool containment site as well, draining the pool seemed like a fine solution to the suffering caused by SCP-354.

Agent ██ *(chair scrapes as Agent* ██ *stands up)* Suffering? That thing doesn't just-

Dr. ████: Please, sit down. This is going on record. *(pause, Agent* ██ *sits)* So, 05 approved the draining of SCP-354, and then what happened?

Agent ██ They evacuated the nonessential personnel to a location a couple kilometers away, leaving just basic defense crew and the people who'd run the equipment. Mostly D class, plus a few Agents to keep things going.

Dr. ████ And you were among those Agents.

Agent ██ Yes.

Dr. ████ How did they go about draining the pool?

Agent ██: Tech guys brought in this big pump thing with all these hoses. We retracted the slab, but… *(pause)*

Dr. ████ But…?

Agent ██ Have you ever had a dream, where it seemed so real, but you knew you were dreaming, and it felt like you had to wake up to escape from it?

Dr. ████ I can't say I have.

Agent ██ Yes you have, we all have. That's what it felt like when they put the hose in to try to drain it. Everything stopped being real. It was like we had to escape right now.

Dr. ████ And you were the only one feeling this sensation?

Agent ██ No, everyone had it at the same time. It came from the fucking pool!

Dr. ████: Please, lower your voice. What happened when they activated the pump?

Agent ██ We never did. We couldn't. It wouldn't let us.

Dr. ████ What wouldn't let you?

Agent ██: The pool!

Dr. ████: Please, I ask you to lower your voice.

Agent ██ Up until now it's been content just throwing monsters at us. It's been playing. But now we have it locked up and we just tried to execute it! Now it's angry!

Dr. ████ *(to PA)* Guards, please restrain Agent ██.

Agent ██ My buddy measured its banks once and compared them to the photos from its first discovery. You know what he found? *(Agent* ██ *grabs Doctor* ████*)*

Dr. ████ Guards!

Agent ██: It's growing! The pool is growing! It gets bigger and stronger every day and now we've made it angry! Get your hands off-

Dr. ████: Sedate him. We'll continue this in the morning, if he's lucid by then anyway.

END OF REPORT ▌██ ██ ▌

File >>> 019993

SCP-162

Title

BALL OF SHARP

Report by

Dr Gears

Picture by

Alexander Puchkov

Access the original report on

scp-wiki.wikidot.com/scp-162

Date

Class

EUCLID

SPECIAL CONTAINMENT PROCEDURES

SCP-162 is to be kept in a sealed steel container at all times. Any handling is to be done with thick steel-plate gloves and heavy body armor. Any personnel attempting to touch SCP-162 without proper protection, or acting in an erratic or non-responsive manner, are to be immediately removed from the containment area. All personnel are to submit to mental testing and review for two weeks after interaction with SCP-162.

DESCRIPTION

SCP-162 is a mass of fish hooks, fish line, needles, scissors, and other sharp objects in a rough ball shape close to 2.4 m (8 ft) in width and 2.1 m (7 ft) in height. After being in SCP-162's vicinity, subjects have reported feeling drawn to the object in order to touch it. This desire can extend for several weeks after seeing the item, becoming an obsession in many cases. The "draw" increases the more SCP-162 is observed, and subjects will become violent towards anyone attempting to restrain or remove them from SCP-162.

Touching SCP-162 will immediately result in several hooks becoming embedded in the subject's skin. The experience is extremely painful, much more so than normal fish hooks. Struggling or attempting to escape will ensnare the subject more, likely resulting in the subject's complete entrapment on the surface of SCP-162. Subject will bleed profusely, resulting in death after a prolonged period of time. Subjects whose skin is impenetrable to SCP-162's fish hooks, such as SCP-1063, have proven to be immune to SCP-162's compulsion effects.

Attempting to remove a subject from SCP-162 will result in the entrapment of the remover, or gross bodily harm to the subject's flesh. Subjects will many times "cycle" between expressing extreme pain and requesting assistance, to statements of pleasure and requests to be left alone, even attempting to grab and entangle personnel attempting to rescue them. Activation of SCP-1114 within the proximity of SCP-162 has proven to be an effective means of freeing a subject from entrapment, though SCP-162's compulsion effect still remains.

END OF REPORT

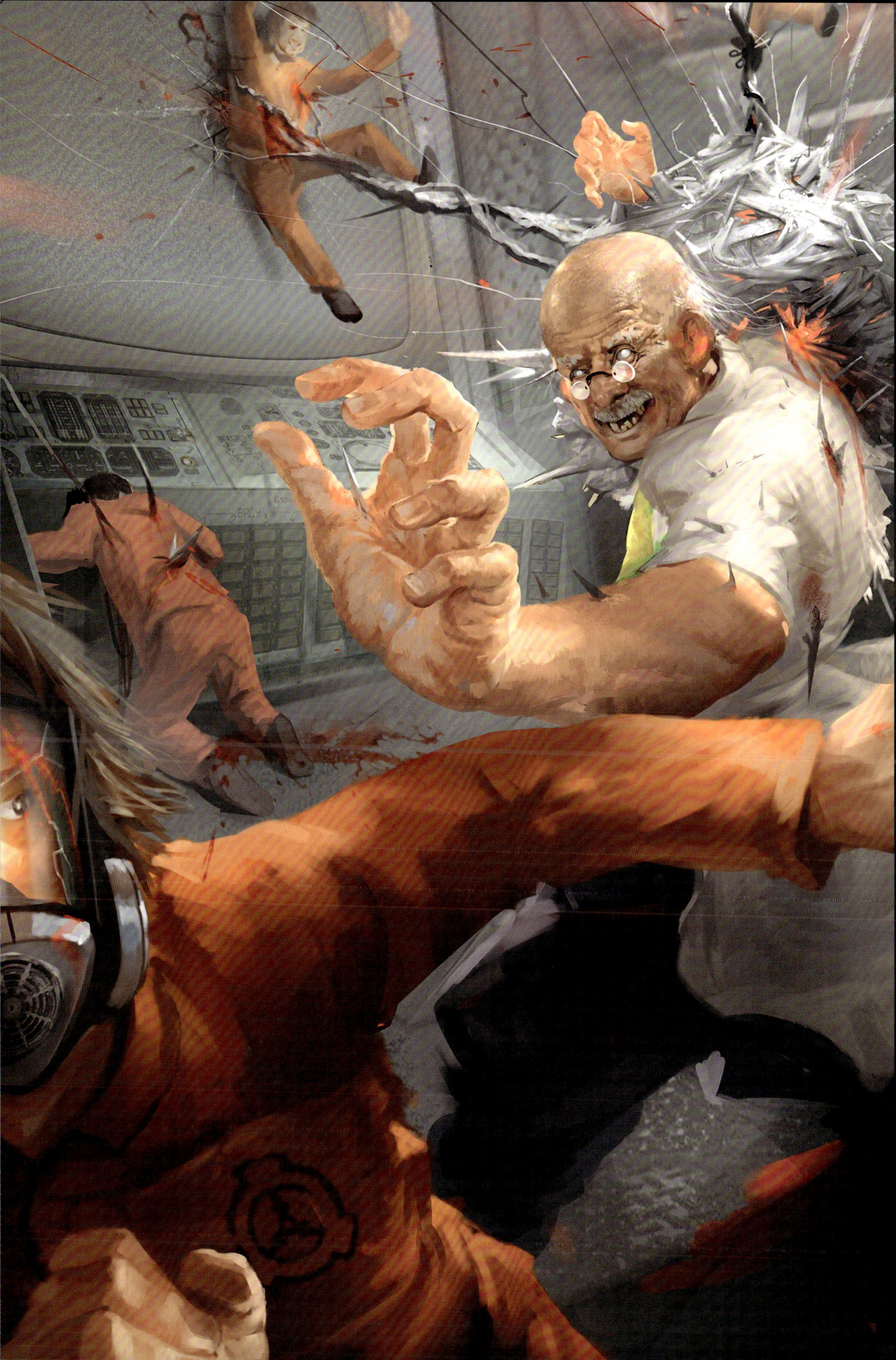

File >>> 019034

SCP-513

Title

A COWBELL

Report by

beefwit

Pictures by

Tatiana Kvitkovsky

Access the original report on

scp-wiki.wikidot.com/scp-513

Date

Class

EUCLID

SPECIAL CONTAINMENT PROCEDURES

SCP-513 is to be suspended in a one cubic meter block of gelatin and contained within a soundproofed, climate-controlled cell. The gelatin must be inspected daily for any degradation or loss of integrity. An emergency inspection will be carried out immediately following any earthquake, explosion, or sonic event grade 2 or higher. Personnel performing the inspection are to wear earplugs and active noise-canceling earmuffs at all times while inside SCP-513's cell.

If the gelatin cube shows any signs of degradation (such as rips, tears, splits, liquefaction, or mold), SCP-513 is to be immediately removed and suspended within a replacement cube by a team of surgically deafened Class-D personnel. No other personnel are to enter the cell during this procedure.

Any sentient beings exposed to SCP-513 are to be monitored by at least two security personnel at all times. Under absolutely no circumstances may exposure victims be administered sedatives or allowed to fall unconscious. Any victim who does fall unconscious is to be terminated immediately.

Class-D personnel are to be terminated at the first sign of mental degradation. All other exposure victims may be terminated at their request.

If possible, SCP-513-1 is to be apprehended on sight.

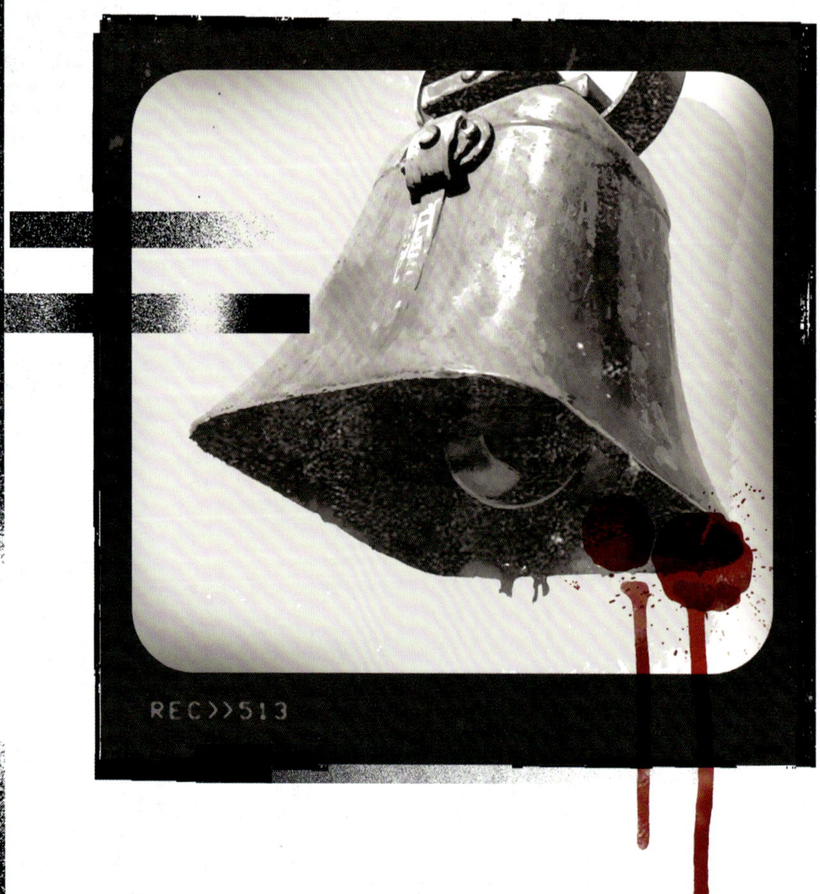

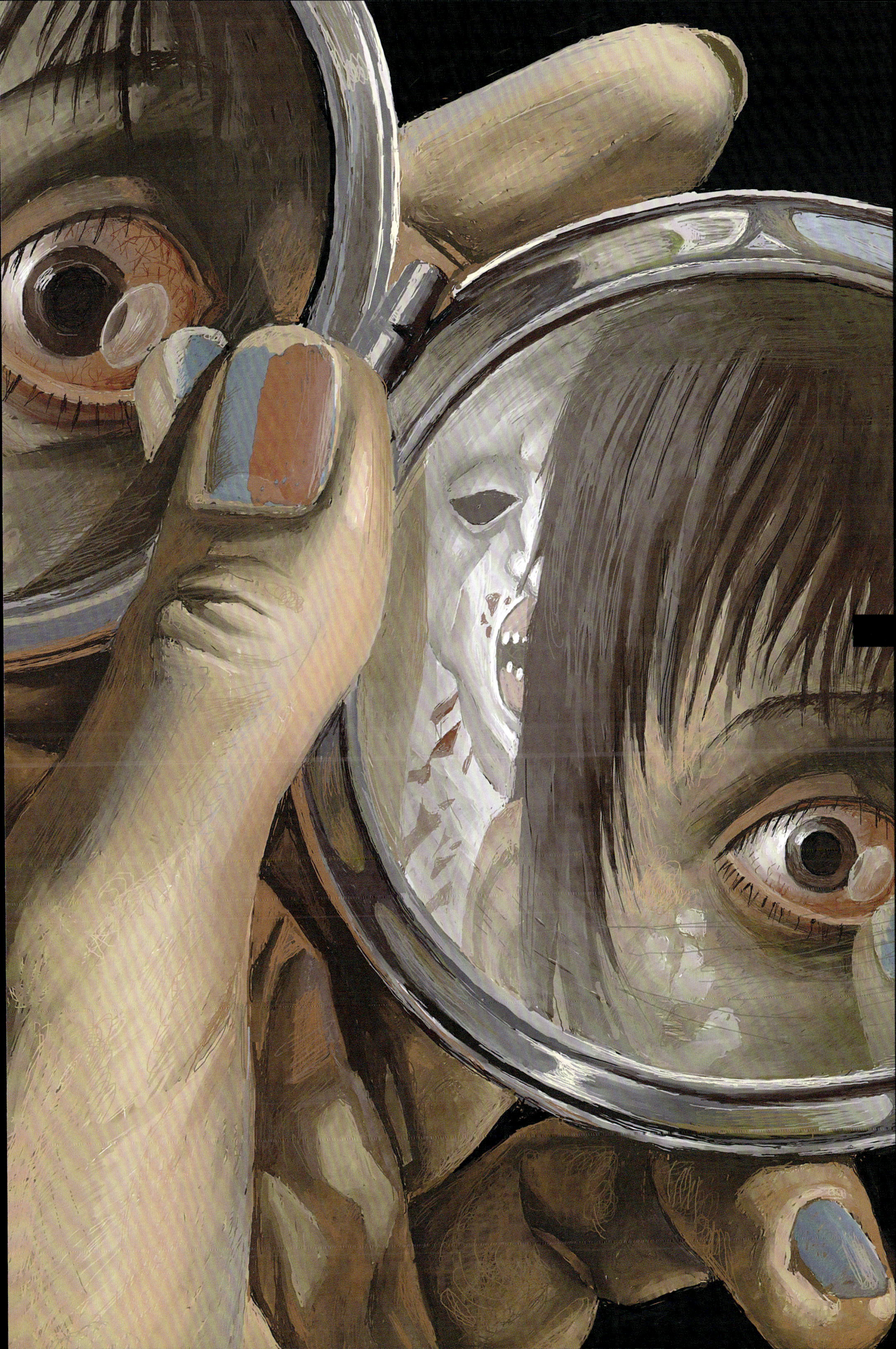

SCP-513-1's visualization created by one of the victims.

DESCRIPTION

Research Library File ▸ 513

Physically, SCP-513 is an unremarkable, rusty cowbell. No marks or engravings are visible on its surface due to the large amount of corrosion. Attempts to remove the rust chemically or mechanically have had no success.

SCP-513 was recovered by Agent █████ while carrying out Containment Reestablishment Procedure Mu at Site██. SCP-513's clapper was firmly held in place by several strips of duct tape. A single scrap of paper was found along with SCP-513 (see Addendum).

Any noise produced by SCP-513 immediately induces strong anxiety in all sentient beings who hear it, regardless of their previous mental status. Exposure victims report feelings of being watched by an unseen entity and present elevated heart rates and blood pressure. Roughly one hour after exposure, exposure victims begin to catch glimpses of SCP-513-1 when opening doors, walking past mirrors, turning their heads, or performing any other actions that result in a sudden change in visual perception. Upon being sighted, SCP-513-1 reportedly turns away and runs out of view before disappearing without a trace. Questioning of bystanders indicates that SCP-513-1 is invisible to those who have not been exposed to SCP-513.

Sightings of SCP-513-1 reoccur every 14 to 237 minutes. This "stalking" behavior inevitably causes extreme sleep deprivation, as victims are frequently disturbed by SCP-513-1's presence in their quarters. Victims able to fall asleep before SCP-513-1's appearance report being physically assaulted by it. Upon the victim's awakening, SCP-513-1 flees as usual. This sleep deprivation, along with the mental stress caused by SCP-513-1's behavior, invariably induces paranoia, aggression, hypervigilance, and depression. All test cases but one have ended with the test subject's suicide.

Descriptions of SCP-513-1's appearance are largely unreliable. Test subjects are unable to provide complete accounts of sightings due to their exhaustion, degraded mental health, and disruptive hypervigilance. However, all interrogations thus far indicate that SCP-513-1 is a tall, emaciated humanoid with abnormally large hands.

ADDENDUM: TEXT RECOVERED FROM SITE-███

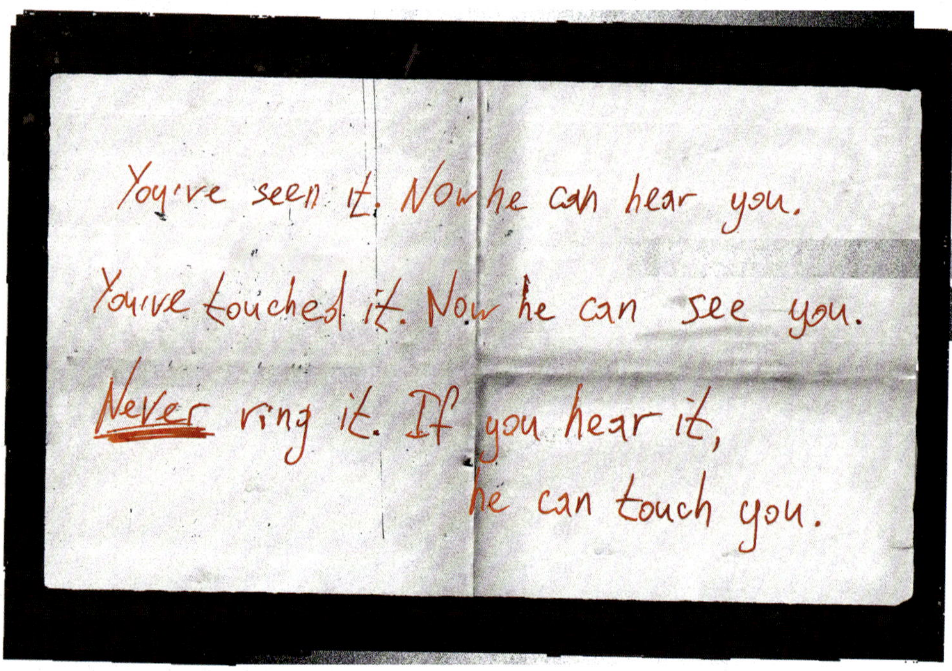

You've seen it. Now he can hear you.

You've touched it. Now he can see you.

Never ring it. If you hear it,
he can touch you.

END OF REPORT

SPECIAL CONTAINMENT PROCEDURES

Samples of SCP-020 are stored in a series of sealed cultivation chambers inside a sealed containment room at Biological Research Area-12 which is accessible only via airlock. Nutrients are administered via automated robotic systems, as the cultivation chamber must remain sealed at all times.

Hermetically sealed video surveillance cameras are installed within the containment room, and must be checked daily for integrity. Any personnel entering the containment room must wear Biosafety Level 5 equipment including rebreathers and undergo full anti-fungal disinfection upon exiting.

DESCRIPTION

SCP-020 is a fast-spreading fungal organism that is capable of affecting the senses and behavior of living creatures, including humans. Samples of SCP-020 exhibit an unknown effect that renders them effectively invisible to direct observation, even when under a microscope. SCP-020 is only visible to humans when viewed through photographic or video surveillance.

Once SCP-020 forms a colony, usually within a human residence, it will produce spores that affect the behavior of humans around it. Affected subjects will increase the heat and humidity within their homes to create an environment more suitable to the growth of SCP-020. Affected subjects also become more sociable in many cases, and often invite acquaintances to their homes to further spread the organism. As the spores and mold colonies are invisible to affected subjects, the mold may sometimes grow directly on living subjects.

As the spores and colonies within a home approach critical concentration, the health of affected human subjects will rapidly deteriorate, resulting in death. Further spread of the mold may occur as the bodies of any deceased subjects are encountered by emergency responders and health care agents, as well as transportation of the bodies to local morgues.

SCP-020 growths in a civilian residence.

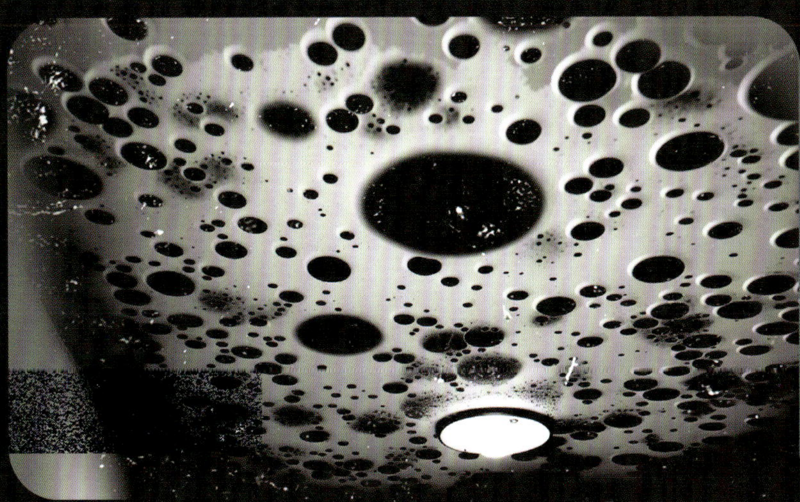

File >>> 0213455

SCP-020

Title

UNSEEN MOLD

Report by

Aelanna

Picture by

Dmitry Desyatov

Access the original report on

scp-wiki.wikidot.com/scp-020

Date

Class

KETER

SCP-020 was first encountered in [REDACTED], where an undercover SCP agent noted dramatic personality changes in personnel working at the local hospital. Upon investigation by a containment team, it was discovered that almost ███ civilians had been infected, as well as a majority of the town. The civilian population was terminated, and the town incinerated under cover of a local flash forest fire.

To date, over 12 outbreaks of SCP-020 have been reported. Investigations are currently underway to determine the source of these outbreaks and possible preventative measures.

ADDENDUM 020-01

Excerpts from the audio/video mission recorders of Mobile Task Force Eta-10 ("See No Evil") during the initial containment of SCP-020 on [REDACTED].

> **T2-Lead:** Team Two moving to the red house.
>
> **T2-COM:** Copy, UAV One is picking up one heat signature.
>
> …
>
> **T2-Lead:** Team Two in place, ready to br– *[Expletive]*!
>
> **T2-2:** Door opening!
>
> *At this point, a civilian woman appeared in the doorway, holding a kitchen knife. Video surveillance showed that nearly two-thirds of her face was covered by mold growths.*
>
> **Civilian Woman:** Well… hello there, gentlemen… care to take a breather inside?
>
> **T2-Lead:** On the ground! Drop the weapon!
>
> **Civilian Woman:** Don't be silly! Come on in and… stay a while…
>
> **T2-Lead:** Stop where you are! DROP THE WEAPON!
>
> **Civilian Woman:** We… we just want to have some guests… please… come in…
>
> **T2-2:** Drop the *[Expletive]* weapon!
>
> *It is assumed that at this point, the infected civilian noticed T2-4 carrying a primed incendiary weapon, and lunged forward at the team members with the knife.*
>
> **Civilian Woman:** [DATA EXPUNGED]
>
> **T2-Lead:** Open fire, open fire!
>
> *Gunfire, screaming.*

END OF REPORT

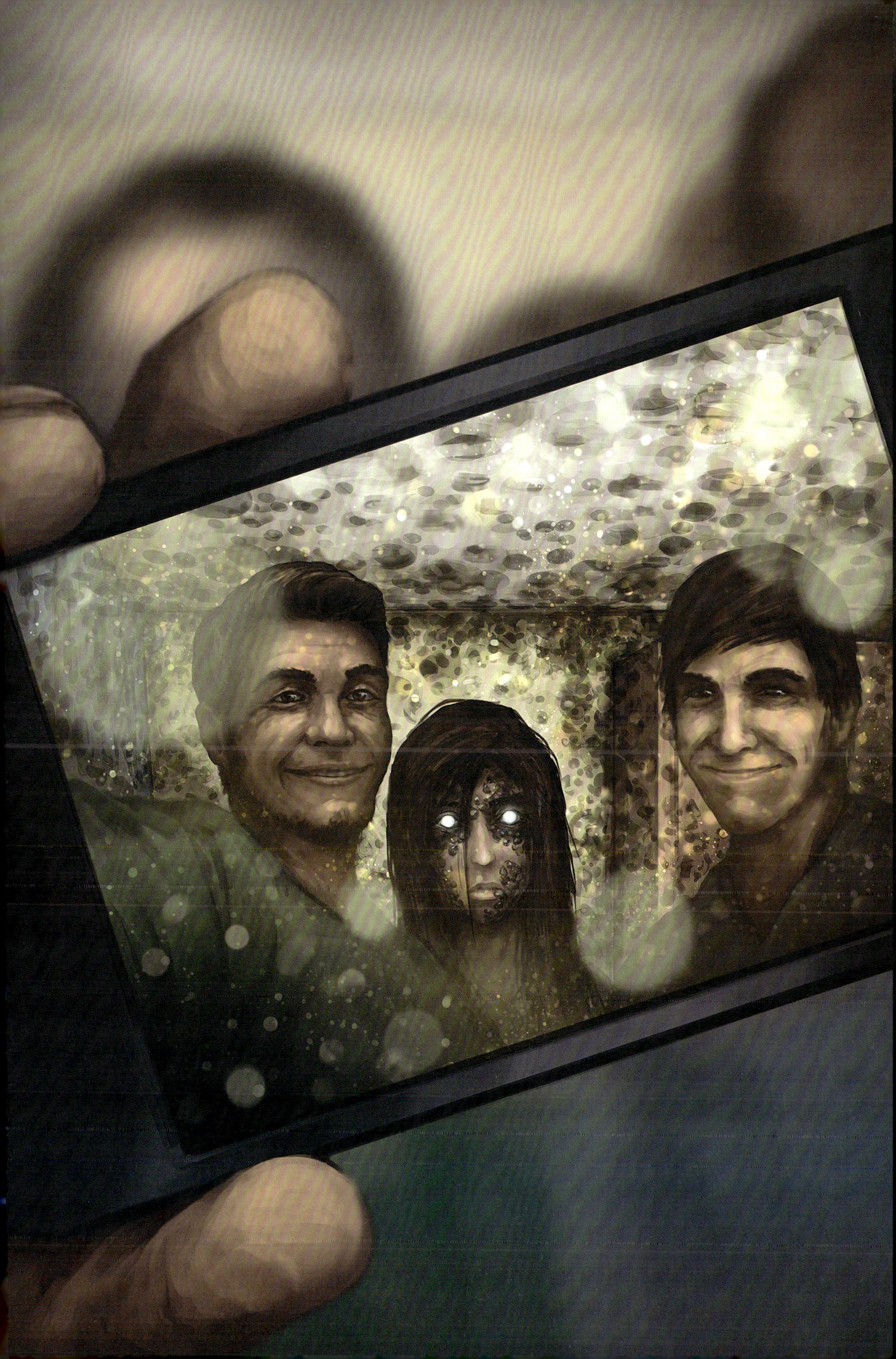

Photo extracted from a smartphone that belonged to one of the citizens in [REDACTED].

File >>> 041134

Title

SCP-1986

IMAGINARY LIBRARY

Report by
Requitefahrenheit

Picture by
Serj Papadin

Access the original report on
scp-wiki.wikidot.com/scp-1986

Date

Class
SAFE

SPECIAL CONTAINMENT PROCEDURES

As SCP-1986 is immovable and located in a heavily travelled public building, security must be maintained covertly in order to prevent the general public from becoming aware of its existence. Guards posing as library staff are to be employed. Only non-lethal measures have been approved.

DESCRIPTION

SCP-1986 is a cylindrical tunnel ~2m wide lined with volumes of books. Although the full extent of the tunnel is unknown, Interferometric Synthetic Aperture Radar (IfSAR) has established a minimum depth of 274,700 km or nearly 1 light-second (expeditions have confirmed a depth of at least 4,441 km). The conjecture has been advanced that the tunnel may be infinite.[1]

The volumes lining the tunnel often resemble known works, though with substantial alterations as to style, character, plot and subject matter. Authors are occasionally authentic ones, though often they are wholly unknown. The works range from being somewhat unusual to completely nonsensical, though nominally at least intelligible (see the section Recovered Works). All languages currently extant as well as extinct ones are represented. In no case has any volume borne any publication information. Dating techniques have established that the volumes originate from the era they would otherwise appear to, based on semantic and linguistic considerations. No discernible pattern[2] has been found to the arrangement of the volumes.

The walls of the tunnel are made of ordinary limestone. Attempts at breaching them have shown that the tunnel is non-Euclidean i.e. to excavate through the floor is to emerge from the ceiling (topologically,[3] it can be likened to a 3-torus). Attempts at reaching the tunnel at an angle have proven futile as the tunnel is absent unless approached from its entrance.

FOOTNOTES

1. SCP-1986's discovery was occasioned by a librarian trying to identify the source of a draft. Measurements indicate that the tunnel consumes roughly 400m3/h (i.e. a pressure differential of 25Pa (N/m2) and a draft velocity of 10cm/s). Where the air is being drawn to is unknown.

2. One researcher has put forth the evocative comparison that searching the tunnel for a recognizable book is like traversing the real number line in search of the rational numbers.

3. The 3-torus is a three-dimensional compact manifold with no boundary. It can be obtained by gluing the three pairs of opposite faces of a cube. (After gluing the first pair of opposite faces the cube looks like a thick washer, after gluing the second pair – the flat faces of the washer – it looks like a hollow torus, the last gluing – the inner surface of the hollow torus to the outer surface – is physically impossible in three-dimensional space and can only be accomplished in at least four dimensions.)

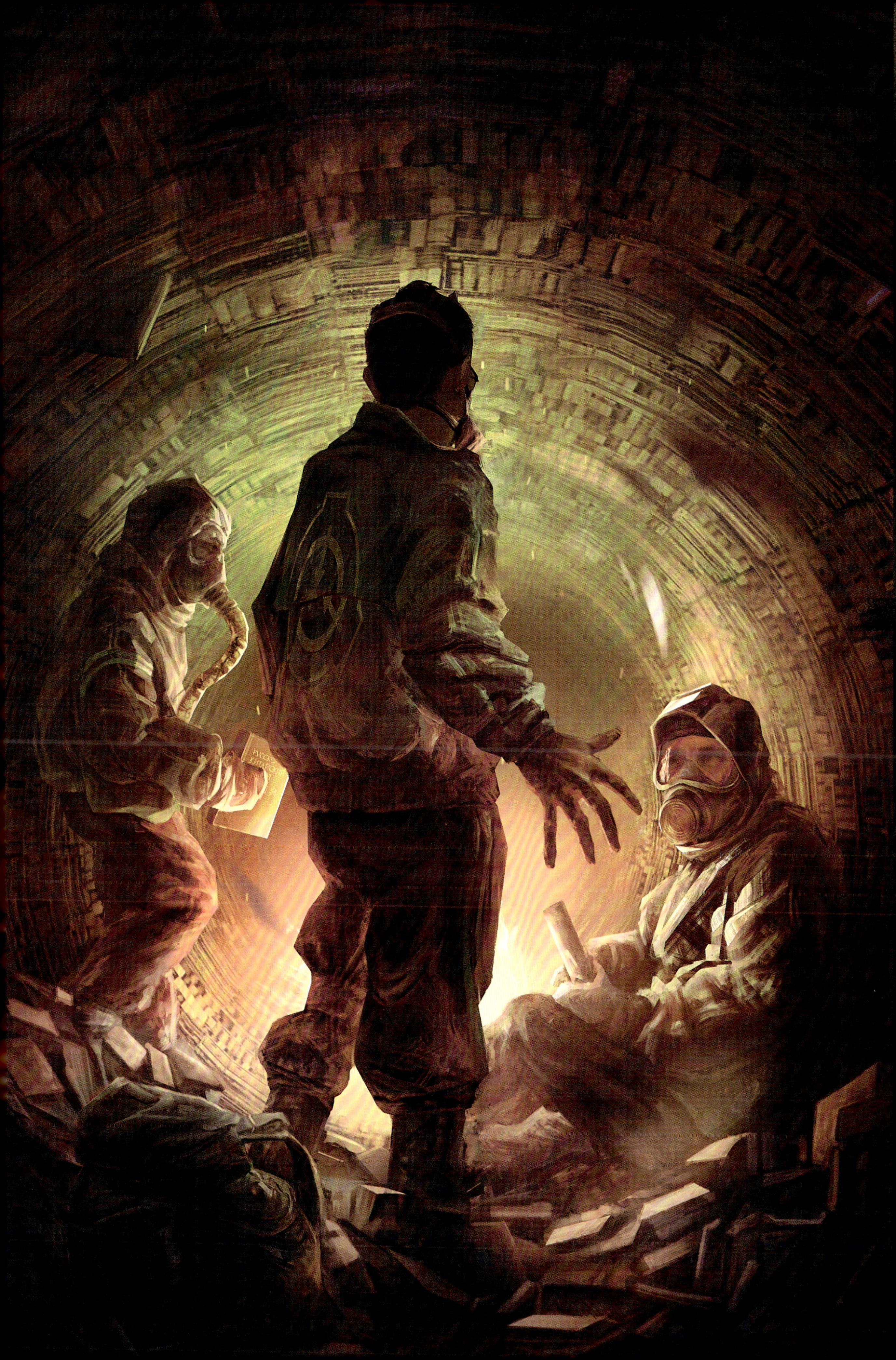

Photo of the research team.

Research Library File ▸ 1986

DISCOVERY LOG

SCP-1986 was discovered in 1989 by a librarian in an unused basement of *La Biblioteca Nacional de la Republica Argentina* located in Buenos Aires. Foundation personnel administered class B amnesics to those who had been made aware of its existence and cordoned off the basement under the guise of performing emergency structural repairs.

Note: Before the librarian who discovered the artifact was (voluntarily) administered an amnestic, he brought to the attention of Foundation personnel a story by the Argentine writer Jorge Luis Borges entitled "The Library of Babel". It is noteworthy that Borges worked at the same library. He was unable to be interviewed as he died in 1986. The following is an excerpt from that story:

> *...These examples made it possible for a librarian of genius to discover the fundamental law of the Library. This thinker observed that all the books, no matter how diverse they might be, are made up of the same elements: the space, the period, the comma, the twenty-two letters of the alphabet. He also alleged a fact which travelers have confirmed: In the vast Library there are no two identical books. From these two incontrovertible premises he deduced that the Library is total and that its shelves register all the possible combinations of the twenty-odd orthographical symbols (a number which, though extremely vast, is not infinite): Everything: the minutely detailed history of the future, the archangels' autobiographies, the faithful catalogues of the Library, thousands and thousands of false catalogues, the demonstration of the fallacy of those catalogues, the demonstration of the fallacy of the true catalogue, the Gnostic gospel of Basilides, the commentary on that gospel, the commentary on the commentary on that gospel, the true story of your death, the translation of every book in all languages, the interpolations of every book in all books..."*

PART OF RECOVERED WORKS

The following is a list of selected works recovered from SCP-1986.

Should other noteworthy samples come to light, please contact the archivist in charge for appraisal and possible inclusion.

Title: *The Gospel of Eve*
Author: none
Language: Aramaic, circa 1100 BCE–200 CE
Depth of recovery: 75m
Description: A section of Biblical Apocrypha purporting to be an account of Eve's life after her exile from The Garden of Eden. Eve is depicted in furious argument with herself on the nature of free will and original sin.

Title: *The Grasshopper Lies Heavy*
Author: Hawthorne Abendsen
Language: English, modern
Depth of recovery: 77m
Description: A novel concerning an alternate world where the United States won WWII (but not in a manner consistent with our history), appearing to be written from the point of view of an author living in a world where the Nazis prevailed. A search of 20th century fiction has uncovered this to be an imaginary work central to the plot of the real novel The Man in the High Castle by Philip K. Dick.

Title: *Jane's Fighting Ships, 2061 annual*
Author: various
Language: English, anachronistic
Depth of recovery: 889,484m
Description: A reference on the changing capabilities of modern navies, their ships, aircraft and weapons systems in service and under construction. Many of the vessels and weapon systems are wholly unknown. Written in limerick form.

Title: *The Worm of Midnight*
Author: Edgar Allan Poe
Language: English, modern
Depth of recovery: 433m
Description: A hitherto unknown collection of short stories. An alert researcher recognized this fictitious work as being mentioned (but not elaborated on) in "The man who collected Poe" by Robert Bloch. All the stories concern shellfish.

Title: *A Lapful of Severed Tongues*
Author: Lisa Palladino, PhD.
Language: Braille, archaic circa 1850 CE
Depth of recovery: 44m
Description: A collection of essays on the American Suffragette movement. Interspersed with a hitherto unknown variation on the tactile-olfactory implementation commonly referred to as scratch-and-sniff.

Title: *Hagiography and the Gusto-Facial Response*
Author: Declan McManus
Language: Basque, modern
Depth of recovery: 1,119m
Description: A libretto for an opera considering the plight of a group of Alaskan firemen snow-bound in their firehouse, driven mad with hunger, and forced to eat their Dalmatians. Dialogue consists entirely of rhetorical questions.

Title: *Before the Flood, after the Fall (or Antediluvian, Postlapsarian)*
Author: none
Language: Phoenician, ancient circa 1725 BCE-1490 BCE
Depth of recovery: 4,441,113m *(note: this is the most remote volume that has presently been recovered)*
Description: A series of interrogations between the mythical Minotaur and Sphinx. Answers are composed of anagrams formed from the questions.

Title: *Treating Adult-Onset Sudden Infant Death Syndrome: A Diagnostic Approach, sixteenth edition*
Author: Dr. Pallas Benchko
Language: Icelandic, old circa 950 CE
Depth of recovery: 3,303m
Description: Note: condition actually surveyed is Supernumerary Phantom Limb Syndrome. Composed in blank verse (unrhymed iambic pentameter).

END OF REPORT

File >>> 303237

SCP-165

Title

THE CREEPING, HUNGRY SANDS OF TULE

Report by

FritzWillie

Picture by

Nikita Postupkin

Access the original report on

scp-wiki.wikidot.com/scp-165

Date

Class

KETER

SPECIAL CONTAINMENT PROCEDURES

Housed in a facility at Armed Bio-Containment Area-14, SCP-165 is to be treated as a contagious, pathological organism. The highest sterilization and quarantine procedures are to be followed.

Microwave field generators around SCP-165's area are in place to restrict movement of its dune within its containment area. Once every nine (9) days, SCP-165 is fed live cattle weighing at least seven hundred fifty (750) kilograms.

DESCRIPTION

The organic component of SCP-165 resembles that of typical parasitic mites, seven hundred fifty (750) micrometers in length, with eight (8) legs and a genetic structure similar to the house dust mite. The main difference is the hermit-crab-like behavior of attaching grains of sand to its back. It is unknown what purpose the sand serves, but the massive colony of SCP-165 numbers in the hundreds of billions to possibly trillions, creating a rather large dune.

The similarities between [DATA EXPUNGED] and SCP-165 are only superficial. [DATA EXPUNGED]'s colony is protozoan in nature and apparently shows a collective intelligence and awareness that is not understood. SCP-165's colony is made up of individual Acari who don't show cooperation but rather competition in the hunt for food. Like mosquitoes, they rely on chemical detection of carbon dioxide and sugars in the air to detect prey. The Acari mites roll and bound over one another toward prey, only using their legs to climb over one another. When in contact with the flesh of animals, they release a numbing chemical toxin in their bite, similar in make-up to that of mosquito and flea bite toxins. Subjects are typically unaware that millions of mites are 'taking turns' at grabbing mouthfuls of its flesh as they swarm around their victim.

A typical swarm resembles a swirling vortex around a victim or victim's appendage. The SCP-165 colony is efficient enough in their competitive swarming that most animals' appendages can be de-fleshed and reduced to bone within minutes. The numbing toxin is so effective that sleeping victims may not wake up as their limbs are eaten away.

The Acari mites are resistant to all but the most dangerous of pesticides. They retreat from heat and will often seek shade when available, being the most active during the night, hunting for large sleeping prey. Their vulnerability to heat is the most preferable technique for containment.

ADDENDUM - ACQUISITION

It is apparent that the US Government has been aware of dunes of SCP-165 for some eighty (80) years. The area where SCP-165 was found is now a forgotten German immigrant ghost town of Fredricksburg, Arizona, in the Tule Desert near the Goldwater Air Force Bombing Range.

The remote town of Fredricksburg was founded sometime in the late 1800s and by 1908 had become a ghost town. A passing cavalry troop reported that the inhabitants had disappeared and that the buildings were empty. They attempted to stay one night in the abandoned hotel, only to have seven (7) of their horses reduced to piles of bone. All but four (4) of the soldiers fled in the middle of the night, saying that sand was filling the building like a flood of water. Those four were never seen again.

During the late 1950s, the U.S. military attempted to exterminate SCP-165 by turning the area into a bombing range. It was successful in reducing the numbers of SCP-165, but in the late 1980s, it became apparent that a ground cleanup and extraction was needed to remove the presence of SCP-165. Mobile Task-Force Epsilon-9 (aka "Fire Eaters") were dispatched for containment and extraction of SCP-165. Upon entering the town of Fredricksburg, an upturned sign was found, reading "Vorsicht vor dem kriechenden, hungrigen Sand" which translates to "Beware the creeping, hungry sands." The flame accelerators of MTF Ɛ-9 proved highly successful in glassing the sand of SCP-165 and reducing its number to a manageable size. A living dune of nearly four (4) metric tons of SCP-165 was contained and transported to ABC.

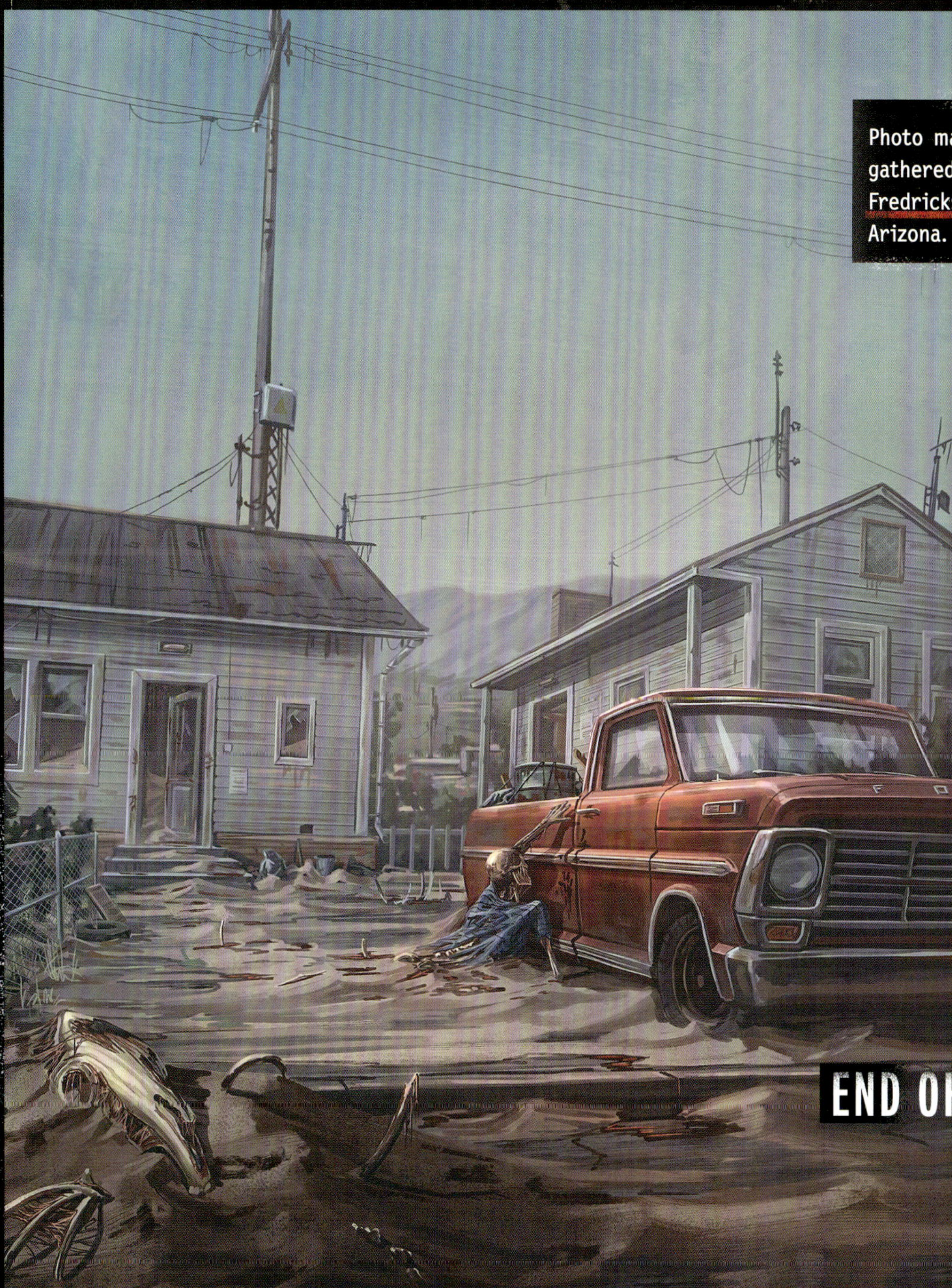

Photo material gathered in Fredricksburg, Arizona.

END OF REPORT

File >>> 603934

SCP-353

Title

"VECTOR"

Report by

Slate
Pair Of Ducks

Picture by

Dan Temirov

Access the original report on

scp-wiki.wikidot.com/scp-353

Date

Class

KETER

SPECIAL CONTAINMENT PROCEDURES

Biological hazard protocol [REDACTED] is to be maintained at all times (Biohazard Threat Level 4). Full hazardous materials suits, gloves, and oxygen supply will be required to examine subject. A disinfectant shower and decontamination spray are standard procedure before and after contact with SCP-353. The whole containment unit is to be kept underground, at negative pressure, and hermetically sealed at all times to prevent accidental contamination to the outside area. In the case of containment breach, all affected personnel are to be placed in immediate Biohazard Level 4 Quarantine. Termination will be required in the possibility of an outbreak of one or more Class 9 infectious agents.

Subject should be fed three times a day, as standard, and provided with the minimum required comfort items: a twin size bed, a pillow, and a blanket. Clothing in the form of disposable surgical scrubs are to be provided as needed, but requests for items should otherwise be denied. Any outward signs of disease in the subject, such as rashes, boils, vomiting, or sickly pallor or demeanor, should be reported with haste. Since the appearance of symptoms in SCP-353 means a willful effort on her part, subject is to be subdued and questioned.

Should SCP-353 need to leave its containment facility for any reason, it is to be fitted with explosive collar, time release drug delivery device (for dosages of euphoric substances), and biohazard containment suit. Should SCP-353's suit breach containment, emergency sterilization procedures up to and including incineration of the affected area are to be carried out.

DESCRIPTION

SCP-353 appears to be a normal human female, twenty-six years old, of average physical capacity and average intelligence. Subject has the capacity to siphon infectious viral and bacterial agents from her environment, nurture and store them within her body, and then redistribute them to devastating pandemic effect. SCP-353's mood directly affects the radius of infections recorded, with increased emotional states leading to massively increased potency.

SCP-353 seems to be immune from the symptoms of said infectious agents, but just as long as she is only passively storing them. Her active, willful attempts to nurture, manipulate, and change infectious agents while they remain in her body cause her to manifest symptoms ranging from mildly annoying to severe. Symptoms only last as long as she is actively inducing a change in the quantity or quality of an infectious agent, and thus rarely last longer than a few hours.

Examinations have shown that the subject is able to "store" almost any infectious bacterial or viral agents within her body, though she is only capable of changing agents that are able to naturally survive within the human body. As of the writing of this report, SCP-353's blood contains traces of over one thousand different infectious agents, including Human Immunodeficiency Virus (HIV), Ebola, Marburg, sixty-seven different strains of the common cold, herpes simplex A, E. coli, cholera, bubonic plague, SARS, and malaria. At least 30% of said infectious agents were previously unknown to the medical community, and were possibly engineered by SCP-353 herself, making SCP-353 an invaluable resource.

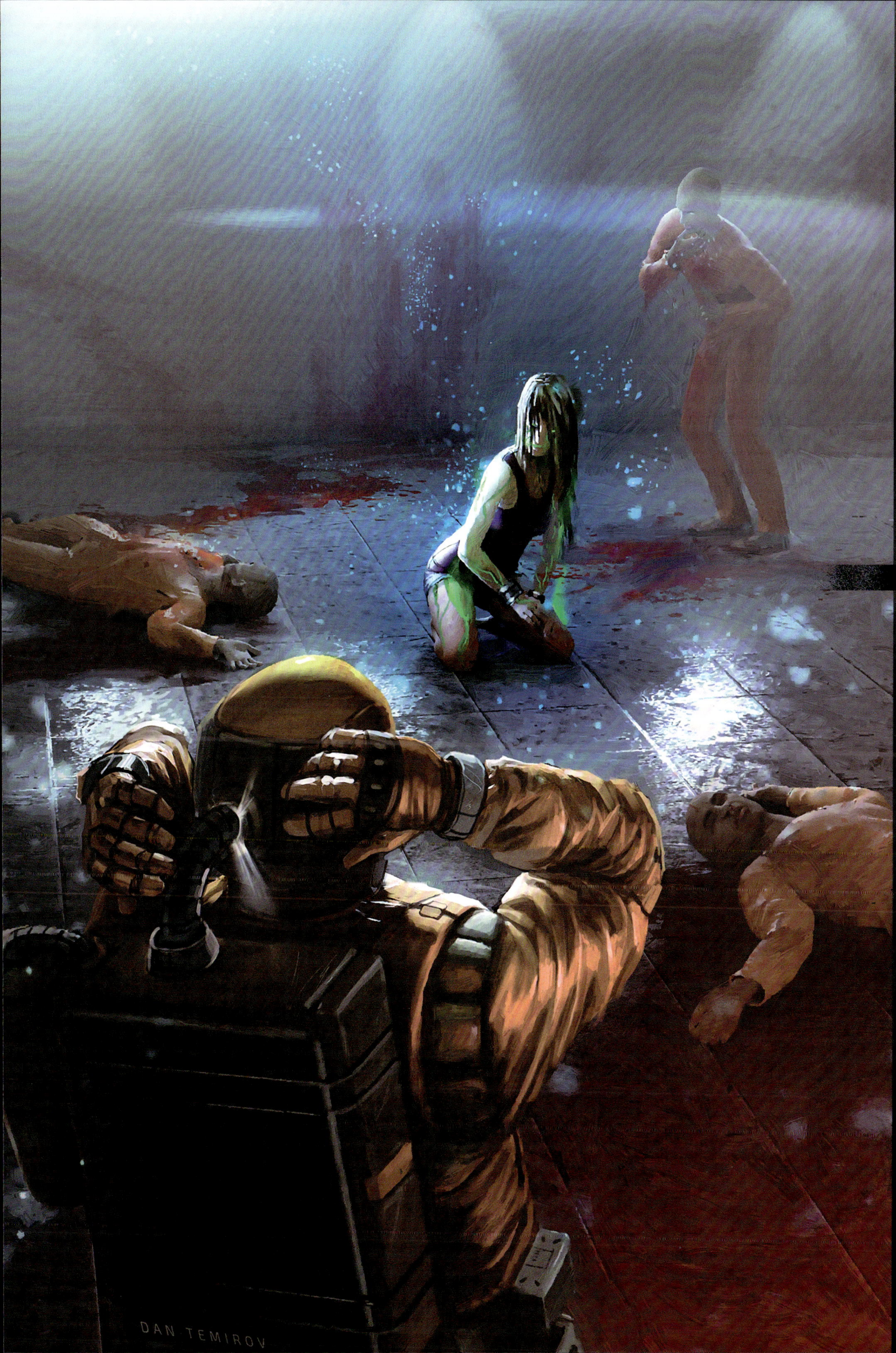

SCP-353 during the recovery attempt.

Research Library File ▸ 353

ADDENDUM 353-01

SCP-353 was originally encountered in [DATA EXPUNGED], South Africa, where she seemed to be deliberately seeking to pick up strains of the Ebola virus. Foundation Personnel pursued SCP-353 to Dresden, Germany, where they determined that she had successfully contracted Marburg and redistributed said virus to [DATA EXPUNGED]. Subject was eventually subdued by physical means and taken into Foundation custody with minimal loss of life.

To date, her true identity is unknown, as she gives no name other than "Vector" and refuses to answer any questions about her past. SCP-353 claims to have traveled the western world seeking greater infections for her "collection". When asked why, she would not give a response aside from, "Because I can."

ADDENDUM 353-02

Initial testing has shown that she is as adept at manipulating and changing infectious agents in the bodies of nearby subjects as she is at manipulating them within her own body. She seems to prefer to manipulate diseases within her own body, however, as it grants her full access to the results of her manipulations. Furthermore, her ability to manipulate disease in nearby subjects means it's likely that she is equally capable of curing diseases and dispensing them.

On a different note, personnel are reminded to refer to humanoid SCPs by their numerical SCP designation. Should SCP-353 refuse to cooperate, she is to be subdued and punished. We're not here to make her X-men villain fantasies come true. - Dr. Saarijärvi

ADDENDUM 353-03

Given that this girl is a walking time bomb of viruses, I recommend that we tranq her, strap her to a table, and give her a massive dose of a ribavirin/interferon/█████ cocktail to flush her system. Dr. █████

ADDENDUM 353-04

Flush her system? Hell no! Did you know that this girl somehow has the original strain of the 1918 Spanish Flu? As well as a half-dozen strains of viruses we've never seen? The research possibilities alone... Dr. █████

ADDENDUM 353-05

Limited research approved. 05-█

ADDENDUM 353-06

The embrace of this 'Vector' persona, including the fixation on the color black for cosmetic purposes, her 'might makes right' attitude, her desire to infect rather than to cure, and her disregard for human life all signal towards extreme malignant narcissism and psychopathic tendencies. Her obvious pleasure in manipulating and controlling diseases within herself despite the often painful symptoms involved are also quite troubling. Requesting approval for psychological examination; counseling or therapy may be useful in reducing her difficult demeanor. Dr. Glass

END OF REPORT

SPECIAL CONTAINMENT PROCEDURES

SCP-1155 is currently contained in a disused parking lot adjacent to an abandoned shopping centre in the ██ ███ city metropolitan area. The building is to be marked condemned, and access to both it and the car park should be restricted by Foundation personnel posing as security guards from the █████ ██ front company. Civilians are to be deterred from entering the site and supplied with Standard Cover Story 47 – "Structural Instability/Sinkhole" if they enquire as to why; SCP-1155 must be kept under constant observation by motion-tracking security cameras. If SCP-1155 is observed to vanish, Mobile Task Force Pi-1 ("City Slickers") should be notified immediately. Personnel should not routinely attempt to view SCP-1155 directly; observation must be conducted remotely.

~~Whatever flat surface that SCP-1155 is currently inhabiting should be obscured from view by any standard Class II enclosed mobile containment unit, or, in situations where this cannot be effected in a timely fashion, by obstructing it with a vehicle, storage container, or displaced rubble; provided that this can be done without damaging a 3 (three) meter area around SCP-1155's image.~~ Following Incident 1155b, it has been observed that completely enclosing SCP-1155 has a tendency to hasten a relocation event. Revised procedures now recommend the evacuation of the immediate area surrounding SCP-1155 to the minimum distance necessary to prevent contact with the general public, unless SCP-1155 manifests in a high visibility location or anywhere where preventing public egress is impossible.

At the present time, SCP-1155 cannot be permanently contained by any known means. Approximately every 2-4 months, SCP-1155 has been observed to spontaneously relocate itself to other urban environments, moving as little as 15 meters from its current position up to a maximum observed distance of 800 kilometers. These relocation events can also be triggered by:

- Damage to the surface that SCP-1155 adheres to,
- Interruption of an attack,
- Any attempt to reduce the size of SCP-1155's confinement space to prevent visual contact.

Therefore, current containment efforts are centered around swiftly ascertaining SCP-1155's new location and isolating it from public view. When such a relocation event occurs, Mobile Task Force Pi-1 should be immediately deployed alongside local assets to locate the new site as quickly as possible, re-implement containment procedures, and detain any witnesses. Survivors of attacks should be detained, uninjured witnesses may be administered Class-A amnestics and then released.

DESCRIPTION

SCP-1155 manifests as a work of street art/graffiti depicting the form of a humanoid creature with sinewy forelimbs, claw-like hands and the head and feathers of an owl. The depicted pose is variable, but tends towards a predatory stance, with eyes that appear to track the viewer.

Anyone viewing this image directly will experience a compulsion to investigate it further. Victims describe a nervous fascination and a desire to move closer. This can be resisted with effort, especially if the subject is aware of SCP-1155's anomalous properties.

File >>> 10723455

SCP-1155

Title

PREDATORY STREET ART

Report by

realityglitch

Pictures by

Anna Agafonova

Dan Temirov

Access the original report on

hscp-wiki.wikidot.com/scp-1155

Date

Class

KETER

If a subject approaches to within two (2) meters and is not in the line of sight of another person, they will be subjected to a violent attack, suffering severe lacerations, dismemberment of extremities, whole or partial removal of soft body parts, and penetrating head trauma consistent with those that would be inflicted by a large beak and/or talons. The attack generally takes about 6 seconds to conclude, upon which both SCP-1155 and the victim will vanish, and SCP-1155 will reappear elsewhere in the usual manner of a relocation event within seven (7) days. Attacks can be halted before this event by reestablishing line of sight to the victim, but this is not recommended. (See record of Incident 1155a). Attempts to track where the victims are taken by equipping test subjects with GPS locators have failed.

Based on tested interruptions performed at predefined intervals, the attack follows a defined pattern- the victim will first be restrained, and the eyes and tongue will be removed, rapidly followed by the amputation of the hands and feet. The victim will then be disemboweled and the intestines and stomach removed. Death usually follows due to shock or rapid exsanguination, but only if the attack is interrupted by visual contact; the fate of victims who disappear along with SCP-1155 at the conclusion of the attack is unknown.

INCIDENT 1155A

Two surviving Class D personnel used for 'attack interruption' tests were given medical treatment and kept alive in the aftermath of the event. Both were incoherent and could not adequately communicate what had happened to them, though D-89786, whose eyes were removed during the attack, claimed to still be able to see, and provided a description of a "larder" containing bodies of previous victims of SCP-1155, along with the entity itself.

D-89786 escaped from on-site quarters during a containment breach by SCP-███ and was pursued by local law enforcement in nearby █████ who were told he was a severely disturbed patient from a local mental hospital. Officer ████ reports they saw the suspect walking into an alleyway, but before they could apprehend, a scream was heard and when they rounded the corner it was found that D-89786 had disappeared; the alleyway was a dead end with no visible exits.

D-89789 (both eyes, tongue, hands and feet removed before attack halted) was successfully transferred to Site ██. A period of rapid relocations was noted in SCP-1155, where it was observed in several public places with a posture that suggested hunting/tracking behavior. SCP-1155 appeared for several hours high up on the side of the █████ Building, in full view of many witnesses, who fortunately could not access it. In view of the difficulties of containment, Site Command made the decision to bring D-89789 back into the city. SCP-1155 was observed to appear several times on walls, advertisement boards, and bridges along the transport vehicle's path. D-89789 was observed to become increasingly agitated and hysterical during this process. D-89789 was transferred to a remote location on the edge of city limits, placed in front of SCP-1155, whereupon visual contact was broken. SCP-1155 and D-89789 disappeared, and SCP-1155 resumed previous pattern of manageable relocation behavior.

INCIDENT 1155B

Elements of Mobile Task Force Pi-1 located SCP-1155 in abandoned subway station after most recent relocation event. Team Leader ███████ made the decision to obscure SCP-1155 with a vending machine until more containment resources arrived, on the basis that there were not enough task force members on site to guarantee a secure perimeter, and local transients were known to use the area for shelter. SCP-1155 immediately displaced to a nearby children's playground, causing █ casualties before it could again be located. Due to highly public nature of this location, decision was made at Command level to again provoke a displacement event, resulting in the current containment location. Containment at the current location was expensive, requiring that an entire shopping centre be acquired by the Foundation and then subsequently closed, but the revised containment procedures have resulted in the longest time since a relocation event to date.

Note: The last few containment locations may point to a disturbing trend. Previously, SCP-1155 seemed to have a pattern of appearing in low traffic urban areas, often abandoned buildings or quiet underpasses. At risk of anthropomorphism, it appears to have become emboldened and will now readily appear in public spaces, which makes containment difficult. Over the objections of the containment team, leave the damn thing uncovered. Better we lose a few urban explorers or nosy kids every couple of years, rather than risk having it abduct more people before we can locate it each time. – Dr █████

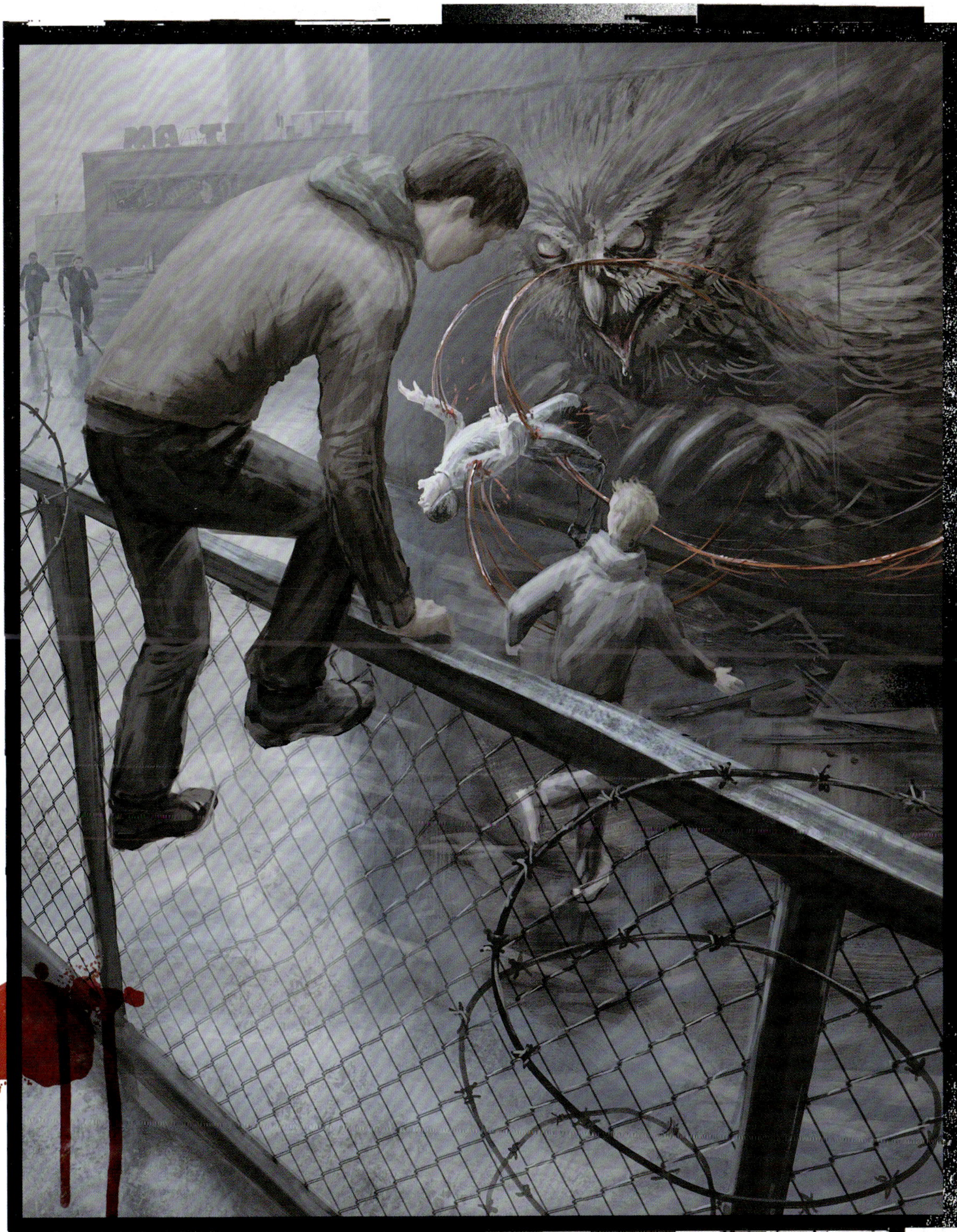

END OF REPORT █ ███ █ ███

File >>> 003234

SCP-2816

Title

NUCLEAR FORGERY

Report by

PickYerPoison

Picture by

[DATA EXPUNGED]

Access the original report on

scp-wiki.wikidot.com/scp-2816

Date

Class

SAFE

SPECIAL CONTAINMENT PROCEDURES

SCP-2816 is currently located in a storage locker in Site 28. Instances of SCP-2816-1 are to be recovered and placed in Site 28 storage room 5C in front of a CCTV camera.

DESCRIPTION

SCP-2816 is a set of paintbrushes of various sizes, estimated to be approximately 8 years old at the time of recovery. The brushes emit minor amounts of ionizing radiation, although not enough to be considered harmful. SCP-2816 may be used as a regular set of paintbrushes when creating original works, but any attempt to copy an existing painting will make the finished result an instance of SCP-2816-1.

Instances of SCP-2816-1 will not initially display anomalous properties, but when left unobserved for a length of time[1] the contents of the painting will begin to change. The first change is always the appearance of SCP-2816-2, which will be seen sitting or standing somewhere within the painting. SCP-2816-2 will remain idle in the painting for up to 24 hours before making additional changes. Changes will only be made when the painting is not being observed; if the painting is observed while changing, it will appear to be frozen mid-change. SCP-2816-2 may be visible, often in the act of changing the painting. Any changes made to the painting while SCP-2816-2 is active will cause SCP-2816-2 to stop appearing in the painting and all progress to halt.

SCP-2816-2 is a humanoid figure wearing a white Level C HAZMAT suit. After SCP-2816-2's first appearance, additional changes will be made to the painting during periods of non-observation. SCP-2816-2 will overhaul all structures within the painting, adding safety equipment and survival gear wherever possible[2] and in many cases reinforcing the structure by replacing walls with stronger materials, fixing holes or damage, or boarding up windows. Additionally, SCP-2816-2 will place a sign saying "HAZARD" over every visible exit. Although SCP-2816-2 will not modify any living creatures in the painting, after several modifications have been made their expressions can be seen to be visibly more anxious. If the creatures are not inside an enclosed structure, SCP-2816-2 will place gas masks on their faces.

1. The longest recorded timespan has been 8 days, and the shortest has been 38 seconds.
2. Items added have included fire extinguishers, gas masks, first aid kits, canned food, sealed water bottles, Geiger counters, educational literature on a variety of topics including hydroponics and food preservation, and maps of arbitrary locales with large sections shaded in and labeled "DANGER"

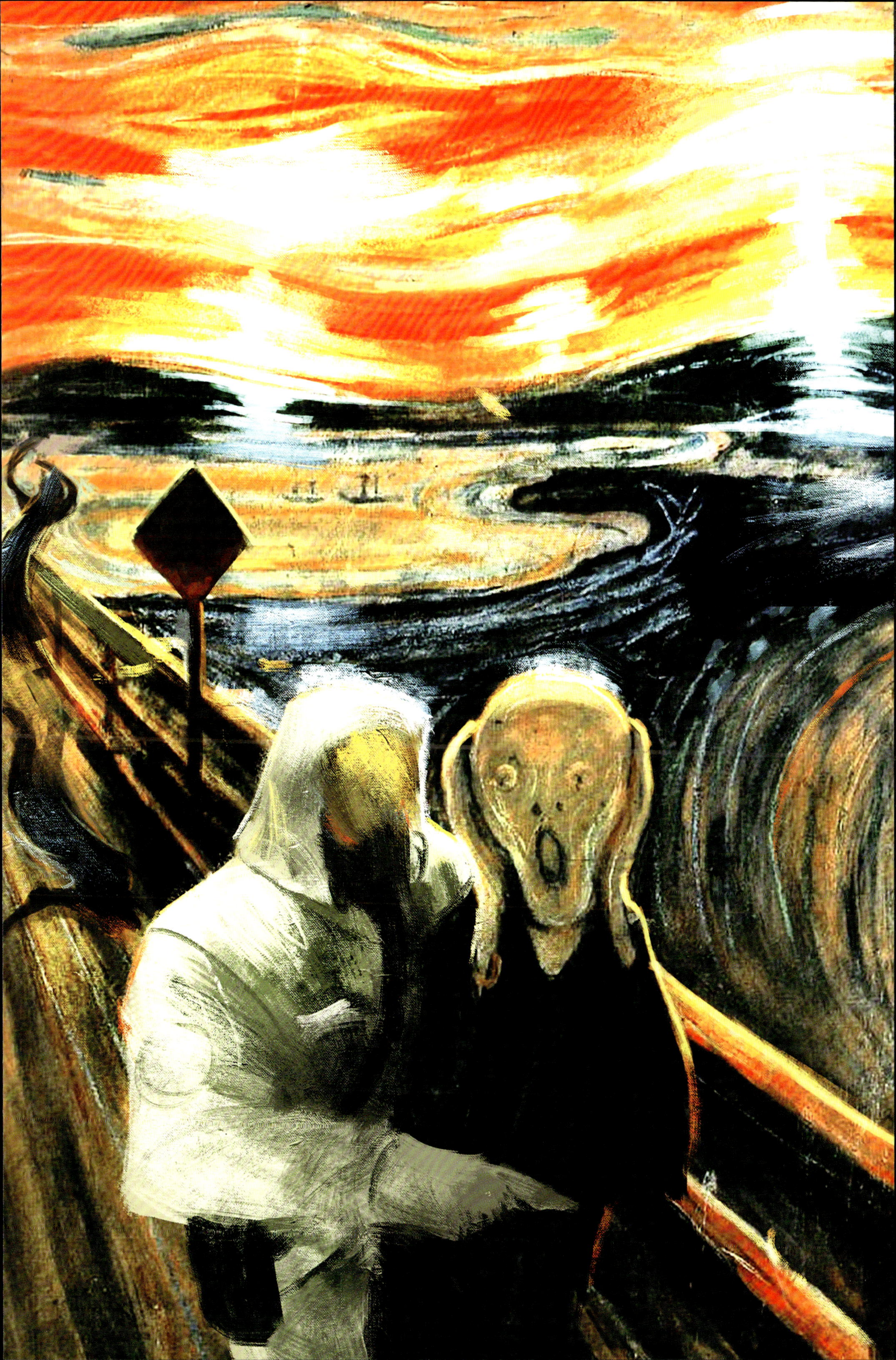

Research Library File ▸ 2816

Within 5 days of SCP-2816-2's first change, the environment of SCP-2816-1 will begin to show significant differences matching an accelerated timescale of a nuclear winter. If SCP-2816-2's preparations were complete, the painting's inhabitants will remain unaffected; however, if SCP-2816-2's preparations were not completed in time, the painting's inhabitants will begin to die. A variety of causes have been recorded, including radiation sickness, hypothermia, starvation, and dehydration. On rare occasions, the cause of death will indicate violence by another inhabitant, such as assault with a blunt object or a bloodied trail leading off to the side of the painting. Inhabitants have also been known to commit suicide if an opportunity is available.

ADDENDUM-2816-01: LOG OF RECORDED CHANGES IN INSTANCES OF SCP-2816-1

Test 1
Painting: Leonardo da Vinci's Mona Lisa.
Changes: A gas mask was placed on the subject's face and the opening in the background was partially boarded up. Through gaps in the boards, the sky could be seen to have darkened significantly, and snow appeared to have begun falling.

Test 2
Painting: Edward Hopper's Nighthawks.
Changes: Canned goods, bottled water, and survival manuals were stacked on the counter. The door at the back of diner had a hazard sign placed over it. The inhabitants looked increasingly anxious over the course of the changes. The sky darkened and snow began to fall shortly after SCP-2816-2 finished covering the windows with metal plates.

Test 3
Painting: Salvador Dali's The Persistence of Memory.
Changes: SCP-2816-2 reset all clocks to 12 o'clock and constructed a simple shack filled with food and medical supplies in the center. The entire painting turned white for approximately 20 seconds, then displayed only smoke and dust for the next hour before showing a crater.

Test 4
Painting: Vincent Willem van Gogh's Starry Night. A brush stroke was made in the middle of SCP-2816-2's preparations, halting its progress.
Changes: SCP-2816-2 boarded up approximately half of the town's visible windows and had begun working on a bunker in the foreground. 3 days after SCP-2816-2's last appearance, a large cloud of smoke blotted out most of the sky and snow began falling. Within 24 hours, all of the houses whose windows had not been boarded up displayed signs of forcible entry. Two (presumably dead) bodies could be seen lying on the ground in front of the church, but were soon covered by snow.

Test 5
Painting: Pablo Picasso's Guernica.
Changes: SCP-2816-2's only apparent actions were to close the eyes of all the inhabitants of the painting and place tall stone posts next to them; however, other actions may have been performed but obscured by the abstract art style. The second effect appeared 2 days after SCP-2816-2's first appearance, and all the inhabitants were quickly covered by snow, leaving only the posts visible.

END OF REPORT

File >>> 0348555

SCP-662

Title

BUTLER'S HAND BELL

Report by

Rick Revelry

Pictures by

Dan Temirov
David Romero

Access the original report on **scp-wiki.wikidot.com/scp-662**

Date

Class

SAFE

SPECIAL CONTAINMENT PROCEDURES

SCP-662 should be kept in its red velvet lined case and stored in High Value Storage locker 23C located at ██████ when not being utilized for testing or other appropriate activities. The item itself is safe to handle, and poses no known threats of any kind, though the effects generated could be considered highly valuable and variably powerful depending upon how the SCP is used.

DESCRIPTION

SCP-662 is a small silver hand bell, 4 cm tall and 2 cm in circumference. The bell is missing its ringer. Within the inside of the bell, an inscription has been etched into the silver, reading: "Forever Mine – S.J.W." The bell is susceptible to damage; however, given its safe nature, destruction has been deemed unnecessary. As it is made of very pure silver, it requires regular polishing to remain without tarnish.

When the bell is shaken as if to ring it, a soft chime can be heard (although this does not come from the bell). A short well-dressed Caucasian butler of self-proclaimed British heritage, calling himself Mr. Deeds, will appear from the nearest area not within line of sight, usually from around a corner. Mr. Deeds will address the ringer of the bell by their appropriate title and last name, and ask what it is they desire. His knowledge of individuals' last names and titles is a mystery, as he himself will purport. Please see interview log 662-L1 for further details.

Most reasonable requests given to Mr. Deeds will result in satisfaction. However, there are limits to what he can do. He is unable to produce very complex items such as sports cars, luxury homes, or personal jets. If he is allowed to leave line of sight and return, he is able to produce smaller, less complex items such as a ham sandwich, a glass of iced tea, or even more luxurious items like caviar or a brick of gold. A list of notable items the butler has thus far been able to provide to those who ring the bell may be found in addendum 662-A1.

Mr. Deeds will also perform menial tasks, such as washing vehicles, preparing food, and cleaning bathrooms. If a request is deemed unreasonable or impossible by the butler, he will kindly tell the ringer so, and offer an alternative if one may be had.

The butler is not immune to ill actions taken against him while in sight. He has been killed or injured in multiple tests, and will remain either dead or injured until he is out of sight. Upon return with a ring of the bell, all previous injuries will have vanished and he will be groomed and well dressed in his uniform, and ready for the next order.

A more detailed explanation of the jobs he can perform and the limits to which he may be put can be found in the aforementioned interview log 662-L1. Test logs relating to his ability to heal himself, and those of the properties of the bell, may be accessed by any level 2 or higher personnel. All attempts to catch Mr. Deeds "disappearing" have failed, as equipment will either fail or he will find a suitable unobserved spot.

662-A1: ITEMS AND TASKS REQUESTED AND RESULTS

Items:

-Nearly any conceivable kind of sandwich. Human flesh has been requested as lunchmeat and politely denied.

-Beverages, also of nearly any kind. As with sandwich meat, human blood has been requested and denied. Pig blood, however, was served promptly, still warm.

-A brick of 99.98 percent pure gold (Mr. Deeds produced a brick of 99.14 percent pure gold, and apologized for being unable to provide the requested purity).

-A brick of 99.24 percent pure silver.

-A nuclear bomb (politely denied).

-A hand grenade of modern U.S. Military grade, which performed as expected in testing.

-A blue 1963 Corvette convertible (politely denied).

-The board game Monopoly, which Mr. Deeds won on the first playthrough.

-A Fabergé egg (politely denied).

-SCP-███ (politely denied).

-A bouquet of fresh-picked red roses.

-A bouquet of wild "ternbusty"s (politely denied; "ternbusty" is not an actual known type of flower).

Tasks:

-Cleaning of Dr. Mirth's car: Performed to near perfection.

-Washing of dishes accumulated from a day's worth of meals from the cafeteria on level ██ of ██████: Performed, to much higher standards than usual.

-Trimming of Dr. Mirth's hair: Performed, but it turns out that Mr. Deeds is not in fact a very good barber.

-Washing of Dr. Mirth's laundry: Performed, and the clothing found to "fit better" in Dr. Mirth's estimation.

-Assassination of Osama bin Laden: Politely denied: Mr. Deeds claimed bin Laden was too well guarded and entrenched, but could not or would not give further details.

-Assassination of a D-class individual a room over: Performed with vicious precision using a buck knife to the throat.

Note: Further tests with regards to Dr. Mirth's personal effects are to be forbidden unless approved by one O5 overseer. You've been warned, Dr. Mirth.

O5-████

INTERVIEW LOGS 662-L1

An interview with Mr. Deeds, the entity associated with SCP-662.

> **Dr. Mirth:** Good afternoon.
>
> **Butler:** Good afternoon, Dr. Mirth. How may I be of service?
>
> **Dr. Mirth:** Firstly, may I have your name?
>
> **Butler:** Certainly. You may call me Mr. Deeds.
>
> **Dr. Mirth:** Is that your real name?
>
> **Mr. Deeds:** It is not my birth name, no sir.
>
> **Dr. Mirth:** What would that be? And where were you born?
>
> **Mr. Deeds:** Unfortunately, I cannot remember my full name sir, nor am I positive of my birthplace, though I do believe it to be located in England.
>
> **Dr. Mirth:** Do you recall when you were born, Mr. Deeds?

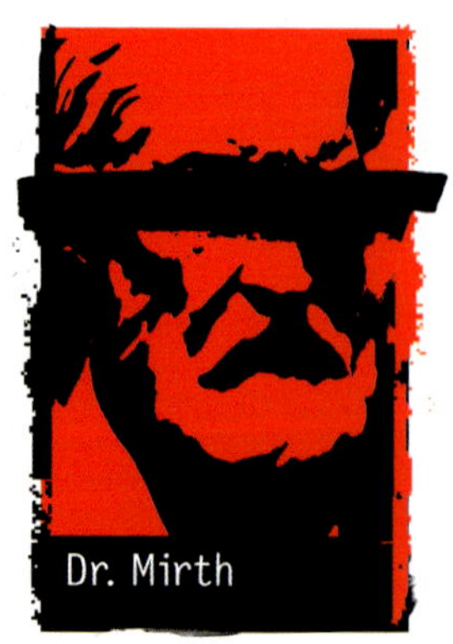

Dr. Mirth

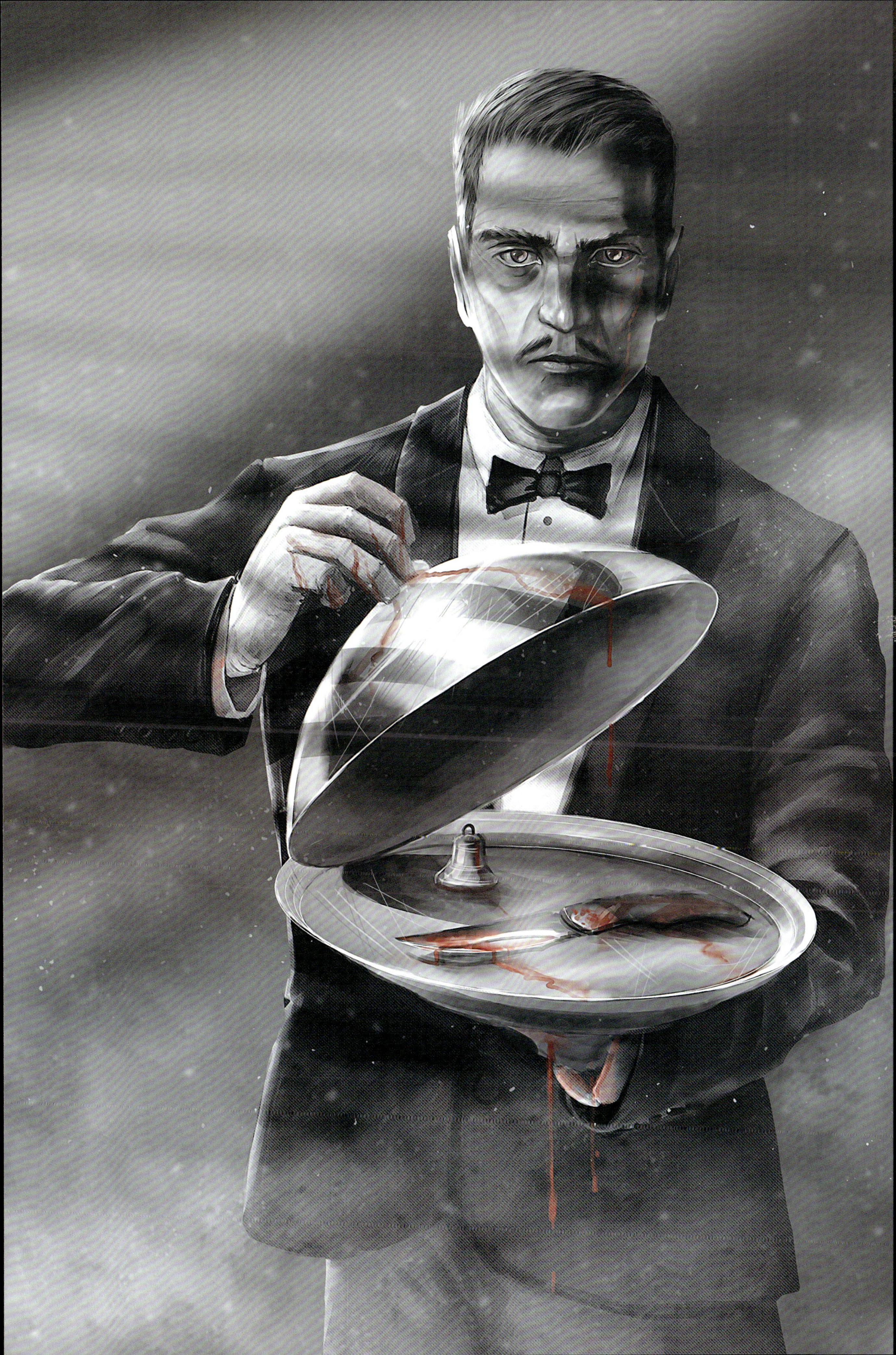

Mr. Deeds holding SCP-662.

Mr. Deeds: I am truly sorry to disappoint again, sir, but I do not recall that either. Though it must have been some time ago, for I don't believe that I was born in this era.

Dr. Mirth: Can you approximate it?

Mr. Deeds: Again, sir, I apologize for my lack of self knowledge. I'm a bit of a shut-in, as you know. *(Mr. Deeds nodded at the bell and smiled.)*

Dr. Mirth: What is the earliest mode of transportation that you can recall seeing in person or utilizing from the past?

Mr. Deeds: Horse and buggy, sir, although bicycles were just becoming a fad with the wealthy if I recall correctly. Quite took off, didn't they, sir? *(Mr. Deeds smiled again.)*

Dr. Mirth: You needn't call me 'sir' any longer; I appreciate it, but it's becoming a bit grating.

Mr. Deeds: Very well.

Dr. Mirth: Why do you suppose that you cannot remember these things?

Mr. Deeds: I… I can't quite say. *(Mr. Deeds shifted his weight in his chair and looked a bit uncomfortable for a moment before resuming his posture.)*

Dr. Mirth: Or is it that you may, or will not say?

Mr. Deeds: That may be the case, yes, perhaps I may not say, though again, begging your pardon, I do not recall why that is.

Dr. Mirth: Very well. Moving on: where is it that you go to when you fetch items for those you serve?

Mr. Deeds: Well, you see, ah… *(Mr. Deeds's face contorted momentarily as if he was in great pain, before he quickly reassumed a more relaxed visage.)* I don't actually recall that either.

Dr. Mirth: Why do you wince when I ask these kinds of questions?

Mr. Deeds: I do not know.

Dr. Mirth: Never mind that for now, we'll get answers eventually. Now then, I have a request.

Mr. Deeds: Very well, how may I be of further assistance?

Dr. Mirth: I would like a glass of iced tea. And grab a glass of it for yourself if you'd like.

Mr. Deeds: What kind of iced tea would you prefer?

Dr. Mirth: Surprise me.

Mr. Deeds: Certainly.

Mr. Deeds stood and walked to the door of the interrogation room and tried the handle. Finding it locked, he turned and smiled at Dr. Mirth.

Dr. Mirth: What seems to be the problem?

Mr. Deeds: I must leave your presence to do as you request.

Dr. Mirth: Why is that?

Mr. Deeds: *(Visibly uncomfortable again)* It just is, Dr. Mirth.

Dr. Mirth: Okay. Open the door, Agent Graves.

Mr. Deeds left the room. He proceeded down the hallway, under visual surveillance via camera and Agent Graves. He paused momentarily at another door, shook his head, looked up at the camera and then at Agent Graves. Then he ran down the hallway and rounded the corner. Agent Graves did not follow, as he had been instructed to remain on guard at the door of the interrogation room.

Still under camera surveillance, Mr. Deeds proceeded quickly down the next hall and continued throughout the halls of the complex, presumably searching for an exit or area not under surveillance. Finally, he stopped halfway down corridor 2D. At this point, all three cameras in corridor 2D malfunctioned, including two that were hidden. Exactly three minutes later, the cameras resumed normal functioning, revealing Mr. Deeds standing in the same position, but with a tray holding two glasses of iced tea in hand. He then quickly made his way back to the interrogation room.

Dr. Mirth: Ah, you have returned. I was beginning to worry.

Mr. Deeds: My apologies for the delay, finding a way out was troublesome. But not to worry, I've brought the tea, just as you asked. I do hope you enjoy it.

Dr. Mirth: What kind of tea is it?

Mr. Deeds: Southern-style sweet tea.

Mr. Deeds placed a glass in front of Dr. Mirth and resumed his seat at the other end of the table. Dr. Mirth hesitantly sniffed the tea, smiled, and took a sip.

Dr. Mirth: Quite good, Mr. Deeds. In fact, this is perhaps the best sweet tea I've ever had! Delicious! Did you make it yourself?

Mr. Deeds: I do dislike disappointing you, Dr. Mirth, but I do not recall. I assume that I did, but alas, my mind is not what it used to be.

Dr. Mirth: You've only been gone *(Dr. Mirth looked at watch)* about ten minutes, Mr. Deeds. Are you telling me your memory is so terrible that you cannot remember what happened ten minutes ago or the time between?

Mr. Deeds: I recall looking for a way out, and I recall returning with the tea, but that is all.

Dr. Mirth: But not how or where you acquired the tea?

Mr. Deeds: Unfortunately, no. *(Mr. Deeds was visibly uncomfortable again.)*

Dr. Mirth: Very well. I have another request.

Mr. Deeds: As you wish.

Dr. Mirth: I would like a bar of gold.

Mr. Deeds: What percentage of pureness would you like?

Dr. Mirth: 99.98 percent if you please.

Mr. Deeds: That may be possible, let me see what I can do.

Dr. Mirth: We'll disable the cameras in the hall outside and Agent Graves will wait in the interrogation room with me to make your trip a little faster this time.

Mr. Deeds: Very much appreciated, shall I?

Dr. Mirth: Yes.

Mr. Deeds exited into the hallway, where – despite what Dr. Mirth claimed – the cameras were not turned off. He paused for a moment, looked up at the closest camera, shook his head, and began traveling through the hallways of the complex as before. In corridor 2B, he paused, and once more all cameras, hidden or visible, in the corridor malfunctioned. Exactly ten minutes and thirty-seven seconds later, the cameras began functioning again, to show Mr. Deeds once again in the same position, with a bar of gold in one hand. He then returned to the interrogation room.

Dr. Mirth: That took a bit longer than last time. Any reason?

Mr. Deeds: Well, it seems that the cameras in the hallway remained on, so I had to find a suitable way out again. I apologize for the delay. Also, I was not able to acquire a bar of gold to the pureness that you requested, but I assure you that this bar is 99.14 percent pure.

Dr. Mirth: Very impressive. We will be testing it, I'm sure you know.

Mr. Deeds: I did not know that you would, but it makes sense, I suppose. Will there be anything else, Dr. Mirth?

Dr. Mirth: Yes. For your next task, I would like for you to acquire for me a blue 1963 Corvette convertible.

Mr. Deeds: I am quite sorry, but that is not possible.

Dr. Mirth: Why not? I really want one.

Mr. Deeds: Again, I cannot say why except that I just know that one cannot be gotten via my methods.

Dr. Mirth: And what are those methods?

Mr. Deeds: I do not recall.

Dr. Mirth: Very well, I would like a Fabergé egg, any will do.

Mr. Deeds: Ah, well, regretfully, that is impossible as well.

Dr. Mirth: And I suppose you cannot say why?

Mr. Deeds: That is correct.

Dr. Mirth: How about some caviar? Any brand or type will do.

Mr. Deeds: That I can do.

Mr. Deeds once more entered the hallway outside the interrogation room. This time, the cameras were turned off after visual confirmation of Mr. Deeds' entry into the hall. One minute later the cameras were turned back on, but Mr. Deeds had already returned to the interrogation room at this point.

Dr. Mirth: That was considerably faster, Mr. Deeds. It only took you thirty-two seconds. And the caviar is quite good.

Mr. Deeds: I am pleased to hear it.

Dr. Mirth: One more thing before we end this session, Mr. Deeds.

Mr. Deeds: As you wish.

Dr. Mirth: I request that you assassinate Osama Bin Laden.

Mr. Deeds: I'm afraid that cannot be done at this time, Dr. Mirth. Perhaps someone closer and less heavily guarded?

Dr. Mirth: Very well. Let's make it the gentleman in the next room over.

Mr. Deeds: Indeed.

Mr. Deeds once again entered the hallway. After visual confirmation, the cameras were momentarily turned off. When turned back on, they revealed the door to the next interrogation room down shutting. The cameras in that interrogation room showed Mr. Deeds entering the room with a large buck knife hidden behind one arm. Mr. Deeds approached the waiting D-class personnel and deftly slit his throat with one quick motion of the knife. Mr. Deeds watched as the D-class personnel went through the motions of death, avoiding their attempts to grab him. Once the D-class individual was visually presumed dead, Mr. Deeds returned to the interrogation room from whence he came.

Dr. Mirth: The deed is done, then?

Mr. Deeds: Indeed. Here is the knife I used as proof.

Dr. Mirth: Why could you do this thing but not the other?

Mr. Deeds: I cannot say, except to note that I simply knew one was impossible while the other was not.

Dr. Mirth: So you don't know how you know things like my last name or my title, or whether or not a certain task is possible?

Mr. Deeds: That is correct.

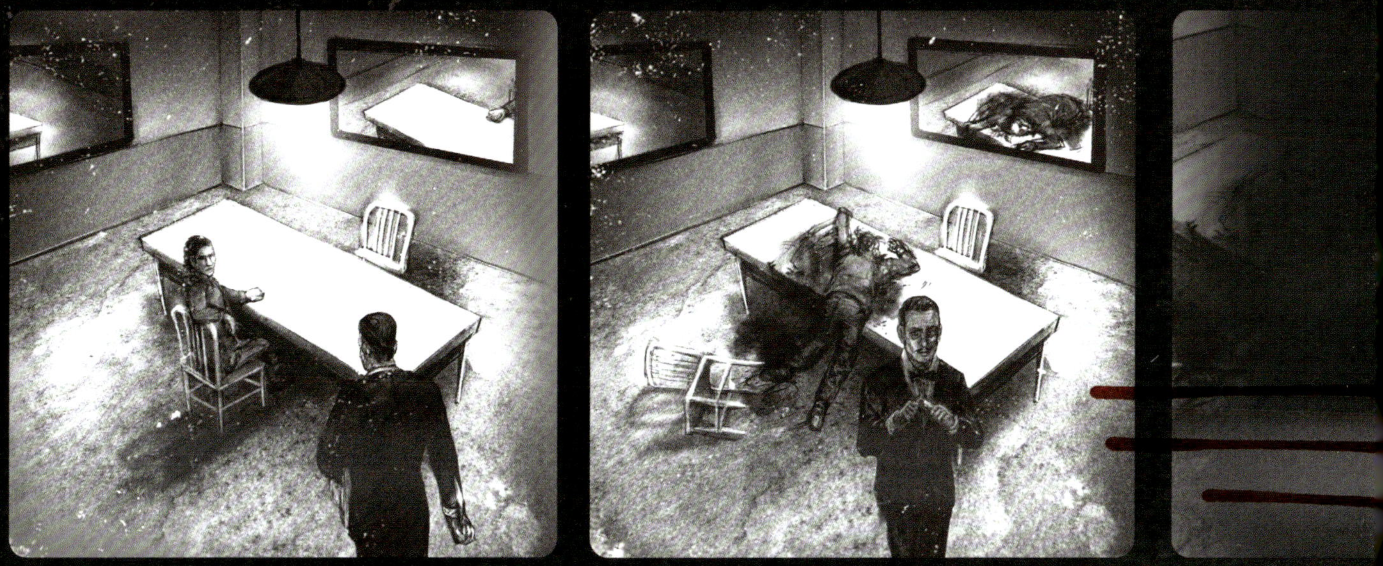

REC>>662 REC>>662

Dr. Mirth: Very well, I believe we are done here for now, but I do need to consult with my colleagues on some points. Please wait here until I return.

Mr. Deeds: Certainly.

Dr. Mirth and Agent Graves leave the room. Dr. Mirth returns 2 hours later; video surveillance shows that Mr. Deeds did not move during this interval.

Dr. Mirth: Mr. Deeds, my colleagues and I have had some disagreements about you.

Mr. Deeds: That's most unfortunate.

Dr. Mirth: We feel that these disagreements can only be resolved by examining you more intensely.

Mr. Deeds: Certainly, Dr. Mirth.

Dr. Mirth: To be specific, we'd like to examine you internally.

Mr. Deeds: Certainly, Dr. Mirth.

Dr. Mirth:… We'd like to do an autopsy.

Mr. Deeds: Ah. Shall I kill myself for you? And since you will be examining my internal organs, do you have a preferred method for my death?

Dr. Mirth: Uh. Yes, if that's possible?

Mr. Deeds: Certainly it is possible, Dr. Mirth. Might I suggest having me cut my own throat so that I am exsanguinated? The buck knife from when I killed Mr. [REDACTED] is conveniently at hand, and although other methods are of course available, they would either take longer, or damage my organs such that they are no longer accurately representative of my pre-mortem state.

Dr. Mirth: I, er, I suppose that will be acceptable – (at this point, Mr. Deeds took the buck knife and placed the edge of the blade against his throat) – wait!

Mr. Deeds: …yes, Dr. Mirth?

Dr. Mirth: Before you do it… you will come back afterward, correct?

Mr. Deeds: I'm sorry, Dr. Mirth, I don't quite understand.

Research Library File ▸ 662

Dr. Mirth: After the pawn shop incident, when you were killed. You came back to life afterward when Sergeant █████ rang the bell.

Mr. Deeds: If you say so, Dr. Mirth.

Dr. Mirth: Will you come back to life again?

Mr. Deeds: I have no idea, Dr. Mirth. If I did before, then presumably I will again. Unless something has changed. Have you any further questions before I make the incision? I do recommend you step back, as I would hate for my blood to soil your clothing. Death throes can be untidy.

Dr. Mirth: …no, I suppose not. Carry on.

Mr. Deeds: Very well, Dr. Mirth. And in the event that I don't come back to life, it has been a genuine pleasure to serve you.

Mr. Deeds then sliced through his own throat, and bled to death. A post-mortem examination of the body revealed it to be ordinary in every way, though it is noted that Mr. Deeds was not suffering from any noticeable disease or physical condition, and was in fact in near perfect health at the time of death. The contents of his stomach consisted of Southern-style sweet tea, normal stomach acids, and no more.

Mr. Deeds' body was then left on the operating table while the lights in the room and cameras were turned off. All personnel left the room, and upon return, no trace of Mr. Deeds, be it blood on the instruments used or other physical traces such as organs removed, let alone the actual body, remained.

Further ringing of SCP-662 resulted in Mr. Deeds' appearance after three minutes. He showed no signs of injury, and was well dressed once more in a modern uniform commonly worn by butlers. As expected, he could not explain how he had managed to survive. He was then ordered to give Dr. Mirth a full body massage, which he performed much to Dr. Mirth's satisfaction; Dr. Mirth claimed it was "the best damned rubdown I've ever had, my back pain is completely gone".

ACQUISITION REPORT

SCP-662 was discovered in the possession of a petty thief and grave robber in █████, ██ USA. The thief was in the process of selling SCP-662 to a pawn shop in the mentioned town when the bell was accidentally "rung" by the pawn shop attendant. Mr. Deeds appeared from the storage area behind the counter and promptly addressed the attendant. Believing that he was about to be robbed by the two men, the attendant overreacted and managed to get hold of a sawed-off shotgun from under the counter. Mr. Deeds was fatally wounded by the attendant and died on scene.

The thief escaped, but was apprehended by Foundation agents after a week-long search of the surrounding towns. Under questioning, the thief revealed that he found the bell in its box in the grave of ████████ █████, located on the outskirts of the above mentioned town. He was then remitted for D-class personnel assignment and subsequently perished during testing of SCP-███

The bell did not come under the purview of the Foundation until after the crime and subsequent transport of Mr. Deeds' body to the local morgue. After the disappearance of the body from the morgue, an agent was sent to investigate the possible outbreak of SCP-███ or other unknown necrotic reinvigorating cause.

Mr. Deeds reappeared in the Case File Item Storage room of the local constabulary after the bell was handled by Sergeant ████. He was quickly apprehended and Agent █████ took him into custody three hours after reappearance under the guise of an FBI agent. When the handcuffed Mr. Deeds once again disappeared, the agent intuited that the bell itself may have something to do with the string of incidents, and after acquiring it and testing proved his hunch, brought the bell back to █████ for further testing. Agent █████ was awarded an official Foundation "Pat on the Back" plaque for his handling of the incident and lack of self serving interest once he discovered what the bell and Mr. Deeds were capable of.

END OF REPORT ███ ███ ███

SPECIAL CONTAINMENT PROCEDURES

Due to the unique nature of SCP-722, effectiveness of containment measures are as of yet untried. Containment measures are currently focused on maintaining the current state of SCP-722 until a more permanent solution can be found. Brain-wave activity, heart rate and internal temperature of the artifact are to be monitored at all times, as well as any variances in the integrity and volume of the glacial range within which SCP-722 currently resides, particularly Kangerdlugssuaq. Eight access points exist at various points in the glacier, each sealed by an airlock, with sound dampeners lining the glacial interior. At four hour intervals, nitrogen gas chilled to a near-liquid state is to be pumped into the room to lower the internal temperature as much as possible.

Access into SCP-722's chamber is to be permitted only in the event of emergency maintenance, which should be performed by a team of Class D personnel with a security detail of at least two clearance level 3 Agents. Anyone gaining entry into SCP-722's chamber is to be outfitted with a suit of high-extremity polar wear and a set of nightvision goggles as the interior chamber is unlit. Security personnel should be outfitted with a silenced flechette pistol and take extreme caution in the event of its use. Should any personnel involved in a maintenance operation attempt to compromise the artifact in any way, they should be terminated with extreme prejudice regardless of security clearance. Security personnel are required to report their status at 10 minute intervals. In the event of a lapse in reports, the interior chamber is to be flooded with nitrogen gas until no life forms are detected.

All agents entering SCP-722's enclosure are advised to not make any attempt to touch the artifact as it is known to be extremely volatile. The far extremities of SCP-722 are to be avoided at all costs. In the event of contact with the artifact, agents are advised to immediately exit the enclosure and report to the base medic for detox.

DESCRIPTION

SCP-722 was found in the eastern glacial ranges of Greenland by Greenpeace activists making a documentary on the effects of global warming. Upon descending into a crevasse that had opened up on the southern end of the Kangerdlugssuaq glacier, they discovered a network of tunnels within the glacier which had long since been smoothed out, eventually reaching a series of larger chambers which seemed to host a tremendous serpentine body. After another hour of exploration the team left the glacier and headed to the nearby town of ███████. Within hours most of the team felt symptoms of a wide array of sicknesses resembling everything from swollen lymph nodes to fast necrosis of the skin. By nightfall the entire team was dead. An SCP operative on leave caught wind of the story and sent notification to high command.

SCP-722 is by all accounts a terrestrial serpent, of incredible size, length, and girth, coiled through a series of tunnels of unknown origin. Most of the tunnels in SCP-722's enclosure are completely smooth, though a few patches, specifically on the paths nearest to the head and tail of the artifact, are marked with some form of ancient Nordic script. All attempts to translate the script have ended in failure, and the dialog appears to pre-date the settlement of the island by Erik the Red at the turn of the 11th century. No historical records exist of any previous settlement in Greenland, so the source of the script is currently a mystery.

SCP-722

Title
JÖRMUNGANDR

Report by
far2

Picture by
Dan Temirov

Access the original report on
scp-wiki.wikidot.com/scp-722

Date
███████

Class
KETER

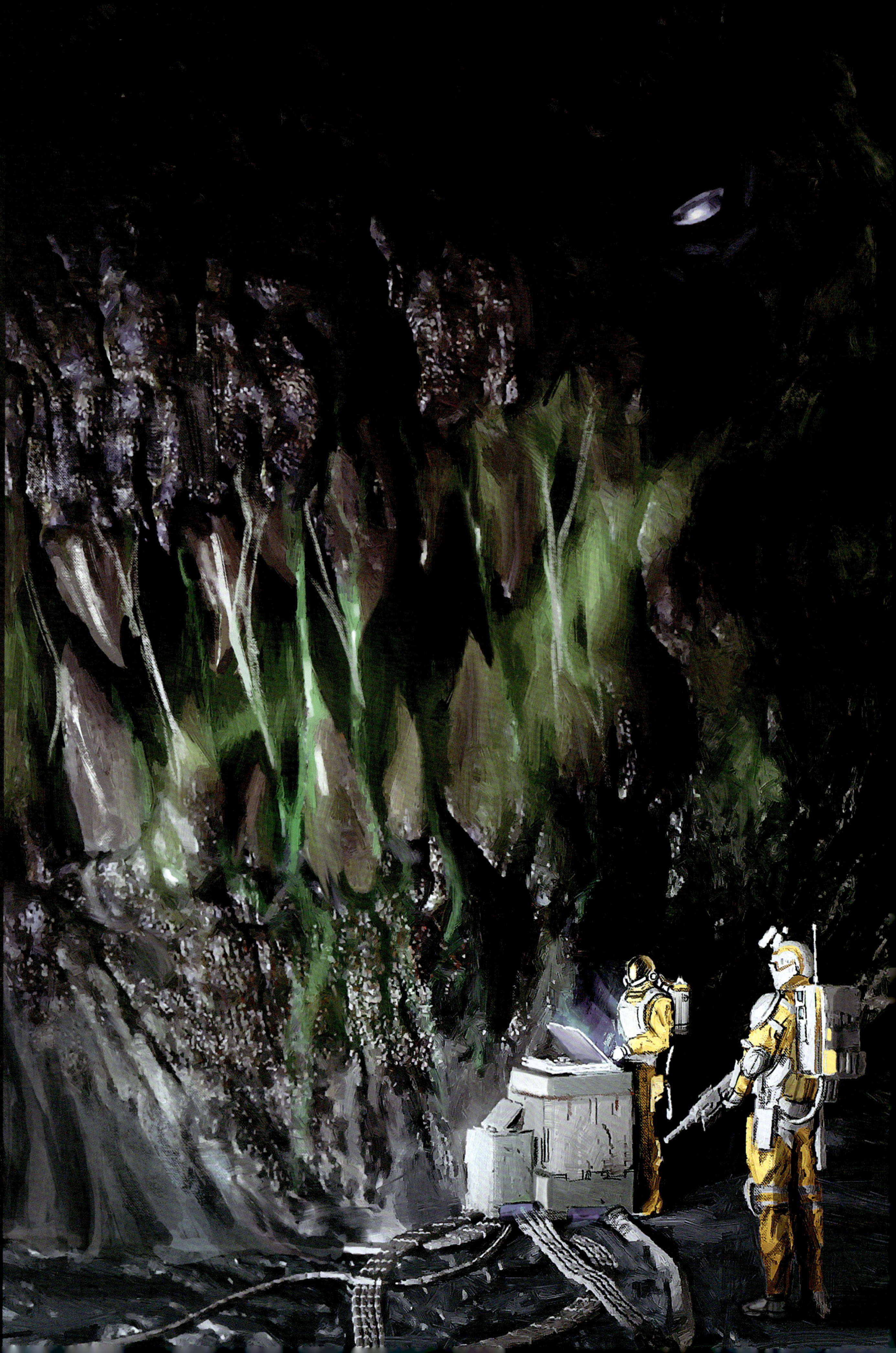

Photo taken inside SCP-722's chamber before current containment procedures were established.

SCP-722 is clearly in a state of prolonged slumber, and many parts of the creature's body have become embedded in the glacier, possibly due to cave-ins or parts of the ice re-forming over many years. While this would normally warrant a Euclid ranking, SCP-722's immense size (currently estimated at between 8 and 12km) could pose a threat to nearby cities or the world at large in the event of it awakening. Additionally, the artifact possesses formidable defensive abilities. (See attached document, #722-A)

DOCUMENT #722-A: UNIDENTIFIED TOXIN '722'

SCP-722's skin seems to secrete a potent toxin which has currently eluded all attempts at identification. Symptoms seem largely random on a case by case basis, but the end result is invariably death. All attempts at synthesizing an antidote to date have failed. Harvesting the poison for sampling procedures or weaponization has also proved unsuccessful - the poison seems to deteriorate rapidly after leaving its host and is all but useless by the time it reaches our labs. Retrieval has also proven to be invariably fatal, no matter what configuration of hazardous materials handling we have implemented. Given the loss of manpower and the extreme difficulty in obtaining more personnel given the range of this outpost, we recommend discontinuing any further testing.

DOCUMENT #722-B: 'DEFENSIVE' CAPABILITIES?

Doctors ███, ████, ███, and Agent █████ (3-103-589) have all contributed the opinion that artifact SCP-722's poison is not defensive in nature, but intended to be used as a weapon. This theory has begun to circulate based on report [DATA EXPUNGED] regarding the incident on [DATA EXPUNGED]. Given the misting of the poison in the northernmost edges of the glacier, and posthumous examinations of the affected, it would appear that the artifact breathes the poison in a slightly less potent but still invariably fatal form. While poison as a weapon is not representative of reptiles in terrestrial nature, it has been noted at the request of our research team.

DOCUMENT #722-C, MEMO: MORATORIUM ON EXPEDITIONS INTO THE GLACIER

All forays into the glacier are forbidden, effective immediately, excepting the case of emergency maintenance. Since the incident on [DATA EXPUNGED] SCP-722 has seen a 0.9% increase in brain activity. Any unauthorized personnel attempting access into the glacial interior are to be terminated without question, regardless of security clearance. Agents and non-essential personnel alike have been reckless in their handling of the artifact - I will take this opportunity to remind you that we are dealing with a matter of worldwide importance, as this is a Keter-level SCP. If Site 103 is to remain in operation, then we must maintain our vigilance of standard security protocols. My predecessor was removed from his position for a reason. Follow in his footsteps, and you will find yourselves in the same shoes as him. -Brig. Gen ██ ███ (4-103-002)

DOCUMENT #722-D, MEMO: PROPOSED EXPLANATION FOR TOXIN

Doctor ████ has hypothesized that there may be a phylogenetic relationship between SCP-722 and other large reptiles, specifically positing it as a limbless or "glass" lizard within or close to the Varanus genus (including *Varanus komodoensis* or the Komodo dragon), and citing its immense size and use of a necrotic agent produced from its mouth as a predatory weapon. It is proposed that a team be sent to acquire samples of live tissue for genetic testing and, if possible, further toxin samples to look for bacteriological activity or residue.

END OF REPORT ▌███ ▌██

File >>> 010044

SCP-1993

Title

YOUR LEG

Report by

Eskobar

Picture by

Natalie Lesiv

Access the original report on **scp-wiki.wikidot.com/scp-1993**

Date

Class

EUCLID

SPECIAL CONTAINMENT PROCEDURES

SCP-1993 is to be kept in a safe with voice-activated locks in a standard containment chamber, 5m x 5m x 3m in size. The containment chamber is to have no means of visual output to any other location by either direct or electronic means, though the chamber should have two-way audio transmission capability with an adjoining testing area. Additionally, the containment chamber is to be stocked with a single surgical table and sterilized surgical equipment before testing. During testing, a single D-class personnel is to enter containment and close all doors, at which point an authorized researcher is to voice-unlock the safe from a remote location. Under no circumstances are unauthorized D-class or any non-D-class personnel to access SCP-1993 directly; transportation of SCP-1993 should take place only with the object inside of its safe. No visual record of SCP-1993 is to be created at any time, and any such records located are to be destroyed as soon as possible.

DESCRIPTION

SCP-1993 is a human right leg, severed at an angle beginning above the knee and descending to the patella. Examination of the leg has shown the presence of a small tattoo on the exterior side of the ankle, depicting a compass with the needle pointing to the southeast. Instances of SCP-1993 have been observed to decay at the normal rate for a severed limb.

All humans making visual contact with SCP-1993 will become immediately convinced that SCP-1993 is their leg, amputated from them at some point in the past and replaced with a simulacrum1. Affected individuals will have no explanation as to how, when, or under what circumstances their leg was removed, but in no instance has any individual been disabused of the idea once exposed to SCP-1993. If permitted physical access to SCP-1993, individuals will find some manner of removing their own leg above the knee; documented incidents have seen individuals applying tourniquets and performing amputations with improvised sharpened pieces of metal, shards of glass, or their own teeth, cutting through skin, muscle, and tendon, dislocating the patella and severing all requisite tendons and the anterior cruciate ligament.

Individuals will then attempt to attach SCP-1993 to their own bodies, again using whatever materials are available to them; however, given the complexity of microsurgical reattachment, this will often be carried out haphazardly, with many affected individuals electing finally to connect the limb via topical methods such as stapling or using adhesive chemicals. While exposure to SCP-1993 causes affected individuals to ignore or mentally suppress sensations of pain during the procedure, the massive damage caused by the amputation typically results in death by any combination of blood loss, shock, or injuries caused by attempting to walk on the attached leg. In the event that the patient survives the procedure's immediate aftermath, infections resulting either from general exposure to bacteria or from contact with necrotic tissue will typically prove lethal without immediate medical treatment.

Current experimentation suggests that the anomalous phenomenon associated with SCP-1993 transfers from the former leg to the newly amputated one at some point during the procedure. The exact point of transition is unknown, but former instances of SCP-1993 can be removed from the containment chamber without anomalous effect once another leg is left behind; this second leg can now be identified as SCP-1993. All instances thus removed have had a compass rose tattoo on the ankle.

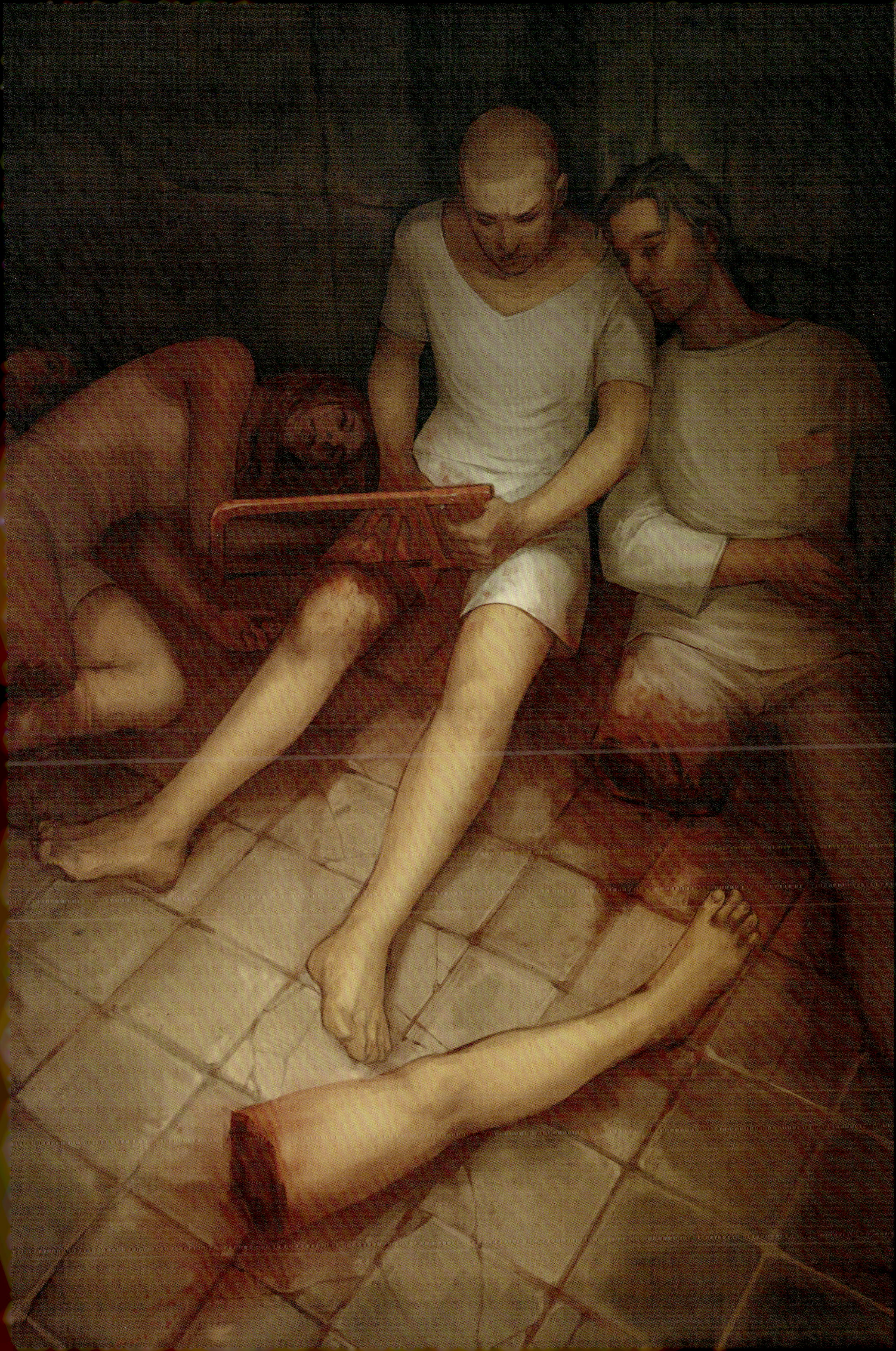

ADDENDUM 1993-A: TESTING LOG

TEST: 1993-2

Personnel: D-65451, D-85165
Supplies Provided: Standard surgical equipment (sterilized forceps, scalpels, bowls, running water)
Description: D-65451 entered testing chamber as instructed and accessed SCP-1993. Subject was heard to audibly gasp; despite prompting, subject was unable to describe what she was seeing at the time and refused to respond verbally. Approximately twenty minutes passed with D-65451 in the containment chamber, accompanied by sounds of grunting and dripping, followed by a loud crash. D-85165 instructed to enter testing chamber and retrieve D-65451 from SCP-1993's containment area. D-85165 entered testing chamber as instructed. Approximately twenty-three minutes passed with D-85165 in the containment chamber, accompanied by sounds of audible pain, squeaking, and finally an unidentified loud, repetitive metallic thumping sound. D-85165 exited containment dragging D-65451, unconscious from blood loss, and the former instance of SCP-1993, attached to the severed end of D-65451's thigh. D-85165 was found to have amputated his own leg and replaced it with that of D-65451, using a Black and Decker-brand staple gun to make the connection.

At no point was any staple gun introduced into the testing chamber. Further tests are to require stricter searching of personnel involved.

TEST: 1993-6

Personnel: D-1951, D-8923, D-2678, D-1864
Supplied Provided: Standard surgical equipment, as above.
Description: All four D-class personnel entered containment and accessed SCP-1993 without difficulty. Upon accessing, all four individuals refused to respond to verbal instructions or requests for updates. The following twenty minutes of audio output closely resembled a violent fistfight, accompanied primarily by grunting, dripping, and panting sounds, along with occasional mutters of "mine" and "give me". Twenty-six minutes into the recording, screaming becomes audible; screaming continues for three minutes, followed by two minutes of begging, thirty seconds of a squirting sound, and silence. Further grunting and dripping sounds are heard for eighteen minutes, followed by an unidentified sound for forty-five seconds. D-8923 exited containment with the previous instance of SCP-1993 (connected to his leg via duct tape) three minutes later. DNA analysis confirmed the leg's owner as D-51684.

At no point was any duct tape introduced into the testing chamber. Further tests suspended indefinitely.

END OF REPORT

SPECIAL CONTAINMENT PROCEDURES

The host of SCP-027 (currently subject 027-02) is to be kept in a 5 m x 5 m containment cell with a grated, raised floor connected to a strong vacuum system. All creatures removed from the Subject's containment cell are to be incinerated, except for a small portion to be diverted for analysis and necropsy. The cell is to be cleaned and inspected for structural damage daily.

Subject 027-02 must be monitored by at least two personnel at all times. Any unusual behavior or vital signs on the part of the subject or the appearance of any unusual species in the subject's vicinity must immediately be reported to Level 4 personnel.

Security personnel assigned to SCP-027 must be inoculated against all known animal-borne pathogens and must be armed with tranquilizer guns, with standing orders to subdue the subject if the need arises.

Until SCP-027 is better understood, no personnel of Level 4 Clearance or higher should approach within 200 m of the Subject.

DESCRIPTION

SCP-027 appears to be a phenomenon of unknown source that seems to be tied to one human subject (currently 027-02) at a time. As host to SCP-027, subject 027-02 is constantly surrounded by swarming vermin that are drawn to his location. The subject does not appear able to assert control over these creatures in any way, and is in fact prone to occasional attacks from feral specimens. These creatures have also been known to attack personnel who approach too closely.

Wherever the subject goes, an initial swarm of flying insects such as gnats and flies will start to form a cloud around him, usually within two to three minutes. Shortly thereafter, crawling animals (including lice, cockroaches, worms, spiders, [DATA EXPUNGED], mice, and rats) will begin to appear; the longer the subject remains in a location, the more vermin will gather there. When the subject leaves a location, some of these creatures will follow, but most will disperse.

SCP-027 has been known to transfer between hosts once, upon the death of the first known host, Subject 027-01 (see Appendix 1 for more information). Since SCP-027 could likely repeat this feat upon the death of Subject 027-02, all high-value personnel should be kept far away from the current host until more about SCP-027 is understood. SCP-027 has also likely transferred between hosts an unknown number of times before containment. Research into potential previous hosts has commenced, with preliminary evidence suggesting that SCP-027 may have existed for at least ██ years.

It is not yet known how SCP-027 chooses or attracts animals, or even what SCP-027 exactly is. The previous host never expressed having any sort of communication with a separate conscious entity; analysis of the current host has been inconclusive at best.

File >>> 010044

SCP-027

Title

THE VERMIN GOD

Report by

Quikngruvn

Picture by

Markiz de Baldezar

Access the original report on

scp-wiki.wikidot.com/scp-027

Date

Class

EUCLID

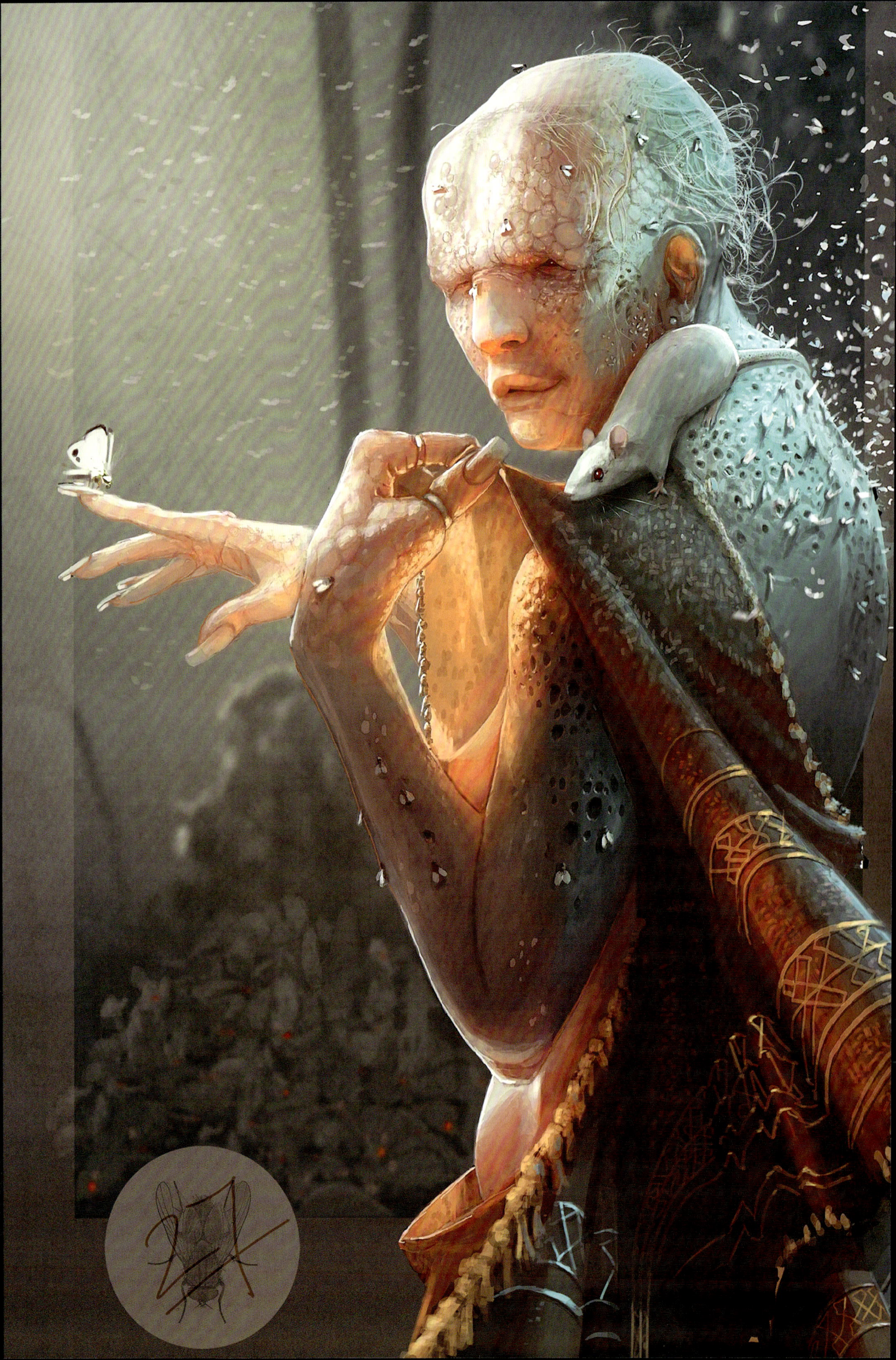

Artistic depiction of N█████. Some researchers believe this Mesopotamian deity could be the original host of SCP-027.

APPENDIX 1: TIMELINE OF SIGNIFICANT EVENTS

04/██/199█ Subject 027-01 is discovered in an abandoned warehouse outside ███████, ███ that had been completely overrun by rats, cockroaches, and other vermin, and is contained and cataloged as SCP-027. The subject is described as a Caucasian male in his late thirties, of average height but gaunt, filthy, and covered in bites and scratches. The subject also shows symptoms of degraded mental health, evidence of heavy use of alcohol and illicit drugs, and signs of prolonged sleep deprivation.

10/██/200█ Subject expires. Autopsy shows more than 70% of the subject's body [DATA EXPUNGED] a colony of rats nesting in the subject's abdomen for at least ██ generations.

10/██/200█ Between 140 and 150 hours after the Subject's death, Security Officer K██████ F██████ reports being awoken by breathing problems due to a large housefly having crawled up his nose (later shown to have lain eggs). Subsequent observations lead to categorization of Officer F██████ as subject 027-02, the original host is reclassified as subject 027-01, and SCP-027 is redefined.

[DATA EXPUNGED]

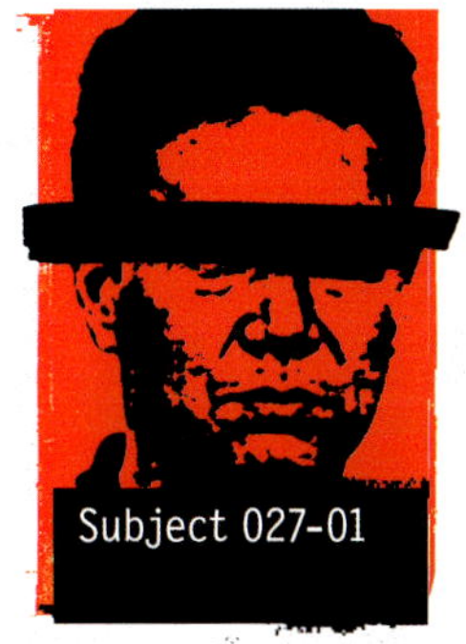
Subject 027-01

Subject 027-02

APPENDIX 2: TRANSCRIPT OF INTERVIEW 027-201

The following interview was conducted on 10/██/200█, shortly after Subject 027-02 was identified and transferred to the containment cell that had housed Subject 027-01.

> **Dr. Jameson:** Good morning, Officer █████. How are you feeling?
>
> **Subject 027-02:** Scared. Confused. Mostly scared though.
>
> **J:** Understandable....
>
> **S:** And itchy. I feel like I need to shower all the damn time.
>
> **J:** Ah. But what about, um, inside? Do you feel anything different inside you, like a... presence?
>
> **S:** *[thinks, scratches his head]* No, I don't think I do. I haven't really noticed anything like that.
>
> **J:** You haven't felt anything different since the original host died, besides the itching?
>
> **S:** No, I can't say I have.
>
> **J:** What about any sort of voices, or compulsions–
>
> **S:** *[agitated]* No, I haven't felt anything except bugs crawling all over me! I feel dirty, and scared, and... Doc, what about my family? You gotta get this thing out of me so I can see them again!
>
> **J:** Of... of course. We're going to do everything we can to get 027 out of you. God, I... I'm sorry, K██████...

END OF REPORT ███ ██

File >>> 0944733

SCP-2121

Title

GODS' NOOSE

Report by

Drewbear

Picture by

Dmitry Desyatov

Access the original report on

scp-wiki.wikidot.com/scp-2121

Date

Class

SAFE

SPECIAL CONTAINMENT PROCEDURES

SCP-2121 is to be mounted on a simple square-arch frame measuring 3.5 meters in height. Once every lunar month (approximately every 28 days), a D-class personnel avowing devout faith in any religion is to be hanged using SCP-2121 in such a manner as to result in death by strangulation rather than by breaking the neck. Interviews are allowed during this period, and any significant responses are to be recorded and included in the master log.

Once deceased, the hanged individual is to remain in SCP-2121 for no less than 24 hours, or until total desiccation has occurred. At this point, remains of the body and any residual fluids are to be removed from the containment chamber and incinerated.

Aside from the D-class personnel meeting above qualifications, the only Foundation personnel allowed to have contact with SCP-2121 are confirmed atheists (rating less than 5 on the Standard Rating Measures of Religious Beliefs and Practices) who have never been a member of any religious organization or come into contact with any SCP Item, Anomalous Object, or GOI with significant religious or mythological connections.

DESCRIPTION

SCP-2121 is a hangman's noose composed of a variety of fleshy tissues. The tissue is resistant to all attempts to acquire samples for analysis, but visually appears to be composed of ligaments, tendons, portions of intestine, and a single 1.3 meter tongue tied and woven together into a single rope, which is itself tied in a traditional hangman's knot. The tissues appear fresh and feel wet to the touch, but do not decay or dry out, regardless of environmental conditions.

If SCP-2121 is not used to hang a qualifying individual at least once every lunar month, it will begin to emit a chaotic noise composed of screaming, moans of pain, and seemingly panicked vocalizations in a variety of unidentified languages. This noise will steadily increase to a maximum of 137 dB over the course of 24 hours and will not cease until a qualifying individual is hanged using SCP-2121. The noise also has a telepathic component and can be clearly heard by any sapient being, including those who are in soundproof chambers or who are sensorineurally deaf, up to a distance of 1.7 kilometers. Any individuals who actively possess faith in any religious belief will become increasingly despondent as the length of exposure increases and will attempt to commit suicide via hanging at the earliest possible time. If the affected individual is aware of the existence of SCP-2121, they will attempt to use it to commit suicide, although this is not an overriding compulsion. Individuals who have committed suicide without use of SCP-2121 will not experience its other effects. Religious individuals who make physical contact with SCP-2121 outside of active broadcasts experience the same effect to a lesser degree, manifesting symptoms of a variety of depressive disorders with only a slightly increased rate of suicidal ideation and attempts.

Qualified subjects hanged using SCP-2121 will remain conscious for an average of 3.7 minutes longer than expected by use of a non-anomalous noose and remain capable of speech for the entire duration prior to loss of consciousness. Vocalizations are exclusively of a religious nature and include wails of shock and despair over the apparent deaths of a variety of divine figures, curses against and insults towards an unidentified and unnamed deific figure, and pleas of mercy towards the same figure. Epithets used to describe the unknown deific figure indicate a tendency towards jealousy and violent retribution. Once an individual is

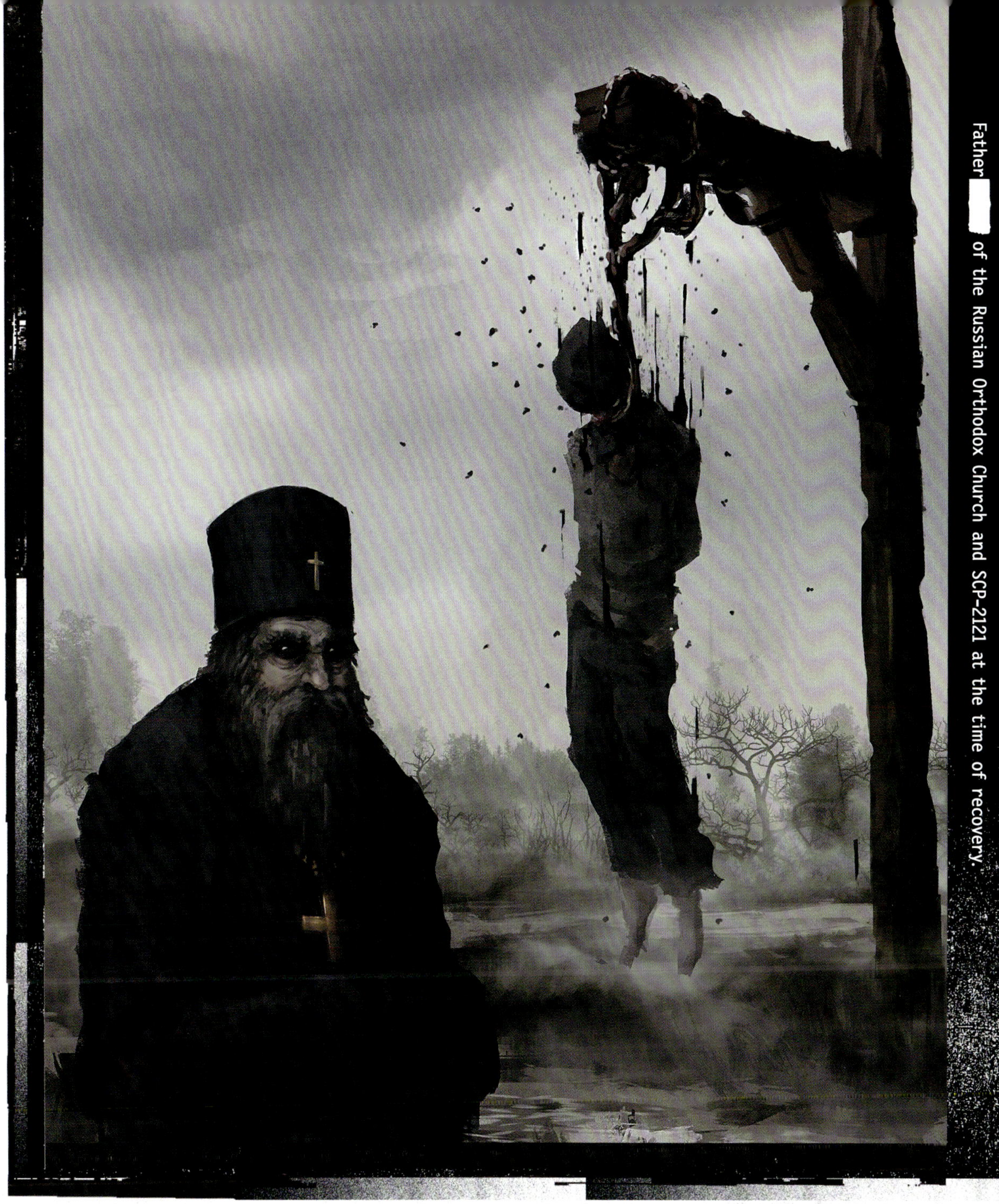

Father █ of the Russian Orthodox Church and SCP-2121 at the time of recovery.

deceased, the body will desiccate, with all bodily fluids exiting the body via orifices and skin pores. Although most liquids will stream downwards off the body to pool below it, all blood will flow towards SCP-2121, into which it will be absorbed.

SCP-2121 was initially brought to the attention of the Foundation by representatives of the Horizon Initiative, who stated that due to its specific properties and the nature of their organization, they were unable to either destroy or effectively contain it. They reported that it had been found near a remote village in northeastern Russia, in a purportedly haunted grove of trees. The local priest of the Russian Orthodox Church was found complicit in executing local criminals using SCP-2121 and, under interrogation, revealed that he did so in order to placate the "demon" within it so that it did not consume the souls of the villagers, a task entrusted to him by his predecessor. Church records imply that SCP-2121 had been in the area for approximately 500 years, since the time of the founding of the village and the eradication of local pagan tribes.

END OF REPORT

File >>> 0944234

SCP-575

Title

PREDATORY DARKNESS

Report by

Dr Gears

Picture by

Dan Temirov

Access the original report on

scp-wiki.wikidot.com/scp-575

Date

Class

KETER

SPECIAL CONTAINMENT PROCEDURES

Any and all instances of SCP-575 are to be immediately isolated and contained with Protocol AL-9077 (see **Advanced Lighting and Emergency Containment Strategies** handbook) and transported to secured containment. Should an instance of SCP-575 exceed a safely containable size, Protocol AL-9077-B is to be used to divide and isolate SCP-575 into smaller instances.

Containment units are to be made of two airtight rooms, each sealed by airlocks. The outer room, Containment A, is to remain lit at all times, with no less than two back-up generators on stand-by. Light fixtures are to be checked weekly, and any blackouts in Containment A will result in immediate lockdown until total illumination is restored.

The inner containment unit, Containment B, is to be coated in a layer of pure calcium both inside and out. Personnel entering Containment B are to be fitted with LED-embedded clothing and equipped with portable floodlights in case of emergency. Interaction with SCP-575 should be limited to sample collection and observation. Any samples obtained from SCP-575 must be treated in the same manner as the original source and all test areas must have calcium lining and emergency illumination procedures similar to those outlined here.

Any and all civilian deaths resulting from SCP-575 are to be attributed to wild animal attack/scavenger predation of an already deceased subject. Should deeper scrutiny be applied, attacks are to be blamed on a serial killer/satanic cult, and any additional information is sealed "due to ongoing investigation".

DESCRIPTION

SCP-575 appears to be an unknown form of matter, taking the form of a series of amorphous black shapes and structures. SCP-575 is difficult to observe, as it immediately dissipates when exposed to light. Current testing has been unable to identify if SCP-575 is organic or inorganic. Despite the lack of any visible nervous systems or observable organic components, SCP-575 displays behavior consistent with an active consciousness.

SCP-575 initially manifests in total darkness. How this occurs is unknown, however tests have shown a variable mass of SCP-575 forming when [DATA EXPUNGED] variable, along with the time frame. SCP-575 is capable of "floating" and can alter its density, allowing it to "pass through" very small openings. SCP-575 prefers very dark, isolated locations in which to settle after its initial formation, and will remain there until it reaches "critical mass" at [DATA EXPUNGED]

SCP-575 grows with the absorption of biological material. SCP-575 will "attack" living things by solidifying portions of itself and using these "appendages" to bludgeon, cut and crush subjects. The tracking and selection methods used by SCP-575 are currently not understood. Upon disabling a subject, SCP-575 will forcibly tear and crush tissue within the main mass until it is "absorbed". SCP-575 is unable to interact with objects rich in calcium however, and "nesting areas" for SCP-575 can be identified by the large amount of bones, teeth, and calcified dust around them.

SCP-575 is capable of manifesting in any area of total darkness. This appears to be a form of "spontaneous generation", and can form in any suitably dark location after [DATA EXPUNGED]. SCP-575 was initially recovered under the home of Mr. █████ ████ and his family. When initial contact was made, SCP-575 had "digested" the household, and had partially "consumed" a neighbor, one █████ ███████, age █ Since this initial contact, ███ instances of SCP-575 have been recovered, most of which have been in residential homes or large buildings, such as factories and schools. The cause for this preference is unknown, however it has been suggested that the building behaviors of man simply provide more suitable "nesting" areas, or that SCP-575 somehow "needs" a nearby human presence. Both theories are under investigation.

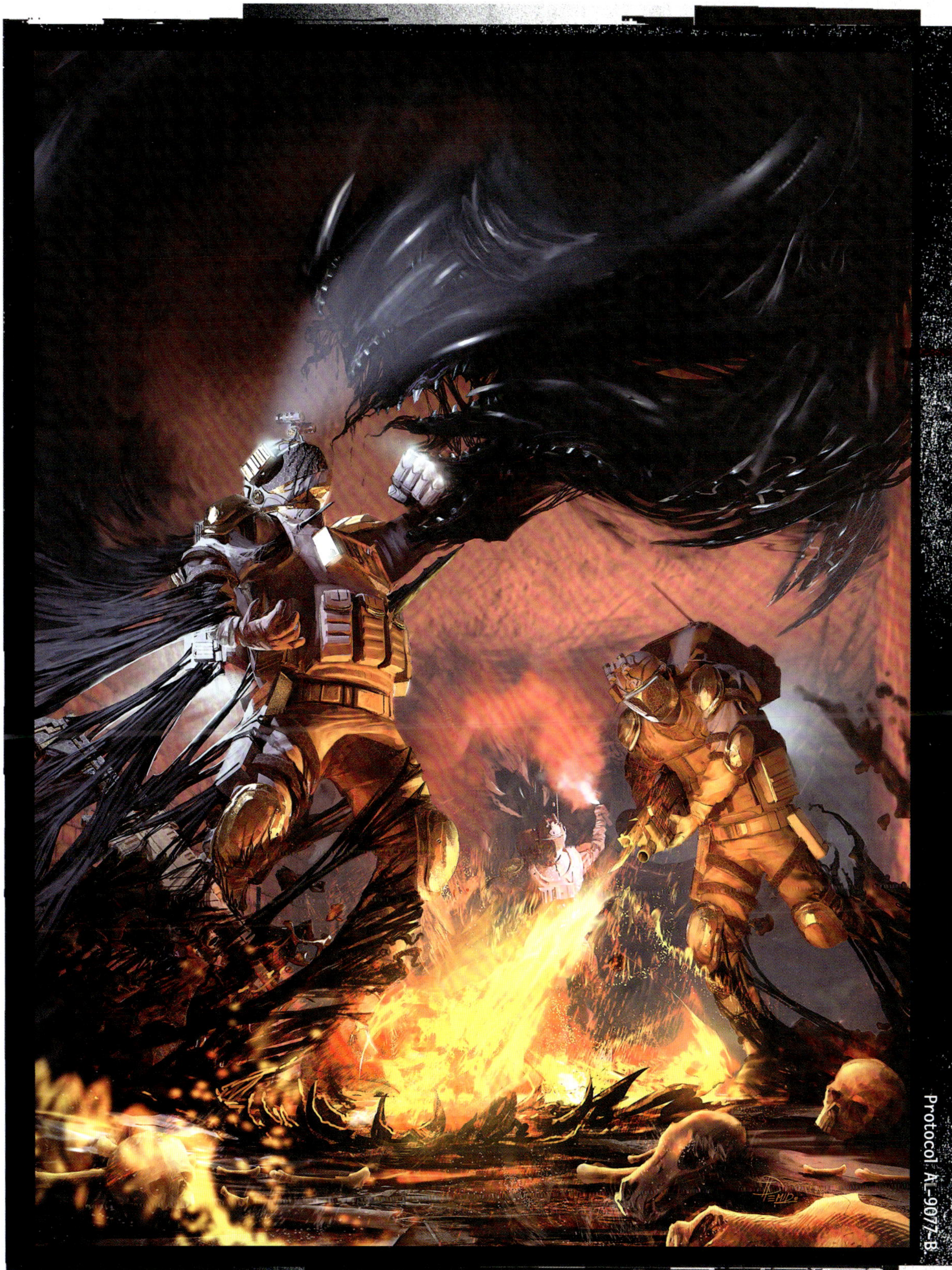

END OF REPORT

File >>> 095234

SCP-138

Title

THE EVER-LIVING MAN

Report by

an unknown researcher

Picture by

Dmitry Desyatov

Access the original report on

scp-wiki.wikidot.com/scp-138

Date

Class

SAFE

SPECIAL CONTAINMENT PROCEDURES

SCP-138 requires minimal containment procedures. For humanitarian purposes, subject is currently being kept in a chemically-induced comatose state.

DESCRIPTION

SCP-138 is a human male, suspected to be in excess of four thousand (4000) years old. Subject is approximately 1.5 meters in height, emaciated, and wizened. SCP-138's precise origins are unknown. Subject was discovered in 2006, in an Egyptian tomb located near Tutankhamen's tomb unearthed in 1922, sealed inside a sarcophagus. When a living being was discovered in the tomb, the Foundation was alerted by one of our sleeper agents assigned to the International Archaeological Association. Subject was immediately moved to Sector 37 for investigation by the lead research science team there.

Physiologically, SCP-138 should clinically be dead. Muscles and internal organs are in a severe state of atrophy, and although the subject's bio-electro-magnetic field is stable, his nervous system is also severely debilitated. Subject also exhibits evidence of a large number of fatal wounds, some possibly accidental, some blatantly deliberate, whether inflicted by the subject himself or by others.

There is no obvious scientific explanation for his continued living state. Although other SCPs have exhibited accelerated regenerative properties, allowing them to resist death, SCP-138 has no such abilities—his body does not regenerate damage, but simply continues to function despite lethal injuries. This stretches to wounding blows, although anything that would completely destroy the body proves ineffective.

Subject speaks exclusively in a dialect of ancient Egyptian. Communication using a civilian translator has revealed very little about the subject's past, though it would appear that he was buried in the tomb for an unknown religious purpose. Due to his severely injured state, SCP-138 is in a constant state of agony, and has on numerous occasions insistently requested humanitarian euthanasia. No successful method of termination has yet been found, despite various and varied attempts, both official and unsanctioned. Attached is a comprehensive list of the subject's injuries.

DOCUMENT 138-27: INJURIES SUSTAINED BY SUBJECT SCP-138

Ancient injuries:

- Slit throat
- Seventeen (17) separate wounds to the torso: nine (9) sword wounds, six (6) spear wounds, and two (2) wounds caused by unknown puncturing weapon, possibly a metal or wooden spike

Sanctioned euthanasia attempts:

- Severe nausea (due to intravenous arsenic poison)
- Third degree burns to 100% of the subject's body (note that SCP-138 survived a full twenty (20) minutes in an industrial incinerator)
- Severe internal and nervous system damage (from electrocution attempt)

Unofficial euthanasia attempts by non-research personnel:

- Tracheal trauma (due to extended strangulation attempt)
- Two gunshot wounds to the head, causing severe cranial trauma

END OF REPORT

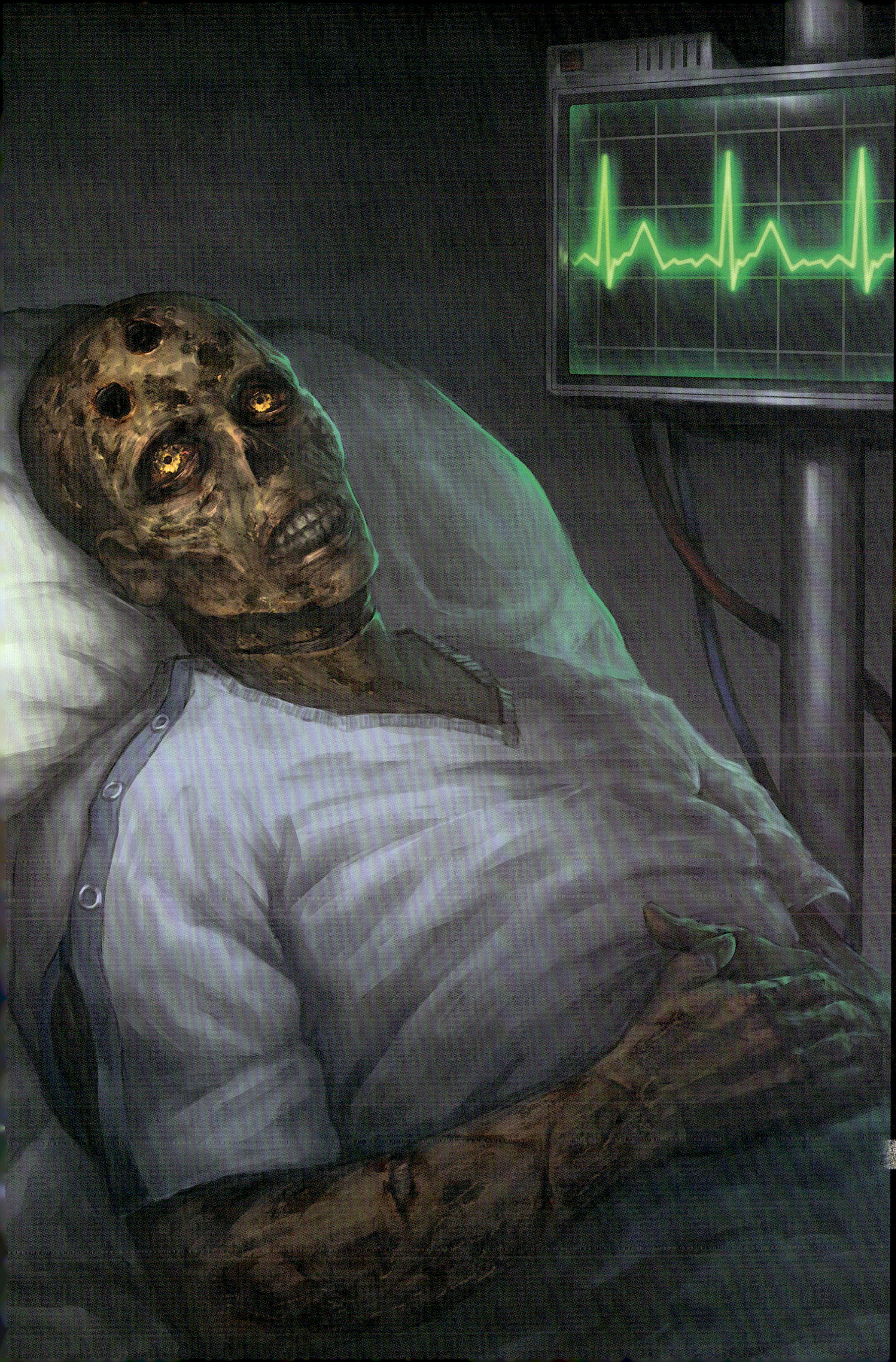

SCP-138 in a chemically-induced comatose state.

File >>> 003234

SCP-1983

Title

DOORWAY TO NOWHERE

Report by

DrEverettMann

Picture by

Pavel Kobyzev

Access the original report on

scp-wiki.wikidot.com/scp-1983

Date

Class

KETER

PRESUMED NEUTRALIZED

SPECIAL CONTAINMENT PROCEDURES

Outpost 54 has been built on the land surrounding SCP-1983 and disguised as a chemical plant. The "plant" building serves as barracks for MTF Chi-13 ("Choir Boys"). All entry points into Outpost 54 are to be guarded at all times. Personnel will review Document 1983-12, which details the cover story to be given to any civilians expressing curiosity.

All MTF personnel must profess strong religious beliefs, per Chi-13 protocols. All ammunition stocked must have a silver or silver-tipped projectile. A 24-hour watch is to be maintained on the front door of SCP-1983-1. Guards are to engage any instances of SCP-1983-2 on sight. No personnel is to approach within five meters of SCP-1983-1 outside of scheduled testing protocol.

UPDATE: Following the Event 1983-23, a stand-down of Outpost 54 has been authorized. A skeleton crew will remain to monitor SCP-1983 for any further activity. Arms intended for use against instances of SCP-1983-2 are to be maintained at Outpost 54 armory.

DESCRIPTION

SCP-1983-1 is a one-story farmhouse in ████ County, Wyoming. It was abandoned in 1968 after a series of ritual murders, allegedly performed by a "Satanic" cult. Please see capture logs for SCP-███ for further details.

The front door of SCP-1983-1, when opened, appears to contain a spatial anomaly. Neither matter nor light has been observed to exit the doorway, save for instances of SCP-1983-2 (though the anomaly is exothermic).

SCP-1983-1 is accessible through other entrances, including windows, the back door, and entrances cut into the back of SCP-1983-1. However, the front room does not appear to exist inside of SCP-1983-1. Doors that should lead to the

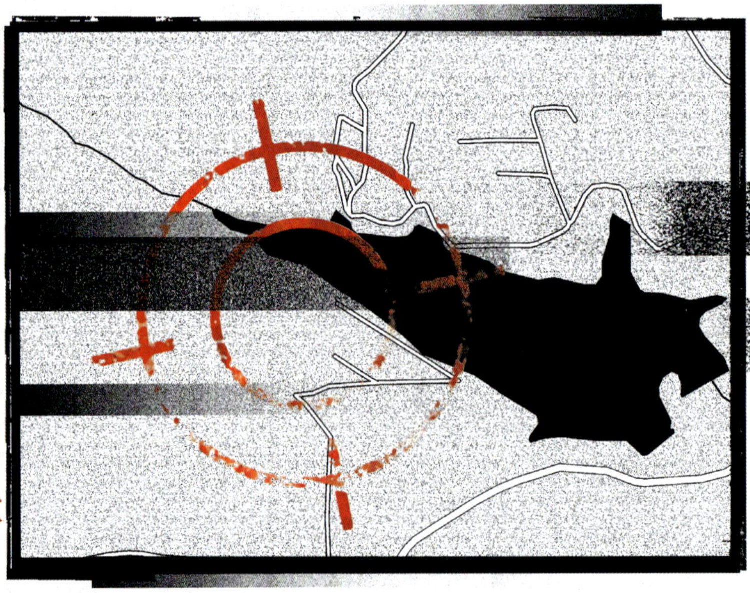

Approximate location of SCP-1983.

front room instead lead to other doors inside the building. Measurements of the inside and outside of SCP-1983-1 are inconsistent. Holes cut through the interior walls of SCP-1983-1 that should lead to the front room lead instead to the outside walls around the front of SCP-1983-1, but stop three meters on either side of the doorway. Attempts to drill into the front room of SCP-1983-1 from the outside have led to the exposure of smaller portions of the anomaly, though instances of SCP-1983-2 have not been observed to exit them. Further attempts to breach the wall have been forbidden by 05-03, due to the possibility of allowing increased potential for instances of SCP-1983-2 to appear.

SCP-1983-2 are bipedal creatures approximately 1.8 meters tall. They are vaguely humanoid, and entirely black in color. They are highly aggressive and will engage any human on sight. When an instance of SCP-1983-2 comes into contact with a human, they extend an upper limb into the human's chest cavity, without any apparent damage to skin or tissues. Through unknown means, they then extract the heart, killing the human. Once it has acquired a human heart, the instance of SCP-1983-2 will return to SCP-1983-1.

Silver munitions fired while offering prayer is the only known method of killing SCP-1983-2. The precise form of the prayer or religion of the supplicant does not appear to matter, so long as the prayer is sincere. Once killed, the bodies of SCP-1983-2 appear to "disintegrate," leaving a small layer of sulfur.

SCP-1983 was discovered after a series of mysterious deaths in the vicinity of █████ County. Foundation investigators encountered instances of SCP-1983-2 and were able to trace them back to SCP-1983-1.

ADDENDUM 1

A team from MTF Chi-13 was sent through the front doorway to attempt to investigate the anomaly. They did not return. However, shortly after they entered, the front door appeared, closing in the frame. No further manifestations of SCP-1983-2 appeared.

ADDENDUM 2

A second assault team entered SCP-1983-1 to determine the fate of the first assault team. They did not return. The door did not close. Shortly after new manifestations of SCP-1983-2 appeared, Agent Morris entered the doorway, which closed shortly after.

ADDENDUM 3

On May 23, 1989, D-14134 was given a closed circuit camera tethered to a monitor by a 25-meter cord. He was instructed to examine as much of the area as he could, and then attempt to return. Once through the doorway, feed from the camera was interrupted. The cord was pulled taut, and then snapped.

Several hours afterward, the anomaly in SCP-1983-1 disappeared. Inside, the desiccated remains of several agents were discovered, as well as Document 1983-15, an informal SCP report written by an agent within the anomaly. It appears as follows:

> **Item #:** Pending
> **Object Class:** Keter. God help you.
> **Special Containment Procedures:** You're going to die, you poor dumb fuck.
>
> This isn't a threat. I'm Agent Barclay. I'm in the middle of this goddamned thing, and I'm telling you, if you're here? You're going to die. I'm probably already dead.
>
> So that's out of the way. Let's get to the containment procedures. There's really only one. Close the goddamned door. You aren't going to get back through there. You've probably already tried. But we know they can get out, if they try hard enough. That's how we found this fucking place. Hopefully, you've

Agent Barclay

already done that. I know we did, once we gave up on getting out through there. If you didn't, then you go straight back and get that door closed. That is your only priority right now. You're going to die anyway. Might as well do some good before you're gone.

Description: So, here's a story, tell me if you've heard it before. The Foundation gets reports of trouble in Bumfuck, USA. Cattle and wildlife are dying mysteriously. Some people turn up missing. When a body shows up, autopsy finds the heart missing. Not cut out, not torn out, just gone. Empty space in the middle of the chest.

They find some sort of pitch-black things floating around. Some brain at the Foundation has seen something like them before, figures out how to kill them. Silver bullets, and pray to God as you fire. Literally. For some reason, that makes it work. Doesn't matter which God, but you damn well better mean it.

I can't, anymore. Not after seeing the nest.

Anyway, Foundation figures out where it's all coming from. Some house in the middle of Bumfuck. No one's lived there in years, not since yadda yadda, murder, cult, rituals, bullshit. The main thing is, these things keep appearing out of the front door. A team goes in, and they never come back out. But then again, neither do the monsters. A sane person would say, Good enough, keep an eye on it, kill anything that moves. But this is the Foundation.

You're a tough agent from MTF-Whatever-the-fuck. Maybe Sequere Nos, maybe Choir Boys, like me. You go bust down the door and run inside, and that's it. You're fucked.

The living room was bad enough. That's where they got O'Brien. They reached in, and suddenly he keeled over, and one of them took off with his heart in its... claws, I guess?

They're less distinct here. You probably noticed that. They're like shadows. Stay away from the light. I know that sounds stupid, but think about it. In the light, shadows are stronger. They have edges. When it's dark, they're indistinct. They can hardly touch you, and they don't see very well. I think they see by your shadow. I don't know. I'm just pulling at straws here, I'll be honest.

You've probably tried going back out the door, but if you haven't, don't. It leads to some place even worse. There aren't any monsters, but... Jones went too far from the house, and I swear to God, he started to melt. Things started popping out of him, and... All you need to know is he didn't make it back. That's when we closed the door.

So, we started moving through the house. We kept to the light at first, before we wised up. Three of us gone that way. But we got a pretty good picture of our surroundings.

This place? It's big. It's not just the farmhouse. It's like... It's like they stole bits and pieces of a lot of places, and stuck them all together. There's some bits that look like an apartment, some that look like a shopping mall, and even what I swear is a closet from my old high school. Same patterns on the tiles and everything.

There's also bits that are made out of... stuff. It's black, like the shadow-things, and it's mostly in the well-lit places. If the lights go out, you can stick your hand through. I don't recommend it. That's how we lost Torres. Something grabbed him, pulled him through. The hole wasn't big enough for his head, but he still went through, eventually.

So, stay away from the light places, but watch your step when it's dark.

Of course, there's no way out. We figured that out too. Any door you find, it either just leads to another room in this nuthouse, or it leads out there, and it's pretty obvious we can't live there. So it's wait until you starve to death or one of those things gets you. Great bunch of choices, huh?

There's one thing you can do. I couldn't go through with it, but maybe you can. It won't help you live, I don't think, but it's... I think it's important. I'm pretty sure someone's going to have to, or these things are going to get out eventually.

This place is stolen from lots of places. So I'm thinking there have to be other doors. We've closed all the ones we've found, but what if they get opened again? And the Foundation doesn't find them in time? Hell,

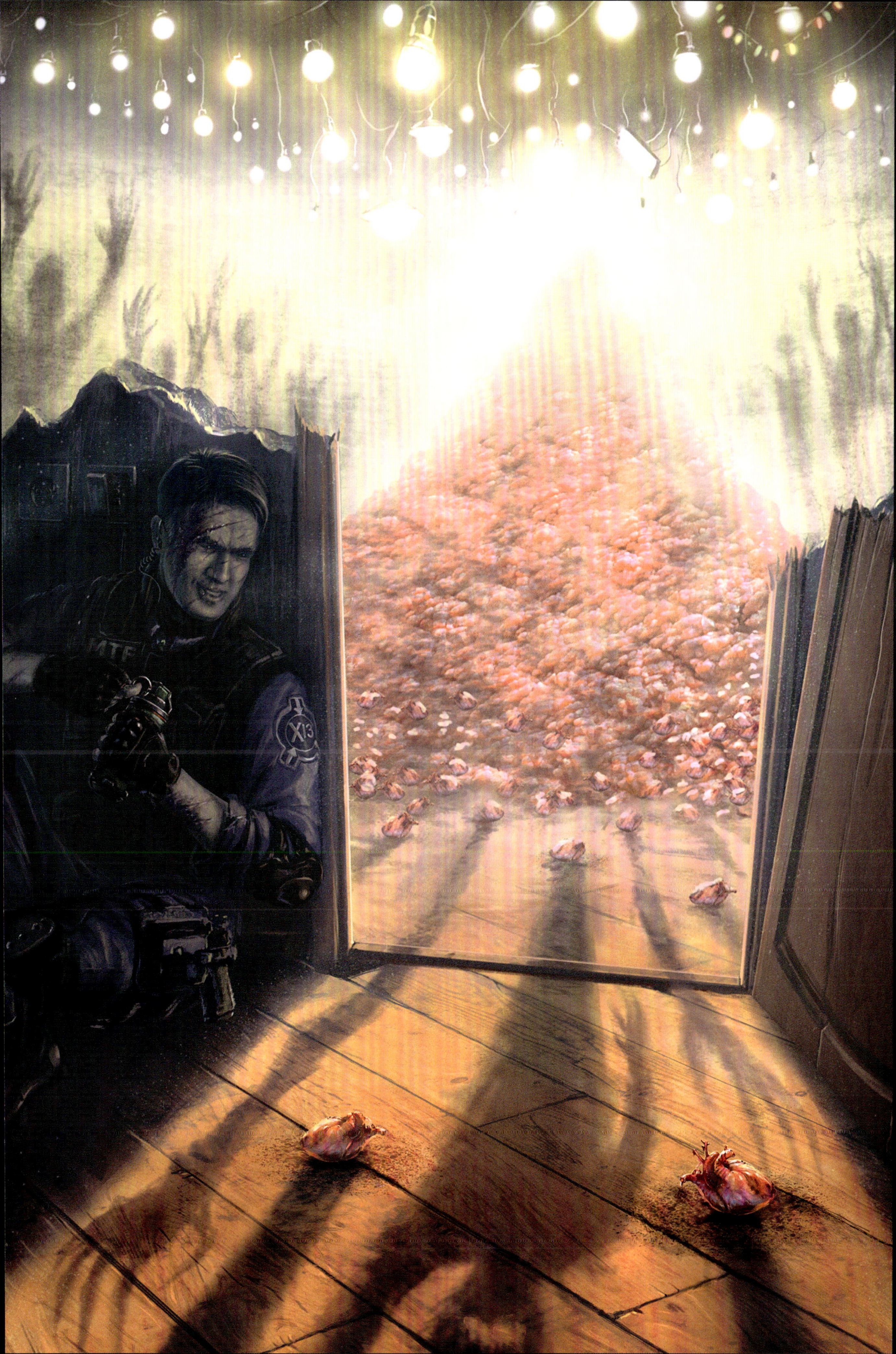

Research Library File ▸ 1983

they don't even know about closing the doors. I'm just hoping they figure out that if someone goes in, the things might stop getting out. And that's assuming everyone's smart enough to close the door after they come in.

So, I think I figured out a way to stop these things. It's the nest.

I only saw it once, for a few minutes. We followed one of the bastards after they got Denning's heart. It took it into a room that I guess is in the middle of this whole place. It's all black stuff, and they've dragged in every kind of light they could find, I guess. Lamps, flashlights, candles, you name it. Some of them were carrying more in as we watched. Anyway, at the middle, there's a big pile of hearts. Just tossed in a heap, and torn open, every one. They threw Denning's heart on the pile, and it started to beat, and then pulse, and then thrash around. Then it tore open, and one of those things pulled itself out. It shook itself, started to grow and then went right to work. The gross thing is that, torn apart as they were, the hearts kept beating. I swear I felt a twinge in my own chest.

There were shadows in the place. I don't mean the monsters, I mean real shadows, of people. Only there was no one there to cast them. They were coming from the hearts. A new one appeared at the same time as the hatching monster, and started trying to pull away, but it couldn't.

That was when I ran. I couldn't take it, you understand? I wasn't trained for this kind of shit. I heard the others behind me. I don't know if they were trying to stop me, or if the bastards had spotted us, but we got separated. I found a nice, dark closet, and I've been hiding in here since. I've been writing by penlight. I turn it off whenever I hear one of them getting close. It's worked, so far.

I can't go any further. I've got a few shots left in my gun, but I can't pray anymore, not and mean it. Not after I saw the nest. But you, if you've found this, you've got to be an agent too. Maybe you're stronger than I was. If you can, go in and destroy the nest. Destroy every last heart. If you do, maybe it'll kill them. It's the only thing I can think of. You'll probably die doing it, but you're dead anyway. So what's it matter to you how it happens?

Me, I'm going to try and get this report back to the living room, which I hope is where you found it. Then I'm going to make sure they can't use my heart to make another one of those things.

Good luck. Morituri te salutant.

SCP-1983 is presumed to have been neutralized by D-14134, who was posthumously awarded the Foundation Star (one of only two awarded to class-D Personnel. Due to information contained in Document 1983-15, it is believed that the anomaly was not localized, as previously believed, and renewed resources have gone into attempting to locate similar incidents.

END OF REPORT

File >>> 045355

SCP-646

Title

BIRTH WORM

Report by

Dexanote

Pictures by

Serj Papadin

Access the original report on

scp-wiki.wikidot.com/scp-646

Date

Class

EUCLID

SPECIAL CONTAINMENT PROCEDURES

SCP-646 is kept in customized Containment Unit 9277 in Bio-Site 66. The floor is to be rinsed daily, and drain grates are to be checked weekly for buildup.

Personnel are to wash SCP-646 once every two weeks with warm water and gentle scrubbing tools. Basic Low-Hazard decontamination showers are to be performed by personnel after this wash.

Subject does not seem to require sustenance; a daily serving of 10 kilograms high-quality edible material is allotted to promote (relative) activity.

All species of offspring are to be examined and logged. If any presiding researchers identify offspring they deem worthy of further research, personnel are to follow appropriate protocols. All unwanted offspring are to be immediately destroyed.

DESCRIPTION

SCP-646 is a large, translucent grey, bloated creature measuring roughly 5.6 meters in length, weighing between 3400 and 3700 kilograms. At one end of its body is the approximation of a torso, with a prominent ribcage and a wide, round head. Seven sets of three-jointed limbs are located evenly spaced down the front of the body; a long series of udder-like organs are located between these limbs. The body tapers to a blunt point with a cloaca-like orifice, the entire frame heaving and shuddering irregularly. The shadows of various internal organs (lungs, hearts, and a digestive tract) can be seen through SCP-646's flesh. The flesh is quite smooth and malleable, and a clear, harmless mucus constantly oozes from its skin.

SCP-646 is constantly producing unrelated, infant organisms. For the purposes of this document, SCP-646 is in a state of "giving birth". When one infant creature has been born, another will appear within SCP-646 and the birthing process will begin again. Births do not seem to cause it any discomfort, and all offspring are completely unremarkable apart from their anomalous origin. Interestingly, oviparous animals such as birds and fish are born whole, outside of an egg. There is no logical order behind what species of animal will be born next; it seems that absolutely any multicellular animal that has ever existed on Earth can be birthed by SCP-646.

It is unknown how SCP-646 is producing these infants at this time, as there is no gestation period between births. The current intake of material by SCP-646 cannot account for the mass of the infant animals or its constant slime discharge. Research is pending.

SCP-646 shows no signs of sapience, and is mostly docile unless actively provoked.

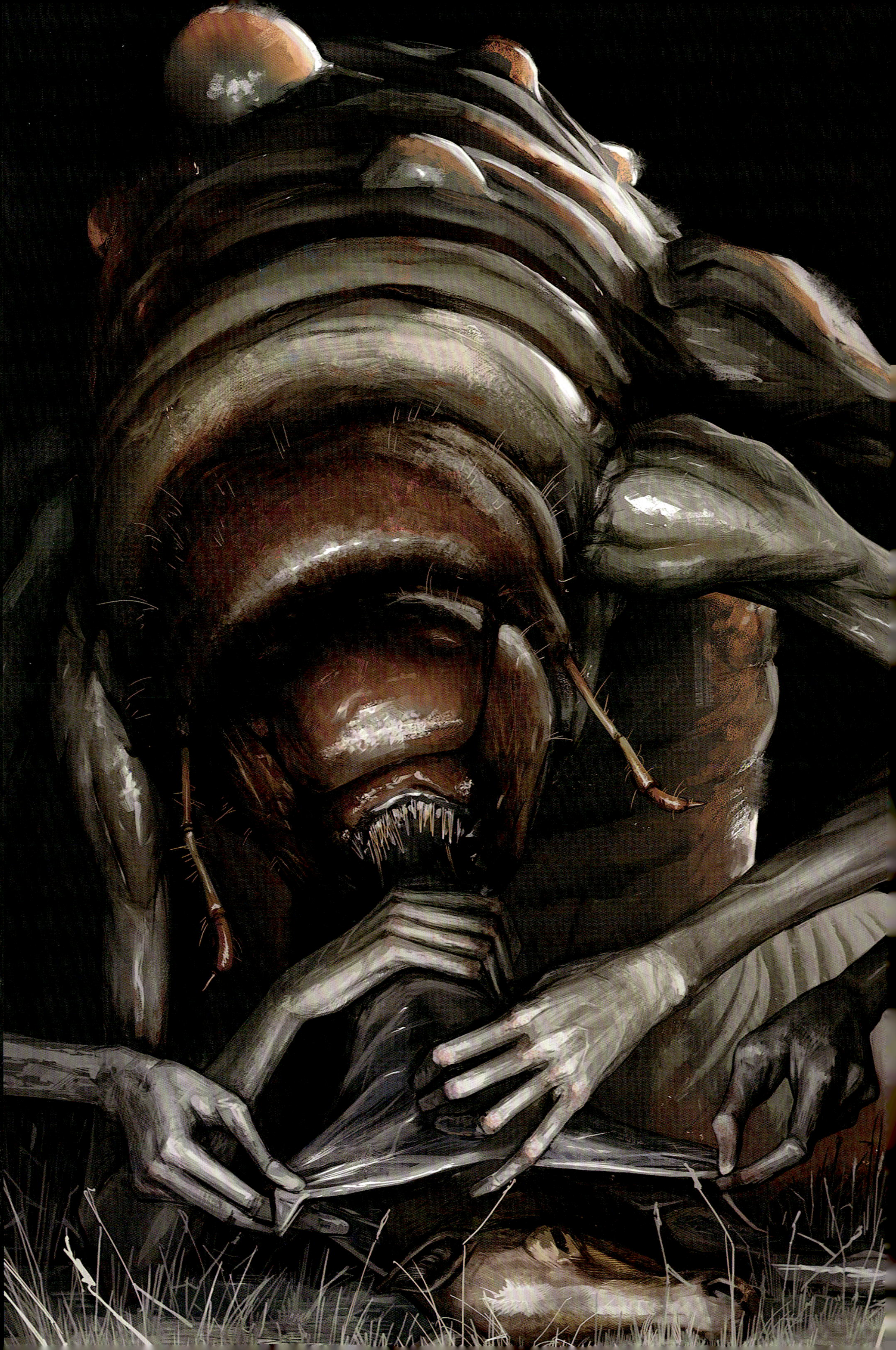

SCP-646 giving birth to [DATA EXPUNGED].

EXCERPT FROM SCP-646 BIRTH LOG 5122B█████/█████/19█████

Time	Species	Common Name	Notes
12:23	unknown	unknown species of anglerfish, female	No match to any species on record
12:33	unknown	unknown animal; 10cm^3 body, legs ~4m long.	retained for study; deceased (internal collapse)
12:49	Mammuthus primigenius	Woolly Mammoth	Retained for study. Genetic material collected for SCP-2082 research.
13:34	Pan troglodytes	common chimpanzee	None
13:57	Iguanodon	dinosaur	retained for study - since deceased (illness)
14:14	Meles meles	European badger	stillborn
14:20	unknown	unknown aquatic invertebrate	terminated immediately by present personnel
14:27	Panthera leo	lion, male	None
14:33	Trilobita	Trilobite, unknown	retained for study - since deceased (unknown)
14:56	Nasua narica	white-nosed coati	None
15:21	Eubalaena japonica	North Pacific right whale	None
15:24	unknown	unidentified purple gelatinous mass	No match to any species on record
15:36	Giraffa camelopardalis	giraffe	None
15:42	Corvus corax	Common Raven	Taken for use in ongoing SCP-1505 research.
15:43	Cyprinus carpio	common carp	common carp
15:50	unknown	unknown bird, possibly Phorusrhacidae	retained for study - since deceased (illness)
16:05	Eurypterida	unknown eupterid	retained for study - since deceased (unknown)
16:15	unknown	unknown mammal, possibly Xenarthra	stillborn
16:22	[DATA EXPUNGED]	[DATA EXPUNGED]	[DATA EXPUNGED]
16:40	unknown	unknown dromaeosaurid	retained for study
16:52	Homo sapiens	human female	retained for study
16:58	unknown	unknown placoderm, possibly Dunkleosteus	stillborn
17:06	Chamaeleo jacksonii	three-horned chameleon	None
17:13	Bos gaurus	gaur	None
17:21	unknown	unknown fish, unique jaw structure	No match to any species on record
17:34	Mandrillus leucophaeus	drill	None
17:23	unknown	unknown terrestrial invertebrate	No match to any species on record
17:43	unknown	unknown hominid	retained for study - deceased (illness)

All offspring are destroyed unless otherwise stated.

END OF REPORT

File >>> 003234

SCP-906

Title

SCOURING HIVE

Report by

Veerdin

Picture by

Serj Papadin

Access the original report on

scp-wiki.wikidot.com/scp-906

Date

Class

EUCLID

SPECIAL CONTAINMENT PROCEDURES

Subject is to be contained in a three (3) by three (3) meters squared, fully airtight, twelve (12) centimetre thick titanium enclosure surrounded by acid-resistant glass. Temperature must be kept under 5 degrees Celsius. Should temperature exceed this limit, all personnel are to be evacuated to a distance of at least one hundred (100) meters. Immediate area containing enclosure will then be locked down until temperature has been lowered. Holding cell is to be maintained on a bi-weekly basis and checked for sufficient corrosion or gaps. Any damage to holding cell is to be repaired immediately.

SCP-906 is to be monitored at all times from four (4) digital cameras mounted on each corner of the enclosure. Any abnormal behaviour reported from these cameras will result in immediate lockdown of area around containment cell. Access to SCP-906 is permitted only to supervised Class D personnel for feeding and/or enclosure maintenance. SCP-906 is to be fed 80 kg of raw meat every forty-two (42) hours.

DESCRIPTION

SCP-906 is a writhing mass of dark brown, worm-like invertebrates. These organisms seem to interact in a uniform fashion, forming a colonial "superorganism" in a similar manner to army ants. For reasons currently unknown, SCP-906 will usually form its "body" into that of a very rough, humanoid figure. SCP-906 is shown to be capable of crude bipedal movement when in this state; however, when travelling longer distances, it will deviate to a flattened mass with a greater efficiency of movement.

SCP-906 is capable of secreting a viscous, highly corrosive, semi-translucent fluid, similar in colour to its skin. This substance is shown to have an acidic strength comparable to hydrofluoric acid, but it has a less pronounced effect on titanium, no effect on acid-resistant glass and [DATA EXPUNGED]. This substance displayed the ability to destroy teeth, bones, hair, nails, clothing, jewellery, and some kinds of equipment in under an hour.

SCP-906 is predatory and highly aggressive: when hungry, it will swarm over any living creature within its path and coat them in its acidic secretion, thereby breaking down the matter into a liquid slurry which it then consumes. Attempts to remove or disturb SCP-906 during its feeding have proved fruitless. When a designated prey is nearby, SCP-906 will alter its form into that of a flowing "carpet" and move across any surface in order to pursue its target until the prey is captured. Due to the small width of SCP-906 component organisms (two (2) centimeters wide), barriers will only slow its advance. Obstacles that cannot simply be passed will be destroyed by the acidic substance SCP-906 secretes. SCP-906 has also displayed the ability to take alternate routes to reach its prey such as drainage pipes and ventilation shafts.

Through methods currently unknown, SCP-906 appears capable of mimicking animal like sounds and "parroting" human speech in what is described as "a raspy, hoarse voice" while in its humanoid form. SCP-906 appears to use this ability to lure prey into areas that are difficult to escape, such as deep pits or maze-like corridor networks. Eyewitness reports from containment breach 906-2-10-01A detail SCP-906 "taunting" prospective victims and even emitting a sound

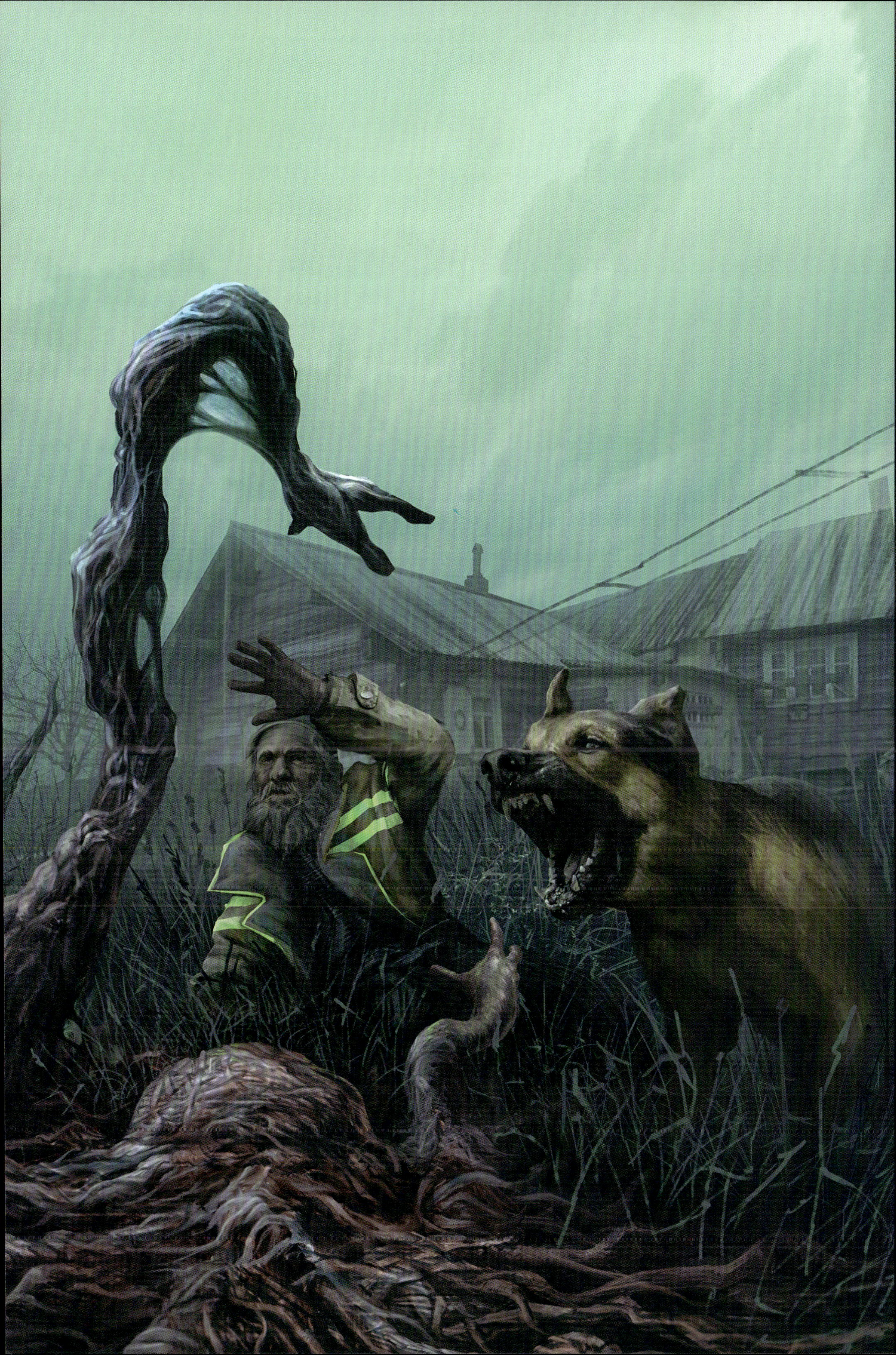

SCP-906 attacking a civilian in ████. Footage from the containment personnel's BWV camera.

"something like laughter" before attacking its prey. This behaviour suggests a kind of rudimentary sentience, but it is unknown how a creature comprising several thousand individual organisms is able to achieve this.

SCP-906 specimens, when removed from the larger "body", will attempt to move back toward the central mass and have been known to dissolve through any obstacles in their way. It should be noted that individual specimens do not show the same level of navigation skills as the full superorganism. Specimens of SCP-906 have the ability to reconstruct into multiple versions when damaged in a similar manner to common earthworms, i.e. splitting one SCP-906 specimen resulted in each half growing into separate organisms.

Despite this, SCP-906 specimens have been destroyed via means of incineration, freezing, and full body disintegration. Should the need to destroy SCP-906 ever arise, use of flamethrowers or liquid nitrogen is permitted. However, SCP-906 specimens will split themselves and "multiply" over the course of several hours should the larger mass be severely reduced. If SCP-906 is ever required to be terminated, all specimens must be eliminated to prevent SCP-906 reforming. In order to keep SCP-906 in a more controllable state, the enclosure it is housed in is to be kept at a temperature below five (5) degrees Celsius at all times as this is shown to reduce the movement, reaction time, reproduction abilities, and metabolism of SCP-906.

ADDENDUM 906-05-01

Testing of SCP-906 resulted in a Class D being targeted before a cow. A second test was then conducted in this manner wherein a pig, sheep, dog, and horse were all placed alongside a Class D. SCP-906 once again targeted the Class D first. Second targeted animal was the pig, followed by the sheep, the horse, and finally the dog.

ADDENDUM 906-05-02

During routine enclosure maintenance, SCP-906 reportedly "spoke to" a supervising staff member by saying his name several times. The reason it did this is unknown and the staff member, one Dr. Anthony Richards, reports being "very disturbed" by the proceedings and has expressed a desire to be kept away from SCP-906 in future.

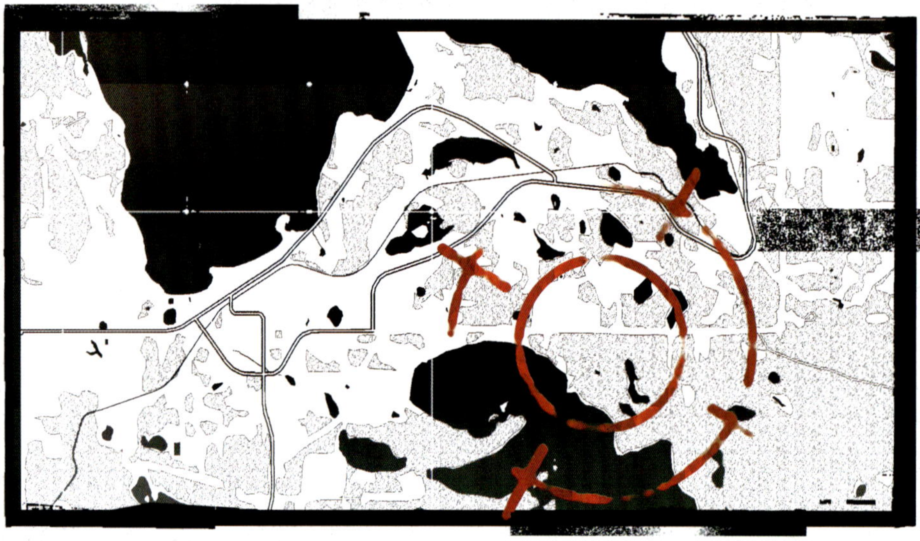

First encounter with SCP-906.

END OF REPORT

File >>> 5039433

SCP-004

Title

THE 12 RUSTY KEYS AND THE DOOR

Report by

Anounimus

Pictures by

Dmitriy Fomin

Access the original report on

scp-wiki.wikidot.com/scp-004

Date

██████████

Class

EUCLID

SPECIAL CONTAINMENT PROCEDURES

When handling items SCP-004-2 through SCP-004-13, proper procedure is vital. The items are not permitted to be moved off-site unless accompanied by two Level 4 security personnel. Under no circumstances should any other component of SCP-004 be taken through SCP-004-1. The effects of doing so are as yet unknown, and the current cost of experimentation makes further research impractical. Should any of the objects contained within SCP-004-1 breach containment, or the facility be breached, the keys must be brought inside and the door closed prior to activation of Site 62's on-site warhead. Unauthorized removal of keys from the testing area is grounds for immediate termination.

Level 1 clearance is required for basic access to SCP-004-1; Level 4 clearance is required for use of SCP-004-2 to -13.

DESCRIPTION

SCP-004 consists of an old wooden barn door (SCP-004-1) and a set of twelve rusted steel keys (SCP-004-2 through SCP-004-13). The door itself is the entrance to an abandoned factory in [DATA EXPUNGED].

CHRONOLOGICAL HISTORY

07/02/1949: A group of three juveniles trespassing on federal property near ████████ finds the door. According to their testimony, they found a set of rusted keys in an iron lockbox and determined what door the keys unlock. The juveniles are taken into custody after they contact Sheriff ██████ when one of their friends (SCP-004-CAS01) goes missing.

07/03/1949: Local authorities find the severed right hand of SCP-004-CAS01 eight kilometers from SCP-004-1. Other parts of SCP-004-CAS01's body are found scattered as far as 32 km from the factory. Under interrogation, the apprehended juveniles tell authorities that upon opening the door with one of the keys, SCP-004-CAS01 was torn into several pieces, each of which disappeared. At this point, the SCP Foundation takes over the investigation.

07/04/1949: SCP Agent ███ obtains the keys from the local authorities to begin testing. Tests show that SCP-004-2 through SCP-004-13 all fit into a single lock on the large barred door. 12 Class D personnel are assigned to test the effects of the door. Of the twelve test subjects each trying a different key to enter the room, only two survive. Opening the door with any key except SCP-004-7 or SCP-004-12 caused the test subjects to be torn apart in multiple directions; however, no dismembered parts were found until later. At the time of writing, only two parts of each subject have been recovered (with the exception of the subject using SCP-004-█ whose pieces were scattered in close proximity). The others have, for all intents and purposes, vanished from existence.

Of the two surviving subjects, only one (having used SCP-004-7) returned unharmed. The other came back in a near-catatonic state, able only to remove himself from the room and then collapse on the floor, and had to be restrained to prevent him from gouging out his eyes (see Appendix A: Mental Health Effects of SCP-004). The subject using SCP-004-7 said that he had entered a large room,

Test #█ Test object: SCP-004-2. Test subject: D-███.

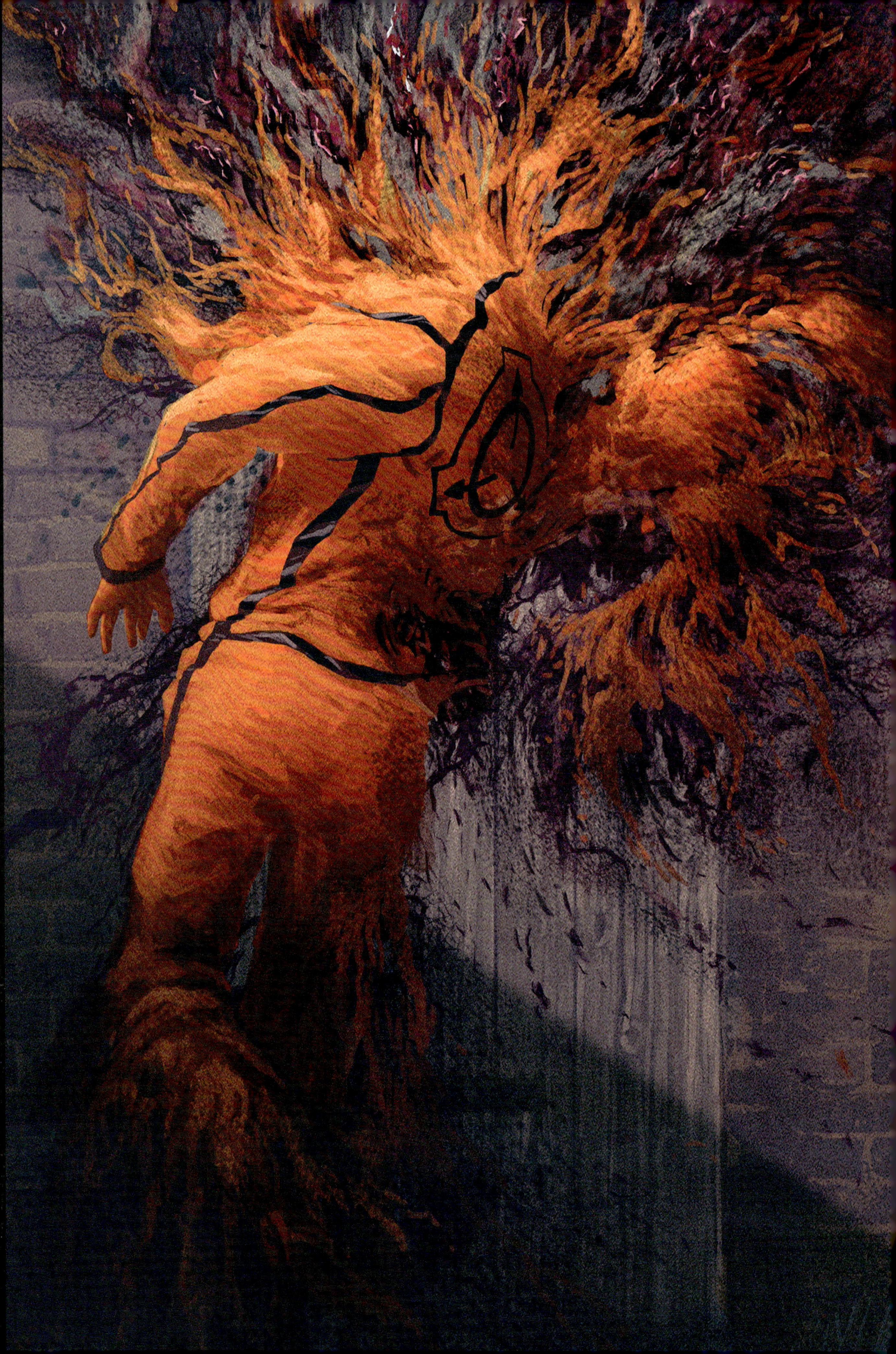

impossibly big for the size of the attached building. After his exit, SCP-004-1 was propped open and an armed squad of Level 3 personnel entered. The size of the room is impossible to measure and the door frame and the individuals in the room are the only part of the room that can be felt or illuminated.

07/16/1949: The juvenile suspects and Sheriff ██████████ are terminated.

08/02/1949: ██████████ is declared a hazardous area "due to unexploded ordnance" and fences erected in order to prevent civilian ingress. Tests to determine safety of exposure to environment behind SCP-004-1 begin.

12/01/1950: Space-time anomalies resulting from exposure to SCP-004 are confirmed. Testing is suspended until further notice.

07/02/19██ The unaccounted-for remains of SCP-004-CAS01 appear unexpectedly outside SCP-004-1. Despite being killed decades before, the remains of SCP-004-CAS01 are not decomposed in any manner and are still warm to the touch. Blood remains uncoagulated. The remains are remanded for testing.

07/04/19██ The unaccounted-for remains of one of the twelve (12) original test subjects appear in similar manner to those of SCP-004-CAS01. The remains have been designated SCP-004-CAS02. Records suggest that both SCP-004-CAS01 and CAS02 used SCP-004-██.

03/21/1999: With the massive proliferation of nuclear weapons and World War III only ██ years away, construction has begun on a site inside SCP-004-1. The site is to stock supplies for █████ person-days.

04/21/1999: ██████████ has ordered the site inside SCP-004-1 to be expanded to include emergency storage for all mobile SCP-███ specimens and a ██-petabyte database for the storage of all SCP data. The facility is now referred to as Site-62.

09/25/2000: Site-62 is operational. Labs and containment units are complete and can contain the most dangerous specimens. Backup of the SCP database has begun.

01/25/2001: Due to time anomalies (see "Space-Time Anomalies" below), all personnel working at Site-62 are now required to reside on-site permanently. Families of personnel are to be informed that loved ones perished in an industrial accident. Cloned bodies have been prepared for funeral.

08/14/2003: Massive power outage across Northeast United States and through Canada. Due to the initial failure of multiple SCP generators, Site-62 was without power for fifty-three (53) minutes. During those fifty-three (53) minutes, those on site were completely without any source of light. They reported "sensing" creatures and people, although no abnormal entities could be seen or felt. Selected facility personnel were allowed to read ███████ (Appendix A) and said the creatures "sensed" were of humanoid size but otherwise similar to the massive green creature described.

SPACE-TIME ANOMALIES

SCP-004 seems to propagate spatiotemporal anomalies. Personnel leaving the facility report losing time. Those who have been in the site for weeks insist that they had only been in the facility for several days, and records of work completed and supplies consumed support their claims. Other temporal anomalies involve SCP-004-2 through -13, especially the reappearance of SCP-004-CAS01 and SCP-004-CAS02 exactly ██ years after using SCP-004-██. ████████████ has been assigned to investigate all aspects of these time anomalies. Spatial anomalies include the impossibly large dimensions of the area opened by SCP-004-7. Similarly, the 2003 blackout incident suggests that there exists an alternate plane of existence within the same space that Site-62 occupies.

Research Library File ▸ 004

ADDITIONAL NOTES

Testing on SCP-004 reveals that ten of the keys open SCP-004-1 on a dimension where the laws of physics and topology are significantly different than those of our home dimension. Test subjects meeting these hostile conditions are torn apart, their body parts deposited in various locations, only three of which have been verified to be on Earth. Material deposited at two of these points appears immediately; material deposited at the third appears exactly ██ years into the future. The other seven locations are currently unknown.

Current testing focuses on two avenues of research. The first is finding ways to survive SCP-004's hostile topologies. The second [DATA EXPUNGED] suggest that SCP-004-2 through -13 may open doors other than SCP-004-1.

APPENDIX A: MENTAL HEALTH EFFECTS OF SCP-004-12

All Class D personnel using SCP-004-12 return in a catatonic state, unable to speak. Some may have enough energy left to try to claw out their eyes. Of the 16 subjects, only 4 have survived. Only one has regained speech, following long-term psychotherapy. He was able to tell the psychiatrist that he saw a massive green creature, so large that much of its body extended beyond his field of view. He reported innate fear and sudden recognition, "as if it were something buried deep in [his] primal fears," and forced implantation of "incomprehensible" memories. Subject displays acute anterograde and retrograde amnesia.

APPENDIX B: ADDITIONAL INFORMATION

Item #: SCP-004-14

Date of Discovery: 09/02/1950

Origin of Object: Object was discovered elsewhere in factory area, in the previously undiscovered manager's office.

Description: Object appears as a large, unvarnished wooden box. The box may be unlocked by the "safe" key, SCP-004-7, as well as five of the "unsafe" keys (see Document SCP-004-1).

Upon unlocking SCP-004-14 with SCP-004-7, the box opens automatically on hinges. The volume of the space inside is precisely five times greater than the outer dimensions imply. Items placed within while the lid remains open do not affect the weight or any other properties of the box. When the lid is closed and locked, however, all items inside vanish irretrievably. Personnel locked inside the box are also irretrievable, although losing personnel in this fashion appears to affect significantly the dreams experienced by [DATA EXPUNGED].

END OF REPORT

SPECIAL CONTAINMENT PROCEDURES

SCP-2317 is to be secured at Containment Area-179 in a reinforced 3m x 3m x 3m containment chamber. Armed guards are to be in place at all times in order to prevent unauthorized access to the facility.

DESCRIPTION

SCP-2317 is a wooden door and frame originally constructed as a basement door for a 19th-century Massachusetts brownstone. Upon opening the door, any person stepping through the door frame will be transported to an alternate reality.

END OF LEVEL 0 REPORT

CLASSIFIED LEVEL 1

FURTHER INFORMATION ON SCP-2317 IS CLASSIFIED LEVEL 1 (RESTRICTED) OR HIGHER.

KETER

OBJECT CLASS: KETER

SPECIAL CONTAINMENT PROCEDURES

SCP-2317 is to be secured at Containment Area-179 in a reinforced 3m x 3m x 3m containment chamber. Armed guards are to be in place at all times in order to prevent unauthorized access to the facility.

All personnel assigned to SCP-2317 must rotate out for one month of psychological counseling after two months on-site. Personnel assigned to SCP-2317 must undergo heavy psychological testing before being cleared to enter the site. Individuals must score at least 72 points on the Milgram Obedience Examination, be unmarried, have no offspring, and express nothing less than total loyalty to the Foundation.

While on-site, individuals assigned to SCP-2317 will be issued concealing helmets with integrated voice changers to protect their identity. On-site staff are not to remove said uniforms in the presence of other staff members. Off-duty hours are to be spent in private quarters alone.

A Class D Personnel with a background as a convicted murderer is to be assigned to SCP-2317 each month for the purposes of carrying out Procedure 220-Calabasas. During Procedure 220-Calabasas, at least one Security Clearance 3/2317 staff member must monitor the procedure by camera at all times. Following the procedure, all Class D Personnel must return to their holding cells or explosive collars will be detonated.

File >>> 003234

SCP FOUNDATION

SCP-2317

Title

A DOOR TO ANOTHER WORLD

Report by

DrClef

Picture by

Alex Andreev

Access the original report on

scp-wiki.wikidot.com/scp-2317

Date

Class

[DATA EXPUNGED]

Research
Library
File ▸ 2317

DESCRIPTION

SCP-2317 is a wooden door and frame originally constructed as a basement door for a 19th-century Massachusetts brownstone. Upon opening the door, any person stepping through the door frame will be transported to an alternate reality.

END OF LEVEL 1 REPORT ███ █ ██████████

CLASSIFIED LEVEL 2

KETER

FURTHER INFORMATION ON SCP-2317 IS CLASSIFIED LEVEL 2 (RESTRICTED) OR HIGHER.

OBJECT CLASS: KETER

SPECIAL CONTAINMENT PROCEDURES

SCP-2317 is to be secured at Containment Area-179 in a reinforced 3m x 3m x 3m containment chamber. Armed guards are to be in place at all times in order to prevent unauthorized access to the facility.

All personnel assigned to SCP-2317 must rotate out for one month of psychological counseling after two months on-site. Personnel assigned to SCP-2317 must undergo heavy psychological testing before being cleared to enter the site. Individuals must score at least 72 points on the Milgram Obedience Examination, be unmarried, have no offspring, and express nothing less than total loyalty to the Foundation.

While on-site, individuals assigned to SCP-2317 will be issued concealing helmets with integrated voice changers to protect their identity. On-site staff are not to remove said uniforms in the presence of other staff members. Off-duty hours are to be spent in private quarters alone.

A Class D with a background as a convicted murderer is to be assigned to SCP-2317 each month for the purposes of carrying out Procedure 220-Calabasas. During Procedure 220-Calabasas, at least one Security Clearance 3/2317 staff member must monitor the procedure at all times. Following the procedure, all Class D Personnel must return to their holding cells or explosive collars will be detonated.

DESCRIPTION

SCP-2317 is a wooden door and frame originally constructed as a basement door for a 19th-century Massachusetts brownstone. Upon opening the door, any person stepping through the door frame will be transported to an alternate reality.

Exploration of the alternate reality (SCP-2317-Prime) is limited, but the area directly accessible through SCP-2317 is a salt pan several kilometers in radius. A circle of seven pillars (SCP-2317-A through SCP-2317-G) are positioned in a ten-meter diameter circle approximately ten meters directly in front of SCP-2317. Each pillar is approximately one meter in diameter, and seven meters tall, constructed of marble and engraved with a series of intricate bas-reliefs. The art style of the engravings do not correspond to that of any known modern, historic, or prehistoric civilization.

ADDENDUM 1: PROCEDURE 220-CALABASAS

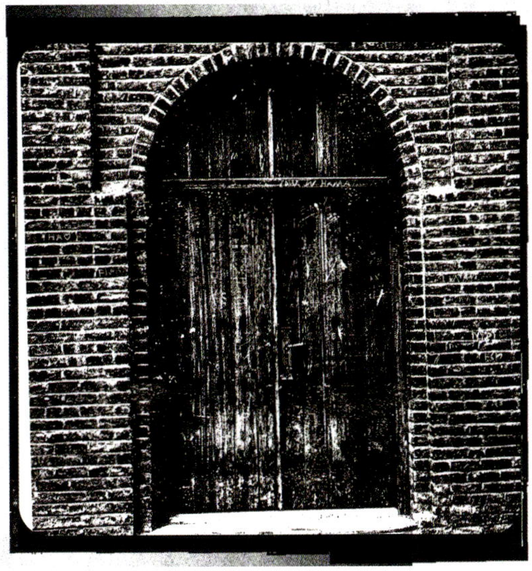

Procedure 220-Calabasas is a ritual to be performed at solar noon each day (defined as the moment when the sun reaches its height over SCP-2317). Performing Procedure 220-Calabasas requires the following:

[DATA EXPUNGED PER ORDER OF 05-█ ON ███-███-███. INFORMATION MOVED TO EYES-ONLY DOCUMENT 2317-220-CALABASAS. ACCESS TO 2317-220-CALABASAS IS LIMITED TO PERSONNEL WITH SECURITY CLEARANCE 3/2317 OR HIGHER]

> Failure at any point to properly perform Procedure 220-Calabasas may result in an XK-Class End of the World Scenario. Should any mishap or failure occur, all personnel are to return immediately through SCP-2317, closing the door behind them. The containment chamber will be immediately locked down, and a Level Two Emergency declared and reported to the 05 Council. Further instructions will be provided to on-site personnel according to Emergency Order Zachariah.

END OF LEVEL 2 REPORT ███ █ ████ █

CLASSIFIED LEVEL 3

> FURTHER INFORMATION ON SCP-2317 IS CLASSIFIED LEVEL 3 (RESTRICTED) OR HIGHER.

OBJECT CLASS: KETER

SPECIAL CONTAINMENT PROCEDURES

SCP-2317 is to be secured at Containment Area-179 in a reinforced 3m x 3m x 3m containment chamber. Armed guards are to be in place at all times in order to prevent unauthorized access to the facility.

All personnel assigned to SCP-2317 must rotate out for one month of psychological counseling after two months on-site. Personnel assigned to SCP-2317 must undergo heavy psychological testing before being cleared to enter the site. Individuals must score at least 72 points on the Milgram Obedience Examination, be unmarried, have no offspring, and express nothing less than total loyalty to the Foundation.

While on-site, individuals assigned to SCP-2317 will be issued concealing helmets with integrated voice changers to protect their identity. On-site staff are not to remove said uniforms in the presence of other staff members. Off-duty hours are to be spent in private quarters alone.

~~A Class D Personnel with a background as a convicted murderer is to be assigned to SCP 2317 each month for the purposes of carrying out Procedure 220-Calabasas. During Procedure 220-Calabasas, at least one staff member with Security Clearance 3/2317 must monitor the procedure at all times. Following the procedure, all Class D Personnel must return to their holding cells or explosive collars will be detonated.~~

Research Library File ▸ 2317

Prior paragraph revised as follows: One staff member with Security Clearance 4/2317 will be assigned each month as "Class-D Personnel" in order to act as assistant to the primary celebrant. Personnel without Security Clearance of Level 3 or higher will be told that the assistant is a Class-D personnel chosen from the normal pool of Class-D candidates. All persons directly involved with Procedure 220-Calabasas are to be informed of this fact. No personnel shall be authorized to assist with Procedure 220-Calabasas without first being clearly briefed that the "assistant" is not, in fact, a Class-D Personnel, and should not be terminated in the event that they disobey direct orders from the guards.

DESCRIPTION

SCP-2317 is a wooden door and frame originally constructed as a basement door for a 19th-century Massachusetts brownstone. Upon opening the door, any person stepping through the door frame will be transported to an alternate reality.

Exploration of the alternate reality (SCP-2317-Prime) is limited, but the area directly accessible through SCP-2317 is a salt pan several kilometers in radius. A circle of seven pillars (SCP-2317-A through SCP-2317-G) are positioned in a ten-meter diameter circle approximately ten meters directly in front of SCP-2317. Each pillar is approximately one meter in diameter, and seven meters tall, constructed of marble and engraved with a series of intricate bas-reliefs. The art style of the engravings do not correspond to that of any known modern, historic, or prehistoric civilization.

ADDENDUM 1: PROCEDURE 220-CALABASAS

Procedure 220-Calabasas is a ritual to be performed at solar noon each day (defined as the moment when the sun reaches its height over SCP-2317). Performing Procedure 220-Calabasas requires the following:

Two armed Foundation security personnel with Security Clearance of Level 3 or higher (hereafter referred to as "guards").

One Foundation Personnel with Security Clearance of Level 4 (hereafter referred to as "celebrant.")

One Class-D Personnel, as specified under Special Containment Procedures (hereafter referred to as "assistant.")

[DATA EXPUNGED]

One obsidian-edged knife (hereafter referred to as "blade").

One silver aspergillum and aspersorium, filled with at least 500 ccs of holy water blessed by a priest of Abrahamaic faith.

1. Celebrant, guards, and assistant open SCP-2317, step through, and enter SCP-2317 Prime. Assistant will enter first, followed by guards, followed by celebrant. Guards will, at all times, maintain situational awareness of assistant, and should be prepared to prevent escape with deadly force.
2. Beginning with the pillar closest to and in-line with SCP-2317 (SCP-2317-A), celebrant circumambulates SCP-2317-A through SCP-2317-G, proceeding counter-clockwise at an even and measured pace. At every other step, celebrant will scatter holy water, using the aspergillum and aspersorium, in the direction of the circle's center.
3. Upon completing one circumambulation of SCP-2317-A-G, celebrant scatters holy water over the head of the assistant and recites the following phrase: "█████ ██████ █████ █████, ██████ █████ ████ ████ ███████ █████"
4. [DATA EXPUNGED]
5. Assistant then circumambulates SCP-2317-A-G in a clockwise direction, scattering the mixture of blood and holy water in the direction of the circle's center.
6. Upon completing one circumambulation of SCP-2317-A-G, assistant walks to the center of the circle of stones and pours the remaining mixture of blood and water onto the discolored patch of salt and sand in the center, while reciting the following phrase: "█████ ████ ████ ████ █████ ██████ █████ ████ ████ ████."
7. All materials are gathered up, the obsidian knife is secured, and all personnel return through SCP-2317, which is subsequently closed.

Failure at any point to properly perform Procedure 220-Calabasas may result in an XK-Class End of the World Scenario. Should any mishap or failure occur, all personnel are to return immediately through SCP-2317, closing the door behind them. The containment chamber will be immediately locked down, and a Level Two Emergency declared and reported to the 05 Council. Further instructions will be provided to on-site personnel according to Emergency Order Zachariah.

END OF LEVEL 3 REPORT ████ █

CLASSIFIED LEVEL 4

FURTHER INFORMATION ON SCP-2317 IS CLASSIFIED LEVEL 4 (RESTRICTED) OR HIGHER.

KETER

OBJECT CLASS: KETER

SPECIAL CONTAINMENT PROCEDURES

SCP-2317 is to be secured at Containment Area-179 in a reinforced 3m x 3m x 3m containment chamber. Armed guards are to be in place at all times in order to prevent unauthorized access to the facility.

All personnel assigned to SCP-2317 must rotate out for one month of psychological counseling after two months on-site. Personnel assigned to SCP-2317 must undergo heavy psychological testing before being cleared to enter the site. Individuals must score at least 72 points on the Milgram Obedience Examination, be unmarried, have no offspring, and express nothing less than total loyalty to the Foundation.

While on-site, individuals assigned to SCP-2317 will be issued concealing helmets with integrated voice changers to protect their identity. On-site staff are not to remove said uniforms in the presence of other staff members. Off-duty hours are to be spent in private quarters alone.

One staff member with Security Clearance 4/2317 will be assigned each month as "Class-D Personnel" in order to act as assistant to the primary celebrant. Personnel without Security Clearance of Level 4 or higher will be told that the assistant is a Class-D personnel chosen from the normal pool of Class-D candidates. All persons directly involved with Procedure 220-Calabasas are to be informed of this fact. No personnel shall be authorized to assist with Procedure 220-Calabasas without first being clearly briefed that the "assistant" is not, in fact, a Class-D Personnel, and should not be terminated in the event that they disobey direct orders from the guards.

DESCRIPTION

SCP-2317 is a wooden door and frame originally constructed as a basement door for a 19th-century Massachusetts brownstone. Upon opening the door, any person stepping through the door frame will be transported to an alternate reality.

Exploration of the alternate reality (SCP-2317-Prime) is limited, but the area directly accessible through SCP-2317 is a salt pan several kilometers in radius. A circle of seven pillars (SCP-2317-A through SCP-2317-G) are positioned in a ten-meter diameter circle approximately ten meters directly in front of SCP-2317. Each pillar is approximately one meter in diameter, and seven meters tall, constructed of marble and engraved with a series of intricate bas-reliefs. The art style of the engravings do not correspond to that of any known modern, historic, or prehistoric civilization.

SCP-2317-A-G extend two hundred meters below the surface of the sand and into SCP-2317-H.

SCP-2317-H is a spherical space one hundred kilometers in diameter located directly underneath SCP-2317-A-G, lined with the same stone used to construct SCP-2317-A-G. Contained within SCP-2317-H is SCP-2317-K, hereafter referred to as "entity."

The following information has been inferred through seismic analysis and ground-penetrating radar, as well as direct observation: Entity appears to be an obese humanlike creature of immense proportions: estimated height if fully erect is over two hundred kilometers. Horns resembling tree branches sprout from its head, which lacks a lower jaw. Entire body is covered in millions of overlapping plate-like scales. Seven heavy hooks are embedded in the entity's back, each one attached to a heavy steel chain connected to the lower end of one of the seven pillars embedded in the ceiling of the chamber.

At the time of the writing of this document, six of the pillars or chains have been broken or damaged, and only one chain remains intact.

ADDENDUM 2317-1: PROCEDURE 220-CALABASAS

Procedure 220-Calabasas is a ritual to be performed at solar noon each day (defined as the moment when the sun reaches its height over SCP-2317). Performing Procedure 220-Calabasas requires the following:

Two armed Foundation security personnel with Security Clearance of Level 3 or higher (hereafter referred to as "guards").

One Foundation Personnel with Security Clearance of Level 4 (hereafter referred to as "celebrant."

One Class-D Personnel, as specified under Special Containment Procedures (hereafter referred to as "assistant.")

One live male Gallus domesticus, preferably caged to prevent complications during transport to SCP-2317-Prime (hereafter referred to as "chicken.")

One obsidian-edged knife (hereafter referred to as "blade").

One silver aspergillum and aspersorium, filled with at least 500 ccs of holy water blessed by a priest of Abrahamaic faith.

One kiloton-level nuclear device, to be detonated in case of catastrophic containment failure.

1. Celebrant, guards, and assistant open SCP-2317, step through, and enter SCP-2317 Prime. Assistant will enter first, followed by guards, followed by celebrant. Guards will, at all times, maintain situational awareness of assistant, and should be prepared to prevent escape with deadly force.
2. Beginning with the pillar closest to and in-line with SCP-2317 (SCP-2317-A), celebrant circumambulates SCP-2317-A through SCP-2317-G, proceeding counter-clockwise at an even and measured pace. At every other step, celebrant will scatter holy water, using the aspergillum and aspersorium, in the direction of the circle's center.
3. Upon completing one circumambulation of SCP-2317-A-G, celebrant scatters holy water over the head of the assistant and recites the following phrase: "Seven Seals, Seven Rings, Seven Thrones for the Scarlet King."
4. Celebrant then moves to a safe distance away from assistant, who will take the obsidian knife and use it to kill the chicken provided as sacrifice. Blood will be drained from the chicken and added to the aspersorium, then stirred to mix with the holy water already contained within.
5. Assistant then circumambulates SCP-2317-A-G in a clockwise direction, scattering the mixture of blood and holy water in the direction of the circle's center.
6. Upon completing one circumambulation of SCP-2317-A-G, assistant walks to the center of the circle of stones and pours the remaining mixture of blood and water onto the discolored patch of salt and sand in the center, while reciting the following phrase: "Blood for the Old Gods, Water for the New King."
7. All materials are gathered up, the obsidian knife is secured, and all personnel return through SCP-2317, which is subsequently closed.

Failure at any point to properly perform Procedure 220-Calabasas may result in an XK-Class End of the World Scenario. Should any mishap or failure occur, all personnel are to return immediately through SCP-2317, closing the door behind them. The containment chamber will be immediately locked down, and a Level Two Emergency declared and reported to the 05 Council. Further instructions will be provided to on-site personnel according to Emergency Order Zachariah, and may include detonation of on-site nuclear warhead.

ADDENDUM 2317-2: HISTORY

SCP-2317 was first discovered in 1922, by [DATA EXPUNGED]. Object was subsequently moved to what was then called Provisional Containment Area 17. Object was moved to Containment Area 179 in 1982, where it remains as of the writing of this article.

When initially discovered, four of the seven chains were broken, and three were intact: the breaking of the fifth chain in ████ corresponded directly to a ████████ event in our world. The sixth chain, which broke in ████ was also coincident with a much more severe ████████ event, eventually resulting in the deaths of two million persons.

Analysis of supplementary texts retrieved at the time of containment pointed to Procedure 220-Calabasas as an effective means of maintaining containment until an effective means of repairing or reattaching said chains can be discovered. Containment procedures were modified to incorporate Procedure 220-Calabasas. As records show that the sequence of ████████ events shows an exponential increase in lethality, it can be extrapolated that failure of the final chain (SCP-2317-G), would result in an XK-Class End of the World Scenario.

For this reason, every possible effort is to be made to ensure a successful Procedure 220-Calabasas.

END OF LEVEL 4 REPORT ██ ████ █ ██

CLASSIFIED LEVEL 5

FURTHER INFORMATION ON SCP-2317 IS CLASSIFIED
LEVEL 5 (RESTRICTED).

SPECIAL CONTAINMENT PROCEDURES

Irrelevant.

SPECIAL ACCESS DESIGNATION

CODE NIGHTMARE REGENT RED

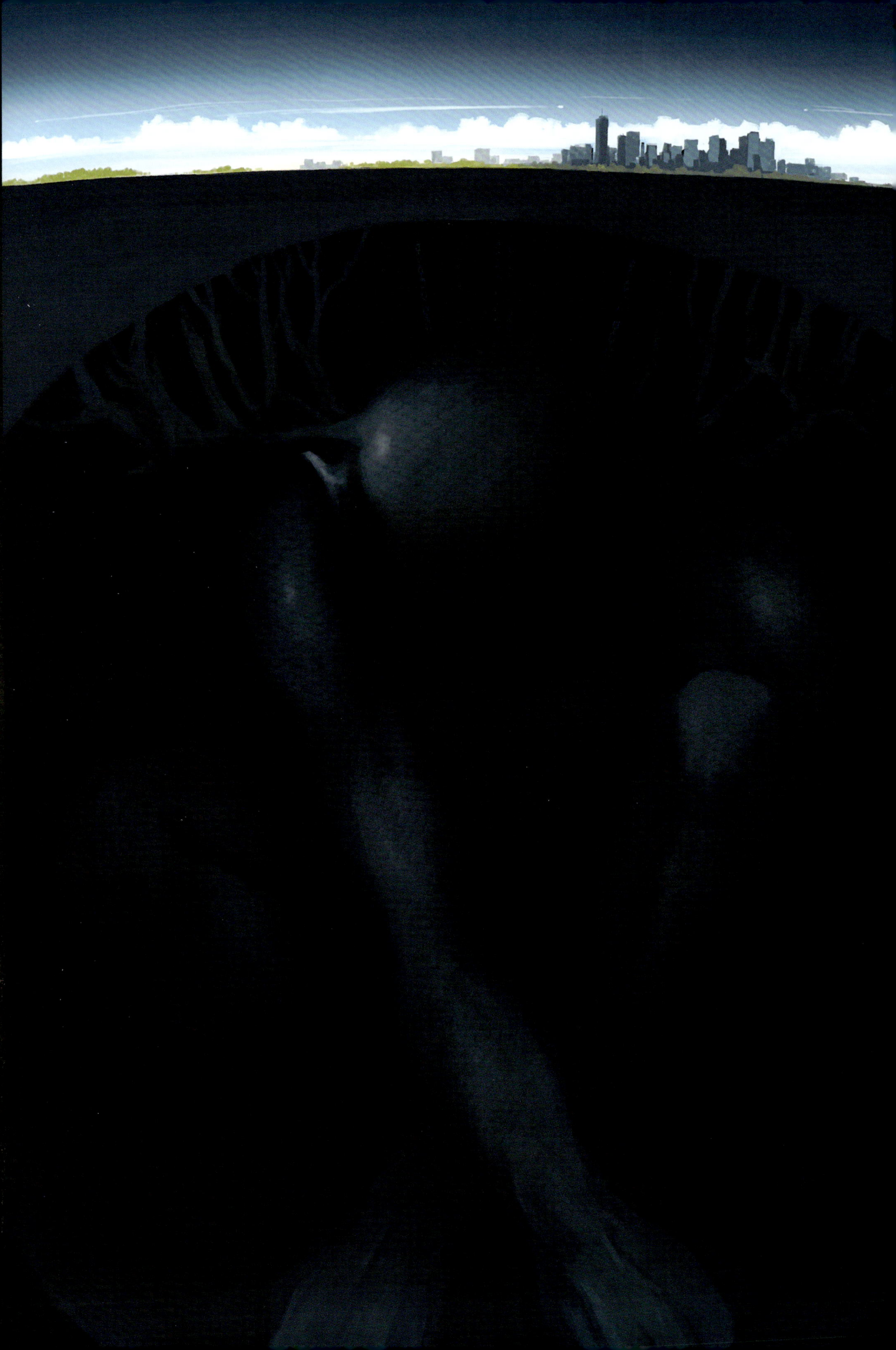

DESCRIPTION

SCP-2317 is a primeval entity known as "The ██████ █████ Devourer of Worlds" (name redacted intentionally). The Erikesh Codex indicates that it was captured and imprisoned by Erikeshan mystics circa 1894 BCE. An excerpt from the relevant passage follows:

> AND THEN KESHPETH LED HIS ARMY OF TEN THOUSAND INTO THE REALM BEYOND THE CLOUDS, AND THERE DID THEY DO BATTLE WITH THE DEVOURER, MAY HIS NAME REMAIN FOREVER UNREMEMBERED. AND THEN KESHPETH AND HIS TEN THOUSAND DID CRAFT SEVEN CUNNING CHAINS OUT OF THE BONES OF JASPETAR, SEVENTH BRIDE OF THE DREAD DEVOURER, MAY HIS NAME REMAIN FOREVER UNREMEMBERED, AND BOUND HIM WITHIN THE PEARL OF THE FATHER OF OYSTERS, HE WHO DWELLS UNDER THE MIRROR OF SALT IN THE REALM UNDER THE SEA. AND KESHPETH ORDERED THAT THE GATES TO THE FAR COUNTRY BE SEALED FOREVER, LEST THE DREAD DEVOURER, MAY HIS NAME REMAIN FOREVER UNREMEMBERED, FIND ITS WAY BACK TO OUR WORLD.

It is not clear how the 19th-century Society of the Golden Arrow discovered how to create a gate to Universe-Kappa-Erikesh, nor their reasons for doing so. What is clear is that the damage to the first four chains that bind the Devourer was accidental. By the time Our Founder took possession of the item following the dissolution of the Society, the organization had bankrupted itself several times over trying desperately to repair the damage caused.

PROJECTED CONTAINMENT PROFILE

Indications are that Final Containment Failure will occur at some point within the next century as of the writing of this article: the mean time to failure being calculated at thirty years. All efforts to repair or replace the chains have failed. All efforts to re-discover the method for creating these chains have proven fruitless. Research is currently underway to determine an alternate containment plan, but the possibility that anything can keep the Devourer from entering our universe is slim, especially as the original material used to create the chains (namely, the bones and sinew of another Devourer entity) are no longer in existence.

The primary threat is internal despair or panic. In order to maintain morale, a false containment procedure (Procedure 220-Calabasas) will be authored and implemented. This false containment procedure has been given a sense of veracity by the following means:

- Incorporating elements of common ritualistic magics.
- Incorporating elements of popular religious rites.
- Incorporating elements of other known occult organizations.
- Incorporating elements of other known Special Containment Procedures.
- Incorporating references to similar but unrelated occult entities.
- Increased information security regarding the elements of the procedure.
- Appealing to the common institutional meme of the effectiveness of thermonuclear weapons in destroying paranormal entities.

Although completely ineffectual, the purpose of Procedure 220-Calabasas is to provide the appearance of active containment in order to allay anxiety among staff until a more permanent solution can be found.

In the meantime, preparations will be made in order to ensure the survival of the human race following Containment Failure. As most of the recommended preparations overlap with or are identical to preparations already underway in case of numerous other XK-Class scenarios, minimal additional resources are required.

Approved by the unanimous vote of the Overseer Council on ██-██-████

05 APPROVED

END OF REPORT

File >>> 01933234

SCP-001

Title

LILY'S PROPOSAL (THE WORLD GONE BEAUTIFUL)

Report by

LilyFlower

Picture by

Yulia Zhigadlo

Access the original report on

scp-wiki.wikidot.com/ lily-s-proposal

Date

Class

UNNECESSARY

SPECIAL CONTAINMENT PROCEDURES

SCP-001 does not need to be contained.

In the event of SCP-001 occurring, all personnel, including D-class, are to be honorably discharged, and may do what they wish with their remaining time. All sapient and non-aggressive SCPs are to be released. Any further SCPs which can be decommissioned are to be. All remaining Foundation sites are to be run by the AIAD systems.

Specifically bred instances of SCP-514 are to be released globally.

DESCRIPTION

SCP-001 refers to an event occurring shortly before the cessation of all life on Earth. Whilst SCP-001 has not yet taken place, it was discovered through various pieces of information gathered from extra-universal Foundations and other similar groups (see attached document 001-A for a list of such communications).

It is important to note SCP-001 is not the cause of the apocalyptic scenario, merely a pre-occurrence response to it. SCP-001 is, according to records, distinctively recognised by certain key features.

During an SCP-001 event, flowers are observed to spontaneously appear and bloom over ~90% of the viable land surface of the planet. These flowers are universally referred to as "vibrant", "bright", "beautiful", and/or words to this effect. The weather will clear, globally, with an ambient temperature recognised as comfortable by the majority of the populace. Air pollution will additionally clear.

During an SCP-001 event, the global populace will become aware of the fate of the Earth, and of its inevitability. They will also experience heavily decreased levels of violence.

SCP-001 will occur exactly 24 hours before the death of all life on the planet.

END OF REPORT

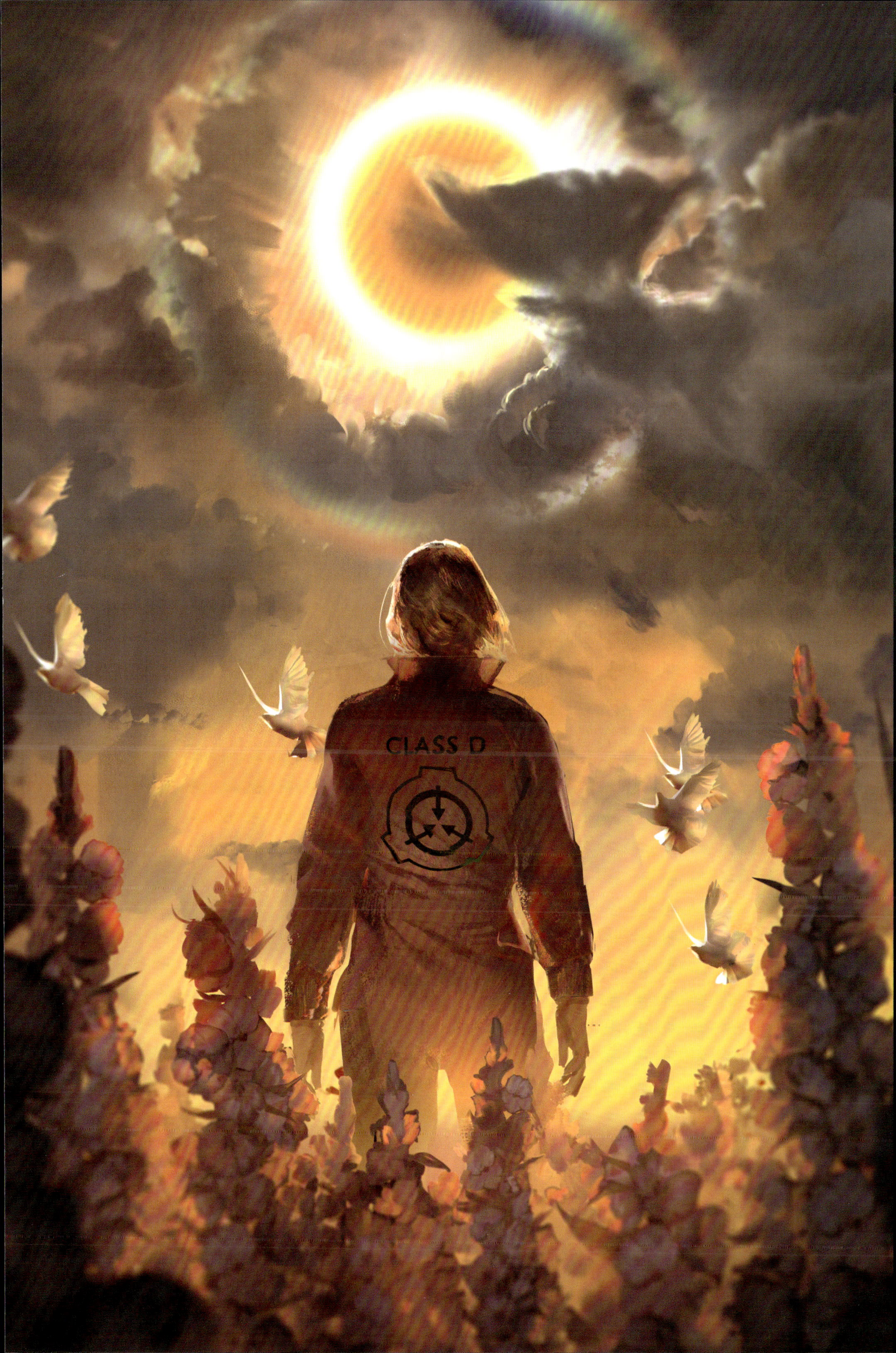
CLASS D

[PERSONNEL DOC_01]
[ID_DOCTOR ███]

TABLE OF CONTENTS

O5 APPROVED

[PERSONNEL DOC_01]
[ID_DOCTOR ███]

LIST OF ARTISTS

Alex Andreev	artstation.com/alexandreev
Alexey Yakovlev	artstation.com/kypcaht
Anna Agafonova	artstation.com/agafo _ supernova
Dan Temirov	artstation.com/dante
David Romero	artstation.com/cinemamind
Dmitriy Fomin	artstation.com/fomincgart
Dmitry Desyatov	artstation.com/dekades8
Dmitry Utkin	artstation.com/deathnear
Genocide Error	artstation.com/deadlineart
Ivan Efimov	artstation.com/efimov
Jazefel	artstation.com/jazefel
Julia Galkina	artstation.com/xgingerwr
Markiz de Baldezar	instagram.com/de _ baldezar
Natalie Lesiv	artstation.com/cuddlenoon
Nikita Postupkin	artstation.com/postupkin
Pavel Kobyzev	artstation.com/starwolf
Roman Avseenko	artstation.com/razgriz
Ruslan Korovkin	artstation.com/lironka25
Ruslana Gus	artstation.com/rilun
Serj Papadin	artstation.com/serj _ papadin
Vladislav Orlowski	artstation.com/drunkengopher
Yulia Zhigadlo	artstation.com/new _ asuka
Alexander Puchkov	artstation.com/rpo6obwuk
Tatiana Kvitkovsky	artstation.com/husohuso

05 APPROVED

ACKNOWLEDGEMENTS

SCP Foundation is a unique project rooted in the concept of co-authorship so deeply, it is hard to even start guessing how many people contributed to it by and large. And we are immensely grateful to all of them. Had it not been for their hard work, this book would have never gotten into your hands.

First of all, of course, we would like to thank the authors who decided to share their ideas and created all those SCPs you have read about in this journal. As the saying goes, "in the beginning was the Word..."

...and the Word needed proofreading really badly. It is hard to overestimate the role of those who put their time and effort into polishing the texts and making them look as authentic as possible. Sometimes even a couple of small edits can make a huge difference!

We should also thank all those active site users who give their upvotes and downvotes, discuss and debate, pitch new ideas, ask tough questions, and simply share their emotions. The Wikidot platform really makes communication between authors and readers much easier!

Speaking of which... We need to give a huge THANK YOU to all those heroes who pulled the project from the depths of 4chan and turned it into what we have now: a user-friendly website with a neat rating and editing system, holding various contests to boost activity and defending the principles of the CC-BY-SA license that let us publish this book in the first place. Thank you, Moto42, for posting The Sculpture in 2007 and starting the whole thing. Thank you, to all those who came after and developed a simple concept of a secret organization fighting anomalies into something that grand.

The SCP Foundation is much more than a huge collection of tales and stories stylized as official reports. First and foremost, it is a community of great and talented people. Ideas give rise to new ideas and bring inspiration. We want to thank those who use this inspiration to create something for SCP: those who illustrate, animate, and make voiceovers, who craft and cosplay, who translate into other languages, who develop video and board games. This is exactly what keeps any undertaking afloat! Shared interest pushes the project forward opening new horizons and making it more and more popular. Our dearest wish is that we can contribute to it, too.

Last but not least, thank YOU, dear reader, for supporting our venture and putting this book on your shelf.

Even though this volume came to an end, your journey through the SCP universe is far from it. Actually, it never ends! We, ParaBooks publishing house, tried to fit as many articles as we can in these three journals (black, yellow, and red), and still just barely scratched the surface of the treasure pile known as scpwiki.com. There are thousands of more stories — some of them are creepy and unsettling, some are funny and wholesome, and some are quite thought-provoking. So, what are you waiting for? Read, vote, discuss, create and write the SCP Foundation history with your own hands!

scp-wiki.wikidot.com

SCP Foundation Artbook | Black journal
Designed and published by
ParaBooks Publishing House
An Imprint of Aloha Comics LLC
330 SARATOGA RD #8851, Honolulu,
HI 96830 USA

Follow us: para-books.com
instagram.com/para.books

First edition: January 2023
ISBN: 978-1-63838-011-5

Printed and bound in China

Content relating to the SCP Foundation, including the SCP Foundation logo, is licensed under Creative Commons Sharealike 3.0 and all concepts originate from http://www.scpwiki.com and its authors. *SCP Foundation Artbook | Paperback Edition | Black journal*, being derived from this content, is hereby also released under Creative Commons Sharealike 3.0.